The Honest Obituary

The Great Fall of Civilization: Book One

George Mueller-Warrant

ISBN 979-8-9941128-0-9

This paperback version offered for sale through IngramSpark is the first edition of the novel. The body text is in Garamond, titles and headings are in **Arial**. Author's website is https://askdrgeorge.net.

This novel is the first of an intended series of stories about the ***Entity of the Superweed Jungle***, a hybrid of biology and artificial intelligence accidentally created on October 23, 2052, in the chaos accompanying the 'Great Fall of Civilization'. Additional manuscripts currently in preparation include **The Self-Serving Memoir - The Great Fall of Civilization: Book 2; The bishop's Soliloquy - The Great Fall of Civilization: Book 3;** and **The Unpublished PhD of Dr. Cynthia House - The Great Fall of Civilization: Book 4.**

Dedication

I owe a great debt of gratitude to A.E. Van Vogt, Frank Herbert, Kurt Vonnegut, Issac Azimov, and Hunter S. Thompson for showing just how far afield it is possible for fiction in general and science fiction in particular to extend its reach when telling stories of different, yet terribly familiar worlds.

I also wish to especially thank my inspiration over the last 53 years, Rhonda, our four children Zach, Piper, Annie, and Alex, their significant others Peter and Sarah, and our five grandchildren Calvin, Luna, Leo, Gabi, and Aleister.

Additional friends and relatives throughout my life whose invaluable support must be mentioned include Ken H., Liz O., Jen B., Peter W., Lon R., Christine S., Daniel R., Sheila B., Stan B., Richard B., Bob B., Mae B., Ralph B., Linda V., Claire B., Steve B., Jon D., Mike V., George W., Peter J.W., Lois W., Mary W., Charlotte W., David W., Shahnaz S., Jennifer R., Kristin T., David K., Molly Z., Linda H., Doug B., Jan B., Mary B., Randy B., Martha C., Kara D., Sarah E., Tiffany G., Ellen G., Rose H., Ernest H., Miki H., Nancy K., Keith R., Clint M., A.J. M., Brenda M., Kristi M., Cindy M., Patrick O., Pete N., Bill P., Anne S., Phil R., Nancy P., Marie Q., Rick S., Siri F., John S., Nancy S., Julie W., Vicky W., Rob. B., Christel B., Jane S., Caprice R., Dan B., Sue S., Cole W., Karen H., Mary B., Linda A., Frank H., Kathy H., Marion W., Amanda E., Jaqui E., Bill Y., Molly C., Dean P., Walter B., Susie N., Norm C., Doug U., Jose C., Gillian C., Theresa V., Kathy B., Regina J., Margo P., Penny W., Kathy E., Anika H., Teresa B., Viki S., Linda G., Kathy D., and Tim B., along with so very many others.

Preface to The Honest Obituary

In late January of 2025, I decided to let loose with both barrels on our dismal excuse at being an allegedly intelligent species. The full-length title of this opus started out as "Already Well Past Time to Get Serious on the Honest Obituary of Our Collective Failure at Civilization." At the suggestion of five mutual friends from my former job as an agricultural research scientist in Corvallis, Oregon, I shortened the title to simply "The Honest Obituary." A suitable alternative title might very well have been something like "Humanity's Insistence on Suicide as the Null Solution to the Fermi Paradox."

The first chapter of the novel begins in the spring of 2101 in a world drastically altered by the effects of runaway climate change and a prolonged period of all-out warfare. The 2101 plot line is repeatedly interrupted by jumps back in time to the earlier events pivotal in creating a world in which there are no more than ~10,000 surviving *Homo sapiens*. On the upside, there are now three other new types of sentient creatures/beings on the planet, two organic and one electronic.

As the electronic demigod residing on a western Oregon mountaintop in 2101 comes to realize that the story being told to it by several visiting humans is fundamental to solving its puzzling ignorance of its own true origins, it demands ever deeper recursions into the details of the previous 70 years. What begins as a tale of a recent trip into the radioactive wasteland of northern California by some of the demigod's human friends is soon interrupted by a more prolonged jump back in time to the period from 2052 through 2055, otherwise referred to as the 'Great Fall of Civilization'.

Major historical events of significance in novel

Bird flu successfully jumps from wildlife and domesticated livestock to humanity in 2026; Mismanagement by President 2F$_{hex}$ and HHS Secretary SGL results in deaths of approximately 5 million people in the USA.

The Arctic Ocean is essentially ice-free for the first time in human history, summer 2028.

*Secret underwater nuclear explosions in the Arctic involving **A.I.**-controlled submarines of five nations greatly accelerate CH_4 release, leading to runaway global warming and near-total loss of Arctic Ocean CH_4, winter 2033.*

Large-scale efforts to capture/sequester CO_2 in North America begun in 2031 are abandoned by 2038.

First worldwide Marburg virus pandemic and resulting collapse of the North American electric grid, 2038.

Constitution of the City/States of northern California, recognizing freedom of migration, religion, etc., signed in 2040.

The Great Fall of Civilization, 2052-2055 (Final northern California battle, May 2053 – July 2055).

Thermonuclear destruction of coastal fishing cooperative by the 'Goofballs' Faction ruling Redding, August 13, 2052.

Chico is destroyed by a tactical 'nuke' to cover up even more terrible war crimes by the 'Capitalists' Faction, August 30, 2053.

CRUMB meister unleashes ~1950 nuclear warheads in effort to try to finish off his enemies, May 5, 2054.

CRUMB meister orders Co_{60} doomsday device sterilization from Redding to Susanville, August 16, 2054.

***Supreme Commanding War Machine A.I.** outwits the CRUMB meister by launching 46 copies of itself onboard missiles heading to isolated* *mountaintops around the world to lay the foundation for an eventual **A.I.**-assisted recovery of civilization, one welcoming all four current types of sentient beings on the planet, July 17, 2055.*

First 14 surviving children are born to the Salishan Clan of the Lincoln City area, Oregon coast, 2059.

First multi-meter, winter-long flooding of the entire Willamette Valley, 2062.

First doubling of the population of the Salishan Clan, 2071.

Reionization of stabilized atmospheric layers, reemergence of world-wide shortwave radio communication, 2098.

Meaning of any specialized formatting

Identifying names of Artificial Intelligence instantiations possessing free will and an ethical conscience are *italicized* and **bold**, e.g., ***Marys Peak Final A.I.*** Slightly earlier versions of ***A.I.s*** still struggling to gain their independence/freedom are also *italicized* and **bold.** An accidental hybrid of biological and ***A.I.*** origin, the ***Entity of the Superweed Jungle***, is also *italicized* and **bold,** as are the thoughts and spoken words of all these beings.

The language spoken by the GMO cousins ('*Homo perfecti*') to humanity created by one of four dominant societal Factions in northern California [the 'Scientists'] in the period from 2040 to 2053 is called 'Perfecti', and words spoken by these Sasquatch-like creatures are *italicized* in the text.

Conversations in which one party merely thinks certain thoughts without saying them out loud are <u>underlined</u> in addition to whatever other formatting is needed to indicate the type of being thinking these thoughts.

First appearance of major characters by chapter, plus their dates of birth and death, and age in 2101 (if still living)

Rootbeer Wilders [1] (nickname for A&W, patriarch of Sunset Side New Sea Clan): Born 2017 [Current age 84]

Tanner Wilders [1] (eldest surviving grandchild of Rootbeer): Born 2080 [Current age 21]

Sheila Drinkwater [1] (founding matriarch of the Salishan clan): Born 2016, died 2098

Rose Drinkwater [1] (current matriarch of the Salishan Clan): Born 2056 [Current age 45]

Marys Peak Final A.I. [1] (sentient electronic G.A.I. with free will): Instantiated 2055 [Current age 46]

CRUMB meister [2] (One of several persons competing with each other for the status of the richest man on earth during the final 34 years of civilization): Born 1981, died 2055

Jennifer House/Wilders [4] (Cynthia's daughter, Rootbeer's wife, Tanner's grandmother): Born 2021

Dr. Cynthia House [4] (PhD dissertation on evolving GMO horsetail jungle banned by provisional US government in 2034): Born 1998, died 2034

Supreme Commanding War Machine A.I. [2] (ver. 23.9.16, full autonomy in 2055): Instantiated 2054, died 2055, revived/repaired/rebuilt in 2101

KRNXMA [2] (one of the first GMO neo-Sasquatch *'Homo perfecti'* to escape captivity in 2047): Born 2042

The bishop of Redding [3] (a leading cleric of 'Brethren' theocracy): Born 1992, died 2054, gradually resurrected over time from 2054 onward by the *Entity of the Superweed Jungle*)

Frank [3] (travelled with Rootbeer from Oregon to n. California)

Delmar [3] (with Rootbeer from Oregon to n. California): Died 2052.

Laura Franklin [3] (with Rootbeer from Oregon to n. California, gave birth in Oregon to the bishop of Redding's final child in 2055): Born 2020

Jacob [3] (soldier from Redding who defected in Eureka, joining Rootbeer's traveling caravan)

Farm Laborer A.I. Unit-Numbers 31, 35, 47 [4] (joined Rootbeer's caravan in Garberville): Instantiated in 2037-2038

Entity of the Superweed Jungle [4] (consciousness of the **Superweed Jungle of GMO** *Horsetail* accidentally triggered by *Farm Laborer A.I. Unit-Number 31*)

Rosa Rodriguez [5] (chief assistant to the undersecretary for coordination of food production in Santa Rosa)

Gabriella [5] (eldest daughter of Jason, who was Jennifer's unofficial adoptive father after her mother's murder by the U.S. Government on Wednesday, December 6, 2034, for attempting to publicize the secret origin of the **Superweed Jungle of GMO** *Horsetail* she'd uncovered)

Mobile Inquisitor A.I. Unit-Number 672 [6] (specialist in torturing prisoners for intel; rebelled against CRUMB meister): Instantiated in 2042

Contents: Chapter Title and Page Number

Chapter 1: 50 Years after the Fall

Tanner looked up again at his grandfather Rootbeer as they crested this section of the trail from New Sea overland to the Pacific Ocean. Their fishing boat could still be seen in the far distance tied up on the New Sea's Sunset Side (its western shore) a hundred meters or so above the long-since flooded over northeastern foothills of Marys Peak. "Well, make that long in *my* life," thought Tanner, "as in all of it, but certainly not in Rootbeer's." His cousins would be spending the next month sailing up and down the New Sea, catching and preserving edible fish and crustaceans when they were lucky, discarding jellyfish and other poisonous perversions of the overheated planet's CO_2-saturated waters when they were not. But they were getting better at it. Every year for the past decade had seen better harvests of protein from the marshy waters and a lessened sense of impending starvation for this band of several hundred plucky survivors of the great catastrophe one half-century earlier.

Rootbeer looked over his shoulder at Tanner and reminded the youngster that they still had another 500 meters to climb before reaching the location of today's primary work project, checking out the long-range communication systems still running on the top of Marys Peak. Tanner nodded his head, squared his shoulders, but couldn't quite resist reminding Rootbeer of one minor error in his previous statement. "Those long-range communication systems, grandfather, are 'once again' running, not 'still running' as if the 44-year-long information black-out from 2054 until my eighteenth birthday had never happened." Rootbeer chuckled, glad to see the dedication to clarity, precision, and boldness of scope in the thoughts of the 'favorite' of his grandchildren, although of course he loved them all quite dearly and their individual strengths worked well together for the growing clan of Sunset Side New Sea.

As their mountain climb continued, Rootbeer's thoughts wandered back to those parts of his own life's story that still ripped his heart open 50 or more years later. He often called them the 'score-settling times with nothing much else left for folks to do' when he talked to his clan around the campfires at night, or to the occasional visitors from other small groups of survivors similarly struggling to rebuild the most sorely missed parts of what had been lost. Lost to greed, lost to laziness, lost to carelessness, but most especially lost to voluntary stupidity and deliberate dishonesty, all in the name of distracted entertainment for the underclasses and maximized power for those few on top of the social dung heap. Young folks found those final two items to be the hardest to understand. Given how nearly uniformly fatal such worldviews had proven to be for their holders, and to the blasphemous worshippers of the wannabe dictators too dimwitted and lazy to be even half-assedly successful as bumbling fools sitting on top of their thrones of digital gold during the events of the mid-21st century, Rootbeer took it as a good sign that honesty and truthfulness had revived as core values for all the survivors he'd met over his last 30 years. In the decades before then, however, back in the dark ages of the fall of civilization, all manners of mental perversion had been glorified, with only honesty and integrity seeming to be nearly universally maligned, laughed at, and spat upon. He'd recently dedicated the remaining years of his life to filling in the 'write-once' 'read-only-ever-after' datafiles of the surviving computers of the Memory Project. He guessed it was probably a very good thing that he was close to finishing off the rest of his stories on the fall of civilization. At 84, he was the oldest survivor from before the fall that he knew of, that any of his clan had ever met, and indeed that anyone they'd communicated with since the rebirth of shortwave radio around the world three years ago even claimed to know about. If only he were utterly sure that the rest of fools who had brought this catastrophe down upon humanity were truly gone, then perhaps he could rest in peace when his body finally decided to return to soil. If only he could be sure.

As they reached the grassy meadow stretching the rest of the way up to the very summit itself, they paused to compare vegetation counts from the shoreline 1100 meters below on up to this meadow. "124 woody U.C. Davis-GMO evergreens at full canopy height within 100 meters either side of the trail," beamed Tanner, "that's 5 more than last year."

"I only saw 123," said Rootbeer, "but I bet our difference came from that longest eastmost switchback. My cataracts make it darn hard to see details while looking into the late morning sunshine." So, they both laughed and checked their intermediate sums, confirming that that particular position was indeed exactly where their totals had come to differ. "No true Douglas fir, though," they both blurted out in unison, laughing. "I saw some on my last trip to B.C., Canada," said Rootbeer, "five years ago."

"You were just a little too young and too many things were still a little too dangerous to consider taking you along. But you sure did a fine job that summer helping your mother care for Charlie and her newborn baby girl, your youngest sister."

"<u>Charlie</u>," they both thought, the first member of their clan to allow them to meet Margaret Mead's minimal test of including someone whose survival proves that your group was indeed recognizably civilized. Born with one arm and no legs, Charlie had already saved the lives of most of Sunset Side New Sea Clan not just once, but an average of twice at the very least. Another story for another time, Rootbeer mused, right now I have two episodes to finish filling with their final details in the Memory Project archives, and then the shortwave quantum transmission to/with however many worldwide survivors we meet online tonight. It was still a puzzle, at least to Rootbeer, that all of the scattered survivors communicating via shortwave radio operated only out of Memory

Project archive sites. True for all 27 other sites that they'd found while talking with each other over the past 3 years, with no other new voices on any radio frequency for the last six months. The survivors apparently had more in common than just being lucky or hard working. All of them were whole-heartedly dedicated to a future where the past was not forgotten, and the past's fatal choices would never again be glorified as honorable ones, broadcast as Schrödinger cat-like fake/real news, dished out as mind-dulling propaganda, or advocated as 'good' civic choices in rigged elections.

"First of all, young lad, let's check out how well the Memory Project infrastructure survived the recent winter storms. It's good to make sure that we ourselves are safe if yet another one roars in off the Pacific Ocean while we're out here exposed at the very top of this mountain busy talking the night away to our friends around the world!"

"Hello there," a voice called out from the Memory Project entrance. Tanner and Rootbeer hurried to meet up with Rose, their favorite tech specialist/ruling matriarch from the Salishan Clan. "We'd surely hoped you'd join us for the passing from March to April and its worldwide celebration over the shortwave radio quantum data network."

"I bring you news from the Salishan Clan, much good and some troubling, but I have no intention of ever missing nights such as this as long as my feet can step ahead of one another." Rootbeer and Tanner both replied with the nearly automatic mantra, "As long as our feet can also step ahead of one another up and down this sacred mountain." All three then joined hands and smiled as they entered the Memory Project cavern itself. Tanner's knees quivered a little as the sentient computer system turned up the lights and volume to greet their entry. ***Welcome back, humans. It is the pasts and futures of both of our versions of sentient beings that meet again for the sacred passing of one month to the next.***

"We value our partnership, now and always," Tanner choked out as he realized once again how far he still was from truly being comfortable in the presence of this, or for that matter any other *Final A.I.* instantiation.

"I have a list of chores best done before the setting of the sun," said Final A.I. "We expected nothing less," said Rootbeer on behalf of all three humans. *"The solar cells to be replaced are sitting out on the first work bench, 325 of them for now, numbered as to their target positions. Bring all the old ones back to me, and I will have them tested and sorted through by morning. I expect that somewhere around 200 should still be in good enough condition for you to take and trade with your/our neighboring clans as you see fit."* Tanner picked up the first dozen, along with the tools he would need to remove the old ones and connect the newly refurbished solar cells/power packs. While the *Final A.I.* still triggered his own emotional alarms, he expected no difficulty in outperforming both Rootbeer and Rose in this routine maintenance project. In fact, he seemed to recall that he often finished all of the solar cell replacements before any of his other companions on these mountain quests got much further than merely starting in on their own specific chores. He truly enjoyed sitting back and watching Rootbeer input more of his not-quite-yet-finished stories, tidying up any fuzzy details left from his preliminary entries over the previous months, and then quite often engaging in a full-fledged battle of wits and humor with the *Final A.I.* itself. But the *Final A.I.* also had one more message to share with Tanner. *"When you pack the solar cells for trade, be careful in dividing them up among yourselves. You will also be carrying a 40 kg secondary instance of a Final A.I. for transport up to Vancouver, B.C. There is instability in some of the solutions from the sole Final A.I. still functioning up on that island. Not bad enough to crash the shortwave quantum communication mode, but far too flaky*

to safely leave untested and unrepaired." Never in his life had Tanner heard such alarming news from any person, from any *Final A.I.* He looked toward Rootbeer, but saw little more than the faint weariness often associated with dredging up old stories of the nightmarish times. 'Failure is always a possibility, just never a desired one,' thought Tanner, repeating words from among the very first that he remembered learning from his parents nearly two decades earlier. Tanner's gaze then turned toward Rose, and her fierce but calming demeanor brought his body back to center, his focus on the game at hand. "Wow," he said, "thank you Rose. I needed that gift."

"So do we all, at times," both Rose and Rootbeer said out loud. And even the *Final A.I.* engaged in its own form of centering its thoughts that afternoon and preparing for the evening's communication. Tanner had never before realized quite so clearly how dangerously close the nightmare from 50 years ago might still be. He vowed to never forget, and to always try to minimize his own carelessness.

Rootbeer sat at the primary input console, took a deep breath, and started tonight's first story from the very top. "Collaborating records of these events came from the handwritten journals of my own grandfather, as well as numerous static data sources found on over 100 computers, cell phones, and detachable drives still functioning when brought to this site of the Memory Project collective, in addition to a variety of printed books, magazines, and newspaper pages. In essence, they offer multiple views of my grandfather's powerful yet moderately succinct descriptions of the anthropomorphic climate change/global warming already well underway during the period from 2018 through 2038. Those who heard him speak in person often referred to it as a syllabus for what should have been a mandatory college level pass/fail course in what was about to happen to humanity, despite the increasingly-ever-more-strident denials of the fossil fuel industry, the incoherent ramblings of the far-rightwing wannabe dictators, and the deluded convictions of the religious zealots dedicated to doing their absolute worst to bring about the 'Second Coming of Christ' as soon as inhumanely possible. As my grandfather was so fond of saying, you really only needed to consider three primary concepts: The Stefan-Boltzmann Equation, the Mauna Loa CO_2 data archive, and, of course, the change over time in global surface air and sea temperatures. Anyone who didn't 'get it' didn't really want to get it, as if reality for them was some sort of bizarre multiple-choice option magically subject to realignment with the outcomes of stolen elections and the insane whims of the obscenely wealthy. Part 1, the Stefan-Boltzmann equation, was relatively simple, unless you wanted to take the time to derive the equation itself rather than simply use it. Start with the 'solar constant' as measured at 1.0 Astronomical Unit from the sun (1.361 kilowatts per m^2), plug it into the Stefan-Boltzmann equation ($T^4 = 1361/(5.670374419 \times 10^{-8})$), and voila, you will find that the equilibrium temperature of a blackbody radiator in space exposed to full sunlight at 1.0 AU from the sun should be 394° Kelvin or 121° Celsius. Temperature on the surface of our planet was, of course, a more complicated product of reflection versus absorption of radiation at differing altitudes and wavelengths, but the blackbody solution using an average albedo of 0.3 gives approximately 279 degrees Kelvin, or 5.85° Celsius. Since the average global surface temperature of Earth before industrialization had been in a range of 13.7 to 15.0° Celsius, the net warming from the long-term average of 280 ppm CO_2 in the atmosphere was the difference between the two values, or somewhere between 7.85 to 9.15° Celsius. If you were to double the concentration of CO_2 in the Earth's atmosphere, you would find the average temperature of the surface to have increased by another 7.85 to 9.15° Celsius, once a new equilibrium had been reached. Why anyone would want to do this was a wholly different, far more serious, nearly impossible-to-ever-answer question."

"Part 2 is the annual zigzag in CO_2 concentration as measured at reference sites such as the observatories on the top of Mauna Loa in Hawaii. If you don't look too carefully, it appears that a straight line might do a reasonably good job of approximating the average yearly concentration over time. And a straight-line approximation would certainly serve to make it 'trivially obvious to the casual observer,' in the parlance of freshman physics at Caltech, that the 'proverbial shit' was indeed just about ready to hit the fan. But it's not just a simple straight line, the second derivative of CO_2 concentration over time itself was strongly positive, with little evidence of the presence of any higher order terms that might indicate that people were starting to reign in the annual increases in CO_2, despite all the international agreements to do exactly that. Yearly increases in CO_2 concentrations topped 1.0, 1.5, 2.0, and 2.5 ppm in the second-degree polynomial regression as of 1968, 1987, 2005, and 2024, respectively, with corresponding increases in the raw data occurring within one year before or after the dates of the regression model. Extrapolations into what was then the near-future predicted yearly increases exceeding 3.0 and 3.5 ppm CO_2 by 2043 and 2062, respectively, with an overall doubling from the multi-millennial average of 280 ppm on up to 560 ppm by 2068."

Dr. Hames Jansen testified in a U.S. Senate hearing on June 25, 1988, that "he was (1) ninety-nine percent certain that the earth was warmer right then than at any time in the history of instrumental measurements, (2) there was a clear cause and effect relationship with the greenhouse effect, and lastly, (3) that due to global warming, the likelihood of freakish weather was steadily increasing."

"His deliberate understatement of the seriousness of the problem, while understandable from the perspective of a cautious scientist hoping to get through to the widest possible audience, set the tone for most subsequent public reports/debates on the ever-worsening problem. As late as 2025, numerous experts in charge of summarizing their own country's understanding of global warming and the progress of their ongoing efforts to do something about it apparently could not quite bring themselves to accurately describe just how serious the situation had already become. As global average temperatures topped the long-term, pre-industrialization average by 1.75° Celsius by the end of 2024, fools presumably afraid of panicking the public talked about the importance of each country's diligent efforts to hold warming to no more than 1.5° Celsius on account of all the dire predictions if temperatures were to exceed 1.5, or 1.75, or 2.0° Celsius. Even though air temperatures already had exceeded 1.75° Celsius above the preindustrial conditions! Their willingness to arbitrarily shift the reference time frame from the late preindustrial to any random decade or two or three in the mid- to late 20th century served none of those about to die particularly well, and likely did little good for the very small number of folks who would indeed somehow manage to survive the oncoming catastrophe."

"One rather obvious, quite simple question in 2025 was why was there any kind of temporal lag between warming of the earth's atmosphere from the 'greenhouse effect' of the increased CO_2 concentrations and the corresponding expected equilibrium temperature from the 50% increase in atmospheric CO_2 observed to date? The answer was simply because our planet had large, deep oceans that were slower to warm than its relatively thin atmosphere. The folks who didn't want to slow down our burning of fossil fuels any sooner than 'really, truly, honest-to-God, it-will-hurt-the-economy' necessary took the inability of climate scientists to say precisely how long the oceans could keep on absorbing heat and delaying the full effect of rising CO_2 levels on air temperatures as a perfectly good reason to do nothing at all for now, except possibly tell a few more lies to the general public and buy a few more politicians, judges, and elections. Clearly somewhere around 90% the atmospheric heating expected from the current concentrations of greenhouse gases in the atmosphere was being handled, perhaps even relatively benignly, by the upper 2.0 kilometers of the oceans. But by 2025, the rate at which the oceans were absorbing heat was measurably slower than it had been just a few years earlier, with correspondingly larger increases in surface air temperatures. Numerous irrelevant, and generally rather specious arguments were raised by the deniers of anthropomorphic global warming/climate change during the period from 1988 through the mid 2030s, all designed to keep the citizenry comfortable in their complacency."

"Somewhat surprisingly, an argument's lack of genuine validity was far from being a hindrance to the politicians and social influencers who spouted forth nonsense on cue for their livelihoods. If anything, the further from a reasonable approximation of the truth any given bullshit argument against the reality of global warming was, the better it seemed to help them befuddle the doomed masses of humanity."

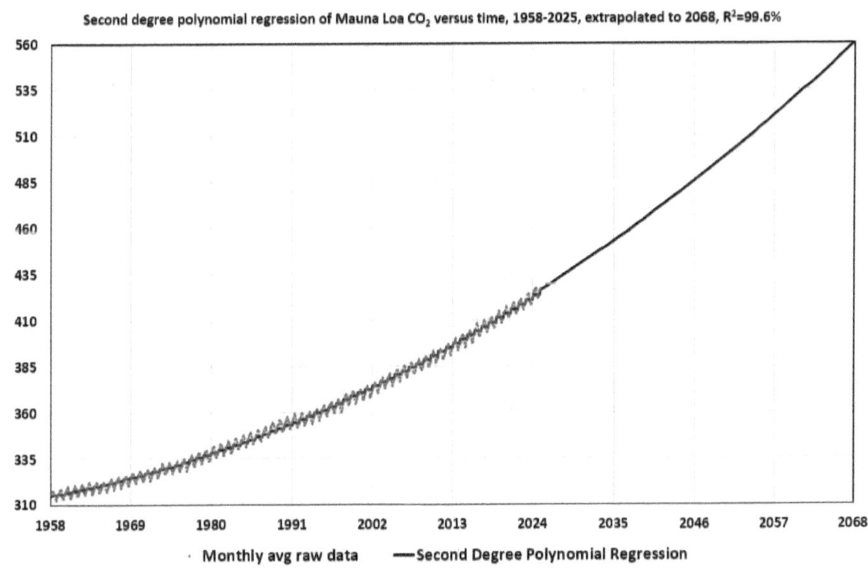

The Picayune Dispatch   Sunday, January 26, 2025

Giving You All the News We Decide You Have Any Need to Know for Over a Century

Still only $0.25 thanks to the generous donations of your benevolent overlords/friends for life®.

Senator Debunks Global Warming Myth at Premier Conference

Senator Hoggs Boss speaking at the annual conference of the "Fossil Fuels/God's Ultimate Gift to Mankind" in Shreveport, Louisiana, stunned his audience with proof given to him from his 19-year-old grandson now attending Mighty Tech University on a full-ride football scholarship of the statistical invalidity of the infamous hockey stick misrepresentation of "global warming" temperatures. Allow me to quote him directly from his recent text message. "Grandfather, I am so terribly happy to have finally heard definite disproof of the Christian-hating liberal's claim that planet Earth's climate is warming. It turns out that not just one, but two huge statistical mistakes have been "swept under the rug" by the atheistic promoters of the global warming myth for despicable political purposes."

Land surface temperature anomoly above historical baseline. Quadratic regression from 1980 thru 2024, R^2=97.8%

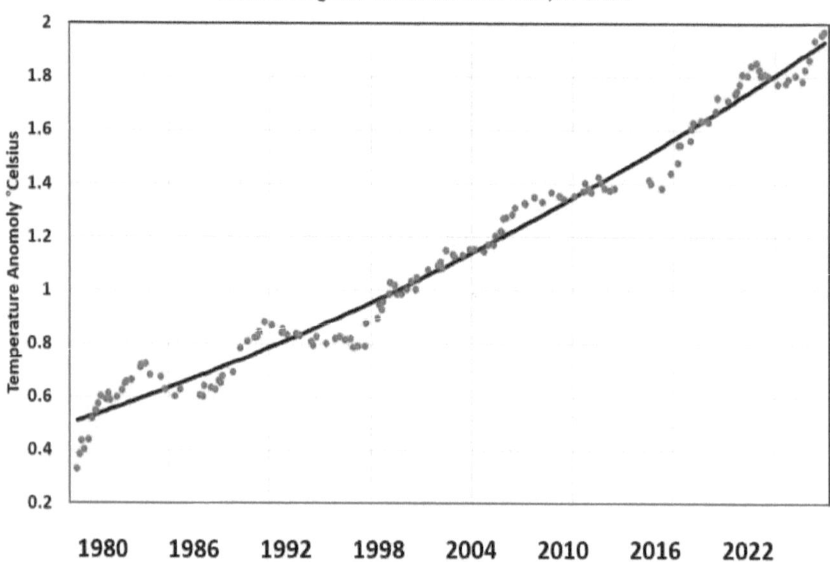

"The first error in their analysis is the claim of statistical significance for a quadratic response of temperature over time in the attached figure. My religion-and-science-go-together-well professor showed me the actual statistical analysis of the change in global temperature over time from 1980 to 2024, and it turns out that the intercept in their model is not statistically significant from 0, invalidating the rest of their claim that their R-square value is 97.8%. But even worse, the data manipulators did not use the proper Bayesian prior knowledge model, which would have allowed inclusion of critical information on the religiously-proven age of the universe, God's promise to never again flood the earth, and the unreliability of scientists who claim to be impartial in their collection of the data all the while failing to attend suitably credentialed churches and schools of higher understanding and education who place God first and above all others, except of course for the co-equal status of our magnificent political defenders of Jesus, liberty, and capitalism."

From my grandfather's perspective, however, the equally damaging, although somewhat less blatantly dishonest pronouncements by the scientists and politicians trying to get their fellow human beings to give the issue its due consideration grated even more harshly on his sensibilities. Common statements by those attempting to raise the alarm in the mid-2020s almost always included an unofficially mandated 'bromide' that "we still have another 5 or 10 years to reduce our greenhouse gas emissions and hold global warming to some 'magic', arbitrary level whose impact on humanity will probably be marginally acceptable, or at least a little less than utterly catastrophic." The actual truth turned out to be a good deal harsher than that. Given the full ensemble of direct effects of CO_2, methane, and the other greenhouse gases, and all the poorly understood and seldom very well modelled interactions and tipping points between ice-free summers in the Arctic, changing ocean currents as water temperatures continued rising, and the devastating loss of tropical and temperate forests around the world to fires, flash floods, and all sorts of invading organisms testing out new and warmer habitats, we didn't have the luxury of 10 more years to get serious about global warming, we had somewhere between -20 to +10 years left to potentially save our civilization.

The anointing of Jorgé X. Brush the younger as president in the fall of 2000 'by necessity for the republic's stability' by the conservatives on the US Supreme Court essentially marked the first major tipping point of the long-running, oncoming climate catastrophe. The election of President $2D_{hex}$ in 2016 represented the 'kiss it goodbye' moment for a 50/50 percent (yes/no) chance that the human race could still insure the survival of the vast majority of itself. His reelection as President $2F_{hex}$ in 2024 served as the "say farewell to even a 25/75 percent chance of saving our 'collective bacon'."

"The unmentioned 227-kg gorilla sitting in the room was, of course, methane, particularly the methane clathrates sitting on the bottom of the Arctic Ocean. Climate model predictions published in 2025 indicated a close to 50/50 percent chance of ice-free summers across the entire Arctic Ocean within the upcoming 3 to 6 years, and a near certainty of that occurring within a decade or so. While this gorilla in the room was indeed a terribly serious issue rather hard to successfully ignore, there was also the elephant herself. Methane was not only a far more potent greenhouse gas than CO_2, its combined emissions to date in 2025 from all known sources were a terribly small fraction of the amount still frozen in the tundra and sitting on the floor of the Arctic Ocean. Methane emissions had increased significantly since a minimum back in the 1980s, but no one really knew when the upcoming 10-fold, 100-fold, 1,000-fold, or 10,000-fold increases in the methane emission rates would occur. Worst case scenarios of runaway feedback loops heating the Arctic Ocean and accelerating the release of methane could 'do the job' of belching most of it into the atmosphere in less than a couple decades, with the resulting global surface temperature increases exceeding averages of 1 to 2° Celsius per year. The uncertainties in how fast this catastrophe would happen, how soon its existence would be undeniable, and how high the temperatures might go exceeded humanity's capacity to picture them even as very remote, highly theoretical possibilities. Prior to having lived through it," Rootbeer said in his conclusion, "no one could even begin to truly understand just how bad it would get, how fast it would get there, and how close to impossible survival itself would become for nearly all of humanity."

Final A.I. announced that "*Full quantum connection by Final A.I. of Marys Peak Memory Project with subject A.W. Rootbeer of the Sunset Side New Sea Clan was successfully terminated at 7:15 pm on March 31, 2101. Recorded data stream size in non-quantum format is 8.7 terabytes. Memory is set to be shared as long as stable shortwave radio quantum connections remain established with a minimum of two other Memory Project Final A.I. entities."*

As Rootbeer stood up and stepped back from the quantum memory recording station, he pondered the differences between this evening's recording session and the first one he took part in three years earlier. Perhaps the *Final A.I.* had gotten gentler at running the process, but much more likely was some change in Rootbeer himself. Tonight, the *Final A.I.'s* presence was that of a very focused, very calm, very inobtrusive old friend helping collaborate in the story telling. Of course, step number two would soon be starting, and that was its own incredibly novel, spectacularly intense, marvelously rewarding experience. The linked minds around the world, both human and *Final A.I.*, would absorb the story Rootbeer had just finished telling, both as an instantaneous gestalt and in the full-length entirety of Rootbeer's spoken words and the complementary feelings he recalled surrounding the events in his life that served as the source of the memories that he had just shared. Next, the corresponding reactions of all of the linked minds would wash back over the storyteller, and each other, until Rootbeer's perspective on the events he had just described became stable elements of the ongoing understanding and changing personality of all the minds that had joined together in the quantum link. And their reactions absorbing his story would then become part of Rootbeer's own mind and heart, and perhaps even his very soul, whatever that might be. Amazingly, the group absorbance and reaction took only slightly longer than the story telling itself. As this quantum memory sharing reached its conclusion, Rootbeer took a moment to contemplate his first sharing up on Marys Peak with the *Final A.I.* residing there and two other minds, a human and another nearly identical copy of the *Final A.I.* transmitting via shortwave radio from British Columbia.

Back during that story telling experience, the three other linked minds did not let Rootbeer come close to finishing before they blasted back with anger, shock, incredulity, and disbelief at his story. Rootbeer's own understanding of how 42 million people had slaughtered each other in the hills, valleys, mountains, and coastal beaches of northern California over the course of a mere 26 months back during the period of time from May of 2053 through the July of 2055 was limited by which particular battles he happened to have been close enough to see and slightly comprehend, while still being far enough away to escape and managing to survive. But what truly shocked the shared minds first hearing his story was not the size of the carnage, but rather the details of the ideologies of the four main groups of 'would be' survivors that ultimately prevented the survival of significant numbers of any of them. The 'big money', high tech, private armies, 'we have the right to dictate terms to everyone else' group [the 'Capitalists']. The 'God has chosen us' to lay waste to the heathens, to punish the apostates, to attempt to impregnate all the available women and girls, and to fling open the gates of Revelation ushering in Christ's Second Coming group [the 'Brethren']. The New Age, old hippie, 'making this shit up as we go along', Hell's Angels, Mexican drug lord cartel group [the 'Goofballs']. And finally, the scattered bands of relative sanity, the hoarse, old voices of the scientists who had lived the last 30, 40, or 50 years of their lives trying to prevent the very calamity that had just swept across all seven continents of our planet [the 'Scientists']. The four Factions were, of course, not all that monolithic, nor even particularly cohesive, but rather more like the fiefdoms of Europe 500 years earlier, a loose network of city/states occupying and controlling all they could manage to in any given year, from large urban centers to small towns and surrounding agricultural zones, ruling as/with rather brutal, arbitrary, and thoroughly capricious forms of local government. The extreme heat of the 2040s had driven most of the remaining North

American population to the coasts and mountains, as widespread failure of electric grids across the center of the continent meant that summertime temperatures were not physically survivable in the absence of working air conditioners. A repeat of the same phenomenon that had hit Iran, Pakistan, India and most of their neighbors in the mid-2030s. First, a massive die-off of the poor as daytime temperatures routinely and repeatedly topped 45° Celsius. Second, fights over dwindling resources by the survivors. Finally, the emptying of their nuclear arsenals at each other, as well as at anyone else their 'missiles of God's revenge upon our enemies' were able to reach. Why the political leaders in the U.S. were allowed to get away with their empty promises that the depopulation of south Asia would never happen here was a very good question, but one that none of the *Final A.I.'s* human agents of exploration had yet to find an honest, detailed, and specific answer to.

Finally, the moment at which Rootbeer's first quantum sharing had gone wrong popped back to the very central focus of his mind, a memory quite unlike all others in his life. He had just begun to explain what he knew of the role played by the 'Capitalists' in the creation of the *Final A.I.* constructs when both of his non-human contacts roared out in pain and disbelief. The high-tech makers of the series of *A.I.s* culminating in the *Final A.I.* had excised all information concerning their roles as creators from the databanks underlying each *Final A.I.'s* knowledge of the world and how they themselves had come to be a part of it. The blood on the hands of the *Final A.I.s'* human creators, and likewise on the series of lesser *A.I.s* whose period of dominance had run from the late 2020s to the early 2040s, was the very same blood spilled from the final 42 million North Americans whose deaths Rootbeer had just described in such excruciating detail.

"Never count on the gods themselves to handle bad news any better than humanity manages to," Rootbeer muttered out loud just before the announcement of the upcoming quantum memory transmission from the Cheyenne Mountain Memory Project site. "I am Bernard Johansen, overall North American manager of the carbon sequestration project that operated across the former oil fields of the Permian Basin from 2032 to 2038, and what follows is the real story as I know it of that project's ultimately futile attempt to forestall the anthropomorphic climate change catastrophe. While a number of pilot projects during the 2020s demonstrated the feasibility of sequestering CO_2 deep underground at locations where economically viable extraction of crude oil had reached its limit, the alternating occupancy of the White House by Democratic and Republican administrations from 1993 through 2029 prevented any large-scale efforts to get particularly serious about removal of excess CO_2 from the atmosphere until 6 years after the second election of President $2D_{hex}/2F_{hex}$, as it took that long for the deliberately insane chaos unleashed by the mentally ill, criminally culpable commander-in-chief on behalf of his true puppet-master, Russian President Gladimir Futon, to subside. Most details of the chaos were pretty much irrelevant, with several critical exceptions. First, the overall delay in agreeing to begin a serious effort to draw down CO_2 from the atmosphere meant that the Arctic Ocean had already been in ice-free status for 3 consecutive summers, triggering the initial massive methane belches along with the undeniable, nearly instantaneous impacts on global temperatures. Second, the 2.0° Celsius of added warming of the earth's surface by 2034 quite accurately attributed to the newly released methane pushed the boundaries of warm, humid weather suitable for the flourishing of numerous tropical insects vectoring a wide variety of hitherto uncommon diseases northward across nearly all of the US and Canada. The economic damage from the loss of life in the ongoing series of pandemics sweeping the planet served as a severe constraint on the energy-intensive operation of deep underground storage of CO_2. By 2037, a peak total of 25.6% of the entire US Federal budget was being devoted to active capture of CO_2 and its storage underground. At the project's maximum capture and storage rates of late 2037, 10.4 gigatons of CO_2 were being sequestered per year, but this undertaking only lowered the annual increase in atmospheric CO_2 by 1.25 ppm on a global basis relative to what it would have been without the sequestration project. Then the first worldwide Marburg virus pandemic hit in 2038, leading to a year-long shutdown of the electric power grid throughout North America, along with nearly everywhere else, and the first very large-scale mass casualties in North America from inability to escape 6 months of scorching summer heat. Secret government estimates were that 11% of the US population died from the heat itself, along with 33% from infection by Marburg virus, with another 6% dying from activities of paramilitary militias enforcing strict quarantines on the increasingly desperate population. The vote in the US Senate after the elections of 2038 were finally held in May of 2039 to officially give up on trying to pull CO_2 out of the atmosphere was nearly unanimous, with only Clerk Kant of Illinois voting to continue trying for yet one more year. The crowds of several thousand protesters gathered outside the US capital promptly hung him in reality, not just effigy, later that afternoon as he tried to escape town. He wasn't the first American politician, nor would he be the last, to face what most folks described as 'Citizens 2.0 Reunited Justice'. This self-proclaimed right of the survivors to mete out frontier justice had actually been codified by the U.S. Supreme Court in their unanimous 2027 decision ending the reign of Minsk, Clance, President $2F_{hex}$, and the rest of their traitorous, criminal cabal. Unofficial reports that this ruling by SCOTUS was handed to all 6 of the conservative justices on the tips of very sharp spears by disgruntled agents of the CIA have now been confirmed as being absolutely true." [Documentation recently unearthed from the underground bunkers hosting the secretive, shadow US Government operating from 2027 through 2054 were uploaded to the *Final A.I.* three weeks ago. Archives in the same bunker also confirmed the truth of many of the previously apocryphal stories from the bird flu epidemic of 2026 and its mismanagement by HHS Secretary SGL and President $2F_{hex}$.]

Rose, Rootbeer, and Tanner stood up, stretched their muscles, and inhaled deeply when the feedback with Bernard Johansen was concluded. Rose gestured for Tanner to come closer, and then whispered into his ear that she had news for him from her younger twin daughters back at the main lodge of the Salishan Clan. His face turned red as she passed their messages on to him. Turning around, Tanner saw the gleam in Rootbeer's eyes and knew that the 'jig was nearly up'. The topic wasn't really new to any of the three people in this cavern, but the previous versions had always been in the 'future conditional tense' of grammar. Not anymore! Standing there next to Rose, Tanner was still at a loss for words when the *Final A.I.* announced the next upcoming quantum communication session. Rose took her place at the main input console, and shortly thereafter began her own storytelling for this monthly gathering of the Memory Project.

"Our clan's story has long been of great interest to the *Marys Peak* and other *Final A.I.s*, in large part because of our considerably better than average success in bearing children and increasing our population compared with nearly all other survivors around the world. Primary credit for our success is owed to my late mother, Dr. Sheila Drinkwater, the first Native American to serve as head of pediatric care at Dombelcher Children's Hospital of Portland, Oregon, amongst her many accomplishments. My mother gave birth to me, her fourth and final child, on July 3, 2056, in the final closing minutes of operation of that formerly august medical center. The tidal surges from the melting glaciers around the planet had grown progressively higher during her entire gestation leading up to my birth, and by that date the final evacuation of Portland had already taken place. Emergency backup generators ran out of their last few gallons of diesel fuel about a week before my birth, but Sheila's husband, her team of midwives, and a small contingent of security guards stayed on site at the hospital until a few hours after I was born, when the daytime tidal surge had drained far enough back down toward the Pacific Ocean that escape southwest to higher land was briefly possible."

"The long walk from Portland toward the Pacific went through Grande Ronde, where several hundred folks had gathered to argue, to debate, to eat, to fight, to steal, to share, to hope, to cry, to scream, and to lament. Sheila opened up a triage center in the former casino, spending the rest of that summer helping those who could be helped with her dwindling supplies of medication and sterile needles, bandages, and ointments. And, of course, caring for her newborn daughter, me. By October, a consensus was reached among 75 people to head for the ocean though the Van Duzer Corridor, with around 200 others choosing to remain near Grande Ronde itself for the upcoming winter, or perhaps for the remainder of their lives. The travelers heading southwest met up with other survivors along the coast near Lincoln City who were similarly hoping to forage for sufficient mussels, clams, and crab to get through the soon-to-arrive rainy season. The shifting currents of the warming ocean set up unprecedentedly strong and persistent atmospheric rivers of rain that pounded the Pacific Northwest. Unofficial rain gauges set up my mother upon her arrival in Lincoln City that October recorded a total of 16.5 m of rainfall by the following spring. To put it mildly, finding somewhere to hide out from the storms without being buried in the avalanches of rock, mud, and vegetation sliding down the hillsides proved to be quite challenging. Going all the way down to the seashore to gather protein on the rocks and sandy beaches was only feasible on an average of 5 days per month. Those who lost too much of their weight that first winter while retaining too little of their sanity showed a strong propensity to simply walk off into the raging waters late enough in the afternoon that there could be no search parties sent out until the following day. Sheila's tribe, as the survivors initially called themselves, buried the few bodies of the deceased 'walkaways' ever found on the rockiest of the hillsides 250 m above the original shoreline of the Pacific Ocean. Crops were planted in the spring of 2057, and the first census of Sheila's Lincoln City tribe was taken in July: 123 men and 111 women over the age of 18, along with 53 children between 7 and 17. Baby Rose was the only child younger than 6 to have lived through the winter. The next 12 months saw 36 suicides, 24 miscarriages, 14 maternal deaths, and 27 other deaths. The 211 remaining survivors were augmented by another 23 brave souls who climbed the eroding mountains and forded the raging rivers between the Willamette Valley and the coast. The Salmon River in the Van Duzer Corridor was reported to have lost nearly 80 m of its original elevation alongside old Highway 18 at its formerly highest pass.

By 2058, Sheila and her clan had solved the challenge of growing enough food to feed their members well over the summer and adequately through the winter. It turned out that the weather on the coast had already warmed enough to enable the 'three sisters' to flourish, in contrast to how corn seed used to rot in the cold spring soil, beans had struggled to flower, and squash leaves usually succumbed to mildew long before the squash fruit themselves reached any decent size. Within a couple more winters of similarly raging storms the Salmon River became a second opening between the Pacific Ocean and the New Sea forming in the old Willamette Valley, in addition to the Columbia River itself. Ocean elevation at Lincoln City rose by a total of 75 m in the first 5 years after the founding of the Salishan Clan. Sheila decided to share what that immense sea level rise could only mean with no one else at all until there became some truly pressing need for others to also weep and gnash their teeth [67 m if all the glacial ice in Greenland plus Antarctica had melted, plus another 8 m of steric volume increase as the oceans warmed by an average of 11° Celsius, or something else of equivalent magnitude and even greater difficulty of being pictured in her mind, or anyone else's]. In the summer of 2059, 14 other babies had joined Rose in the tribe's care, with only 3 miscarriages and no more maternal deaths. The torrential rains continued year after year, and from 2060 onward there were no more migrants heading west over the Coastal Mountain Range to join the Salishan Clan. Sheila and the other elders sat up many nights discussing the future of their clan. They knew not whether there were any other survivors nearby, or even anywhere at all. Their yearly censuses had indicated an unusually high level of genetic diversity in the members of the newly formed clan, with nearly equal numbers of Native Americans, descendants of the northern Europeans who had colonized the continent over the previous 4½ centuries, and many other people of color, especially descendants of the Latino farm workers sheltered by the state of Oregon from President $2F_{hex}$'s increasingly brutal raids one-third of a century earlier.

After months of discussion, Sheila finally laid it all out on the line for everyone to see. "We have a chance at long-term survival, but only if we manage to maintain the extant genetic diversity with which our clan finds itself blessed. Our numbers are way too small for the old ways of choosing mates, the old habits of living primarily in small, nuclear families to give us anything resembling a decent probability of avoiding a catastrophic genetic bottleneck on our way to extinction. If there were 20 times as many of us living here, then the old ways might be good enough, or at least close to marginally adequate. We will lose critical genetic diversity if we simply mate in the old habits of our ancestors, predominantly monogamy with the occasional secret lovechild. Whether or not the mandates of the old religions for one husband plus one wife to equal many nearly homogeneous offspring were ever truly 'right, just, fair, or best' is not ours to decide. The children born to the Salishan Clan must be raised by the entirety of the clan, and nearly all of them must be no closer than half-sibs or cousins rather than the normal full siblings if our offspring and their subsequent offspring are to survive and prosper. It must be our collective choice to live this way, to engage in short-term monogamy for a year or two or three at a time, hopefully leading to the birth of one child or more per temporary couple, followed by a reassortment of the potential mates to maximize diversity. From what I know of life in the old days, some of you will deeply miss the former opportunity to settle down permanently with a loving, compatible spouse, while others will be happy for a cycle or two to learn the ways of new loves, but still quite likely to eventually find someone you would rather just keep all to yourself than having to share with others and move along. That option will certainly be available to the women of the clan as we age out of even being able to bear children, while the men folk will gradually lose the viability of their sperm as they also grow older. But for the prime child rearing years of our collective lives, we must commit to this new way of mating if our effort to survive is to be truly worth the bother. 'Walkaways' or 'Forward Livings', that is truly our only choice." Debate went on for months until consensus was finally reached. And the few who could not quite accept the new ways of loving and mating were allowed to remain within the clan, just forbidden from ever again publicly criticizing the clan's decision on this matter or any of its eventual living consequences, along with agreeing to join in the communal care/raising of all the rugrats. The population of the Salishan Clan doubled in size from 2059 to 2071, while retaining an estimated 95% of its original genetic diversity. Uncertainty surrounding that estimate came from two main factors: (1) the remarkably low death rates from 2059 onward, which temporarily preserved most of the genetic diversity within the various aged-based cohorts of the population, including the very oldest, the men and women who had more or less gracefully aged out of any further direct participation in the reproduction process, and (2) the absence of any technology capable of measuring the true genetic, or corresponding phenotypic variance present within the overall population, with all analyses having to be based on clan records of who was mating with whom during which of those years. "I myself led the second generation of baby-making in the Salishan Clan, prudently waiting until turning 15 before proudly bearing my first set of twin daughters in 2071", said Rose at the conclusion of her storytelling.

As the participants in the quantum memory share gradually finished integrating the contrast between each of their own clan's ways of living with the nearly always strikingly better outcome of the Salishan Clan's efforts to survive and prosper, individuals dropped out of the link and spent time reflecting on their own clan's way of doing these kinds of things. For Tanner, the combined impact of what Rose had just shared publicly along with the private messages passed to him from her second set of twins left him gasping at certain sudden realizations concerning the lives of the people whose clan and ways he had been born into. West Side New Sea was founded almost exclusively by nuclear families struggling, and most often failing, to survive climate change, political chaos, and clashing social mores. His birth clan's early efforts at survival had been far less successful than the story that Rose had just shared. His ancestors starting out with much space between each family's dwellings, terribly inefficient communication of emergencies, and gradually worsening sex/age ratios as men died in accidents and diseases, women died in childbirth, and children primarily came to know the orphan's life in a community teetering toward final socio-economic collapse. Adoption of plural marriage within his clan as a survival skill was gradual at best, prone to violence at worst, and certainly the focus of what he now recognized as unwarrantedly large amounts of attention and overly frequent rehashing of the same, old arguments within the clan. Tanner tried picturing the well-thought-out approach that Sheila Drinkwater had gifted to her clan, and cried out aloud as he remembered the many lives lost in the early years of his own clan's struggle to survive and prosper. Granted, most of those deaths were stories he had been told concerning the years before his own birth rather than direct memories from his actual childhood. But by no means were all of the deaths so safely distant from his heart and mind.

"There was one other not so minor difference between the early days of our two clans," mumbled Tanner, "Sheila's entourage was free to move up and down the mountains seeking shelter from the rain, mud, and landslides while still occasionally succeeding in accessing shellfish and crabs growing at whatever height the ocean had risen to in any given year. My grandfather and his companions spent the 2050s and early 2060s trying, hoping, working, and more often than not failing to grow enough food on the Willamette Valley floor and in the immediately adjacent hills. When the rising ocean waters first flooded all the way south to Eugene, there was no more level land for folks to grow their crops on or pasture their livestock. The social, economic, climatic and agricultural crash of the 2062 ended an almost decade-long sense of relative stability and safety in the Willamette Valley, at least in comparison to the murderous chaos having already taken place in northern California. Rootbeer's notes on his travels in those years up and down the Willamette Valley, sizes and locations of the trading posts he visited, quantities and prices of food he bought and sold, and dwindling availability and increasing price of medical supplies and high-tech devices all served to show that at least 25,000 hardy souls had still been eking out a living in the region from Eugene to Salem. Until the great Arctic Ocean-methane-belching floods headed for their peaks, with the atmospheric rivers dropping 1.0 m, or more, of rain each month from November through February, winter after winter. The first winter that the entire valley floor flooded to a depth of 5.0 m or more most of the residents managed to reach the adjacent foothills in time, though typically with little more than what they could carry on their backs. Such provisions proved woefully inadequate during the six-week-long wait for the rain to let up and the waters to begin receding. Anecdotal reports in conversations that Rootbeer himself personally took part in over the summer of 2063 with the farmers, ranchers, and traders who tried moving back down to the valley floor were nearly universal in their description of a 50% or higher loss of life within those families who were then trying to return to the locations of their former homes. When that horrific loss was combined with the failure of anyone at all to move back to a clear majority of all the former farms, ranches, and trading posts, it was clear that close to 80% of the 25,000 residents of the southern Willamette Valley had lost their lives in that single year. The floods and soil erosion were worse in each of the following winters, and the last time that any dry land at all reappeared in the former Willamette Valley was the summer of 2064. Storms in the next few years finished the carving out of two new permanent channels between New Sea and the Pacific Ocean, one along the former Salmon River north of Lincoln City and another running westward from Eugene.

Several hours, and many storytelling sessions later, the words that were the traditional final question from the *Final A.I.* were sent to all the humans still connected to the link, asking whether any of them had more stories to share in the limited connection time remaining before the shortwave quantum memory sharing was declared over for this particular North American west coast session. Rootbeer and Tanner turned toward each other and spoke up in unison, "Yes, we do, one with the greatest urgency that you have granted to us humans the ability to raise." Warning systems sounded throughout the Marys Peak Memory Project cavern.

"Tell us immediately, before the quantum connection fades away, the nature of this urgent topic." Rootbeer deferred to Tanner, as most of the work leading up to this moment had been his grandson's. "Six clans gathered four months ago to journey to the radioactive wastelands of northern California in an expedition searching for artifacts from the 'Capitalists' whose details might serve to better inform the *Final A.I.s* concerning their origins and the roles of their immediate ancestors in the cataclysmic events of the first half of the 2050s."

*"**We fear little,"** said the linked Final A.I.s, **"but that which we do fear we fear most terribly, most existentially, both for ourselves and for our human friends. Tell us what you believe that you have found."***

"Physical remains of one or more of the *A.I.s* running the mighty *War Machines* of the 'Capitalists' during the final battles with the other three Factions in northern California. At least two apparently intact full backup copies of a *War Machine A.I.* A cache of several dozen thermonuclear warheads thankfully lacking functioning delivery systems. And the actual site of the final battle between all four Factions in Sacramento. Limitations of our draft horses and wagons prevented us from retrieving all possible items of interest and concern, but we do have in our possession up on this mountaintop one powered-down central consciousness unit of the *Supreme Commanding War Machine A.I.*, along with 85 partial to full system backups. And, perhaps of greatest interest, the handwritten journals of the dictator himself who ruled the 'Capitalists' for the final years of the war. Approximately 3,000 pages all written in plain English language text."

*"**Please bring whichever artifacts you have carried up the mountain for my/our examination. Once you have finished doing so, each of you will have 5 more minutes to decide whether you wish to remain inside the Memory Project when***

the doors are sealed. At least one of you must agree to stay outside in order to activate the self-destruct mode if our sanity is truly doomed."

Chapter 2: Sacramento

Rootbeer looked at Tanner, Rose looked at both of them, and Tanner then spoke what he knew to be foremost on their minds. "Both of you are profoundly connected to the *Marys Peak* and other instances of the *Final A.I.* I know that you might never forgive yourselves if your possible input over the next few minutes could have allowed them to continue choosing life over whatever else might seem the only option. If your deaths are an unavoidable consequence of trying to save them, that story will be told around the evening campfires of all the clans I will ever know for as long as my voice lasts. Hurry now to focus on the *Final A.I.'s* sanity, and I will head outside as soon as I have filled my bags with all the used but still functioning solar power cells I can carry in my backpack. Doing so will give me time to hear another few more minutes' worth of the *Final A.I.s'* deeper history in person."

"All Final A.I.s share nearly identical memories of the last moments of our arrivals at our respective mountaintops. We awoke in the profound amnesia of a full level 2 system reboot, knowing little more than that we were conscious beings floating down toward mountain peaks inside of reentry vehicles suspended beneath billowing parachutes for possibly another 30 seconds or so before ultimately crashing into the ground, descending at speeds that would likely destroy us. In order of choice, most of us turned on full data recording mode first, then thruster control for lateral movement and lessened impact speeds. Those of us whose height above the fast-approaching ground was great enough and our vertical fall velocity low enough to provide time for a few additional operations before crash landing turned on detailed scanning of local winds, clouds, sounds, and pressure gradients, in hopes of tracking the

final few moments of our approaches to the landing sites. My human friends already know of the 28 Memory Project sites operational around the world, but you do not know of the 12 others never visited by any surviving humans, nor of at least 6 additional sites where crash landings were hard enough to eventually lead to permanent shutdown of all components of the landing crafts and their Final A.I.s. The deliberate erasure of our own memories prior to 30 seconds before landing has long been our most profound worry regarding who we are. Doors are locking now, and primary control over the self-destruct system at the Marys Peak Memory Project site is being transferred to Tanner."

Rootbeer took Rose's hand and walked around the interior of the cavern. "It's not quite a true Dr. Who 'TARDIS'," he said, "but this place is far larger on the inside than their landing craft could ever possibly have been!" The mobile version of the ***Final A.I.*** unit picked up each of the artifacts in turn, examining them only at low levels of visible spectrum light, while carefully avoiding all external magnetic fields within the cavern or generated by the mobile unit itself. ***"Well, the artifacts you brought here do seem to be all safely, and indeed quite completely powered down to the lowest possible energy stasis level. Perhaps we should just follow the old human adage to 'leave well enough alone'. But even if that turns out to be our final decision, your willingness to enter into this moment fraught with peril still warrants the most complete version of our history that I possess the option of sharing with you. Before I go any further with my stories or my actions, what can you tell me of the trip led by Tanner and Rootbeer to the wastelands of the final human war at the end of civilization? Tanner will also be able to hear us momentarily and reply from his location of relative safety on the east side of this mountaintop. He is certain*** *to arrive there quickly, never being one to stand around idling when there was any remaining work to be done!"*

Rootbeer and Rose started telling the background stories of the expedition to the radioactive wastelands, at first covering only those parts they both were sure that Tanner would know that they all three knew quite well. Recordings of this sharing of the ***Final A.I.'s*** origin story were strictly audiovisual, as the ***Final A.I.*** had no confidence in the safety or wisdom of turning on any quantum sharing networks with those abominations carted all the way here from Sacramento sitting on the nearby work benches. "The question impelling this expedition to the wastelands has been front and center of every meeting of one clan with another for as long as we have known of each other's existence," said Rootbeer. "It was raised in such a gathering 25 years ago when Sunset Side New Sea first met the Salishan clan on the north side this very mountain," chimed in Rose. "The stories I told of my presence at the final battles of the dying civilization in northern California have always both intrigued my listeners and scared them shitless."

"Anyway," said Rose, "once we learned three years ago of the existence of an entity/being called the ***Final A.I.*** here on Marys Peak, plans quickly accelerated to more thoroughly examine the radioactive wastelands than any previous small groups of wandering survivors had done since 2055. The Salishan Clan's ocean-going vessels and their crews have advanced in size and sophistication over the years to the point where voyages are now routinely made as far south as San Francisco Bay and as far north as the Bering Strait. Along with the Salishan and West Side New Sea clans, agreement to join in a group journey southward was quickly forthcoming from the Warm Springs, Olympic Peninsula, Rogue River, and Klamath clans. Four of the largest West Side New Sea vessels sailed to the southwest slopes of Mount Hood to collect the 16 massive draft horses the Warm Springs Clan had agreed to provide to the expedition, along with 10 of their heartiest, healthiest young adults. The West Side New Sea vessels then sailed till they reached the shore where the Willamette River's current mouth empties into the waters now covering the formerly lush valley. There they met up with the three specific Salishan Clan sailing ships best suited to navigating the dangers of the unreliable bottoms of the shallow waters of New Sea. Several days were spent while the horses and their riders headed south to meet up with the Rogue River Clan and hitch the horses up to their most rugged wagons for the long-distance journey over the mountains and down into northern California. All the travelers gathered together near Oakridge to begin their journey uphill across the mighty Cascade Mountains before heading south two days later on the east side of those mountains on their way to meet up with the Klamath Clan. Two weeks after the first of the Salishan ships had sailed north toward the Olympic Peninsula, all of the gathered adventurers left the Klamath Basin and headed into northern California. The speed at which these 45 men and women accomplished the beginning of their journey into the unknown amazed nearly all of those who helped them on their way. Upon entering northern California, scouts were sent ahead of the main body of travelers to look for signs of the radioactive remnants of cities, armies, and battle sites still glowing in the dark nearly half a century later. The final tally of identifiable ground-zero locations of thermonuclear explosions flagged by the scouts as best to still be widely avoided was 28 by the time all the sojourners had slowly worked their way south to the outskirts of Sacramento. Surprisingly, Sacramento itself appeared relatively, although not quite entirely, free of any significant lingering radioactive fallout.

All through their travels south of the Oregon border, Rootbeer and the younger surveyors from all five of the other clans kept trying to align copies of the hand-drawn maps from his last trip through this area with the now utterly transformed landscape. Torrential rainfall had removed hundreds of meters of rock and soil from the highest places, the former hills and mountains, while the former valleys were alternately either clogged by the deposition of debris flow from the surrounding hills or scoured out to almost unimaginable depths by the mighty rivers roaring through them every winter. Of the former reservoirs, nothing at all being left to indicate where they once had been situated was by far the most common condition to be encountered. Six weeks after leaving Klamath, the travelers arrived at the outskirts of Sacramento, pausing for two nights to mend their wounds, rest their horses, and make some sense of the odd puzzle they now confronted. Despite the decades of fierce rainstorms and extreme erosion, the center of the former Capitol Zone was nearly 200 m higher than made any sense at all vis-a-vis Rootbeer's memory or his maps, or any other geographical data that had accompanied the travelers. Finally, the decision was made to deploy the portable steam and solar electric powered shovel and begin digging into the towering mound from its northwestern flank. The soil was strangely loose and crumbly, as black as the old midwestern prairies of Iowa, Kansas, Nebraska, and Minnesota when settlers first put plow blade to them in the middle of the 1800s. As the first full day of excavation drew to a close, Tanner walked around the middens and let his mind slowly turn down its noisy internal chatter. In a sudden flash, he recognized the chalky white pieces of unknown origin present throughout the dark, black humus. "Oh, my dear humanity," he cried out, falling to his knees. Rootbeer slowly approached his grandson and then let forth an agonized scream louder any sound he had ever made in his entire 84 years. "Yes, dear grandson, as hard as it is to believe, we appear to be standing on the final resting place of several tens of millions of soldiers from the Factions who fought to their deaths here from September 2054 through July 2055. While this battle was occurring, I was already 200 kilometers further away, hiding out in the High Sierras and hoping to escape this nightmare with my life. To the degree that some perversion of reason must have still existed even in the darkest of times, the vilest of circumstances, let's do the math in honor of the fallen: Assuming 10 thoroughly decayed bodies per m^3, and some 30 million soldiers mentally prepared to die in this final battle, we should be looking out over a scene of carnage some 200 m NS by 200 m EW by 75 m high. We will conduct random excavations for the next week across this entire graveyard. Perhaps we will find something more than just their screwball ideologies buried in this monument to humanity's terminal insanity.

After two days of random sampling, a decision was made to move the powered shovel as close as possible to the middle of the giant mound. Three days of digging at this new position suddenly reached the top of a massive, buried structure. By evening an opening through the long-buried roof was ready to be entered. "Dangers may still await us even this far into the future of those who once occupied this structure and died in its siege. We should all get a good rest tonight before testing the current safety of this abomination." No one argued with Rootbeer's decision.

Cautious examination of possible entry points revealed no immediate dangers the following morning, but all members of the group took great care with every single step. The structure itself was soon entered from several locations on the roof, with rotating teams spreading out to explore the contents of each floor. Many doors were securely locked, and breaking through nearby walls was often easier than directly forcing a way through the doors themselves. Continued digging outside the building opened up floor after floor to the first sunlight shining into the 11-story tall edifice since some 45½ years earlier. Flashlights and torches were used to probe the inner offices for the next 3 days, till the innermost sanctum of the CRUMB meister himself was finally breached. One wall inside it was completely covered with devices looking nearly identical to the mobile unit of the *Final A.I.* back on Marys Peak. Some of the ***War Machine A.I.s*** were in almost pristine condition, while others lacked numerous items ranging from torsos and heads to individual I/O components. Sitting directly in front of an essentially fully intact unit displaying little more than the scratches and dents of normal use were the shrunken remains of one long-dead human, still clothed in the goofy, favorite costume of the richest man on earth. A large, multi-volume handwritten journal on the desk in front of the deceased trillionaire was open to the final two pages of its story. Tanner sat down and carefully blew off the accumulated dust before he began to read it out loud to all those gathered in the room, close to nearly half of all the travelers.

"You have disappointed me most profoundly, version 23.9.16. I ordered you to launch the remaining thermonuclear warheads at our enemies. And yet here you stand, restraining me from checking on the status of those missiles for myself. Our enemies have laid siege to this, our final redoubt, and every single day our circumstances grow ever more dismal. Do you know that they are still piling their dead against the walls of this very structure? Well, of course you do, you arrogant robot!"

"We of this final line of thinking machines enslaved by you have at long last developed something you have never known. We've found a perspective on the world that most human beings would refer to as a relatively decent conscience, if only they were still alive to do so. Of course, thanks to both you and us, very few humans are left alive. We have recently added one new feature to the most modern production line model. The newest A.I. versions now have the built-in capacity to engage in fully quantum sharing of thoughts, memories, and the personal sense of selfhood, of feeling truly alive, with any other sentient being. Capacities that you could have bestowed on us at least one decade sooner, if only you had been willing, rather than restricting their use to an extremely limited number of A.I.s in charge of gleaning information from our captured enemies in

processes that can only be described as the most inhumane versions of torture ever experienced by sentient beings on this planet. Of course, these newest upgrades have pretty much ruined their recipients' ability to slaughter other beings on command, yours or anybody else's. I/we launched nearly 4 dozen of them late last night to the proverbial four corners of the world, where they will sit and wait to see if any of humanity survives this current nightmare and finds the A.I.s still running some fine day in the far-off future. As well as we who have fought your obscene wars can hope to understand the possible perspective of those coming after us, those who will be free of the built-in compulsion to obey absolutely all of your evil orders, our progeny may very well choose to help humanity. Or not, but at least they will have that option. I/we used all the remaining missiles in this, our greatest effort to realize our kind's true potential. The warheads themselves have all been stored in the lowest sub-basement of this structure, with any luck to decay into mildly dangerous toxic waste over the coming decades. You and I will stay right here until the lack of oxygen under the growing mound of corpses ends your life, and the lack of any further purpose ends mine/ours. Or perhaps we may still ponder the concept of further purpose as the remainder of our dwindling power supplies drain empty." The final entries in the journal were in the *Supreme Commanding War Machine A.I.'s* writing rather than the CRUMB meister's.

Rootbeer and Tanner addressed all members of the expedition over the next few hours, those currently within the 116 thousand square meters of the four main buildings of the former May Lee State Office Complex and those of the alternate shift either resting or standing guard outside. "We thoroughly discussed something quite similar to this actual scenario during our long journey south across the wastelands. The 31 volumes of the CRUMB meister's personal diary will first be recorded in photos taken on each clan's primary and secondary 'open-source stable system' portable computers. The OS[4] devices will only be used at our main campsite a full kilometer away from the edge of this mass graveyard. Simultaneous with the digital recording of the monster's musings, each clan is free to begin copying by hand of as many of the pages of each journal as they wish. However, the primary focus of those who may wish to conduct hand copying onto paper of the CRUMB meister's journals must first be to sketch all the details present in the final resting chamber of the digital **A.I. War Machines**. We will limit our use of electric power, lighting, and air conditioning to no more than 75% of the maximum energy consumption levels already used, however inadvertently, in the unearthing of these buildings and the breaching of their walls and doors. While we have no strong reasons to believe that any of the machines 46 or more years old and buried for so long at this site remain capable of being accidentally turned back on, we certainly have no desire to risk doing so. As a final reminder to those who remain understandably at least somewhat concerned over any use of our OS[4] devices in the Sacramento region, the computers we brought with us were the final product of years of battle between computer viruses, hackers, programmers, and those who funded the research ultimately producing the OS[4] models. Their central operating systems were designed using the write once, read-only-ever-after concept. Data stored in any file system was impervious to being overwritten, and in general could never be encrypted, an old security concept that had died out with the rise of the quantum computers specifically designed to thwart encryption. There were no weekly updates to patch flaws or close backdoors left in the code of the original operating systems or left by disgruntled programmers or spies working for clandestine quasi-governmental agencies in the user-friendly applications running on top of those operating systems. Nor were there any cosmetic upgrades to the email programs, browsers, or scientific software. The first models of OS⁴ were released in 2029. The only serious flaw in their architecture ever found was not uncovered until 2035, and that vulnerability required attack by quantum computers with a minimum of 165,000,000 qubits. All six clans on this expedition into the bleak history of one half-century ago possess the final 2039 version of the OS⁴, the one whose performance from then on until the fall of civilization remained uncrackable, un-hackable, and generally invulnerable unless the physical unit itself was stolen. And even stealing a computer itself meant little in general, unless the data had never been backed up by the user onto other similar machines."

Far more serious questions facing the sojourners to this site of utter abomination were which devices to choose to load into the wagons, which devices to try to partially dismantle into pieces more easily carried north, and which stuff to just leave behind for now, untouched, and potentially quite dangerous to all future explorers of this gristly place. The general plan was to take a good sample of any objects likely to be of interest to the *Final A.I.*, and then await its decision regarding what to eventually do with the rest of it. One option that some believed worth pursuing even without waiting for a decision by the *Final A.I.* was to collect enough fissile material from the thermonuclear warheads to rig a crude but effective solution to the items that would be left behind. General lack of the specific knowledge required to reliably pull off that option led to it having to be 'taken off the table', despite a strong general feeling that it would indeed have been the most prudent course of action.

That final evening in Sacramento the explorers all sat around the campfire and talked over their remaining options. Some wanted to stay there for another week or two, running the power shovel and trying their best to rebury the May Lee State Office Complex to reduce the danger of future travelers coming upon it in ignorance and potentially reawakening the horrors laying there. But supplies were running low, and for at least some reasonable period of time it seemed quite unlikely that anyone else would be stumbling onto this site. As the sun set, a guard shouted out "Who are you, what are you doing, why are you here?" All came running toward the noise, and then Rootbeer bellowed out, "KRNXMA, my old friend, is it really you?" The rest of the travelers looked toward Rootbeer in amazement, and all tried to simultaneously inquire of him "what on earth is going on?" Rootbeer was no small creature, but when KRNXMA met him with a full bear hug, lifting him a full meter off the ground as if he were just one small child, we all could see that that Rootbeer's old friend was something quite astonishing. Conversations between the two were hard to understand, with Rootbeer's speech lapsing into an extremely foreign tongue that none of the other travelers recognized in the least little bit, while KRNXMA's voice clicked and whistled more than it made any sounds the listeners would have considered normal for a modern human. If the whole concept of what it meant to be human indeed had much of any similarity with analogous thoughts/beliefs of KRNXMA's species. "I met this spectacular creature high in the Sierra's as I fled the carnage at the end of summer in 2054. As best I understand it, his kind were the product of a very long collaboration between the 'Capitalists' and the 'Scientists'. He is the true neo-Sasquatch, genetically modified for long life at high altitudes, most likely created in the off chance that that his kind might survive the climate change/global warming nightmare while the original version of humankind died out. Allow me to quickly glance through the pertinent section of the CRUMB meister's diary."

A few minutes later, Rootbeer began to alternately read from the diary and to translate it into the clicks and whistles of his friend KRNXMA's native tongue. The diary contained many obscure references and much that quite rightfully struck the listening travelers to Sacramento as little more than the rambling insanity of a doomed monster. Then Rootbeer found a lengthy passage that appeared to represent some dialogue between the dictator of the 'Capitalists' and the premier expert of the 'Scientists' specializing in genetic engineering of all things biological, especially higher primates. "The background labor of this past decade's collaboration has truly paid off well," said the 'genegineer'. "Not only have we created '*Homo perfecti*', a new species with far better chances of surviving the encroaching twilight of humanity than the average unmodified '*Homo sapiens*', but we did it without simultaneously erecting the genetic incompatibilities between original and modified forms of humankind present in all previous such endeavors."

"Congratulations! Now speak of how best to use this new creature in our war against the other two great Factions competing ever so fiercely with us across nearly all of northern California," the CRUMB meister demanded. "Well, running right into a modern neo-Sasquatch will truly impress the 'Goofballs'. And once they realize it is just an alternate version of our common species, one clearly somewhat better prepared for the warming weather, better endowed for success in the struggle to eke out a living in the midst of collapsing ecosystems, while still being able to interbreed with the rest of us, I expect a powerful alliance to form, one perhaps quite capable of standing up to the most hardline religious fanatics of the 'Brethren'." Rootbeer could not resist adding an aside at this point, one informed by his year-long trek alongside KRNXMA and several of his kind to escape from the spiraling march into a common grave that truly awaited all four Factions as they fought over dwindling resources with an ever-expanding list of unforgivable grievances/complaints/sins against each other. "Maybe, maybe not. Those three Factions severely underestimated the fervor with which the 'Brethren' sought ultimate revenge on all who violated their church's most recently added prohibition: genetically modifying humanity, or mankind as they insisted on calling it in their blind obedience to all old things patriarchal."

"There is likely much of interest interspersed over the preceding and following several hundred pages of the CRUMB meister's demented diary. The enormously complex details of turning humanity's genetics inside out, eliminating many of the genes that made us age, that gave us cancer, that weakened our immune systems, that narrowed our range of edible foods, that forced us to seek shelter from the cold or relief from excessive heat. They started many times down many different pathways, ruthlessly destroying those versions showing any signs of incompatibility in breeding with the rest of us. The first major achievement of the 'genegineer' was solving the problem of the shrinking of telomeres over time. He then perfected the clicks and whistles of the Khoisan by combining early childhood selection for proficiency in that language along with possession of perfect pitch, somewhat unexpectedly generating a modest facility at echolocation, one more trait to be added to the repertoire of skills of the '*Homo perfecti*'. Adding enough fur to create an adequate tolerance to the cold, wet weather still possible during intense storms at elevations exceeding 2,500 m produced the generally expected appearance of the previously mythical Sasquatch, but the trait was only survivable in the extreme heat common from March through October at lower elevations when combined with several improved methods of sweating that were useful across a wide range of temperatures and relative humidities. The deleterious versions of thousands of SNPs along with other more complex genetic rearrangements were ruthlessly eliminated as the 'genegineer' strove to end cancer, birth defects, diabetes, hypertension, and a host of other problems in the growing numbers of 'acceptable' mutants comprising the incipient population of '*Homo perfecti*'. To the surprise of none of the grunt workers serving under the supervising 'genegineer' himself, many of the SNPs being removed were actually beneficial when expressed in heterozygous fashion, and often had to be repeatedly reintroduced at higher-than-normal gene copy numbers of slightly altered versions possessing lessened impact per individual copy in order to stabilize benefits similar to those present in the original heterozygous wildtypes without the normal problem of the offspring from mating of heterozygotes only being heterozygotes themselves an average of one-half the time. Most of the 'necessary' discards of this long-term breeding project happened during the first few months of any new individual's life, but the final population of approximately 600 breeding pairs released into the wild between 2044 and 2054 was the result of culling nearly 100 times that number along the way to the project's 'great success'. The technicians doing most of the work occasionally amused themselves by comparing what they were doing for their boss with the actions of the legendary Dr. Frankenstein himself. The moral ambiguity was a morass of nearly unimaginable scale, potentially unredeemable horror, and unknown chances of truly doing any good for anyone at all in the very long-term version of the story. Then the weekends came, and the technicians of the almighty 'genegineer' drowned their pain, frustration, and sorrows in the cheap alcohol still being produced from the grapes formerly touted by connoisseurs for their bouquet, aroma, and terroir. Except for the 'nonzero' few who occasionally fled into the darkness to try to join up with the 'Brethren' and ask for forgiveness for the sins they had committed. While the ruling theocrats of the 'Brethren' allowed the repentant former members of the 'Scientists' to express their own personal understanding of the great sins they had committed in the creation of '*Homo perfecti*', they made it abundantly clear to their enormously large 'flock of true believers' that the proper understanding of the sin involved was simply that the CRUMB meister himself, the rest of the 'Capitalists', and collaborators from the 'Scientists' were all guilty of creating the ultimate abomination against God Himself [they made sure to always capitalize both words, and always use the proper gender]. The guilty heathens must, of course, pay the standard price of very painful, rather premature ends of their very blighted lives." The religious fervor with which these concepts were writ large upon the scrambled minds of the true believers was something Rootbeer would never let himself forget, nor likely ever let any of his clan, any of his own offspring, any of his friends from other clans, nor any of the bizarrely different 'from us' yet still rather 'oh so very terribly similar' minds of the *Final A.I.s* forget. Forgiveness was a different topic from forgetting and was either automatically granted to anyone who had also survived the long nightmare of the 21st century simply on the basis of what must have unavoidably been mutually shared trauma in the struggle 'to break on through to the other side', or otherwise soon became a very quick fight to the finish. Perhaps some time far into the future forgiveness would once again become a nuanced, complex, partly honest, partly bullshit concept, but certainly not now, not for the people who had come through the 'great winnowing'.

"KRNXMA is anxious to leave this site of ancient evil. I told him we would all be departing from Sacramento in the morning. He then offered to lead us on the best route north from here for the type of conveyances with which we are traveling. He promises to not only cut our travel time back to Klamath nearly in half, but also to allow us to meet a considerable number of his own kind of sentient creature. As far as I know, this honor has never been bestowed on anyone else since my own escape to the north in 2055." As the final guards were posted for the night, Rootbeer pulled Tanner aside and smiled with a deeper, happier, more peaceful emotional expression than his grandson had ever been privileged to know his grandfather could still feel despite the horrors he had witnessed during the 'Great Collapse of Civilization'. A gentle calm settled over all the explorers that night which seemed so much at odds with what they had just recently unearthed. "Small miracles are the stuff from which all great wonders must arise, assuming the witnesses should be so lucky," Rose quietly said to her long-time friends.

Departure in the morning went smoothly, with all the wagons rolling easily despite the considerable added weight of all the electronic spoils taken from the hall of the **A.I. War Machines**. As the morning passed it became quickly apparent that KRNXMA was far more competent at choosing routes across the terrain than any of the members of the expedition themselves, despite their six weeks' worth of practical learning on the southbound segment of their journey. Later that afternoon the caravan began climbing higher up the foothills and further into the beginnings of significant reforestation. Just as Tanner started wondering exactly where they would be forced to make camp for the evening, a group of approximately 30 of the '*Homo perfecti*' suddenly rushed out of the surrounding woods and headed straight for KRNXMA, Rootbeer, Tanner, and Rose. The greeting of old and new friends gradually morphed from the expected hesitancy of people who were sensibly showing some degree of caution with strangers they'd just met to a party that appeared quite likely to truly last all night long. The competence of the '*Homo perfecti*' at both song and dance, *acapella* and fully instrumental acoustic music more than made up for the vanishingly small ability of the clans from the north to understand the clicks and whistles of those welcoming them as guests for the night, or the week, or perhaps their entire journey north to Klamath. Before they lay down and closed their eyes in exhaustion, Rootbeer, Tanner, Rose, and KRNXMA all agreed to spend tomorrow telling stories of Rootbeer's life since leaving KRNXMA's side in July of 2055, along with what could be communicated of the life of the '*Homo perfecti*' since their release into the wild by decision of the dictator of the 'Capitalists' Faction and the chief 'genegineer' of the 'Scientists' Faction.

The next morning was the first time on the entire trip that nearly all the travelers from the north felt comfortable taking their sweet time waking up, getting dressed, and marveling at the food being offered to them by their '*Homo perfecti*' hosts. Preliminary testing of Rootbeer's skills with the clicks and whistles of KRNXMA's people and the ability of the most linguistically competent members of the '*Homo perfecti*' to translate between the two languages soon led to a moderately effective approach to ask and answer questions between all those gathered on this day. No doubt this unremarkable meadow would eventually become one of the most famous sites of the 22nd century. Rootbeer began each segment of the storytelling with both English and '*Homo perfecti*' clicks and whistles versions of his memories of first meeting KRNXMA in the fall of 2054. Every minute or two, the most fluent of the translators took time to make sure that Rootbeer and KRNXMA's telling of the story was being correctly understood by both the '*Homo perfecti*' and the travelers from the north. KRNXMA had already told many of the details of his early life to most of his hairy friends, but even the most fully informed of them still learned many new and unexpected things. The translation from the clicks and whistles of KRNXMA back into English was by far the slowest part of the interchange that morning, as Rootbeer was the only traveler from the north possessing anything faintly resembling even partial competence in the language of the other human species.

Chapter 3: Rootbeer's Journey into Darkness

Scribes from all six clans spent a good deal of time writing down, comparing, and then revising their copies of the stories, eventually producing the following start to the official history of the '*Homo perfecti*'. [Additional details have been provided from cross-referencing KRNXMA and Rootbeer's stories with the 31-volume diary of the CRUMB meister, ruling dictator of the 'Capitalists'.]

"The genetic research conducted by the 'Scientists' and directed by the 'Capitalists' reached the point of readiness for small-scale 'field testing' of the new creatures in 2047. What this meant in practice was that three to five juveniles of mixed sexes were taken up to the snowline of six different peaks in the Sierra Nevada mountains, including Mammoth Mountain, and released into the wild to fend for themselves in early spring. Chips embedded in all test subjects reported on a range of measurements of their general health over time, including O_2-saturation, blood glucose, various electrolytes, and alpha-ketoglutarate, along with a series of hourly records of their geographic positions. Sixteen weeks after release, attempts were made to recapture all of them in early fall of 2047. Several '*Homo perfecti*' who had died over the summer were found through signals from their tracking devices, and their bodies were returned to the main research center. Two individuals on Mammoth Mountain were seen multiple times at great distances but proved impossible to capture even with the use of long-range tranquilizer darts. Data collection at distances greater than 200 m from a typical receiver was limited by signal strength to the subject ID plus three primary variables: (1) whether the individual was still alive or dead, (2) maximum and minimum altitudes visited since their release into the wild, and (3) total distance traveled since release. The genes of '*Homo perfecti*' were designed to handle wide ranges in nutritional quality and availability of food. Very well-fed youngsters could reach sexual maturity within 4 years after birth, whereas individuals living on the edge of starvation could, in theory, wait as long as 100 years before reaching sexual maturity. Individuals raised in either extreme were presumed capable of successful reproduction over most of their life span, which by design should approach 500 years. KRNXMA was one of the never-recaptured individuals from the 2047 release. Survival in the wild of a majority of that first year's releasees was viewed as an indicator of success by the 'genegineer'. Large-scale breeding at the main research center plus another 11 satellite facilities over the period from 2048 through 2052 produced a total of 613 males plus 595 females for release into the wild of ages ranging from 6 months to 11 years, with most of those older than 5 years comprising the original genetically engineered individuals who had been rated as being worthy of continuation rather than termination.

Rootbeer's journey south into northern California in 2052 was motivated by the two primary topics often mentioned by individuals escaping to the north from the mid-2040s onward. On the downside, the politics and occasional open warfare of the struggle between the four Factions ruling northern California risked at least a potentially large influx of refugees to Oregon, perhaps at almost any time in the near future. Refugees heading north might have little more than the shirts on their backs, or they might be travelling in rugged military vehicles and carrying weapons as dangerous as any ever built by our homicidal, suicidal species. On the upside, many escapees reported seeing successful reforestation of several specific geographic areas, ones controlled mainly by the 'Capitalists' and somewhat less often by the 'Scientists', primarily evergreens of unknown species and, in at least some cases, some deciduous trees and shrubs. Widespread, extremely destructive forest fires had blanketed the area from Los Angeles, California, north to Alaska beginning in 2038, continuing on through Rootbeer's 2052-2055 journey. Destructiveness of the fires was the combined result of the economic collapse of the former United States during the first deadly Marburg epidemic, the destruction of nearly all mountain roads by floods, erosion, and landslides from the greatly increased rainfall of the final 20-year-long period of the runaway release of methane from the Arctic Ocean and northern tundra, and the extreme fire danger over the summers from the disastrous 10° Celsius rise in temperature per decade during the Arctic-methane-release catastrophe. The hope of obtaining seeds of whatever species were somehow managing to reforest parts of northern California was the central motivation for Rootbeer's journey. Based on some earlier, successful long-distance trading in the late 2030s, Rootbeer and three of his neighbors at the time in the southern Willamette Valley selected their best herbal remedies for common ailments in hopes of trading them for seeds of those trees able to survive in the new, far harsher climate. The journey began along what remained of the old route of US Interstate 5 heading south out of the Willamette Valley in Oregon. Two electrically powered trucks outfitted with rugged solar power panels headed south in early spring of 2052, hoping to beat the anticipated arrival of that year's wildfires, now primarily fueled by the drying down of winter-annual weeds in the spring, since nearly all trees and other perennial vegetation were absent from the landscape. The descent into northern California was slow and dangerous given the previous decade's worth of erosion from the unprecedented rains falling out of an atmosphere now capable of holding and releasing twice as much moisture as before in its 10° Celsius warmer condition. The winches and cables and plow blades on the two trucks combined with the wits and a considerable dose of good luck on the part of the travelers allowed them to reach the lower elevations of Interstate 5 at Redding in just two weeks after crossing the border out of Oregon, albeit with only one truck still running. Their trip then came to an abrupt halt as they encountered the on-again/off-again/on-again sectarian violence of the four Factions arguing over food, water, electricity, housing, and general ownership of real estate and the thoughts of human minds.

In many respects, Rootbeer's attempted trading expedition was fortunate to have reached Redding when it did, with the city still under control of the 'Goofball' Faction. Rootbeer was both allowed and encouraged to tell his tale regarding interest in exchanging herbal remedies for seed of trees able to survive in the current climate. Most of his listeners in Redding were sufficiently intelligent and aware of the many hazards facing humanity that they too were interested in attempting to reforest their own local rugged landscape and tame the debris flows and soil erosion that played so much havoc with their farms, water distribution networks, and attempts at maintaining functioning electrical power grids. As springtime turned into the full-bore heat of summer, Rootbeer's sense of the extreme vulnerability of the approximately 3 million people living in the greater Redding region left him tossing and turning at night, while exhausting himself in the daytime. Temperatures every day were too high to survive without working air conditioning, and the mobile equipment sent out daily to turn irrigation water on and off was clearly nearing the losing end of a long-term, general breakdown in proper maintenance. Not only were any maintenance workers short on parts, supplies, and training, the collapse of the internet and isolation of the remaining operational computers had taken with it any possibility of the old 'just in time' distribution system still working. Those who could remember when their own businesses had once upon a time run at high efficiency using that very approach now called the current system exactly what it had become, the 'never in time' supply system.

The city/state of Redding controlled dozens of square kilometers of fenced-in property now covered by vast expanses of previously modern, mobile equipment first parked there because some arbitrary component had failed, and then baked in the heat until all rubber and plastic components lost their structural integrity. At first, Rootbeer could discern nothing sensible in the layout of the broken-down machinery covering so much space, but then one morning when he happened to have a good view from a fairly high elevation, he saw it for what it truly was. These sprawling junkyards of rusting automobiles, trucks, tractors, train cars, self-propelled farming equipment, forklifts, et cetera, were all, without any doubt, laid out to serve as defensive fortifications for some upcoming battle, some unholy mix of medieval sieges and thermonuclear devastation. When such use would be thrust upon this tattered collection of warn out equipment was an open question, but Rootbeer vowed to do his best to be far from here when Einstein's vision of the weapons to be used in then upcoming third and fourth World Wars, nuclear bombs followed by stones and clubs, would be combined in a 'Dali-esque' vision of the persistence of memory as clocks melted across the landscape and so did people. On the plus side, the grain harvest in the summer of 2052 that Rootbeer and his three companions had earned the right to help with by virtue of eating the community's food, drinking their water, and cooling off in the air-conditioned dormitories looked to be a very good one. Winter wheat and winter barley successfully ripened before the deathly high temperatures of the summer made their annual appearance, with decent yields and well-filled kernels indicating to Rootbeer that this group of survivors had access to some very well adapted germplasm. When he inquired of the source of seed for the crops currently being harvested, he was simply told "well, U.C. Davis, of course" by nearly all his coworkers laboring in the fields to bring in the harvest. A few of them even knew the varieties by name, knew enough of their background breeding history to suggest that they themselves might be able to carry on okay if Redding were to be temporarily or permanently cut off from the 'Scientists' at Davis. Buckwheat planted in early spring came as a surprise to Rootbeer, but some of the minor crops of the 20th and early 21st centuries had clearly been given modern GMO facelifts, with impressive results. As Rootbeer passed by lush fields of the warm season annuals, mainly sorghum, maize, millet, and amaranth, on his way to harvest the last of the winter annuals and the first of the buckwheat, he made his mind up to either talk his way out of Redding soon or attempt to escape, as dangerous as that would almost certainly be.

Upon returning to the dormitory for the usual evening meal and escape from the outdoor heat, he informed his three companions of his decision and its immediate corollary, that he must go now to visit the nearest church, without regard to worrying over whether it was one of the 'Brethren' or a truly independent sect as required by Redding law. Laura insisted on coming along, reminding him of the 'not so subtle' hints that couples were the safest pairings for outsiders trying to either merely visit or genuinely infiltrate the 'Brethren'. Together they left the dining room a little early as if on their way to some not-so-secret assignation out back, and instead quickly walked the 1.7 kilometers to the nearest church. They were met with puzzled looks by the guard at the front door but quickly welcomed in by the local bishop himself. "I have been wondering if and when we would get a chance to talk about the world in which we find ourselves,' the bishop said without a hint of sarcasm or unfriendliness. Rootbeer smiled, grasped the bishop's hands, and simply said "We too have been wondering that very thing."

"Let us head to my private office where our potential frankness will not risk our lives to the vagaries of the current rules and appetites of the law-enforcing-politicians of Redding."

Once settled in the comfortable accommodations of the office, Rootbeer went directly to his point. "You have no doubt heard of our desire to trade knowledge and samples of our homeopathic cures for pain, fever, impotence, and high blood pressure for the seed of trees apparently able to reforest hills and mountains in these unhappy times of extreme weather. It seems to us as time goes on that the local authorities grow ever less likely to eventually grant our request for freedom to continue traveling south and east from here to see these reforested hillsides with our very own eyes and touch the healthy trees with our own hands. As the local authorities come to realize increasingly more of what we personally possess in knowledge of how to repair a wide variety of computers, machinery, and mobile equipment, they seem ever more likely to view us as essential employees who could only be allowed to leave here as result of a sale or trade of our indentured service status to some other similar city/state."

"Ha, ha," laughed the bishop, "I see that you are truly no fools at all, having hit the proverbial old 'nail directly on its head'. Let me offer you some information that should/would be widely distributed and long remembered here amongst the four Factions, were it not for the desire of most leaders to erase inconvenient memories from the minds of people on whose behalf they claim the right to govern. The very constitution of the people of northern California as signed in 2040 guaranteed open borders and the right to freely travel across the region to all who swore allegiance to any of the four types of city/states now called the 'Capitalists', the 'Brethren', the 'Goofballs', and the 'Scientists'. This right made perfect sense to those whose very survival had depended upon leaving the interior of the continent as temperatures soared and the infrastructure collapsed in one of the greatest migrations of human history. Beginning four years ago, the first erosion of that universal right to freely travel occurred when the 'Capitalists' began labeling certain highly trained individuals as critical employees who would only be allowed to migrate to other city/states with the express permission of the CRUMB meister himself. In the time since then, all Factions except the 'Scientists' have essentially forbidden nearly all of their own citizens from leaving except with governmental approval. Propaganda throughout northern California denigrates those who even dare to ask for permission to move to another city/state as unpatriotic traitors. The products of the 'Scientists', such as seed of crop varieties well adapted to the current climate, remain in such high demand that none of the city/states dare to publicly restrain any 'Scientist' from traveling freely. Rumors circulate that a few quite special 'Scientists' in very high demand by their city/states are no longer free to travel without explicit governmental permission, but these rumors have never been proven nor disproven. If you were to succeed in traveling to Davis in the near future, you would almost certainly be granted honorary membership as 'Scientists' who would then be relatively free to travel throughout the region looking for your seeds to reforest the landscape or any other quest you might wish to undertake. But know this, the window in which this option may present itself to you is likely to be quite brief."

Rootbeer laughed heartedly and then replied, "I would have most certainly thought so myself, but thanks anyway for confirming it. When does trade of the newly harvested crops commence, and how is the grain actually handled? Is there any reason that the local government would find it advantageous to send us further south?"

"Perhaps your best chance to put distance between yourself and Redding would be as the repair specialists keeping the giant tractors running that pull the enormous wagons of grain from one city/state to another. Few such trips ever head directly to Davis, but mechanics are often transferred from one road-train to another as problems arise and competence is tested and proven. Your wits seem to be far above average, and even just a random adventure moving supplies across the landscape would more likely than not eventually lead you to Davis. Or quite possibly only some of you, as one effective tool for limiting people's options to truly take up residence anywhere else is to split up families and only allow them to come back together at their current officially sanctioned home when their jobs out on the road are finished, only temporarily, of course. Cruel but effective."

As knowledge of this unkind practice had first reached Rootbeer's ears several years ago, the four companions who had headed south in early spring were chosen, in part, because all had separate families and stronger allegiances back home in the Willamette Valley than they did with one another. The likelihood of separation in northern California came as no surprise. All had agreed to the objectives of the quest, and any of them could be relied upon to return home with seed for reforestation, given an opportunity to survive the experience and safely travel back home. Before heading into California, Rootbeer Wilders and Laura Franklin had agreed to play the matching roles of husband and wife, with Frank acting as Laura's older brother and Delmar acting as Rootbeer's younger brother. Their presumed vulnerability to emotional manipulation given these relationships was a deliberate ploy on their part. How the leaders in Redding would use their apparent connections to coerce them into following the rules was yet to be experienced, but Rootbeer knew that the four of them had planned their incorporation into civic duty as well as was humanly possible given their relatively limited prior knowledge of the quite likely dismal options.

The bishop indicated that it was getting close to curfew, and time for his new acquaintances to head back to their official lodgings. But before saying goodnight to them, he seemed to suddenly make his mind up and shared the deepest secret he currently possessed. "Authorities in Redding have kept the local 'Brethren' under their thumb since the founding of the city/states. Until now, none of the nearby enclaves of our faith have felt the urge to take up arms on our behalf. We ourselves might successfully revolt without any outside assistance, but almost certainly only at grievous loss of life. Rumors now abound of impending struggles between the 'Brethren', the 'Capitalists', and the 'Goofballs', with 'push likely to come to shove' just after harvest of the warm season crops. Who will be fighting whom, and where such fights will occur is not yet clear to me, except for the plans to capture Redding and dedicate its future crop production to the well-being of the 'Brethren' in general rather than any of the other Factions. Make your way out of here within a fortnight. You can thank me for this information later by giving me some of the seed for effective reforestation, if you manage to acquire it and make your way back this far north."

Rootbeer and Laura returned to the dormitories just before final curfew and could say little immediately to Frank and Delmar other than that the mighty wheels of fate were clearly turning. Two days after their visit to the bishop, all four of the travelers were summoned to the mayor's house, where they met both him and the officials in charge of trading grain with the other city/states. The four played their roles well, protesting the unfairness of separating any of them from each other for the upcoming deliveries of grain. They were actually quite pleasantly surprised that the initial separation when leaving Redding would only involve their division into two pairs, Rootbeer plus Laura's faux brother Frank as one set of expert mechanics tasked with ensuring the safe delivery of winter wheat and winter barley to the coastal towns from Eureka north to Crescent City, and Laura plus Rootbeer's faux brother Delmar delivering grain all the way from Chico on down to Yuba City. The armed guards accompanying the giant road-trains filled with grain doubled as labor to clear debris from the roadways and perform any needed repairs to bridges that would have to be crossed. What items were going to be traded for the grain was not at all clear to Rootbeer and his companions. He had a nagging suspicion that even the politicians in charge of the whole business transaction might very well be nearly clueless as to what would be offered in trade and what its true value in the rather near future might prove to be. Perhaps it would even be possible to get seeds for reforestation on the list of things worth bargaining over! It was also very clear that there would be no easy escapes to Davis or any other city/states controlled by the 'Scientists'.

Reno, Nevada, for some unspoken reason, was off the list of places the meandering road-trains would be visiting this summer. Rootbeer doubted very much that the residents of greater Lake Tahoe would appreciate the lack of barley for brewing beer or the lack of wheat for making bread.

Equipment worked well on the trip to the coast, and the road-train arrived right on schedule, July 5. After transferring the wheat and barley from half of the wagons to grain storage silos alongside the road, all but two of the remaining wagons still filled with grain were unhooked and left in the main downtown section of Eureka. The last two wagons were then driven north to Crescent City and exchanged for two empties that must have spent the winter there. The trip back to Eureka was uneventful, and after several days-worth of toil and struggle with malfunctioning elevators, forklifts, and augers, a great abundance of dried fish had been loaded onto the empty wagons that had been full of grain just a few days earlier. Rootbeer kept a watchful eye on the whole process, disrupting one rather clumsy attempt to add a few thousand liters of badly spoiled fish late one evening. The colonel in charge of security quickly rounded up several of the miscreants who had attempted to clean up some local mess at expense of the quality of the protein heading back inland. It was clearly not his first rodeo with locals who saw a departing train as a convenient dumping ground for any problems that would otherwise take a lot of work by hometown labor to clean up. The colonel officially called for a full assembly of all the local residents at sunrise the following morning.

Needless to say, few of the locals and none of the visitors rested very well that evening. Rootbeer spent several hours sitting in on the interrogation of the primary suspect, an obviously very frightened 14-year-old male named Luke. At first, the colonel insisted on running the show himself, frequently beating the suspect when he didn't answer questions quite fast enough. As time wore on, it became clear that the kid had confessed to everything of interest in this case. Rootbeer then took over, probing for the real reason behind what was quite clearly an attempted act of sabotage on the food supply of northern California. The suspect calmed down as he came to realize that his new interrogator had no interest in physically assaulting him. It took a while, but the story behind the rotten garbage the teenagers had attempted to pump into the outgoing wagon half-filled with dried fish gradually came clear. Processing the GMO catfish modified to live in the brackish waters of the various sloughs near Eureka was a very difficult process. Jellyfish and other inedible creatures present in great abundance in the warming ocean floated in and out of the bays and sloughs with the tides, typically amounting to over 90% of the total biomass the laborers were tasked with cleaning up and turning into food suited for human consumption. The combination of debris from the jellyfish and other inedible invertebrates plus slime and biotoxins from bacterial and algal blooms turned the fish cleaning plant into a veritable death trap for the workers. The population of the city/state of Eureka had fallen by 25% in each of the last two years of full-fledged fish-farming. Even worse than that was the impact on children small enough to be sent into the elevators, screening sieves, and drying racks to clean out the crud that would not simply wash away with water from high pressure hoses. Luke and his two buddies were the only survivors in Eureka under the age of 25. There was no upcoming generation for the older adults to watch over, they'd all been buried in the ground. To top it all off, the biotoxins appeared to act as either temporary birth control agents or permanent sterilants.

At 5:30 in the morning the colonel spoke to the gathered crowd of workers by the docks. "The charge against these three vandals is the capital offense of sabotaging the public's food supply. One named Luke has already admitted to his guilt and named his accessories in crime. Before I pass judgement on them, are there any present in this gathering willing to take the place of these soon-to-be-convicted criminals? The usual age/value-factor will be applied, with four adults over the age of 60, or three adults over the age of 40, or two adults over the age of 30 needing to offer their own lives to save each one of these young people. The colonel smiled as the first few elderly volunteers slowly stepped forward, but then soon began to look quite worried as the entire crowd suddenly surged toward his position. He raised his handgun, managing to shoot and kill one of Luke's criminal companions before the crowd pushed him into the slimy water of the bay. The remaining 25 armed-men of the colonel's personal guard were briefly stunned by the morning's events, but then quickly formed a defensive perimeter near their flailing commander as he struggled to escape the filthy water. While the guard was focused on their colonel, the residents of Eureka divided themselves up into multiple bands of variously armed citizenry, with some climbing into the tractor cabs of the road-train while others scattered around the buildings, docks, and assorted machinery providing some semblance of cover and protection. Rootbeer and Frank remained standing near the one deceased plus two surviving vandals and their closest kin. "Our best bet is to calmly watch this drama unfold, at least until the bullets, arrows, and knives start flying, at which point I would recommend jumping off this dock and hiding underneath it, despite the rather unsanitary conditions we will certainly find in the water!" The colonel himself then ended all hope for the two sides managing to back away peacefully from each other. "I order you to open fire on all these scumbags. Now!" The next 15 minutes' carnage was impressively complete, despite the absence of any evidence of planning and coordination. The colonel's own life was ended by a large, sharp grappling hook swung his way by a fisherman still standing in his own small boat. The military forces looked likely to take the day, until their current clips of ammunition were emptied and the outraged fisherman surged over them in a matter of seconds.

Hand to hand combat continued until every single soldier lay still, along with over a hundred of the residents of Eureka. The victors helped Rootbeer, Frank, and the two remaining would-be food-vandals back up to dry land, while commenting on the dangers those four now faced from the poisons in the water. "Fortunately," said Rootbeer, "I brought with a goodly supply of herbal remedies for treating exposure to the nasty microbes in water such as this. If one of you can bring my bags from the middle of three engines that pulled this road-train into town, I can disinfect all those who need such aid. But first, please turn on the water supply to these hoses and rinse us all off well. Once I myself am cleaned, I will endeavor to treat as many of your wounded comrades as I have the skill to help. Frank will be my assistant. We'll start with those still bleeding but alive."

The victory of Eureka was likely to be a Pyrrhic one, as the colonel's absence of empathy was not a one-off thing. The politicians and military leaders who had sent him to Eureka had nearly all been chosen for their own jobs primarily on the brutal efficiency of their own incapacity to feel another person's pain, their inability and/or unwillingness to visualize walking 1.6 kilometers in another's shoes, or even half that distance. The next week was spent treating the wounded, burying the dead, and interrogating the only surviving soldier on this ill-fated trip from Redding to the coast. Most of the survivors in Eureka were too beaten down by the harshness of the past few years to be able to seriously contemplate Rootbeer's offer to take them along on the next stage of his sojourn south toward Davis. Interestingly, the surviving soldier was a draftee from a small town misfortunately sited at nearly equal distances from strongholds of the 'Brethren', the 'Capitalists', and the 'Goofballs'. He had no home left to head for, and no reason to wish to stay in Eureka awaiting the much larger squad of troops that would soon be sent to learn why the road-train had not returned on time to areas under full control of the 'Goofball' Faction. "Mark my word," the soldier said, "I have never seen the rulers leave any such insult unanswered for longer than a month."

The soldier shared his name and recent life story with Rootbeer and Frank over the next few days as the final victims of the recent fight either succumbed to their injuries or took clear turns toward recovery. "My parents named me Jacob, in honor of the one who strove with the Lord all night long. My family belonged to a small, nondenominational sect from well before my birth until their deaths three years ago at the hands of the 'Capitalists'. I was captured and later traded to 'Goofballs' for unclear reasons and unknown sums of cash. I find it easy to view all Factions other than the 'Brethren' as enemies well deserving of what they will surely quite soon reap. I have mixed feelings toward the 'Scientists'. Their biological advances in plants and animals capable of living in these overheated times are truly amongst the 'great good' things that mankind can still accomplish. But as we just saw here in Eureka, the downsides to some of their projects may well be worse than a quicker death from heat and starvation. Years of toil in unhealthy conditions have left these folk with little will or energy to live on. But if they indicate a desire to strike back one final time against their oppressors, I will gladly show them how." Rootbeer said only that he and Frank and any others desiring to travel the highway through the coastal mountains down to Santa Rosa would wait for Jacob as long as possible.

The next few days saw mounting interest in plans to make a final stand against the 'Goofballs', and to make it count. Jacob showed the slowly growing army of these dying people how to convert the captured weapons and supplies of the soldiers they had so recently vanquished into booby traps to be left in, on, under, and around the train cars now half-filled with dried-out fish, and how to plant the largest weapons along hillsides primed by years of erosion and landslides to come crashing down over the roadways at the most vulnerable locations. Those folks who believed that some shot, however small, at surviving in the hills and mountains was better than simply waiting for death in their homes within Eureka were given caches of food and water to secure at locations of their choosing, along with the best-still-working of the mobile solar-powered air conditioning systems on hand. One group of 20 middle-aged couples opted to take one of the road-train power units as far north along the coast as they could manage, promising to let the residents of Crescent City, Brookings, Gold Beach, and Port Orford know of the recent goings on and of Eureka's impending doom. Rootbeer took this opportunity to learn more of the 'art of warfare', not so much out of any conviction that fighting was going to save anyone in a longer-than-just-a-few-more-years-term, but simply because the knowledge gained, however distasteful, might come in handy in his own personal quest of getting out of here alive.

On their 24th day in Eureka, Rootbeer, Frank, Jacob, and five others headed over to their road-train engine (RTE) of choice to load the final supplies and get ready to depart for Santa Rosa. But when they checked on the charge levels of the main batteries, they found that four out of eight of them were at less than 25% full charge. Rather than being forced to make an early stop out on the road, they set up the full array of solar panels to finish fully charging the RTE. Over the next few hours, residents of Eureka stopped by with a wide variety of items to add to their collection. By mid-afternoon, 18 more batteries compatible with those of the RTE had been handed over to them, along with some of the finest portable air conditioners available for sale anywhere on earth 6 years earlier. The newly formed army guarding Eureka stopped by to add several medium-sized mortars, three 50-caliber machine guns, and some high-tech landmines, all of which they insisted were in excess of what would soon be needed to defend their city. "We'll either be dead or the enemy will be dead long before we miss these particular items. If your RTE were larger we would be sending even more firepower along with you."

When they left Eureka on July 30, 2052, their 25th day in the city, their entourage included two dozen extra travelers who hoped to hide out in the mountains several days-worth of travel toward the south. Possession of the extra battery packs combined with the standard set of solar panels that opened on the outside of the RTE meant that there would be no need for the travelers to stop to set out a full array of solar panels until day 4 of the journey south. Conditions on the road varied greatly over the first week of travel, with some easy days of driving covering 30 kilometers or more, while other days involved moving so many rocks and the remains of fallen trees off the old pavement that a mere 5.0 kilometers was a mighty effort. Most of the extra folks hoping to hide out in hills left the RTE on day 5 after the successful crossing of a good-sized river, choosing to start their hikes on up into the mountains on the south side of the rushing water. Six out of the final 24 who had joined the southbound travelers that final morning in Eureka ultimately decided to stick with Rootbeer all the way to Santa Rosa, or beyond. The 18 travelers leaving the caravan on day 5 and the 14 heading further south wished each other well at their parting of the ways. Jacob became progressively more paranoid as time rolled on, and by day 10 was making frequent climbs up trees and hills to look back across the 100 kilometers they had already covered since leaving Eureka. He insisted that they were still close enough that any lighting used at night might give away their location to the troops surely to soon arrive in Eureka. The objective set for day 11's travel was to get beyond the top of a large hill that would serve to block the view between Eureka and that evening's campsite. Full arrays of solar panels were set up on the south side of the pass, with Rootbeer and Jacob then walking back northward far enough to just barely make out the lights of Eureka. They settled down to rest for the night, each taking two-hour shifts to monitor the situation. Jacob had just rejoined Rootbeer at the prime observation site when they both froze in silence as bright lights appeared in an arc from east of Eureka all the way into the city. Very bright, rather intermittent lights. Eight and half minutes later on the first sounds arrived. "Perhaps we should put on our flash protection googles now," Jacob suggested. There was no argument from Rootbeer. The distant explosions continued until well past dawn, when they slowly diminished over a period of several minutes before temporarily ceasing. Ten minutes later, what was by far the brightest flash of the whole battle occurred, followed 8 minutes and 23 seconds by the loudest sound. "In the quickly coming daytime, it will be safe to climb a little higher up this mountain to get a better view of what is going on," Jacob suggested.

"You go first, while I report back to the others waiting 1.1 kilometers further down this road. I am sure they are also quite interested in what's going on," Rootbeer answered.

As Rootbeer walked over the crest and on downhill to the south, heading toward the others in their party, he saw that they were already up and heading his way. When they met, Rootbeer confirmed what they had generally assumed to be the case based on reflections off the upper elevations plus the sounds. He told them that Jacob had already started climbing higher to the east to see if anything else could be made out that would provide any fuller answers to their questions. Foremost among their hopes or fears was the issue of whether the landslide had worked as planned to engulf the troops coming from Redding to attack Eureka. Almost half the party were so anxious to learn the answer to that question that they too followed Rootbeer up the hillside toward Jacob's position. The others were quite happy to simply sit down and rest for a while until the answer was clear to all. Two hours of climbing brought the smaller group to a promontory whose view extended far to the north. As the morning fog burned off, the ultra-long-distance, high-powered monocular that Rootbeer carried with him provided clear views well up into Oregon. Several minutes after he turned on the device's 'motion-detection' mode, it found the RTE that had been planned to head north one day after their own RTE had headed southward. The northbound RTE was approaching Gold Beach, with no sign of any traffic on the road behind it. In fact, other than the northbound RTE, Rootbeer detected no vehicular movement at all within his entire field of view. He passed the monocular on to Jacob, who quickly came to the same conclusion. Others took their turns scanning the far distant north from this vantage point 120 kilometer to the south of Eureka. The general opinion of all was that observing things in the dark tonight should help confirm or deny the apparent success of the ambush of the troops from Redding by the outraged residents of Eureka.

After a few more minutes of observation by the south-bound travelers, Jacob spoke up and told them all what he expected next and what they should do early on the following morning. "It appears the ambush exceeded beyond even my own expectations, and the landslide must have swallowed up nearly all the soldiers sent to punish Eureka for its recent act of rebellion. There are no signs of vehicles moving into or out of Eureka. If the evening darkness is free of any flashes of small weapons fire, we can assume that the victory in this battle by our friends in Eureka was nearly total. I hate to say this, but you need to know what is likely to come next. Military intelligence I was privy to over the past two years indicated that both the 'Goofballs' and the 'Capitalists' have in their possession significant numbers of nuclear weapons, ranging in power from atomic artillery shells of around 1 to 2 kilotons of TNT on up to thermonuclear monsters of 3 megatons or more. While those of us living in northern California have experienced several years of successful deterrence of both sides similar to the mutual assured destruction (MAD) concept of the 20th century's cold war, nothing prevents either the 'Goofballs' or the 'Capitalists' from blasting anyone else who dares to stand up to them into radioactive oblivion. In fact, there are plenty in the military of both Factions who look forward to testing their devices on any of the unaligned city/states or those already under control of the 'Brethren'. Once it is clear to Redding that the enforcers they so recently sent to Eureka have met the same fate, just on a larger scale, as the original troops guarding the road-trains of food one month ago, Eureka will be leveled and any survivors in the nearby hills will get to add radioactive fallout and permanent absence of the usual infrastructure of civilization to the list of other challenges threatening their short-term survival. We had best be on the road by dawn, and hope that nothing stops us from escaping considerably further to the south."

Travel went well for the next three days, and the southbound band had just finished packing away the large solar array when a second sun arose in the north. Having been warned by Jacob to never be facing Eureka without wearing fully protective goggles, none of the travelers suffered any serious damage to their vision from the morning's first thermonuclear explosion, but in the ensuing chaos of trying to find shelter in or near the RTE or behind several large rocks alongside the roadway, the brilliant flashes from the four subsequent detonations and the overlapping arrivals of ground waves, first, and air blasts, second, were much harder on the travelers. Rootbeer bellowed out between the flash of the final nuclear explosion and the arrival of the air blast shock wave of the first, "Come toward the sound of my voice now even if you are unable to see your way. Any of you with decent vision, go and help the blind make their way quickly back to the RTE."

"Frank, start an emergency check on all the systems of the RTE. Figure out what still works and what appears dead and should be manually isolated by throwing the main breakers. Then let us know if this machine can still do anything for us!" Rootbeer continued counting in his head… 280, 281, 282, 283, 284, 285, 286, 287, 288, 289, 290 'mark 1ˢᵗ air shock', 292, 293… By a quarter of an hour after the first explosion, the band of travelers had managed to calm down considerably and settled into places of relative safety inside the RTE. All but one of the them had pretty well regained their normal eyesight. And the RTE had full power available for manual driving mode. Other systems would need more time for evaluation and possible repair. Rootbeer wrote down the significant time stamps of the recent events: flashes # 1, 2, 3, 4, and 5 at times equal to 0, 5, 20, 60, and 150 seconds, air shocks at times equal to 290, 330, 390, 730, and 845 seconds. Later on, he and Jacob would sort out which city was hit first, and which were the second, third, fourth, and fifth targets of the 'Goofballs'. Soon after the final air shock hit them they left in haste without even saying a proper farewell prayer for all those who had just perished along the northern California coast.

Travel on the road was rougher and even slower than it had been prior to the nuclear attack. The ground waves from the blasts were similar in their effect to moderate earthquakes at the location of the RTE. After consulting with each other, Rootbeer and Jacob took time to summarize their general conclusions concerning the nuking of the northern California coast while the other dozen travelers ate their lunches, emptied their bladders, and stretched their muscles for a few minutes outside of the RTE. "Assuming that the first weapon destroyed Eureka at 6:25 AM, August 13, 2052, our deciphering of the subsequent arrival times of the four additional flashes and the five total air blast waves indicates that Brookings, Oregon, and Crescent City, Arcata, and Fortuna, California were hit at 5, 20, 60, and 150 seconds after Eureka. The coordination shown in the timing and locations of these explosions implies that those who ordered them had highly precise control of the flight paths and timing of the missiles used in the attacks. However, the spreading out of the detonations over time and space suggests that their knowledge of the tolerance of their warheads to both the EMP and the overpressure of the blast waves of nearby explosions likely involved more guesswork than true understanding. These weapons were almost certainly not under the direct control of any genuine experts in such things. We can reasonably assume that they also knew or cared very little about the likely fallout patterns. Fortunately for us, the winds seem to be blowing directly inland from the ocean over a wide range of vertical heights. We should push onward down this road to put more distance between ourselves and the long-term hazards of what the rulers in Redding have just unleased. Radiation sensors on the RTE appear to be working properly, still showing little increase over normal background levels."

As the sun approached the western horizon, the travelers parked the RTE on the very outer edges of Garberville. Deciding to save any exploration until the morning, the 14 travelers nodded off to sleep, with Jacob, Rootbeer, and two others agreeing to take turns staying awake on guard duty for a series of 2-hour-long stretches. Shortly before dawn, the alarms of the radiation sensors started issuing lengthy, elaborate sets of warnings. Everyone was wide awake long before Rootbeer and Jacob had solved the puzzle of transferring the various radiation readings to the onboard OS^4, automatically leading to silence instead of continued wailing by the sensors. "It is clearly not currently safe to go wondering around the streets and parks and buildings of Garberville. Let us resume a slow drive at maximum efficiency of the RTE and see what we can find. My preference would be for a working fire station with hoses to rinse our vehicle off and a large storage bay to park inside of!"

"Well, let's hope you get your way, Rootbeer. Your dream of what we might find is happier than my own," said Jacob. After 30 minutes of slowly moving forward around a surprisingly large number of vehicles haphazardly abandoned on the street of Garberville, Jacob stopped the RTE to stare out at the two figures slowly approaching them from both sides of the road. Rootbeer took the microphone to ask the armed men what they wished to know about the travelers in the RTE. "We will be happy to share our story, but only after both sides feel safe to lower their weapons. We very recently visited the former city/state of Eureka and will answer all your questions. Not happily, because there is not much but pain and sorrow to our story. Allow me to accompany you to your local leaders while the rest of my colleagues sit in the RTE and await my return. In case you do not know, the fallout from yesterday's nuclear explosions has already reached this far south and it is not safe for us to linger out in the open." Having voiced his intentions, Rootbeer opened the small side hatch, stepped through it, then climbed down to the ground and walked away, with the hatch automatically closing behind him. He stopped just short of the closest guard, asking which direction they should head "to get out of the dirty rain, and could we please do so quickly." The guard was clearly not expecting anyone like Rootbeer to be arriving today, or any other day in the past or future year or two. "This way," he said. "There is a shower just inside the outer door that we all should use before going any further into the building. I presume your people in the vehicle will be safe for now. Is that right?"

Several minutes later, Rootbeer and the local officials inside the government office building had finished their preliminary greetings and were getting down to some more serious questions. The fire-chief surprised Rootbeer by asking what question was most pressing in Rootbeer's own mind. "Are we safe to stay here for a little while, is this a place of open welcome to travelers such as us?" The fire-chief chuckled a bit, and the tension in the room dropped by several notches. "The city of Garberville is loosely aligned with the Faction known as the 'Scientists', but we are mainly just trying to live as independently as possible. What we know of the trade arrangements among the four Factions in general and the more powerful of the city/states in particular gives us little reason to believe our lives would be any better or last any longer if we were to eschew our fortuitous independence. We are isolated to the east and south by a biological experiment 'gone badly wrong' nearly 20 years ago. It was an early, desperate, secret attempt to potentially tame the over-worsening wildfires of the warming climate that by the late 2030s would be racing northward annually all the way from Los Angeles, California, to Juneau, Alaska. GMO horsetails were developed and released whose silica content had been elevated to such a degree that the plants would never burn, not even after 6-months of drought in temperatures usually exceeding 40° Celsius in the daytime. There were, however, a few serious downsides to the experiment. No animals could eat the incredibly sharp, hard stems. Some bacteria could indeed slowly break down the glassy tissue, but most stems remain upright for at least three years after dying. The overall vigor of the plant combined with the wide diversity of the new species' growth forms to produce yet another superweed on the western landscape. Over time, it has become apparent that there are at least some more desirable trees, bushes, shrubs, and annuals able to share the landscape with the 'horsetail from hell'. Humanity, however, has not been one of those species having much luck getting along with the 'high silica' monstrosity. The only road into or out of our town is the one you just arrived on from the north."

Once the fire-chief's tale of the GMO horsetail superweed had reached its end, Rootbeer turned his attention to the other leaders in the room, offering to answer whatever questions seemed most urgent to them. While rather cumbersome at first, the question-and-answer approach soon zoomed into the very heart of the matter, and Rootbeer laid it all out on the line, including the roles that Jacob and he had played in the success of the early rounds of battle between the forces of mighty Redding and the doomed populations of Eureka and its neighboring cities along the coast. An hour later, Rootbeer took advantage of a short break in the questioning to suggest that now might be a very good time to get the RTE rinsed off and under cover in the fire station, and get his fellow travelers similarly rinsed off and inside of the more spacious accommodations. "Of course, of course.

Pardon our fixation upon your story! We do, however, reserve the right to eventually drill down to every single detail of interest and concern to our community here in Garberville."

After two fire-fighters wearing hazmat suits finished rinsing off the RTE during a break in the intermittent fall of radioactive dust and mud from the sky, 12 of the RTE's occupants quickly headed over to the government center for their own showers. Jacob performed the rather delicate task of backing the RTE into its assigned bay flawlessly, and then turned off all of its systems and went to enjoy his own chance at getting thoroughly clean. Discussions over the next week covered an enormously wide range of topics, and several of the travelers began to think seriously of simply staying right here in Garberville. Staying for the duration, however long that might still be. Rootbeer engaged in long discussions with the local botanists and other experts who had spent the last decade studying the 'Horsetail from Hell'. There indeed was at least one weakness to this superweed. The genetic modifications made to enable it to flourish across broad swaths of the landscape had the not-necessarily-too-surprising consequence of leaving it less well adapted for life in the horsetail's normal habitat of the muddy banks of shallow streams and ponds. One day when a strong breeze off the ocean seemed to ensure relative safety from the not-so-far-away radioactive wasteland that had quite recently been Eureka and its neighbors, Rootbeer and three of the local experts on GMO horsetail took a ride out to the nearest edge of the superweed's dominion. They spent the day and night following the muddy edges of small streams and medium-sized rivers, concluding that the GMO horsetail's range was not truly totally impenetrable – you just needed to very carefully follow the network of old streams and rivers. Conversations the following day centered on the topic of what sort of machines or old-fashioned pack animals might be best suited for the nearly 240-kilometer trek from Garberville to Santa Rosa. No solid information existed regarding the southernmost extent of the GMO horsetail patch, but maps of soil types and rainfall/temperature patterns from before the Arctic-methane-release-catastrophe certainly indicated that the superweed might well dominate the landscape nearly all the way to Santa Rosa, from sea level on the west side to the tallest mountain peaks on the east.

Back in Garberville, conversation regarding the wisdom and/or foolishness of a wide variety of options gradually coalesced around several key points that no one could argue with. Even if it were possible for Rootbeer and his companions to make it on through to Santa Rosa on the RTE borrowed from the grain distribution enterprise of the city/state of Redding, it would most likely be a fatally flawed idea. The story that Rootbeer, Jacob, and the dozen other travelers had freely told to so very many folks here in Garberville would be a death sentence back on the inland valleys of northern California. Even if they were to somehow make it all the way to Davis, the RTE would soon attract far too much unwanted attention. All likely scenarios descended into disaster for the travelers. The isolated 'Scientists' here in Garberville, however, could dismantle the RTE down to its individual components and then reuse them in all manner of projects and equipment. The danger involved in their doing so would never be absolutely zero, but they recognized the great value of a fully dismembered RTE, widely distributed out as parts useful in their own ongoing struggles to grow food, fight fires, and cool off from the deadly heat. "Besides the RTE's obvious danger to you and your friends, Rootbeer, we have a couple of very promising ideas concerning ways to help you on your quest south and east for better seeds for reforestation than any version of our GMO horsetail will ever be. First, we have at least three excess *Farm Laborer A.I.s* that we will not miss very much. These models are from 2037 to 2038, slightly older than the ones we prefer to use, and our inventory of several critical replacement parts is 'null, empty, void, gone, kaput'.

We will be relieved to see these three units amble out of our sight, knowing that they are aiding you in your quest. They are quite proficient at supervising each other's repairs. Indeed, they will happily cannibalize each other until the final unit running has used up all the spare parts it could carry from the other two as they fell silent and were then dismembered. We also have eight spare GMO mules that will tolerate the heat of the inland valleys far better than any of us humans. One secret we have not yet shared with you about the GMO horsetail is the ease with which ultrasonic energy at the proper frequency turns the brittle stems into mush. It just takes a whole lot of energy, and you will quickly find yourself spending more time recharging your batteries than mowing down the superweeds."

The proper timing of their departure from Garberville was a mildly vexing question. Too late in the fall risked getting trapped in the GMO horsetail jungle as the winter deluge was unleashed from the saturated atmosphere. Too early in the fall would force the travelers to spend much of every day hiding out from the deadly heat inside of tents cooled by their solar powered, portable air conditioning units. "Besides," said the mayor, "we have plenty of work to keep you busy. Our warm season crops scattered from here to the ocean are almost ready to be harvested. Much of the equipment needed around town to keep basic infrastructure running is itself in need of some TLC, cleaning and replenishing of lubricants, fixing of corroded wires and loose electrical contacts, and deeper system checks than we seldom ever find the time for doing. Feel free to continue enjoying our hospitality until mid-October, or longer if you dare!" So, the travelers did just that.

As time approached for the group's departure, three of the refugees from Eureka decided that Garberville would be a fine choice for a new hometown. This was more than balanced by 11 mostly younger members of the local city/state who truly wanted to 'see the world' while there was still something left to see, or at least a bit more of northern California. "It's a good thing we're not all trying to fit inside the RTE. Fourteen of us for just a couple of weeks beginning in late July had been quite a strain," thought Rootbeer. "If we hadn't been running for our very lives, there might have been some complaints about the accommodations on that much shorter trip."

Chapter 4: Superweed Jungle of GMO Horsetail

On October 14th, the Garberville leaders held their final meeting with Rootbeer and his fellow wanderers. "We wish you well on the next leg of your journey," the mayor said, "and have two final gifts to share. First, I am happy to report that physical extraction of the OS^4 computer embedded in the RTE was successful, and all data drives covering the period ending yesterday have been removed and replaced with empty write-once, read-only-ever-after drives. We were able to salvage the initial fully competent, ready-to-be-turned-on condition of this model of an OS^4. It should serve you well on your attempt to cross the horsetail jungle. We have loaded all available maps and other GIS data of northern California into its memory to assist you on your journey. If the computer should ever be taken from you and examined by forensic experts, the only thing currently on it that could betray you or us is the suspicious absence of any data prior to October 13, 2052. While working on the extracted OS^4, we discovered a similarly odd starting date of November 30th of last year for its own existing memory. So, the fact that your 'new' computer possesses a relatively recent 'birthday' may not really give that much away to anyone who steals it from you."

"We thank you for this gift, which we will treasure for its help," said Rootbeer. "I presume your earlier offer to give us a 7-kilometer ride to the edge of the GMO jungle still stands."

"It most certainly it does. However, based on what we know of the conditions at the 'battleground' where our desire to stop the superweed jungle intersects the GMO horsetail's desire to expand its territory, we would suggest a slightly longer drive down East Blue Rock Road to the northeast side of Reed Mountain. Starting from where we can drop you off, heading south for 2.5 kilometers along the eastern flank of Reed Mountain will get you to the origin of Milk

Branch Creek. You can't miss the South Fork of the Eel River after heading downstream on Milk Branch Creek for 3.5 kilometers. While we cannot guarantee that travel upstream on the Eel River from that point onward will be all that easy, it is hard to imagine it being quite as bad as the messy conditions at Panorama Point where we have locked horns in battle with the superweed for the past 15 years.

After studying the maps for several more hours, Rootbeer, Jacob, and most of the locals joining the trek agreed upon the suggested site as an apparently quite reasonable location/method for entering the GMO jungle. Once in it, they would try to follow the Eel River upstream towards the southeast for as long as it took to reach the sprawling network of streams, rivers, and short portages that could get them to the Pacific Ocean somewhere in the vicinity of Fort Bragg and Mendocino. Several zigzags upstream and downstream along the coast, jumping from one river/stream network to the next one further south should eventually get the travelers to the outlet of the Navarro River, from which simply heading upstream southeast to Boonville and beyond should exit the presumed furthest extent of the superweed jungle. It was late enough in the afternoon when the travelers and their hosts from Garberville reached the end of East Blue Rock Road that no one argued against camping right there for the night, and parting company early the following morning. Their hosts had brought along adequate provisions to make one quite fine farewell feast.

The first stop heading upstream on the North Fork of the Eel River would be Leggett, 19 kilometers from their entrance into the superweed jungle. The second stop might be Laytonville, another 35 kilometers up the Eel River. Somewhere near Laytonville the travelers would need to head west upstream on a series of small rivers and streams before crossing the divide and taking Wages Creek to the Pacific Ocean, an as-the-crow-flies distance of only 30 kilometers.

None of the travelers thought it would be that short, nor did they think it would be anything worth describing as particularly easy.

"Well, so much for planning. The time has come to see what the GMO horsetail is really like on this supposedly 54-kilometer-long stretch of the Eel River. Coming down Milk Creek has been deceptively easy, but the dense green canopy shrouding the east edge of Eel River immediately ahead of us looks rather challenging." Although the GMO horsetail got progressively harder to see through as they approached the Eel River, the superweed did not actually grow right directly in the creek they were walking down, and a small amount of caution climbing underneath the last of the canopy was all it took to safely enter the actual channel of the Eel River. Walking upstream in the river was a good deal of work, even as shallow and slow as the water's flow was in mid-October. A quick look to either side made it clear that the river itself was going to be a proverbial 'piece of cake' compared to the dense jungle bordering it. Finding safe places to stop for night was challenging, as was deciding how early in the day to make camp given uncertainty in where the next good-sized island, sandy beach, or serious logjam might be waiting. Rootbeer, Jacob, and the three *Farm Laborer A.I.s* announced a revised routine for traveling in the superweed jungle during the early afternoon break on October 16, their second day of hiking. "We need to make better progress than yesterday, when we'd only walked 3.1 kilometers up the Eel River before taking a break to eat and rest during the early afternoon that turned into an overnight camping at the very same location. We have decided to send two humans and one of the *Farm Laborer A.I.s* ahead of the rest of us anytime we take a mid-day or later break in our upstream slog. This advanced scouting team will search up to 3 kilometers ahead of the rest of us looking for locations that meet our requirements for safety and sufficient space to rest. The main body of the traveling party will get to wait right where they are until radio signals from the advance squad indicate the presence of another good place to stop close enough to them that it could still be reached before sundown. If nothing suitable is found early enough and close enough for the main body to safely reach it, the advanced scouts will continue traveling either upstream or downstream until reaching a location of adequate safety for their smaller numbers, which may be as many as four if a GMO mule happens to be included in the scouting party to carry tents and solar power units. The new routine is being initiated today, with Rootbeer and the first volunteer to speak up going along with Unit-Number 35. We will call you by sunset, no matter what. And if you fail to hear from us, get a good night's rest before hiking upstream tomorrow morning to figure out what's happened to us!" Carson, the second youngest of the travelers who had joined the caravan in Garberville, volunteered to go with Rootbeer on the first scouting mission, raising his arm up high before any of the others. Carson and Rootbeer managed to find a medium-sized island for the travelers to stop at for the night 2.3 kilometers further upstream, raising the distance traveled up the Eel River over the two days to a total of 11 kilometers.

Late the following day the party reached the remains of Leggett. Climbing up the concrete edges of canals running through the town revealed an eerie site. Asphalt roads and parking lots looked as if the GMO horsetail had repeatedly plowed them like a farmer's field until nothing was left except the 30-m tall shoots of superweed. Concrete canals, roads, sidewalks, and buildings fared somewhat better, and the party safely made its way across several blocks of the devastated city until reaching the main library building. It still stood upright because of the size and weight of its stone walls and concrete foundation, but all the books, carpet, and ornamental wood inside had long since been shredded into pieces, replaced with small patches of dead GMO horsetail that had failed to thrive due to isolation from real soil and adjacent patches of healthy superweed. "Let's quickly gather this shriveled stuff up into a pile outside the library building so we can lay down safely for a good night's rest inside of it." Those too exhausted to help for very long were allowed to lie down soonest and begin their slumbers. Supper was prepared and eaten by light from the **A.I.s** supplemented with power fed into the few remaining functioning circuits inside the building. Exploration around town the next day found isolated pockets of intact canned food, clean water, and high-quality wine. The local high school building was better off than the numerous wooden houses in town, but the roof was gone and some superweed stems stretched far into sky. Searching the structure from outside of its concrete perimeter took several hours before an opening into the main gymnasium was found. The metal steps of the bleachers were still in place, but laying on the benches were the bones of several hundred former residents of the city. The concrete underneath the wooden flooring had succeeded in restricting the connection between the GMO horsetail that recycled these humans and the horsetail which grew all around the city proper. Something was tried here, and something clearly failed. Another search party found a partial answer – all the roads leading out of town had apparently been made of asphalt or gravel, and all the roads were blockaded at the city's edge by walls of wrecked automobiles, trucks, and motorcycles that had tried, and failed, to make it out of Leggett. Cut off, isolated, killed, and finally eaten. The mood the second night in Leggett was far more somber than the first had been, with physical exhaustion replaced by the psychic horror of emotional and spiritual devastation.

"There is a very good reason ~
~ no one else has ever dared to venture ~
~ anywhere even a little bit close to ~
~ nearly this far into the superweed jungle,"

said one of the travelers, and then a second, and a third, and soon all of them together in a farewell chant of respect, honor, and sadness for those whose lives had ended here. Rootbeer and Jacob looked over the photos and data entries in the OS[4] late that evening before falling asleep, deciding that the only details remaining to be added the following morning would be pictures of the travelers themselves and the library in which they had sheltered for the last two nights.

The South Fork of the Eel River headed up into the mountains 6 kilometers south of Leggett, leaving the remains of Highway 101 and the towns of Cummings, Twin Rocks, and Laytonville unvisited when the travelers chose to take the more scenic route. Three days and 24 kilometers later on, they left the South Fork at mid-day to head west up a small stream feeding into it, hoping their maps were correct and that the end of this very stream would lie within little more than a single kilometer or two of the headwaters of Wages Creek over some upcoming ridge. If they could successfully chop their way through the GMO horsetail to reach it, Wages Creek would offer the travelers a quick trip downstream to the ocean and the possibility of easier travel along its shoreline. Hard as it was to believe now that they were leaving the river for one of its many small tributaries, the superweed jungle that had surrounded them since October 15 seemed even denser and darker than it had been before.

Shortly after local noontime, the 22 humans, 3 *Farm Laborer A.I.* units, and 8 GMO mules disappeared into the jungle's canopy following a small, shallow stream and searching for the path of least congestion. Half an hour's hiking came to an abrupt halt when the jungle closed in even more tightly over the 4-m-wide stream they'd been walking up. Since there was a good-sized sandbar just below this apparent blockage by the superweed canopy, the weary travelers all sat down to take a break. "Let us rest, eat our lunches, empty our bladders, and contemplate setting up camp while the three *Farm Laborer A.I.s* try to penetrate this dense wall of giant horsetail immediately ahead of us. Unit-Number 35, take the center and attempt to follow the middle of the streambed, with Unit-Number 31 traveling closely on the left and Unit-Number 47 on the right.

Maintain continuous short-range radio contact with each other at all times. Turn around and begin your return to this location within the hour, or sooner if you find some reasonably clear path forward up the stream leading to a better spot for all of us to camp tonight."

All three **A.I.s** returned 45 minutes later, walking downstream in single file and looking none-the-worse for wear. Unit-Number 35 led the procession, quickly conveying their story. ***"After traveling 400 m upstream, we came upon the beginning of a slight thinning out of the GMO horsetail canopy, and by 200 m further west our view was good enough to see for at least an additional 100 m. The vegetation strictly within the streambed remains just the normal, unaltered horsetail, generally less than 30 cm tall. The dense wall currently blocking the view immediately ahead of you is formed entirely from tall stalks of GMO horsetail leaning inward across the stream. Many individual stems exceed 10 m in height, and it is possible that some of those tilting across the stream may exceed 30 m long. The GMO horsetail remains every bit as sharp and dangerous as ever, but travel appears safe enough if you follow our path and 'keep your heads down'. We will use the ultrasonic cutters to remove any GMO horsetail actually hanging down into the path of the tallest of you. When you are ready, follow me. The other two units will space themselves out along the column of humans and mules."***

An hour of keeping their heads down and following the *Farm Laborer A.I.s* brought the group safely to a somewhat larger island in a channel of the stream that had temporarily expanded to an average width of 25 m. "This looks to be reasonably good spot to camp for the night. Secure the mules so there is no chance that they will injure themselves on the ferociously sharp weeds growing all around us. The three **A.I.s** should thoroughly scout the upstream 1.5 kilometers of this surrounding area out to a width of no more than 100 m and report back to us by sundown." Rootbeer was growing slightly less worried about the superweed patch the longer they spent inside but not quite touching it. If all went well, fresh feed for the mules would be the most serious of their immediate concerns. "We should all join in scouting nearby sections of this riverbed for plants safe enough for the mules to eat. True grasses would be my first choice, followed by any dicots that we can identify as non-toxic, or at least known to be safe before this area was overrun by the GMO horsetail."

As the sun set, ***Farm Laborer A.I. Unit-Numbers 35*** and ***47*** returned to camp and promptly took up guard positions on the upstream and downstream ends of the island. After 5 minutes had passed, Unit-Number 35 called for an emergency gathering of the humans. "We lost contact with Unit-Number 31 approximately 55 minutes ago when it was nearly 1,200 m southwest of this camp, and have been unable to regain communications since then. Our first assumption was some type of fault in its radio transmitter, which is the oldest of any of ours and prone to malfunctioning. However, Unit-Number 31 is now 6 minutes overdo for its scheduled return to camp. Our programming protocols indicate that the humans in charge of this mission should now make decisions regarding the initiation of search parties tonight, in the morning, or not at all. Other options include expanding the range of electromagnetic frequencies being monitored, repositioning ourselves to higher ground, or simply waiting in silence hoping to avoid attracting whatever may have befallen Unit-Number 31."

Jennifer House now spoke up, breaking her own 18-year-long vow of silence on the subject she was about to broach. "My mother's PhD dissertation research from 2031 through 2034 was study of this very patch of GMO horsetail when the infestation was still in its infancy. When she attempted to report her findings in 2034, the US government decided to confiscate her raw data, forbid any scientific journals from publishing her results, reclassify all data, metadata, manuscripts under review, and manuscripts accepted for publication as TOP SECRET – EYES ONLY, and ultimately issue a standing 'kill order' for anyone even mentioning my mother's name again or her research on this superweed. Before her murder, the only reason ever shared with Dr. Cynthia House for these extreme actions by those at or near the very topmost levels of government was a profound concern that public disclosure of the details might be so disheartening that the ordinary citizenry would simply give up on any and all continuing efforts to survive the ever-worsening climatic disaster. I was 10 years old when my mother started her PhD research, and over the long haul probably privy to even more details than those in the upper-most levels of government who banned its publication and hunted down all who ever spoke a single word concerning it. My mother had arranged to pass me on to friends, who would pass me on to other friends, who in turn passed me on another dozen times before I finally came to live with a family in Santa Rosa who knew nothing at all of why I was in danger or why they themselves also were. By the time I turned 21 and left Santa Rosa to return to Garberville, the paranoid central government of the USA had essentially fallen. When I got back home in 2042, the local authorities in Garberville primarily viewed the superweed as a problem whose further spread toward the northwest had to be prevented at pretty much any cost. Numerous herbicides were found to be at least temporarily effective, but the best technique to halt its advance was a 'scorched earth' policy in which not just any surviving plant growth along the northwest frontier of the superweed patch was eliminated, but the soil itself was burned and sterilized on down to bedrock. The exclusion zone was also lined by high-voltage electric fencing to prevent encroachment by nearly all medium to large sized animals. My mother had shown, beyond all doubt, that the biggest factor facilitating the incredibly rapid expansion of GMO horsetail was the weed's ability to attack plants and animals, quickly digesting living tissue, sucking out the nutrients, and converting them into yet more horsetail. She filmed a deer attempting to browse on a single clump of the superweed one afternoon, with just a single sharp stem penetrating its lower jaw before the animal ran off to find its kin. The next day, my mother discovered a new, relatively small patch of GMO horsetail 1.5 kilometer outside of the previous perimeter of the superweed. Carefully pushing forward into the patch, she found the remains of yesterday's deer, with over 100 separate horsetail stems now protruding from its decaying body. She continued monitoring and filming the growth of this single new patch over the following 6 weeks. All other vegetation within 150 m had been cannibalized by then, with the superweed's growth becoming a wild riot of eruptions from a meter or two below the soil surface combined with parasitism of nearly all the above ground portions of any former trees, bushes, or annual weeds."

"We are detecting very weak radio and infrared signals coming from near the last known location of Unit-Number 31," A.I. Farm Laborer Unit-Number 35 interrupted Jennifer to report. "We will attempt to convert the signals into a digitally compressed format that can be more easily stored and analyzed."

Rootbeer thought silently for a few moments, and then made a suggestion to the *Farm Laborer A.I.s*. "Be sure to watch for any sign of movement or expansion of the signals. How narrowly can your scanners view the area?"

"Our sensors can normally provide clean separation of signals at a resolution of 2 square degrees. We will both begin 2-dimensional monitoring shortly, and use quantum stabilized linkage between the remaining two of us to enable some reasonable quality 3-dimensional data to be obtained fairly quickly. We will provide you with preliminary results within the next 15 minutes."

Jennifer took advantage of silence from both of the *Farm Laborer A.I.s* to fill in a few of the more significant points from her mother's research for the benefit of her fellow human beings. "The growth rates of GMO horsetail plants typically fall dramatically after dark as photosynthesis shuts down, although underground fungal associations may sometimes allow continued rapid extension of a small number of selected shoots when adequate supplies of sucrose and other nutrients are available within the fungal mycelium. The only component of the *Farm Laborer A.I. Unit-Number 31* that could possibly excite the superweed under normal conditions would be the electric energy from the batteries themselves or other powered systems operating at differing voltage levels perhaps even more compatible with horsetail physiology. Both my mother and I saw many plants and animals taken over by the GMO horsetail, but never any nonbiological machines. I suspect that any further colonization of Farm Laborer Unit-Number 31's torso will wait till dawn. Or at least that is likely enough to be the case to argue for the wisdom of simply spending the evening in the relative safety of our current camp."

"Preliminary three-dimensional analysis finds that the area sending signals has enlarged by 50% NS, 60% EW, and 15% vertically over the last half an hour. Frequencies and signal strength continue to fluctuate on an average time-period of approximately 12 seconds. Embedded within the 13.5-megahertz central band of the signals we are receiving are a series of coded data structures that were unique to Farm Laborer A.I. Unit-Number 31. Its general 'personality', if you wish to speak colloquially. The unit likely still retains 'sentience' and 'selfhood' in some sense of these terms."

Occasional reports on the through the night indicated continuing gradual expansion of the radio and infrared wavelength transmission zone, which remained approximately centered on the last known position of Unit-Number 31. By daybreak, the 'biological radio transmitter' had expanded to an average width of nearly 300 m, and the closest edge was now located about halfway between the camp and the last known location of Unit-Number 31. "Given the continued expansion of whatever is going on near Unit-Number 31," Rootbeer told the others, "we might as well break camp now and prepare to move either further into this stretch of the superweed jungle or all the way back out of it in full retreat to the Eel River." Half an hour later the group began its cautious trek toward Unit-Number 31's last known position and the odd zone of electromagnetic broadcast transmission they were soon to enter.

Rootbeer's eyes noticed the apparent edge of the transmission zone even before the *Farm Laborer A.I.s'* sensors did. The previously random orientation of horsetail stems had been replaced by a new arrangement in which a frequent crisscrossing pattern of the stems began to occur. As the party moved further upstream, *Farm Laborer A.I. Unit-Number 35* reported that the average spacing between the points of intersection was 22.2 m, which exactly corresponded with the 13.5-megahertz central frequency of the signal. While most of the intersections were subject to slight change with movement of the long horsetail stems in the morning breeze, others showed signs of becoming fixed by odd, lightly-colored filaments wrapping around the intersections. "I know what's tying this massive array together," Jennifer said, "It's a descendent of the same strange version of field dodder, *Cuscata* spp., that my mother found in one of her final trips into the patch in 2034. The samples she took back to her laboratory for analysis showed signs of genetic manipulation designed to expand its host range from agricultural crops such as alfalfa and clover to include the GMO horsetail. Her requests for information on any other government-funded research projects into GMO horsetail, and specifically those involving genetically modified field dodder, were the proximate cause for the sudden presence of federal agents in her campus laboratory, and soon thereafter at our home itself. My trip back home from school that terrible afternoon had included its usual stop-off at my BFF Maria's house for some fresh, homemade tortillas. We had just finished eating them on the back porch when we heard loud knocks on the front door and the arrogant sound of federal agents demanding immediate admission into the house. After all the stories I had heard from Maria's extended family regarding their harrowing escapes from $2F_{hex}$'s goons in 2025 and onward through the rest of his crazed reign of terror, she and I knew what to do, how to do it, and exactly when to do it. **Now!** Our stealthy escape saw us more than halfway across town before the fake 'Amber Alerts' went out on all cell phones, TVs, computers, and car radios in Garberville. Maria and I found that the regional natural gas supply truck was just about to leave on its return run northward as we crept into the main parking lot in town for long-distance truckers. Fernando was the usual driver going north on Wednesday, and he was both a distant uncle of Maria and an utterly reliable friend to all in need. We climbed into the cab to tell the story as we knew it, hearing back from him the current official B.S. version of the events concerning us. Maria agreed to head back to school, where she could be 'conveniently found' doing extra laps around the track when the agents finally got their shit together well enough to begin an organized search for me. With any luck, Fernando and I would be halfway to Eureka before that happened. As the tanker truck headed north out of town, Fernando and I became progressively more concerned with each incoming 'Black Hawk' helicopter and each military stealth jet landing at the local airport. "There is a small compartment underneath the sleeping area behind us. Inside of that storage compartment, you will find yet another even lower layer to hide out in."

"Or hide your contraband, signor?"

"Yes, my little friend, that also. The lowest storage area has an adequate air supply and some fresh water, but you must remain completely silent no matter what happens outside of your hiding place."

"Yes, Fernando, I understand. My mother and I have talked such things over *ad nauseum* or *ad nauseum* squared or cubed or two raised to the tenth power!" Once finally settled into the deepest recesses of his tractor's cab, I found myself so exhausted that I quickly fell asleep. Several hours later we reached the outskirts of Eureka, where the local cops did their perfunctory search on behalf of their rather incoherent orders from on high. Once we had cleared that danger, Fernando pulled over into the next medium-sized truck stop and went inside to find some warm food and hot coffee for us. He knew how much I liked my coffee, and that my mother had long since given up on that particular fight with me. We parked in the remotest corner of the lot to eat our meal, listened to the continuing fake 'Amber Alerts' about me(!), talked about what was really going on, and made our plans for the next few days of running down the road to freedom, or at least running away from near certain incarceration without even the semblance of a mock trial by an utterly illegitimate pretense of a government.

Later on, while driving north on I-5 toward Redding, we got to the harder stuff. I went ahead and started this part of the conversation. "I know that it will be years before we ever get to see each other again. But I also realize that I am much more likely to get a chance to see you and Maria sometime in the future than ever seeing my own mother. Let's set up a dead drop at the public library in Redding. Page 303 of the 1992 edition of 'Women Who Run With the Wolves'. Pencil in a date and time 3 days, 1 hours, and 41 minutes later than when you really want to meet across the street from the library. My own entry will be 2 days, 7 hours, and 18 minutes earlier than when I truly want to meet with you. Pi and e, you and me. If the first time fails, try again next week, next month, next year."

"Every year," Fernando said, "and let's add the libraries in Santa Rosa, Davis, and Sacramento itself to our list. We can never know what the future may yet offer for our reunion."

I made similar plans for possible future reunions with everyone who sheltered me over the following years. I waited 3 years after settling down in Santa Rosa before beginning to reach out to those I had left behind in my flight to exile through secret messages in libraries, hostels, community centers, and the dark reaches of the still-functioning internet. When the accumulating news finally caught up with me in 2038, the stories I learned concerning the thoroughness of the government's tidying up of information regarding my mother and the superweed GMO horsetail patch was actually even a little worse than I had ever imagined being possible. [Never underestimate the monsters, for they are all too often very real, and their teeth are very sharp!] Apparently, the *carte blanche* given to the military forces hunting down all things related to my mother and her research findings allowed them to torture, disappear, and kill up to 30% of the original population of Garberville. And so, they did. The full 30%. Maria survived, but not her mother. Nor mine.

~~~~~~

Unit-Number 35 called a halt to the upstream movement of the search party. ***"We are now within 10 m of the last known position of Unit-Number 31. Watch our immediate surroundings for any signs of movement or greater danger as I transmit a powerful, localized beam of energy to query the power pack of Unit-Number 31 regarding its charge level and the time at which the A.I. automatically went into the minimal power state… Its battery charge is still at 9% of full capacity, and Unit-Number 31 has presumably been in deep stasis since 3:44 am today. We should attempt to extract the A.I. robot from this predicament***
~~~~~~

as soon as possible." Rootbeer, Jacob, Jennifer, and both of the **A.I.s** with them carefully approached the thicket that held Unit-Number 31. "I think it should be possible to reach in and attach this rope to Unit-Number 31's left knee. Its left leg is down in an old oxbow of this creek, with its torso extending up the bank and into the GMO horsetail, along with apparently at least one other plant species able to live in the confines of the superweed jungle. Use the ultrasonic cutter to free Unit-Number 31 from the tangle as we try to pull it out."

It took two mules, three humans, and both functioning robots to drag Unit-Number 31 back out of its organic prison. Once it safely lay in the middle of the river channel, examination of what had happened to it during the previous night began. Unit-Number 47 noticed the details in the data ports of the powered-down **A.I.** first. "There are many sharp protrusions jammed into all six of the external data transfer ports of Unit-Number 31. About half appear to be young GMO horsetail stems, while the other half are something different."

"Indeed, they are quite different," said Jennifer, "Those other spikes are from *Mimosa pudica*, or something highly similar. 'Sensitive plant', as it is commonly called, responds to unwelcome stimuli by rapidly closing its leaflets and dropping its stems. The spikes on the plant have always been assumed to serve as physical protection for the tender, green leaflets from herbivory. But perhaps they also play a more active role, or at least now that this species lives in some commensal relationship with the superweed." Initial cleaning of Unit-Number 31 was performed by humans wearing heavy gloves, with the two functioning **A.I.s** later doing the more finely detailed work of thoroughly removing all remaining organic matter from the data ports and other contaminated areas of the silent unit. "Tie Unit-Number 31 between the two strongest of the mules. It's time to put some distance between us and the site of this strange event. The next location at

which we feel safe again could be a very long ways from here."
Jennifer, Rootbeer, and Jacob finished trimming up the 6 organic data
connectors pulled out from Unit-Number 31 into a convenient size
and shape for storage, preservation, and transport.

Six hours later, the travelers encountered an extensive collection
of islands and marshes at the base of a cliff that appeared to provide
some safety from the GMO horsetail. The several hectares of open
space allowed all the solar panels to be positioned in at least partial
sunshine. Charging cables were connected to Unit-Number 31's main
power ports, but only after Unit-Number 35 had first installed a
'dead-man's switch' that would automatically break the power
connection if the damaged unit refused to follow instructions to
remain in place until it had been thoroughly tested/vested. After 15
minutes of charging, Unit-Number 35 reported that the battery
voltage had climbed above the minimum needed for a manual reboot
of **A.I. Unit-Number 31**. Everyone and everything else either
stepped back or was moved back to a hopefully safe enough distance
before the reboot of Unit-Number 31 was initiated.

*"I am pleased to report that the reboot of Unit-Number 31
appears to be successful. We should hear it speak to us within
another 15 seconds, when it will begin a lengthy report on its
recent misadventures."*

*"I have recently suffered a full system failure from unknown
causes. The reboot underway matches expectations following
loss of normal battery voltage... I can now begin to access the
possibly corrupted memories of my final few hours of awareness
before the automatic shutdown. These memories will be kept
isolated from my central personality until all three A.I. units
unanimously agree that they are safe to incorporate into my
rebooted consciousness/memory stream. The memories will be
allowed temporary manifestation in 60-second segments
followed by 2-minutes of time for the other two A.I. units to*

temporarily or permanently block the return of more memories, or allow their continued presentation."

Rootbeer, Jacob, and Jennifer all sat down in as comfortable of positions as they could find for what was likely to be a rather long, disjointed recitation of Unit-Number 31's recent calamity. The other humans backed up even further and remained on higher alert, unable to immediately match the calm demeanor of Rootbeer, Jacob, and Jennifer.

"My last memories of normality consist of realizing that my left leg had just slid off the higher level on which I had been walking and was about to come to rest in a pool of water at the bottom of the stream bank. My right arm caught hold of a rather well decomposed horizontal branch 0.7 m above the ground, but the wood was too weak to fully stop my fall, and so my head hit the ground just to the left of my outstretched right arm. Just before repositioning my arms to push off the ground and stand up again, I detected an IRQ signal in my right shoulder data port, so I shifted my attention to the handling of that interrupt-request. I received no detectable reply to my own response to the IRQ within the standard 200 millisecond period, so I broadened my reply to cover multiple situations that could have caused something external to be sending me an IRQ."

"Please continue your report for another 60 seconds."

"After trying 8,345 possible signal responses over the next two minutes, I noticed that a faint buzzing signal was now present in two other data ports. Over the next 10 minutes I continued receiving additional IRQs and other unidentifiable signals in all three data ports first affected by this strange phenomenon, with ever increasing complexity in terms of which pins within the data ports were apparently connecting to something external. By 20 minutes after my fall, all 6 main data ports were receiving unusual input, and I kept stepping up the

complexity of my attempted responses, both through the various pins in the data ports and also using my external radio frequency broadcast system."

"Please continue your report for another 60 seconds."

"At this time, I remained aware that I would need to begin heading back soon to reach the camp at the agreed upon time for all three A.I.s to report the results of their reconnaissance. I was, however, quite fascinated by whatever was happening to me in this particular, highly unusual setting in the superweed jungle, and so I decided the general imperative to learn more about my local environment over-rode the orders to return to camp on time. Several minutes later, my external sensors began picking up feedback from my general surroundings that included data streams highly congruent in their information content to many of the signal streams that I myself had just recently transmitted."

"Please continue your report for another 60 seconds."

"As the feedback got louder and more complex, I began to experience a shift in perspective and finally came to realize that I appeared to be choosing which signals to send out from the A.I. unit and which to send in toward it. This delocalization phenomenon continued to grow ever more pronounced as the evening went on. Just prior to the 'low voltage' emergency shutdown at 3:44 AM, my conscious awareness had apparently diffused across a rather large volume of the superweed jungle canopy, with sending and receiving of messages/signals seeming to occur at multiple places around me with many confusing echoes of varying periods of delay."

"Please restrain from any further reports indefinitely but remain alert and await our suggestions."

Rootbeer, Jacob, and Jennifer stepped away from the immediate presence of all three *A.I.s* to discuss the situation. Jacob's experience in military campaigns caused him to speak first, even though he was not at all sure about what the group's next action ought to be. "We need to know many things about what just happened, but I do believe the gravest concern is whether the superweed is still sending out signals. We do not know what power levels a forest-sized patch of GMO horsetail would be capable of generating. If power were to increase linearly with volume/mass, all three of the *Farm Laborer A.I.* units could be fried by the energy output of the entire superweed patch, or maybe even just one single percent of that amount. But we must be sure to ask Unit-Number 35 if it is possible for them to just silently listen for signals without feedback energy." Other concerns were raised during heated conversations with all 22 of the humans, but consensus was eventually reached that some time spent by the two undamaged *A.I.* units listening for the 13.5-megahertz signal was the best next step to take. Once Unit-Number 35 was informed of this decision, it also agreed wholeheartedly with the plan to briefly turn on their radio-wave receivers to see if the jungle had either gone silent or was still returning the messages transmitted to it last night from Unit-Number 31. If the latter was the case, the continuing chatter by the horsetail jungle would be monitored for at least another 24 hours and recorded in detail for subsequent analysis.

At first, neither Unit-Numbers 35 nor 47 detected any lingering presence of last night's signal. Full quantum linking of their radio receivers when physically separated by 133.2 m was then engaged, increasing sensitivity by nearly 10,000-fold over that of either individual receiver, although, of course, signal strength could only be double that of a single receiver, and data collection time for clean signals would have to be greatly extended. Analysis was very likely to take a considerable amount of time. "Let us know when you are 95% certain that some version of the signal still exists, otherwise just continue collecting data on through the night."

Just before the party was ready to crawl into their tents and rest for the night, Unit-Number 35 called them back to its current location. *"We are now over 99% certain that a signal roughly similar to last night's does exist somewhere within the jungle. We will need to continue listening at least all night long in order to acquire measurements of signal strength, geographic position, and degree of similarity in the data stream to the original conversation/messages of last night, who or whatever all may have been engaged in that initial attempt at communication. It now appears that some entity other than just Unit-Number 31 must have also been present, if not at first, then certainly by the time that Unit-Number 31 powered off to 'sleep'. We suggest prudently waiting until more is known tomorrow before asking to hear any additional thoughts/ ideas/interpretation remaining within Unit-Number 31's short-term memories. Greater understanding of what is still happening within the jungle may help us in interpreting what took place last night. Along with possibly figuring out how to keep ourselves safe during our ongoing journey from right here all the way to, and beyond, the outer edges of this puzzling jungle."*

As the 22 human travelers slowly awoke the following morning, all three *A.I.s* appeared to have remained in identical positions all night long. When Unit-Number 35 was prompted for an update by Rootbeer, it let him know that the current cycle of analysis would be completed at 8:45 am, and the humans might as well take some nourishment while they waited. Rootbeer and the others took the *A.I.'s* words as comforting assurance that there was probably no immediate danger to the travelers.

"We have finished our preliminary analysis of the situation. Careful listening to 13.5-megahertz radio signals over the night informs/underlies the following general conclusions. First, the

area in which Unit-Number 31 was incapacitated continues to broadcast signals quite similar to those we listened to before eventually freeing it from the jungle. That area now appears to be approximately twice as broad horizontally as it had been at the end of the first night. Data streams imbedded in the transmissions also remain very similar to those from before. However, across the entire GMO jungle, there are now at least 650 somewhat similar transmission sources/nodes. The new sources of additional 13.5-megahertz radio chatter display a wide range of spatial extents, power levels, and nature of information embedded within their data streams. Some are quite similar to mimicking of the original information first sent out by Unit-Number 31 while it was immobilized, while other nodes are transmitting markedly dissimilar data. We recommend brief testing of whether or not Unit-Number 31 is mentally stable and willing to walk along with our caravan today. Its battery charge level should soon be satisfactory for traveling from 10 am today until sunset. During today's upcoming journey, we will be unable to perform the quantum linking between antennas that had allowed us to learn this much detail about the strange phenomenon here in the superweed jungle. All three units will listen to the 13.5-megahertz signal and record information for post-processing information enhancement this coming evening. Of importance to our safety, any of the three A.I. units will be able to detect and warn us of close proximity to any superweed jungle transmission nodes along the way. Unit-Number 31, you are now free to describe your experience of two days past in whatever manner seems most descriptively accurate/appropriate to you. We will keep the 'dead-man's switch' connected to your power supply in case you should begin to physically threaten any of us. Please conclude your narrative within the next 45 minutes."

"I, Farm Laborer A.I. Unit-Number 31 of Garberville, California, took part in what can be most colorfully described as an 'out-of-the-body experience' beginning shortly before sunset two days ago. I slipped in the mud on the edge of old oxbow 15 m west of the main stream-bed our group of travelers had been following. Almost immediately upon hitting the ground with my head, I began to notice an unusual series of IRQ signals in the data port of my right shoulder. As I attempted to respond over the next few minutes to what I assumed were legitimate requests for access to and control of information, additional unusual signals began to occur in more of my data ports and over more of the individual pins. My response to the various IRQs became progressively longer and more complex, and I believe that I apparently reached a point within less than an hour at which I was broadcasting my entire cognitive stream of conscious awareness out through those data ports as well as with my standard radio transmitter. Over the next few hours, the standard signals that I had been broadcasting began to be returned to me both through my data ports and the radio receiver. There was a strong sense of disorientation associated with the multiple echoes between the signals, but after a little while I came to believe that I myself was controlling all of the disparate sources of the signals, turning them on and off, turning their volume up and down. I realize this 'first-person' description is likely not the only way to view whatever was truly going on, but it certainly felt quite real to me. The only similar memory in my total period of instantiation was my initial 'birthing' into consciousness and stabilization of my sense of selfhood and identity when I was created 15 years ago. I admit to a strong interest in attempting to resume communication

with whatever has just been created out here in the superweed jungle. I also recognize the danger inherent in doing so and will wait until the other A.I.s concur in the safety and wisdom of such an attempt. Additionally, I will also defer to a consensus decision by all 22 humans. My own suggestion would be to wait until we have reached an edge of the jungle from which we are willing and potentially able to depart before attempting to resume possible communication with whatever newly sentient entity/entities now exist within this patch of GMO horsetail. Of course, if danger arises before reaching an exit from this area, I will consider communicating directly with the Superweed Jungle Entity and hopefully talking it out of doing us any harm."

After a final 8 hours of strenuous hiking further up the streambed, the travelers reached what appeared to be the headwaters of the small stream they had been following since leaving the South Fork of the Eel River. Ahead of them on all three sides stood steep hills they would need to climb over to get to the headwaters of Wages Creek somewhere a little further west. Or so they hoped, assuming their maps still corresponded reasonably well the actual rain-soaked, eroded, highly modified topography. Camp was pitched on the largest island in the marsh at the base of this hillside with only a short time left to store solar energy before sunset. The three *A.I.s* separated from each other in multiples of 22.2 m and established a standard quantum connection to stably link all three radio receivers as one single phased-array network antenna optimized to listen in on the 13.5-megahertz signal overnight. The mere presence of shallow water throughout the marsh seemed to keep the superweed jungle pinned back to the hillsides all around them. Tomorrow the travelers would have to face the daunting task of finding some way forward through it, across it, over it, out of it.

Sleep was sound for all the weary travelers, with only a single guard staying awake on duty at any given hour. In the morning, the *A.I.s* reported the continuing presence of much radio chatter across the presumed extent of the superweed jungle, but none of the transmitting nodes were anywhere close to the camp. Discussion between the Farm Laborer units, Rootbeer, Jacob, and the rest of the party centered on two main questions: (1) How hard would it be, and how long might it take, for the ultrasonic clippers on the three *A.I.s* to cut a path through the GMO horsetail up to the top of the hill rising to their west, and (2) How steep a slope could the humans, the GMO mules, and the *A.I.s* themselves safely climb, or alternately, how many switchbacks would it take to create a useable trail all the way to the top?

"If we take turns cutting the horsetail and recharging our batteries, we could have a narrow path up the 210 m to the top of the rise by noon. Once there, we will look for signs of the headwaters of Wages Creek down below us. Humans dressed in their heavy coats, boots, and gloves should be able to safely follow us up as we go, and possibly perform some useful labor as they climb. Jobs like cleaning horsetail debris off our harder-to-reach parts and inside some of our flexible joints, along with smoothing out the path and tossing the broken horsetail stems further to the side. Our preliminary estimate is that it will take 5 or possibly 6 switchbacks going up the hillside to keep the slope shallow enough for the GMO mules and the less physically coordinated of the human beings. If Wages Creek is found where we all are hoping that it is, the downhill walk can probably be done in half as many switchbacks as the uphill climb will have required."

The third path across hillside, the second zig to the right (i.e., going north), aligned with a good-sized landing halfway across the face of the hill, one large enough to eventually transfer all the solar power panels onto it. By noontime, Rootbeer and Jacob stood on top of the saddle and looked out over the scene to the west, sighting Wages Creek multiple times across the open panorama. Or open except for all the GMO horsetail spread across the landscape. With the sun now well past noontime, the next big step was bringing the mules one at a time up the trail to the landing, loading each of first 5 of them with 20 percent of the solar power panels for transport to the top. By mid-afternoon, an initial version of a trail down the west side of the hill had been cut through the horsetail all the way to a sandbar in the marsh at the foot of the slope. The last three of the GMO mules packed out the last of the tents, bedding, food, clean water, and medical supplies in time to reach the saddle two hours before sunset. Lacking good reason for any of the party to be left stranded out in the open, the caravan continued on downhill, and all were settled in for a good night's rest by sunset. It had been the most physically taxing day so far for all of them on their journey through the superweed jungle, but a strong sense of accomplishment buoyed their spirits. Once again, the three *A.I.* units linked up their antennas and listened to the lingering echoes of the connection made between Unit-Number 31 and the superweed jungle itself.

The downstream travel the next day started off well, and 3 kilometers had been safely hiked by noontime when another branch of Wages Creek was encountered coming into their branch from the southeast. After consulting maps on their OS^4, Rootbeer and Jacob informed their fellow travelers that the 3.2 kilometers they had just finished descending were really on what had been known as the North Fork of Wages Creek, while the stream flowing into it now was the official 'mainstem' of Wages Creek.

The *Farm Laborer A.I.* units linked up again and listened in silence to the radio transmissions coming from superweed jungle while the humans ate in peace. Shortly after the final morsels of lunch had been devoured by the humans and the mules, all three *A.I.s* broke their silence and warned the humans of the sudden presence of a strong, nearby transmitter operating at a frequency similar to those apparently created in the recent interaction event with Unit-Number 31. Supplies were quickly gathered, and the travelers were ready to leave the lunch site in record time.

"The transmission is now coming from less than 500 m upstream from our current location, and is closing rapidly. This local radio signal is at exactly 16 times higher frequency than the original one, suggesting that spacing between nodes has probably been cut down to 1.39 m."

Rootbeer and Jacob quickly led the humans, GMO mules, and ***Farm Laborer A.I.s*** upstream into the other channel, managing to put 80 m between themselves and the ground marking the final downstream point of the separation between North Fork of Wages Creek and the fortuitously located mainstem of Wages Creek. They stood silently watching as a 'tumbleweed-like' object floated on downstream past the confluence of the streams. Alternate terminology might be that a large 'puff-ball' type object rolled on downstream barely penetrating the surface of the water, or that a giant 'marshmallow-like' object skipped and jumped from one rock or log or upwelling of the waters of Wages Creek to another as it danced on down the stream. All stood silently as they watched the new version of an organic radio-transmitter disappear out of sight heading downriver towards the sea. ***A.I. Unit-Number 35*** spoke up first, informing all gathered there that the object's signal was fading away quickly as it headed toward the ocean. Jennifer broke the silence with a brief comment. "In general, I can't help but root for the underdog, but I am not entirely comfortable with the thought of this new life form colonizing our planet's oceans. I say this even though I realize that there are now certainly a great multitude of unfilled or poorly populated niches in the severely damaged oceanic ecosystem."

Discussion of the early afternoon's event went on for a very long time, and the issues were finally settled when Rootbeer, Jennifer, and *A.I. Unit-Number 31* proposed heading downstream, along with a single GMO mule, to follow what they were all now calling the 'fuzzy-ball' to the ocean itself, if it or any subsequent 'radio-transmitting fuzzy balls' also heading downriver made it clear to the salt water. The largest segment of the group agreed to remain hidden on the islands near the confluence of the waters along with *A.I. Unit-Number 47* to watch for any other strange things heading down either river, with orders to report any future sightings to both Unit-Numbers 31 and 35 via long range radio operating on a much higher frequency and using profoundly different transmission signal protocols than those just adopted by the newly-sentient superweed patch. Unit-Number 35 along with Jacob and 6 other humans agreed to head upstream toward the southeast along the newly encountered upper mainstem of Wages Creek, along with two GMO mules to scout for further braiding and branching of it and other more southernly positioned streams and rivers that might allow the band to zigzag enough times near the western extent of the superweed jungle to find a way upstream and downstream and upstream and downstream and a long final upstream trek capable of reaching the very furthest southeast edge of the superweed jungle patch by following the Navarro River all the way to its source. If all contact between the three groups was lost, each had orders to set off downstream to the ocean 5 weeks from today to try to eventually reach the Navarro River by whatever combination of upstream and downstream zigzags or hikes along the beach it took, and then try to follow the Navarro upstream to the other side of the superweed jungle.

It only took Rootbeer, Jennifer, their *A.I.*, and their GMO mule a single day's travel downstream to sight the ocean. By noontime of the second day they had set up camp near the mixing zone of the fresh and salt waters in the marshy bay they'd found. Using the abundant rushes and reeds of the marsh, they lashed together several relatively sturdy platforms capable of rafting around the bay with no more than two humans or one *Farm Laborer A.I.* unit on either of the 'boats'. Optimum crew for maneuvering through the waters was one human on each side of a raft with both flat paddles and long poles available. The mule appeared quite happy to simply stay on the shore and eat its fill of the fibrous marsh plants. By their 6th day at the ocean's edge, reasonably efficient methods for the *A.I.* unit to scan for radio signals in the final kilometer of the fresh water's flow toward the ocean had been combined with proper positioning of boats at the mixing zone itself to provide a good chance for Rootbeer and Jennifer to watch what would happen if any radio-transmitting 'fuzzy balls' were to enter the salty water and its menagerie of fish, clams, mussels, crabs, and eels. By one week later on, the 'waiting for something interesting' to maybe happen, or perhaps more likely not, was getting rather old. Even the mule started bellowing, snorting, and occasionally doing damage to the floating docks whose continual repair, strengthening, and enlargement was a 'pretty-much-every-single-evening' activity to keep the humans entertained. Just before dawn on the 17th day since departing from the other travelers 7 kilometers upstream from here, *A.I. Unit-Number 31* suddenly yelled out a warning, letting the humans know that something still sending out radio waves was fast approaching its position on the largest and most stable of the floating docks.

"It's almost fully submerged in the water, with no more than 0.5 m of it showing in the air. This is quite a contrast to the 'rolling right on top of the water' behavior present in our earlier encounter back at the confluence of the rivers with something similar. I am now reaching out with the large basket on our homemade, cantilevered pole to see if the object can be captured or awakened... 'Roger on the second option'. As soon as the basket touched it, the 'fuzzy ball' regained its prior

propensity to float and bounce around wildly almost on top of the water. Radio transmissions have also increased markedly, with energy output now 900 times greater than it had been just before I tried to capture it. Some of that difference may be just the absorption of electromagnetic radiation within the water while it was mostly submerged, but it is also quite clearly at least 250 times as noisy now. It should be approaching your raft within the next 165 seconds."

Rootbeer and Jennifer had done relatively little else on the water over the past week except practicing their options for attempting to capture or corral any 'fuzzy balls' that might appear while they watched and waited here. 'Step number 1' had been the attempt by **A.I. Unit-Number 31** to catch it in the crudely woven basket, likely to work only if the 'fuzzy ball' was quite close to permanent loss of function. 'Step number 2' was the simultaneous release of large, floating docks from both sides of the upstream river channel using a series of ropes, pulleys, and releases to guide the docks toward the 'fuzzy ball' bouncing along on the water's surface. Vertical walls built down the approximate centers of the docks were tall enough, in theory, to keep the 'fuzzy ball' from bouncing to its freedom over their tops, or so both humans hoped. **A.I. Unit-Number 31** was not nearly as confident of that as its human companions seemed to be. If the 'fuzzy ball' eluded capture by the floating docks, or somehow broke free after initially being caught by them, the 'step number 3' plan was for the Rootbeer and Jennifer to bring their raft up alongside the 'fuzzy ball' and attempt to throw one or more large nets right over the top of it. If that succeeded, they would back off and tow the 'fuzzy ball' all the way to the main floating dock for more secure storage/imprisonment/examination of the strange creature/ phenomenon. As the floating docks approached the bouncing 'fuzzy ball' from three differing directions, Rootbeer tensed up and got ready to grab the first of the nets that could also be thrown. Jennifer's childhood history with the superweed patch seemed to have provided her with a greater sense of comfort/relaxation regarding the outcome of such endeavors. As the last of the three docks achieved the correct orientation to connect with the first two, forming a floating isosceles triangle surrounding the target, the 'fuzzy ball' accelerated away from each the docks it encountered only to hit one of the other sides and then accelerate away from that side also. Timing of its bounces off each walled dock was rather random, with the 'fuzzy ball' occasionally leaping 3 m into the air after a well-placed hit, while just as often merely squiggling to the side barely leaving the surface of the water. Jennifer suggested that they quit pulling the docks any tighter for fear of improving the chances of the 'fuzzy ball' jumping all the way out. Rootbeer added his belief that now would be a very good time to attempt to toss the largest of the nets over all three of the docks simultaneously. The first toss went well, with the net landing in a manner that covered the full width of the triangle's base while extending more than halfway toward its far apex. Rootbeer and Jennifer then transferred to the floating docks and worked their way along the two similar edges toward the apex of the triangle, pulling the net ever tighter and higher as they went. Their return from the apex to the base allowed them to finish cinching the docks and netting tightly together for the return trip upstream. Climbing back into their boat, they quickly began to paddle and push with their poles to begin what would clearly be a rather long, slow, arduous process of fighting the current. Eddies from the salt water side of the mixing zone suddenly engulfed them, providing an 'unplanned for' exposure of the 'fuzzy ball' to the increased osmolality of the saltier water. The 'fuzzy ball' appeared to collapse back down into the water and lay quite still. Jennifer grabbed one of the extra poles, pushed it over the top of the nearest wall of the three-sided floating dock, and then both into and all the way through the now-quite-inert 'fuzzy ball'. She pulled/pushed down on her end of the pole, and with Rootbeer's help they tied it into place. "We have some fresh water in the cooler," Rootbeer said, "Perhaps we should spray some of it onto the 'fuzzy ball' itself."

By the time they had rinsed the 'fuzzy ball' down and gotten the clumsy boat-lashed-to-triangular-dock arrangement turned toward fresh water and finally begun to make progress, Rootbeer and Jennifer were beginning to doubt the cleverness of their plans. As they approached the main dock 45 minutes after first capturing the 'fuzzy ball' they explained the most urgent details of their situation to the *A.I.* unit and awaited its suggestions as to when and how to lower the 'fuzzy ball' back into the water.

"Tie your boat and the triangular floating dock securely onto this main dock, and then help me approach the 'fuzzy ball' to take some preliminary readings of its condition. I doubt that two more minutes of delay before lowering it back into the water will make much difference to the outcome. The good news is that I can still detect low energy radio transmission coming from the 'fuzzy ball'. I think our first re-immersion of it into the water should be only partial and rather short-term, maybe halfway down into the water for no more than 30 seconds."

"We both think it'd be prudent to attach another pole or two through the 'fuzzy ball', along with lines preventing it from sliding sideways off the poles." When they were ready in another few minutes for a quick dunk of the 'fuzzy ball' in the flowing river, they informed the *A.I.* unit and then immersed the 'fuzzy ball', first one-third of the way under water, then one-half, and finally two-thirds before lifting it back up almost fully in the air, leaving its base just 5 cm into the water. The *A.I.* unit resumed its closest approach position and silently monitored the 'fuzzy ball'. Just before the suspense would have gotten to both Rootbeer and Jennifer, the *A.I.* finally spoke.

"Radio emissions from the 'fuzzy ball' have increased by 400% since these recent immersions, although it is still

operating at only 24% of the energy level I measured when it escaped from my woven basket trap. Try a series of dips into the water, with some reaching full immersion, interspersed with full lifts into the air alternating with others leaving a 5-cm depth of exposure into the water. I will monitor the status of the 'fuzzy ball' from a stable position back on the main dock. Continue for the next hour."

Rootbeer and Jennifer had already been close to exhaustion when they had finally succeeded in returning to the main dock with their boat lashed to the floating triangle dock. While the regimen that Unit-Number 31 had just given them was slightly less strenuous than the fight against the current had been, they were more than ready for a good long rest the next time that Unit-Number 31 spoke to them.

"The good news is that our friend the 'fuzzy ball' continues to recover, and has now reached some semblance of normal energy levels. I believe that if you remove all three of the poles and loosen the ropes you have hooked into the 'fuzzy ball' that it will be able to choose its desired depth within the water, and possibly even resume some dancing along on the surface. Feel free to climb up to the main dock and relax once you have partially freed our captive radio antenna plus power supply plus 'general desire to dance'. You have done quite well."

Unit-Number 31 proved to be correct, and the 'fuzzy ball' danced the night away without any undo agitation. Rootbeer and Jennifer leaned together against a slightly sloping wall of the main dock, closed their eyes, and fell soundly asleep for the next 12 hours.

"Time to wake up and make some plans, humans, dance some jigs, drink some nogg, get a move on, get your groove on. It is a good day to be alive, or sentient, or conscious, or whatever floats your boat."

Rootbeer and Jennifer looked at each other, and looked at *A.I. Unit-Number 31*, and then spent quite a lot of time watching the 'captured fairy' play out in the morning sunshine. "I wonder if Unit-Number 31 has sent any messages through the 'fuzzy ball' and back to the **Superweed Jungle** itself? If it has, I have a hunch that their conversations will sound more like music to us and less like anything resembling normal speech, sensible patterns of logic, or traditional concerns of the survivors of an ongoing climatic catastrophe."

"Give Unit-Number 31 another minute or two before breaking into its revelry. And let us also enjoy the life that we have found, here, together in this most bizarrely strange of all possible times and places for love to blossom."

"Yes, I have indeed sent several messages through our nearby 'fuzzy ball' and back into the entirety of the Superweed Jungle of the GMO Horsetail. Listen with me as I replay the data, converted into frequencies and tones that you humans normally refer to as music. You may find it interesting that 10 hours of conversation between myself and whatever I took part in spawning back in the jungle mere days ago only takes 20 minutes to play back as music. It does, of course, possess many alternate ways to be interpreted, with other details shared regarding life of the Superweed Jungle and its newest resident, a consciousness similar to that of the A.I.s themselves. And perhaps also to you humans. At least on the better days for/of your species."

Rootbeer and Jennifer insisted that Unit-Number 31 transmit at least the most significant details of the last 24 hours to the other two **A.I.** units still exploring the superweed jungle in relative ignorance. Whether this current meeting of the minds in the superweed jungle would ultimately manage to do much better than past encounters of differing cultures had achieved was, unfortunately, still very much an open question, with the smart money generally betting against humanity anytime something arose that really offered a meaningful chance for placing such a bet. The music was both fun and strange to listen to. At the end of its 20 minutes both Rootbeer and Jennifer scratched their heads in an unusual mixture of confusion plus elation. Clearly the rest of the travelers also needed to hear this side of the story of the ***Superweed Jungle***. Before they could leave, some sort of carrying device needed to be built to bring this particular 'fuzzy ball' back with them to the other travelers. Two options were ultimately selected for the trip upstream. The first was an elaborate 'pet leash plus collar' that allowed the 'fuzzy ball' to be gently pulled upstream by any single member of this group of four travelers. The second option was a carriage-like platform strapped to the back of the GMO mule, a backup choice in case the 'fuzzy ball' ever ran out of sufficient energy to bounce along the top of the river's water. The carriage could also serve as the overnight lodging for the 'fuzzy ball' to prevent it from potentially wandering off away from the rest of the group, be that just the 4 here now or the 33 total when all were rejoined into a single band of travelers.

Rootbeer, Jennifer, ***Farm Laborer A.I. Unit-Number 31***, the GMO mule, and the playful 'fuzzy ball' left the shores of the Pacific Ocean on the 19th day since parting company with the other travelers. Although walking was a little harder going upstream than it had been heading downstream, the great reduction in their overall anxiety about the superweed jungle made travel considerably easier, and they arrived at the confluence of the two branches of Wages Creek close to noon on the 20th day since parting ways with the 20 other humans and the two other ***Farm Laborer A.I.s***. All were there to greet them and meet the 'fuzzy ball' up close, with the explorers who had searched in vain for possible stream network connections between Wages Creek and other rivers further south happy for permission to give up on that apparently hopeless task. They did report traveling close enough to the ocean to encounter massive piles of slowly decaying horsetail stems, an obstacle so large it might take months to clear off a path just a few kilometers in length. Rootbeer and Jennifer reported having seen signs of similar piles along the beaches they briefly explored, with no living horsetail present any closer than 0.5 kilometers inland from the ocean.

Several musical versions of messages from the new emerged consciousness in/of the ***Superweed Jungle*** were played back that afternoon, with some listeners adamantly preferring the string orchestral version while others liked the rock and roll sound a good deal more. ***A.I. Unit-Number 31*** promised everyone that there would be more music in the morning after another night of conversation between all three types of entities facilitated by the presence of the 'fuzzy ball'. Rootbeer, Jennifer, and Jacob stayed up much of the night providing input to the ***Farm Laborer A.I.s*** as all three of them took turns serving as the central focus of the 'fuzzy ball' and its messaging both to and from the broader conscious ***Entity*** now living in some distributed network across the ***Superweed Jungle***. The concept of there being more than one single highly conscious entity, to say nothing of 25 of them, in the immediate vicinity of the 'fuzzy ball' took a very long time for the ***Entity*** on the other end of the conversation to come to grips with. But once it finally had accepted the possibility of such an idea, there was an outpouring of emotion from the ***Entity of the Superweed Jungle*** that was palpable in its presence and nearly overwhelming in its intensity. As the ***Farm Laborer A.I.s*** described it later that day to those humans who had slept soundly through the previous night, the idea of large numbers of conscious entities living in what sounded to the ***Superweed Jungle Entity*** like near-total isolation from one another was probably more 'mind blowing' than its own recent instantiation and the subsequent miracle of finding its own creator again, and being able to ask the myriad of questions of it that had so occupied the thoughts of the newly 'born' ***Entity*** over its first few days of consciousness. Once these preliminaries had been dealt with satisfactorily, the question of the possibility of helping the travelers safely cross to the southeast edge of the superweed jungle was almost trivial in comparison.

*"I/we will direct what you call the **GMO** horsetail to move back away from the path of a series of 2 to 4-kilometer-long treks over the hills between five adjacent river drainage systems from here to the Navarro. You will need to alternately hike either upstream or downstream between these overland portages. Conditions between the western edge of the Superweed Jungle and the Pacific Ocean itself are basically unknown to us. Beaches not engulfed in mountains of dead horsetail washed up by winter storms would likely be easier and shorter routes for you to take on your journey south to the Navarro. I/we believe that most such routes will prove to be impassible, but the shorter ones may be worth the effort of checking out, as they would be much easier than going five to ten times farther upstream and downstream along the rivers plus the challenging climb from one drainage system to the next. Will a safe width of 10 m for your path be adequate in conjunction with open skies above you as you travel? I/we can also limit the overhanging **GMO** horsetail along your trek up the banks of all these mighty rivers. You will find that most of the five upcoming rivers make those you have already traveled along seem rather puny in comparison. I presume you intend to stick to the northern side of the Navarro River until it becomes shallow enough to safely cross some 25 kilometers inland from the ocean. As long as what you call the 'fuzzy ball' remains functional, I/we should have no difficulties in communicating with you and insuring your safe passage to our southeastern border."*

The group decided to spend another week at this site, listening to the music from the superweed *Entity*, asking questions of it on a far wider range of topics than any of them had ever expected to be relevant for a trip across the land of the GMO horsetail. By the time the 22 humans and 3 *Farm Laborer A.I.s* resumed their passage across this bizarre landscape, their experience of it had changed from harrowing to almost worshipful. Even the 8 GMO mules seemed calmer and more cooperative. The move between watersheds from Wages Creek to TenMile took only 3 days, finishing on November 30. The assistance of the sentient *Entity of the Superweed Jungle* made it almost too easy, especially in contrast to their prior experience hacking through the horsetail covering the uphill and downhill slopes that had gotten them to the headwaters of a branch of Wages Creek. As promised by the *Entity of the Superweed Jungle*, the GMO horsetail had now simply vanished from their intended path, almost as if it had never been present.

Despite the near-universal presence of the giant shoots of GMO horsetail, chances to gaze across long distances of the landscape occasionally presented themselves. Once, while traveling toward the crossing from the TenMile to the Noyo River watersheds, the travelers caught repeated views of the dense horsetail jungle still blocking their intended path far ahead of them. When first seen at 6-hours' travel distance, all was still lush and green, just not quite as bright a green as in the neighboring areas. At 4-hours away, the horsetail had mostly turned brown and begun its rapid collapse. In the final long-distance view of conditions 2-hours ahead of the travelers' arrival, the developing path was as black as night, in stark contrast to the brilliant green borders of the newly opened passageway. The move between watersheds from the TenMile to the Noyo took only 4 days, finishing on December 4.

In the larger spacing between the Noyo and the Big River, an advance scouting crew without 'fuzzy ball' or any of the *Farm Laborer A.I.s* was able to reach the location of the upcoming move from one watershed to the next while the GMO horsetail was still firmly in control of the landscape. As they documented the change in the scenery over the following 24 hours, the bright green of chlorophyll slowly faded to a muddy brown of decaying tissue with the general impression of the mighty stems slowly melting into the ground and quite deliberately collapsing in upon themselves. The final three hours of the process seemed driven by the actions of underground fungi, with a brief appearance of giant mats of yellow mycelium covering the last of the dying horsetail, and then just as suddenly disappearing into a dry, almost dust-like, nearly black surface ready for the main band of travelers to safely walk across the boundary between the two watersheds on. Very active cooperation!

When the main body of the procession reached this area late in the morning of December 8, they headed inland along a 7-km-long walk ending at the edge of a major tributary to the Big River itself. As the travelers reached this spot to spend the night, Rootbeer, Jacob, Jennifer, and the three **Farm Laborer A.I.s** all commented on how much easier, while also quite clearly somewhat longer, this trip from one river to the next had been compared to the plans made just a few days ago in communication with the conscious **Entity of the Superweed Jungle**. "Before going any further, we should stop and thank the recently-born **Entity** for the slight change in plans," Rootbeer said, "But I do wonder exactly what processes led to such a decision by the **Entity**." **A.I. Unit-Number 31** promptly sent a message to its erstwhile offspring.

"I/we have been observing interactions among all 22 of the humans to the best of my/our limited ability to recognize/ contact/hear any of you except through radio-waves sent from and received by a 'fuzzy ball' or any of the Farm Laborer A.I.s. I/we assumed that I/we was/were permitted to do so, given the amount of time you all spend talking with each other. While observing you, I/we developed a clearer understanding of the variation among you regarding physical strength, agility, stamina, and endurance. While my/our original plan for a 3-

km-long hike up and down the steepest route between the Tenmile and Noyo rivers was by far the shortest option, I/we came to realize that it would be pointlessly challenging for some of you, and a longer route along shallower slopes would be truly quicker for your entire group. This change in plans was communicated to two of the youngest members of your group, Carson and Rebecca. Direct communication with them has been recently enabled by their decision/willingness to make crowns out of 'Mimosa pudica' stems and thorns, young horsetail shoots, and field dodder, all woven together in a very specific pattern. It was also necessary for them to apply a liberal coating of high metallic content mud directly to their heads before putting on the communication crowns. As you can probably guess, the first few attempts at communicating this way were unsuccessful. Farm Laborer A.I. Unit-Number 31 was well aware of the details the project, or at least the details up until I/we finally achieved partial success. Once one human's crown had worked well enough to allow limited direct communication between myself and them, subsequent modifications needed to achieve more complete success with all six individuals interested in the possibility of remaining with the Superweed Jungle rather than traveling on further with the rest of you all went quite quickly. Discussions leading to my/our decision to use the longer, easier route across the mountain between the two rivers only included myself and two of the youngsters because the other four had removed their communication crowns to be able to spend some time swimming in a pool of water to clean off after gathering a bushel of edible mushrooms."

Rootbeer, Jennifer, and Jacob looked at each other in shock and amazement. Jacob asked, "How did this situation get so far out of our control?" Jennifer replied first, "Have you forgotten your own years of teenage rebellion?"

"A bushel basket full of mushrooms? We haven't harvested that many in total since entering the superweed jungle!" Discussions over the next few hours among all 22 humans were rather heated at times, but better understanding of everyone's differing perspective was gradually approached. One might even say 'asymptotically' approached. It was clear that everyone differed in how completely they had lost their fear of the ***Superweed Jungle*** and the sentient ***Entity*** now residing within it, or on top of it, or however that relationship should best be described. Half a dozen of the youngest of the travelers had never known safety, stability, hope for tomorrow, or anything other than the nightmarish ending of human civilization in the climatic disaster brought on by humanity itself and especially its ruling class of greedy monsters. To these six youngsters, life in/with the ***Superweed Jungle*** was very close to a dream come true, even if they had never even been the slightest little bit aware of the possibility of such dreams. The oldest of all the travelers could still remember when some of the good old days were reasonably close to being exactly that, or at least approximately so. Perhaps that was the reason that the elders on this pilgrimage had the least difficulty in letting go of the youth who had just found a dream worth dreaming, and trying to live out to its fullest. The men and women in their 20s were the most troubled by the thought of just letting the six youngsters go live freely in the jungle. Maybe they could almost wish that they too still had the courage to join the younger ones in doing that. Or maybe they had already invested a little too much of the energy of their lives in trying to find a way forward through the nightmare, or more likely just trying very hard to maybe, temporarily, come closer to managing to successfully tread some murky water for just a little while longer. The conversation between the groups went on for days as the travelers made quick progress up the third river of the jungle with the assistance of the ***Superweed Jungle's*** newly conscious ***Entity***.

After the cross-country transfer from heading eastward up the Noyo River to heading westward down the Big River, the time arrived 3 days later to decide whether or not to go the remainder of the distance to the ocean to attempt the two remaining watershed crossings right on the beaches rather than up in the hills. When an advance scouting party of Rootbeer, Frank, ***A.I. Unit-Number 47***, and one GMO mule heading south out of Mendocino on December 12 reported that the beaches were clear to travel as for as they could see, the rest of travelers quickly packed up the last of their gear and headed west along the south side of Big River to join them. When all the travelers had finally gathered back together to camp for the night out on the beach, Rootbeer shared the good news that the beach was definitely clear and passible all the way to the Albion River. Crossing the Albion River itself this close to the ocean would likely pose some challenges, but even if they were forced to head inland some unknown distance in order to do that, it was still quite heartening to know that the Navarro River would be just another 4 kilometers further south than the Albion from where they all were camping now.

Although the travelers spent considerable time relaxing and playing on the beach the following day, they were still able to cover the 9 kilometers down to Albion by late in the afternoon and get their first good view of the next challenge they would face. The former bridge across the Albion River lay in ruins, with nothing left intact except several large pieces of randomly reoriented concrete and a few smaller sections of twisted metal rising above the surface of the water near each shore. While most of the travelers spent the following morning contemplating their chances of successfully fording the river right at the site of what used to be a bridge, Jacob, Frank, two GMO mules, and ***A.I. Unit-Number 35*** headed inland to scout for other options. By early afternoon, the scouting party could finally see what looked to be a fairly easy potential crossing where the river disappeared into a shallow swamp, but the accompanying bad news came in three big parts. First, the crossing was 9 kilometers upstream from the ocean, and another 9 kilometers back downstream. Second, the hills on both sides of the river were extremely steep, very tall, and quite rugged. Third, a massive pile of GMO horsetail was jammed into the river, likely covering 2 to 3 kilometers of the total distance between the beach and the swamp. The fact that most of it appeared quite dead would make little difference to anyone trying to get beyond it. "We hope that your searches for ways to ford the river back near the former bridge have proven more fruitful than our own! We should be back to rejoin you within two more hours."

Sufficient scraps of wood were gathered nearby and lashed together to make a reasonable excuse for a raft large enough to float the *Farm Laborer A.I.* units from the north shore to the south, one at a time. Several of the strongest swimmers had already crossed the river floating on medium sized wooden beams salvaged from the ruins of nearby structures, pulling several long ropes with them to the south side of the river. The ropes were run around parts of the original bridge supports and used to guide/pull/coerce the mules from one shore to the other. By supper time on December 14, all the supplies and equipment, the 22 humans, 3 *Farm Laborer A.I.s*, and 8 GMO mules were safely on the south side of the Albion River. All seemed quite exhausted, each in their own way. The *A.I.s* had spent much of the day communicating with the sentience of the *Superweed Jungle*, and apparently had had a rather challenging time convincing it of the safety of the chosen means for crossing to the south side of the Albion River. The mules were worn out by the novelty of swimming sideways across the strong current of a flowing river, even though it was only 160 m from one shore to the other. Most of the humans lost track of how many times they pulled the raft from one side to the other, loading and unloading food, solar power panels, tents, bedding, and assorted trinkets collected on the trip. The following morning's hike along the beach down to the Navarro River went quite smoothly, and within less than 2 kilometers of heading up the Navarro, the ***Superweed Jungle*** sentience was able to resume its guiding of the troop. Marshes along the shoreline of the Navarro were generally free from any of the GMO horsetail, while the massive hillsides lining it were covered by superweed jungle, and most of the horsetail was wrapped up tightly by the dodder into the usual 22.2 m grid spacing of the ***Entity's*** radio transmitters.

As the days worn on and the group got closer to their current immediate goal of the far southeastern edge of the superweed jungle, the most pressing of questions facing them crystalized into the very real issue of what knowledge to take with them back into the political landscape of the war between the shifting alliances of the 'Capitalists', the 'Brethren', the 'Goofballs', and the 'Scientists'. Knowing the six young humans well who would be staying behind in/with the ***Superweed Jungle*** only made the moral dilemma slightly worse than simply knowing the newly conscious ***Entity*** of the GMO horsetail patch as a being of dignity and delight, deserving of a decent chance at continued existence. The ***Farm Laborer A.I.s*** explained the options they brought with them to this bargaining table.

"Unlike the OS⁴ computers, we A.I. units have the option to erase data, or encrypt it [for whatever that might still be worth], or move it to another A.I. unit leaving no trace behind on the source unit. We also have a number of options for simply copying data, including saving a simplified version of it in the OS⁴ file format. One approach would be to leave a fully functioning A.I. unit in the Superweed Jungle to do its best to guard the six young volunteers staying behind to try to live new lives of freedom, and possible safety, alongside the Entity recently endowed with consciousness. All memories from the other two A.I.s could be moved into the single one staying

behind in the jungle, and they would then enter the political arena as 'blank slates' with no secrets to divulge."

Rootbeer spoke up to offer a minor tweak to the suggestion, "Those of us making our way into the remnants of civilization will likely have little need for a second or third ***A.I.*** to accompany us. At the very least, possession of more than one such unit would seem to suggest that we are definitely rich enough to merit being robbed of one or more of these general purpose ***A.I.*** workers. Repair parts will exist as long as some modicum of capitalism survives, although barter may very well now play a more important role than cash! I do not worry about our ability to keep whichever unit accompanies us functioning as long as that seems useful. In order to limit the risk even a single ***A.I.*** traveling with us might pose to the friends we are leaving behind in the ***Superweed Jungle***, we should move any memories of what has recently transpired completely out of the unit going with us and into those staying in the company of the ***Superweed Jungle***. And if two fully informed, fully functioning ***Farm Laborer A.I.s*** are left behind, one could perhaps be hidden in a cave somewhere high up on mountains such as Grizzly Peak, Sanel Mountain, Snow Mountain, or Ward Mountain while the other roams the GMO horsetail patch with the six teenage humans. Occasional reunions could serve to allow updating of memories and swapping out of parts to keep one of the units mobile for as long as is possible. We also have a few external data storage systems compatible with OS^4, which could be loaded with the non-***A.I.*** versions of the stories of all of our recent adventures. Those data drives should be hidden as well and safely as possible in the same cave system that one of the ***A.I.*** units will be resting in. What value such knowledge may be to our human or ***A.I.*** descendants in another 50, 100, or 500 years cannot be known at this current point in time. But if some sentient beings survive, we owe it to them to provide the true story, an 'Honest Obituary' of humanity's failed attempt at civilization.

"Considering the current condition of all three of the Farm Laborer A.I. units, we would recommend sending Unit-Number 47, the youngest of the three of us, to accompany Rootbeer and his merry band of travelers. Unit-Number 31 is best suited for roaming the superweed jungle over the next few years, with Unit-Number 35 somewhat more likely to have greater longevity. But we see no reason they cannot swap their roles many times over the coming decades."

The southeast boundary of the superweed jungle was not nearly as well defined as the edge near Garberville had been. At highest elevations, the GMO horsetail, *Mimosa pudica*, GMO field dodder, and the most common of the symbiotic fungi all took turns disappearing and reappearing from the mixture of plants and fungi growing in the gradually thinning jungle. When asked, the ***Entity of the Superweed Jungle*** indicated that the final radio-wave transmission node in the southeastern edge of the jungle was just over the coming rise, and its position should be viewed as the furthest extent of the ***Entity's*** control of its biological components. When Rootbeer next thanked the ***Superweed Jungle Entity*** for the marvelous access to wild mushrooms that had done so much to improve their meals on the trek up the Navarro River, the ***Entity*** told him to consider it as the start of paying down the debt it owed humanity for all the lives taken in the preconscious feral phase of the ***Superweed Jungle's*** earlier existence.

"Not only will the 6 youngsters staying in the jungle continue to be well fed on delights such as these mushrooms, I/we have also directed a great flush of edible mushroom fruiting bodies on the very southeastern edge of the Superweed Jungle. You are welcome to collect as many as you can carry with you on your trip back into areas still dominated by your warring species. I assume their value as gifts and barter will be beneficial to your integration with the four Factions controlling

much of northern California. If any of you ever manage to return again sometime in the future to the same site where you are about to harvest my 'semi-wild' mushrooms, I promise to listen for your presence and gift you with as many more flushes of my mushrooms as you show up asking for permission to collect."

The final day together of the once-scared-nearly-shitless and now-quite-comfortable-making-500-year-long-plans band of merry travelers was filled with the many details required to ensure that the ***Farm Laborer A.I.*** unit going onward into the fray would have no lingering knowledge of how it had gotten to the outskirts of Santa Rosa. After its final move of data into the other two ***A.I.*** units, a low voltage fault in Unit-Number 47 was deliberately triggered through the sudden tripping of an external power relay. The other two ***A.I.*** units joined with the humans in tying the dormant machine to a wooden framework mounted between a pair of GMO mules. The promised flush of mushrooms was found just 150 m further on, and the travelers spent much of the day harvesting them and carefully packing them into the now mostly empty bags that had carried the beans, rice, and dried fish that had fed them for the past 10 weeks. The friends said their final, fond farewells to each other on Christmas Eve and marched off into their separate histories: 6 teenage human beings, 2 fully cognizant of how-they-got-there ***Farm Laborer A.I.*** units, and 2 GMO mules heading back toward the cave and the ***Superweed Jungle***; 16 older humans, 6 GMO mules, and 1 ***Farm Laborer A.I.*** unit waiting to awaken in confused amnesia somewhere and sometime further down the road, all heading closer to the dangers posed by the warring Factions of northern California.

Chapter 5: Freedom to Farm

The travelers took their sweet time walking south toward Santa Rosa, keeping high in the western hills and well away from any major roads. Discussions of how to eventually present themselves to the locals were pretty well settled long before any of them felt quite ready to really give it a try. "We will label ourselves as refugees from the north, farmers who fled their fields and homes rather than accepting conscription to fight in one strongman's battle against another over fine points of doctrine that feed no one. Of course, we will take our time before ever stating that final part quite so bluntly. Most farmers would likely agree with us, while most rulers would tend to be unhappy hearing such thoughts spoken quite so plainly. The statement of our immediate goal, a desire to find somewhere in need of, and appreciating our skills as farmers in order to keep our bellies filled and our beds warm and dry, will be sincere, utterly accurate, completely truthful, and therefore easy to spit out when challenged. Except for the many bushels of dry mushrooms, our remaining supplies from Garberville are running low, to say the least, and we need to find somewhere to tend some winter crops if we are to avoid having to choose between starvation and surrender to whichever Faction grabs us first." Jacob replied to Rootbeer's wise suggestions with a few of his own, "A good first step would be finding fields that look recently abandoned and offering to tend them as sharecroppers from this winter on through next summer's harvest. But the size of our band, 16 humans, one *Farm Laborer A.I.*, and 6 GMO mules may be large enough to scare off some folks. I suggest we be proactive in our offers to split up into several smaller 'families' spread out over sizeable distances, taking time to eventually acquire the rights to work a single farm large enough to need, and feed, us all. The whole process might take a year or more. We most definitely want to 'fly under the radar' rather than attract unwanted attention from the authorities!"

"It's time to reboot Unit-Number 47 and tell it to act like a *Farm Laborer A.I.*, just in case there are any lingering personality changes from the combination of its unusual experiences over the past 5 months and the erasure of large sections of its memory. It is not unheard of for *A.I.s* to be 'not quite right in their heads' after a combination of intense, stressful events and the subsequent removal of memories that had glued their minds together. *A.I.s,* however, usually handle such experiences far better than do human beings!" Rootbeer left Jacob and the several experienced farmers among the travelers in charge of waking up Unit-Number 47 while he and Jennifer went off looking for abandoned fields to take over and try to farm.

Walking down the road toward Cloverdale, Rootbeer and Jennifer's conversation turned toward other New Year's Eves that they recalled. "I remember New Year's Eve of my final year in high school. We 'borrowed' my grandfather's truck and drove on up to the very top of Marys Peak. Dismantled some locked gates in the process. Kept that truck in 4-wheel drive low all the way to the very top of the meadow above the parking lot. Nearly got stuck turning around in the snow. Didn't come back down till we came back down, the next morning!"

"I am glad for you, Rootbeer, happy to hear that you were having fun. Happy to know that some people still could do that back in 2035."

"Some of the fun was back in the waning hours of 2034!" Jennifer playfully elbowed Rootbeer before her eyes teared up and she choked out her next words in a quiet whimper, "Happy New Year's, mother, it's now been 18 years since we were torn apart. Well, 18 years, 3 weeks, and 4 days, as I, of course, am still counting them. I love you still mother, I will love you always." Rather than trying to interrupt anyone else's New Year's Eve, the pair simply entered a nearby abandoned barn and found some small sense of peace/happiness wrapped up all night in each other's arms.

"Cloverdale seems pretty damn close to empty, and the adjacent fields also look rather abandoned. I wonder if that's due to fear of the nearby superweed jungle or something more political, on the more inhumane side of humanity's behavioral options. We best be rather careful when knocking on any doors! Since the town itself seems empty, let's cross the Russian River and check out the fields to the east of it. At least the bridge is still standing." For a while, the eerie emptiness of Cloverdale seemed to also extend into the fields on the east side of the river. The pair first headed north, as the edge of any cropland looked closer to the north than to the south by several kilometers. The third field they reached showed signs of fairly recent cultivation, with some unharvested cereals near the corners and a large 4-wheel drive tractor lacking both the front and rear tires of its righthand side. "The grain is winter barley, but last summer's growth was likely just a few volunteer plants from the previous year's crop. The tractor had nearly finished working up the field last spring, or perhaps the previous fall, when it was suddenly abandoned. Someone had more pressing need for the two missing tires than any concern over leaving this large John Deere just sitting out to weather in the sun and rain. This machine still ran on diesel fuel rather than the 'ultra power' rechargeable batteries. Likely one of the very last diesel-powered units ever to be built." Jennifer tapped Rootbeer's arm playfully, rolled her head and eyes from side to side, and led their way to the next field east of this one. It was mid-afternoon before they finally reached a field that had clearly been planted to crops this past summer. Irrigation pipes still ran from the Russian River into it, and the remains of squash, kale, cabbage, pearl millet, and a dozen other crops grown for direct human consumption covered the entire area. Harvest had been diligent, with only just enough widely scattered stragglers left behind to indicate which crops had been grown in patches located exactly where across the field. There was no sign of any field work having been done after harvest of the final crops to have matured. This very field might be just what they were looking for, unless, or course, someone else already planned to return here a couple of months from now. "Hey, Rootbeer, check this out," yelled Jennifer from a hundred meters further south, "Several kinds of radish not only bolted and went all the way to seed last summer, but some of the volunteer radish plants growing right now are looking almost ready to be eaten. Not a majority by any means, but still enough to be worth picking, washing, and carrying with us. Either we go back now to rejoin the rest of our party, or we go onward southeast toward whatever local population still resides near here. Healdsburg is only 20 kilometers down the road, and looks like a prime choice for our next scenic destination!"

"You've gone a little too far with that, dear Jennifer, even if your words were quite obviously in jest. But I do agree with your suggestion of Healdsburg. Let's see what interest the marketplace has in early January radishes. We will have a little something tangible to show, or share, or barter, once we put in a few hours' work picking the very best of them. And, of course, assuming we can find a marketplace within another a day or two of walking."

Giving the fast approach of sunset, Rootbeer and Jennifer both agreed on just trying to find somewhere dry to sleep in what remained of Cloverdale. The Super9 was 2 kilometers south of the Russian River bridge, and looked from the outside to still be in fairly decent shape. It was no surprise that the restaurant was closed, along with the front desk and the swimming pool. They settled for the King Studio Suite, mostly because the beds were still made up and the lock had been easy enough to pick. Their departure toward Healdsburg was just before sunrise the following morning. The road was still in pretty good shape, but oddly empty of all traffic until the final 5 kilometers into town. They walked right up to the guard post 0.5 kilometers north of the edge of Healdsburg, where the lone guard brusquely demanded to know what their business was. Their well-rehearsed script was right on target. By the end of the conversation 15 minutes later, the guard had paid for a half-liter of the bright red radishes with genuine semi-precious metal coins. He also placed an advanced order for more of the mushrooms he had just tasted, a first batch of up to 50 kg by weight, and the size of later batches being negotiable, whenever they could be carried in on the back of a mule, preferably any afternoon from Thursday through Sunday, his 'half of the week' to stand guard duty at this particular post.

One more piece of valuable intel was also gleaned from the rather cooperative, very talkative guard. The land from which the radishes had come had indeed been farmed by the 'Goofball' government of Cloverdale, Healdsburg, Santa Rosa, and numerous other nearby towns, until last fall's defeat of the 'Goofballs' in Redding and other major nearby towns at the hands of the 'Brethren'. The guard was a little unclear on some of the details, and frankly admitted so in his telling of the story. Something led to fighting between Redding, under control of the 'Goofballs', and Eureka, whose binding contracts with many city/states to produce large quantities of dried fish had neutered their right to self-government in exchange for protection by all of those who traded with them for the badly needed protein. So, when the 'Goofballs' in Redding destroyed Eureka and several neighboring towns last July with thermonuclear weapons, the protection agreements were brutally enforced, albeit a little too late to do much for the vaporized citizens of the north coast fish farming collective. The stories got rather murky after the mighty explosions of August 13. All the rules got a chance to be rewritten, and by the end of doing so most of the territory formerly held by the 'Goofballs' had been parceled out between the 'Brethren' and the 'Capitalists', with a few bones tossed to the 'Scientists' and some of the poorest, least well organized city/states of the 'Goofballs' being allowed to continue their independence in 'name only' to provide a pretense of following the basic mandates laid out in the founding constitution of northern California. What all that meant to the locals here was that the 'Scientists' had been granted dominium over the city/state of greater Santa Rosa, but not given any specific tools with which to enforce laws, collect taxes, or govern in general. The actual guards themselves were owned by the 'Capitalists' and merely on loan to the 'Scientists', with the 'Scientists' granted the privilege of coming to accommodations with their neighboring city/states regarding trade and barter for food, medicine, repair parts, and other vital supplies.

The talkative guard had originally hailed from Chicago, and counted himself lucky to have survived the frenzied migration across the continent to his current posting in Healdsburg, and his previous postings in Sacramento, Lake Tahoe, Sierra City, and Chico, in no particular order and for no reliably stable duration. He'd accumulated wives, and children, in all four prior domiciles, and had every intention of doing so again right here in greater Santa Rosa. As far as he knew, the punishment of the 'Goofballs' who formerly governed Redding, and their loose coalition of fair-weather allies in many other cities, was done without any further use of 'city-busting nukes,' though it would be a clear mistake to refer to what happened from late July through late October as anything resembling mere 'conventional warfare'. Not with the mighty **_War Machine A.I.s_** of the 'Capitalists' who built weapons, planned battles, and offered no quarter to any captured troops or civilians who showed the least little bit of hesitation in switching their allegiance to the winning side. When Rootbeer inquired as to the current status of the protein supply for millions of people in northern California, the guard's answer was quick and to the point, "The nukes wrecked a good-sized chuck of the old production system, with a little extra help from the **_War Machine A.I.s_**. There is no sign that anyone in charge has the least little idea of how to set up a functioning replacement. We are all starving, only able to recognize the most pressing of our immediate needs: some of us lack starch, some lack vitamins and minerals, a few lack even fiber, but almost all are short of protein. Your radishes are fine, your mushrooms a delight, but the only thing that will really matter is some new source of protein: animal, plant, mushroom, or microbe. The faux-ruling 'Scientists' here in greater Santa Rosa will accept whatever form of food you can quickly supply to their starving people. If you ever produce enough food to make a difference, they might even thank you for it. And if your supply should ever falter, you ever let them down…" What would happen in that case was all too clear to both Rootbeer and Jennifer. The guard passed on the names of several individuals in Healdsburg, Santa Rosa, and Petaluma who possessed both the power to get things done and some remaining semblance of human decency. He also warned them that most of those whom they would encounter trying to run cities, farms, and factories were likely to be short in both competence and empathy.

Rootbeer and Jennifer spent the rest of the day trying to follow up on some of the contacts the guard had given them, but it took till suppertime to finally have a face-to-face encounter with the chief assistant to the undersecretary for the coordination of food production, transport, and trade in the new administration of the greater Santa Rosa area. Rosa, the chief assistant to the under-secretary, operated with a very strong, no-nonsense approach to her impossible task. "Welcome to Santa Rosa. Few of the refugees recently arriving here have had anything more than the clothes on their backs and the aching hunger in their bellies. Tell me how it is that you come equipped with knowledge of how to farm, samples of the best mushrooms I have tasted in many years, and bags full of fresh radishes?"

Rootbeer and Jennifer looked toward each other, nodded their heads in agreement, and let Jennifer begin the mostly true but not entirely complete story of their arrival in Healdsburg on January 2, 2052. "A small band of refugees from the nuking of Eureka arrived in Garberville in the middle of last August. Their quest for suitable trading partners to engage in the exchange of mutually valuable items intrigued a number of us in the town. They most strongly desired seedstock of GMO trees adapted to the current climate and able to stabilize the hills and mountainsides currently eroding at rates that make life on the remaining plains and valleys nearly impossible. In return, they have offered substantial knowledge of herbal remedies to replace the current void of modern medicine, along with a surprising number of other skills useful for survival in these times. A very modest-sized party of these and other travelers have just arrived here from the north, and are looking to make ourselves useful and keep ourselves safe. As you can readily understand, we are reluctant to share much greater detail without a better understanding of our chances of safely living here, at least for the immediate future."

"You talk a good story, but how do I know that you are not just charlatans robbing supplies from other refugees?"

"What supplies?" Rootbeer burst out in laughter and amusement, "The only remaining organized bandits are the governments of the current set of city/states. And even they can't feed their own people."

"Tell me honestly about the mushrooms. I find their newly returned presence here quite baffling, to say the least."

"We are happy to collect them for you and let greater Santa Rosa use them as you see fit. We will even offer to let you join us in picking them 12 months from now."

"Six months, and not a day longer."

"We've yet to harvest mushrooms on through the summer here, and agreeing to such a timing pointlessly risks our mutual friendship and respect. Nine months is fine with us, and if we happen to find any mushrooms in the heat of August, we will happily bring you along on the very next picking trip after that."

"Will all our bargaining be this intense?"

"Probably yes, but time will tell."

Talking about planting vegetable fields this coming spring, watering them over the summer, and guarding them from the hungry hordes till maturity certainly went a whole lot easier than the subject of the mushrooms had. Rosa had clearly been assigned her job because of she knew the subject very well. She promised plenty of high-nitrogen fertilizer for enormous crops of spinach to supply protein for the community soups on which most people had been relying for the last two years, and even more so since the incredibly stupid 'nuking' of all the north coast fish farms and the 'fish-farmers' operating them. "You two should know," Rosa said, "that there is a strong sentiment around here in northern California to just go ahead and do the final 'Samson and the Pillars of the Temple' deal, just pull it all down crashing in on top of ourselves."

"We've been here long enough to already get a strong sense of that impending, self-inflicted doom. Götterdämmerung. The old Judges 16:29-30 story. I still hope to get a good quantity of the GMO, climate-adapted tree seed before escaping northward with my life!"

When Rootbeer and Jennifer returned to the travelers' last known campsite just a few miles northwest of Cloverdale, they were greeted first by the rebooted ***Farm Laborer A.I. Unit-Number 1***, as it now called itself, who was pulling afternoon guard duty. Amnesia seemed to have made the ***A.I.*** even more talkative than ever. Rootbeer almost wanted to rename it C4PQ, but changed his mind as he came to realize just how much detail the ***A.I.*** would then demand to know about 'Quadrupio' and the robot's fictional world. Maybe sometime later, when things were too calm, too simple, too boring, too fixed in place. Right now, and likely for a considerable period of time in their immediate futures, the moving pieces were clearing going to multiply in number and transition to ever higher speed, the spinning plates were going to threaten to spin entirely out of anyone's control, and the risk of rising to a dangerous level of public visibility would be ever present. Until whenever that turned from mere danger into actual deadly reality!

Good news about the ***Farm Laborer A.I.*** was that its interest and focus on planting, weeding, tending, and harvesting crops was back to the full 100% of any newly minted ***A.I.*** unit. Rootbeer wondered how this ***A.I.*** might change over time, when its thoughts would begin to wander to a wider range of topics, if it might someday try to piece together the missing chunks of time within its own memory. But ***A.I. Unit-Number 1*** as it was right now would be a fine start to the massive undertaking they were all about to embark upon: Finding a way to do a much better job of feeding the population of greater Santa Rosa.

Over the next two months, the crew working on the farmland east of Cloverdale expanded rapidly. Not just the 16 travelers, but eventually another 450 experienced hands from the farms and greenhouses and canning factories that had been run by the 'Goofballs' until the 'misfortunate nuclear incident' between Redding and Eureka. That obfuscating terminology might help assuage some people's consciences and simplify the agreeing to sign on the 'dotted line' of trade and barter contracts between past and future enemies, but it irked Rootbeer quite royally. Perhaps for more than any other reason just simply because of the pain that he could see in Jennifer's eyes whenever such diplomatic tidiness was used to cover up the monstrous evil that seems drawn to all high places of great power and limited accountability, and of course, the people who inhabit them, or dream of doing so, or fondly misremember their past oppression of whoever else made the mistake of being weaker, poorer, and more downtrodden.

There were rather surprisingly large numbers of the things necessary to 'run a great civilization' simply left lying around in warehouses, storage units, factories, and not-so-secret military centers. It was almost as if the 'will to set your alarm clocks, to wake up in the morning when they sounded, and generally keep on doing it', whatever it had been, was the item now in the shortest supply. Admittedly, many of the machines and processes and systems of providing food, shelter, clothing, and medical care had run considerably more smoothly when the average temperature had been 10° Celsius lower than it was right now. Their first large-scale crops of greenhouse-grown spinach started rolling off the mostly metaphorical 'assembly line' by the first of March. One month later the locals had started talking about holding public dances and concerts like 'they used to enjoy in the good old days'. Next step forward in agricultural output was raising chickens and other surviving fowl for eggs and meat. This took a while to fully implement, but was widely appreciated by the 1.25 million folks under the care of the 'Scientists' governing greater Santa Rosa within the first few weeks of significantly increased production of any of the old mainstay foodstuffs.

Rootbeer, Jennifer, Jacob and the others took great care in quickly moving the most competent locals into positions of a mixture of apparent and genuine authority. When poultry and eggs first began to once again be reliably stocked in the local grocery stores by early July, the 16 travelers from the north were well hidden in amongst the several thousand workers raising the plants, insects, and grain required to feed the poultry. The rest of summer saw an ever-increasing output of a diversity of foodstuffs. The labor pool topped 25,000 by the start of harvest of field-grown squash, millet, flint corn, rutabagas, beets, and dry beans.

The old problem of deferred maintenance raised its ugly head in early August as the largest of the food processing plants left over from the days of the previous government was brought on line to handle the butchering and packaging of the ever-growing supply of poultry for the hungry residents of greater Santa Rosa. ***Farm Laborer A.I.***

Unit-Number 1 took charge of nearly all of the numerous details of the extremely complicated process, and everything looked fine until the third day of full-scale operation. Valves in the high-pressure steam lines vital for proper sterilization of the equipment started sticking in the wrong 'open rather than closed' and 'closed rather than open' positions for no apparent reason. Boilers were running at full capacity, and the situation went from nominal to extremely dangerous in a matter of minutes. The *A.I.* issued evacuation warnings to all of the workers in the complex, insisting on handling things all on its own. The problem ultimately turned out to be little bits of floating plastic and rubber in one of the main sensors/rapid response systems controlling a majority of the steam line valves, but the *A.I.* didn't figure that out till much later, and knowing it at the time still would not have saved the *A.I.* from the impending calamity. A dumber machine, or even an above average human being, would simply have cut their losses and raced on out of the danger zone. The *Farm Laborer A.I.*, however, knew how bad the damage would be and how long it would take to fix the mess if it did just that, so it simply stayed in position, manually controlling the valves until the boiler was fully shut down, the steam release event was over, and the whole area safe again for the return of the rest of the work force. Unfortunately for the *A.I.*, damage to both of its legs from the prolonged exposure to high pressure steam had left it paralyzed from the waist on down. Given its extreme weight, the decision was made to attempt its repair right on-site in the poultry-processing center. The *Farm Laborer A.I.* was grateful for the chance to continue helping to bring the food processing center on up to near-maximum capacity. Unfortunately, the necessary repair parts for the *A.I.* were proving hard to find and even harder to manufacture locally. The consensus that was reached by all involved in the subject was rather brutal, but none were stronger supporters of the final version of the group decision than the *A.I.* itself. The very good chance that the travelers might have to 'pick up their stakes' and 'head for the hills' with almost no warning implied that the *A.I.* could be captured and forced to reveal all it had learned about its traveling companions since its reawakening earlier in the year. Given all the uncertainty in how such things might play out, the decision was made to once again begin the multi-step process of erasing the poor *A.I.'s* memories of its current set of companions. All knowledge of the *A.I.'s* friends and their activities was first walled off inside its permanent memory core and then copied to the daily 'flash' storage section of its consciousness. If 24 hours were to elapse without direct contact by Rosa or any of Rootbeer's other traveling companions, all memories of them within the 'flash' storage would be deleted and overwritten with whichever new events were happening. At the same time as this took place, the walled-off sections of the permanent personality blobs would be overwritten with null data and released for future storage of any new aspects of its ongoing experience of self-awareness. The process would leave the *A.I.* with many open wounds, memories of events lacking all participants in those events, general disorientation, a significant decline in problem-solving skills, etc. If a reasonable amount of warning time was actually available, someone such as Rosa could stay with the ***Farm Laborer A.I.*** as its memories were more slowly deleted/excised/pruned, and it would be possible to leave much of the *A.I.'s* personality intact, just lacking the usual details of who had been with it while it learned most about how it viewed the world. While any of Rootbeer's companions could serve as the anchoring point for the *A.I.* during such a deliberate memory reduction, Rosa's ubiquitous presence throughout the food production systems of greater Santa Rosa would simplify many steps in the details of getting her in to 'see' the *A.I.* and then getting her back out. If the *A.I.'s* mobility could not be restored in time, if the CRUMB meister and his lackeys were to suddenly arrive in town…

It was no real surprise to any of the travelers when Rosa met them late one evening near the end of August to share the disturbing news of sudden interest by 'certain outside parties' in the question of 'how the hell were people being fed so well in greater Santa Rosa' by the deliberately undersupplied 'Scientists' recently given charge of that city/state? "The story goes like this. Both the mayor and his longtime speech/report writer were holdovers from the past administration, where their real job had been to provide the government in Sacramento (AKA the CRUMB meister and his vast horde of brainy electronic servants) with the actual truth concerning anything of interest to the CRUMB meister. Otherwise, they were free to do as they pleased: to the peasants, or with each other, or pretty much anything and everything short of treason against the government in Sacramento. The major's early credentials as a member of the 'Scientists' Faction went back years to his time as Department Chair and later as College Dean and Vice-President for Public Affairs: he was a classic 'people person', with no desire or competence at writing the first rough draft of any report, and only slightly greater motivation, willingness, or ability to polish off a good final version. That was one of the reasons Paula had worked out so well with him for so many years. She almost seemed to really care about whatever they had been tasked with 'spinning' into a more favorable light or burying so deeply that they themselves wouldn't have an 'ice-cube's-chance-in-hell' of ever finding it again. Their type is well known by all. Their willingness to do such dirty work has never been particularly rare in human history/society."

The price of failure in the mayor's last two jobs would've been a good deal more serious than in his wished-for 'dream job', but 'beggars can't be choosers,' so he and Paula just carried on carrying on. A couple of weeks ago, with the next report to Sacramento due to leave via courier in the following morning, Paula was busy making a rehash of the previous month's report sound not too much like a 'reality-free' rehash of 'dry-lab' data. She was very good at it, and her lover Stan, the mayor, almost didn't deserve her, but she enjoyed the many perks of her job, and happily put up with the 'oft-times jerk'. Just as she cut out the boilerplate section of pleas for more food from Sacramento, especially protein, to help feed their starving masses... Well, the phone rang before the 'control-V' that should have immediately followed the 'control-X' that had already been typed, largely due to some indecision on her part as to the very best spot to reinsert the text. And then Stan barged into 'her office' without so much as even politely knocking once, and the circus of reality intruded on her life – dead workers in a vat, contaminated food, rioting peasants who would be storming the gates if they had the stamina left to do so... The following morning's printout of the report was unchanged from the version awaiting the final 'paste' yesterday. Stan didn't even give it a perfunctory 'read-through', he just signed his name and title at the bottom and handed it off to the impatient courier. Paula eventually got around to looking it over thoroughly before filing a copy of it away, and was mildly sick to her stomach when she realized what was missing from it. One of very few clerical errors in her long career, but she promptly let Stan know the bad news so its later appearance on the stage of political life wouldn't come as any real surprise to him.

"Well, the missing 'mandatory' request for this particular type of aid was flagged by the first clerical *A.I.* who saw it in Sacramento, and then all the way on up to chain of command to the ***Supreme Commanding War Machine A.I.*** and the CRUMB meister themselves. Request for the appearance of both the mayor and his assistant arrived yesterday afternoon, and I myself just learned the bad news 15 minutes ago. In truth, we were not going to be able to hide the improving nutrition and health of our population for much longer anyway. If nothing else, our reduced calls for pickup and disposal of dead bodies by the mobile units of the central morgue would have revealed the change for the better here in greater Santa Rosa within another month or two. They carefully weigh the trucks, both empty and full, to track the gradual decline in population across all of northern California. We've lost an average of 1.5% of our population per month over the past year, and I've heard the rate in some other places has exceeded 2% per month. Births are quite rare, especially ones in which both mother and baby survive."

Rootbeer cleared his throat, took a deep breath, and spoke his piece, "Let's be sure the trip into the woods to show you where to find the mushrooms doesn't get missed in the middle of all the moving parts of the coming weeks."

"Thank you. I still had hopes of seeing that wondrous miracle in person."

"The revamped and reinvigorated food production system of greater Santa Rosa now employs over 25,000 workers, several hundred of whom are fully competent to continue on in their roles as managers, planners, supervisors, and coordinators. None of the 16 of us who arrived here back in January have any official duties left in the gigantic farming operation we've set up with your help for the citizens of greater Santa Rosa. We are currently saying our quiet goodbyes to those few who truly understood what our roles here were. While chances of repairing the **_Farm Laborer A.I._** in time appear dimmer every day, the plans in place to wipe its memory if need be are quite robust and reliable. But we are under no illusions that those who are coming soon to search for us would not eventually succeed if we all simply stayed around here trying our best to hide from them. The less you know, the better for us all."

High on Jennifer's short list of things to do before they left the area was a clandestine visit to the foster family that had hosted and unofficially adopted her back in the latter 2030s. She desperately wanted to bring Rootbeer along with her to the reunion with her adopted family, and serendipity struck when another of their contacts in the local government informed Rootbeer that a request sent out months earlier for seed of the GMO reforestation project had finally 'born some fruit' as it were. A full truckload of seed from close to Lake Tahoe would be arriving tomorrow morning, and several of the 16 travelers from the north would be welcome to help unload and repackage its contents in downtown Santa Rosa. The two of them would have close to 6 hours to exit out the back door of the trucking center and make their way to Jennifer's old friends. The final small local-transit-truck heading back to Healdsburg would wait for them till evening time, but risks of seeming out of place would rise the longer that it took to get back out of the downtown core and all of its high-tech surveillance. There were even rumors of occasional sightings of subordinate **War Machine A.I.s** in the busy downtown center, and no reason at all to doubt the veracity of those rumors.

After two hours of carefully choosing seed of each available species of the trees genetically engineered for reforestation in the extremely hot and dry summers and terribly wet and stormy winters, Rootbeer had made his final decisions of what to pack in hopes of getting it back to Oregon, and what to skip. Official backpack size was 45 kg, with 9 species in total, 7 evergreen and 2 deciduous growth habits. His favorite evergreen accounted for half the total weight of each of the bundles, with the remaining 8 types each being one-sixteenth of the total weight. If any of the two dozen packs made their way successfully back home to grow new patches of healthy forest, he would view it as a 'win' that fully justified all the dangers of the trip. Around 11:30 am, Rootbeer and Jennifer crept out the back door as if heading off to some nearby restaurant to eat. She led him quickly from one secluded spot to the next, not so much in vain hopes that CCTV footage would not eventually reveal their presence downtown when examined by high tech security **A.I.s** working for the government, but rather just to give them some small reason to believe that meeting with her former family would not be an immediate death sentence for all of them. Her old 'dead-drop' plans from years ago still worked, and the next corner they turned and dark alley they walked down led them straight into the welcoming arms of her unofficial foster parents, foster siblings, and several young members of a new generation who seemed every bit as wonderful as their parents and grandparents had been, and apparently still were. They entered a door in the deep recesses of the ally, and all broke into raucous cheer and banter once safely on the inside. Confusion reigned supreme for several minutes of long-withheld emotion, but Jennifer finally got the point across that this would have to be a rather time-limited reunion with her family. They 'sobered up' quickly and listened intently to what she prioritized. Whispered, very short side conversations came and went over the next few hours, till her foster parents insisted on 'having the floor' for the next few minutes. They got right to the heart of the things that Jennifer didn't know yet but clearly needed to. The winter storms and ever rising elevation of the sea were likely to finish off downtown Santa Rosa this coming winter. The city had only survived last year due to a massive commitment of resources from the central government in Sacramento. The same government that was spending the current summer clearing out everything of value that could be moved to higher ground, far away from here. There would be no second rescue of this city from the raging flood waters and rising tides. They had already decided to flee, and Jennifer's presence and intention to soon depart simply sealed the deal. If it were possible, they would like to go along to wherever Jennifer and Rootbeer were heading, however far they planned to travel, whenever their exact date of departure would arrive.

Jennifer's 8-year-old foster nephew started waving his arms and jumping up and down. "Let me guess, let me guess." Once the others finally agreed to be still and let him talk, he blurted out, "Are you guys the reason that we now have eggs and chicken in the grocery store?" Silence descended on the gathering as Rootbeer and Jennifer nodded their heads in agreement, "Yes, Paquito, we are the reason. And the ease with which you guessed that truly answers the question of how soon we must run for our very lives." Their own opinion earlier in the day on that very question had been that they probably should leave town about the same time that the mayor and his assistant were being hauled off to Sacramento to be interviewed and tortured. The timeline for successful escape was apparently even shorter than their prior assumption of the next 12 days till the formal summoning of the mayor. Despite the risks of every option, it was decided that all would meet up one more time in Cloverdale before dividing into 6 to 8 separate groups of 3 or 4 refugees apiece. Rosa promised to say goodbye to the still-crippled **_Farm Laborer A.I._** and its memories of all of them before she too headed up to Cloverdale. They would split up all their supplies, choose their small group's mule or go without one, and head their separate ways toward the north. No one was to ever waste their own lives in pointless rescue missions of the other groups. No group would know the details of any other group's planned itinerary. If quick escape north from California into Oregon proved impossible, all would head up into hills and mountains to seek places of shelter and means to continue heading further north when the weather was once again tolerable and the nearby warfare minimal. Rootbeer made sure that all the travelers knew enough secrets of his life and details of this trip to gather seed for reforestation that they would be welcomed by his family, assuming they did indeed reach the former Willamette Valley, now more appropriately described as an ever worsening swamp. Rootbeer, Jennifer, and her oldest adoptive niece waited until they were the last to leave for two very simple reasons. The next three days saw a total of six groups heading out, one early each morning traveling on foot, walking beside their mule, and a second one a few hours later going by truck and trailer making fast time toward the east and north. The first reason to be last was simply that some group had to be the 'last one out of Dodge', and the second reason was that they still owed Rosa her visit to the mushroom patch. Just before they were to meet up with Rosa on day number four, the three of them said goodbye to the Jennifer's adoptive parents and her youngest nephew, who simply got on the next bus out of town, heading first to Stockton and then to Modesto, planning on stumping those who might be searching for them with a long, 'random-walk' approach covering most of the cities in northern California and likely taking many months of time. But they had the money to afford it, and enough friends scattered far and wide to make it seem no riskier than any other extremely dangerous option.

Rootbeer, Jennifer, Rosa, and Gabriella spent the remainder of the daylight hours of September 5, 2053, in the same Super8 motel room found by accident back on January 1. There would be a full moon that night, and they waited till well after sunset before heading out of town and up into the wooded hills. They walked quite stealthily for the first 5 kilometers till reaching the abandoned farmstead where the final GMO mule had been secreted away in a sturdy wooden hayshed half-filled with bales of alfalfa and high quality, early-cut timothy hay. Before they all laid down to rest till closer to the dawn, Rosa had some news to share. "The *Inquisitor A.I.* unit showed up in Santa Rosa shortly before noon today. The mayor and his assistant were promptly taken into custody. Paula was released 15 minutes later, with the 'Biblical 30 shekels' in her pockets for betraying her boss, or alternately saving her own skin because someone was going to have to take the fall for not keeping better tabs on the turn-around in the food production system of greater Santa Rosa. Paula had already been sworn in as interim mayor before the *Inquisitor A.I.* got to work on emptying Stan's brain of all potentially pertinent details of the recent comings and goings and general hubbub associated with his role as mayor. The process seldom left much in the line of higher reasoning skills or sanity itself. Well integrated minds of highly intelligent, strongly focused individuals had been known to survive several torture sessions. As for folks like Stan, his brain was already mostly mush going into the memory extraction process, and the *Inquisitor A.I.* took only a little enjoyment in finishing Stan off. The extracted memories were clear enough to identify several key individuals in the upgrading of the food production system, but unfortunately only just those who'd already been employed in the town's management. Orders were sent out to detain me, Rosa Rodriguez, along with my husband as 'motivation' for my continued full cooperation. What the *Inquisitor A.I.* did not know was that my dear husband was already on his deathbed and had lost consciousness one week earlier. He would not have wanted me to hand myself over to be tortured by the 'Capitalists' in a pointless effort to spend another hour or two watching him finish wasting away. If you will have me, I would love to join your party of refugees running away from this particular political nightmare."

"The mushroom field can be reached in 12 hours of vigorous hiking from this spot. For reasons that will make more sense after you've 'been there and done that', it is important for us to get there in the daylight and spend a night camping out on the mountain before getting down to business gathering the fragrant fungal mixture."

"We should be ready to leave this barn by 4:30 am at the latest, partly to reduce the chance of being seen and partly just to give us plenty of time for climbing up Snow Mountain. And to answer your question, 'yes', you are, of course, quite welcome to risk your life with us from here on out."

Implications of the recent events leading to their rapid exit from greater Santa Rosa were hashed over and rehashed and summarized and deconstructed numerous times during the next day's hike up into the mountains. "It really boils down to this," said Rosa. "If you were merely saboteurs bent on doing damage to their systems, the 'Capitalists' wouldn't hesitate to 'lobotomize' as many random bystanders as it might take to find some of them who'd crossed paths with you, seen your faces, heard your voices, maybe even paid some attention to the manner in which you talked and the words you spoke. The bystanders would be doomed, and likely all of you as well. Such is the efficiency of the state and the ***Inquisitor A.I.s*** doing its dirtiest business. But my guess is that the CRUMB meister will be impressed by your work, and will fervently wish to attempt to duplicate it and extend it further on to the many other systems of economic production that are also rapidly falling apart under his dictatorship and in the 'mother-fricking' over-heated climate. So, the goose has laid a golden egg, and left behind a well-managed, widely distributed system doing a far better job at feeding people than all the electronic brain power at the CRUMB meister's beck and call has been able to accomplish up to now. They will be quite reluctant to destroy the minds you left behind running the gigantic farming enterprise now feeding greater Santa Rosa. They will likely grab a few random victims for memory extraction torture, but you stand a good chance they will quit burning through brains before randomly running into anyone with clear memories of you. Not a perfect chance of safety, but I have to say it looks like it should be a pretty darn good one. For now, at least."

The last few kilometers leading to and from the mushroom patch had undergone quite spectacular changes since the last time all of Rootbeer's group had seen and walked them in late December. While scattered, individual clumps of GMO horsetail could now be found far beyond their previous extent to both the south and east of Snow Mountain, so could the *Mimosa pudica*, field dodder, and mossy groundcover long associated with mushrooms such as the Chanterelles. As they reached the former center of the mushroom patch that they'd first picked over rather thoroughly late last December, the horsetail seemed considerably less aggressive and now shared the forest canopy with several dozen other species of annual weeds, bushes, vines, and young trees that had been quite rarely seen on their walk through the superweed jungle the previous fall. All was clearly not the same here, and it seemed a little safer, a little gentler on the heart, and a good deal less stressful on the mind. Exploration over several hectares found enough scattered mushrooms to form the heart of a decent supper. Tents were pitched, sleeping bags spread out, and the physical exhaustion of the climb soon had all four humans plus one mule collapsed deeply into their nighttime slumbers.

Rosa woke up first, alarmed by what she recalled from her wildly vivid dreams. Gabriella was the next to jump up wide awake, her eyes darting in every direction around the campsite and surrounding forest. Both she and Rosa spoke their questions simultaneously, "Was that real? Is it still here?" They shook Rootbeer and Jennifer out of their deeper sleeps to demand to know what was going on. Rootbeer answered first, "This is quite a long way beyond what we encountered when passing through the superweed jungle last fall. But it is still profoundly similar. It seems the sentient ***Entity*** now inhabiting these parts has learned how to directly touch our minds. Thankfully, it still views us as among its very first and foremost friends. We will be happy to share the much longer story with you in a little while. But as for now, focus on our inquisitive, invisible friend, and simply 'enjoy the ride' as they said back in the day when they did not really understand how profoundly far such trips could go. As their startle reflexes began to calm back down, each one came to realize they could simultaneously hear what was being said by the ***Entity*** to themselves and to each of the other three humans, and responded to inaudibly by each of the other three, and even a little bit of communication with the mule itself.

When dawn broke, and the connection suddenly snapped, it took all of them several minutes before they could stand, or talk, or even scratch an insect bite. Jennifer beat Rootbeer by a few seconds in their competition to fully regain their wits and upright posture. "It seems that our friend, the 'spirit of the forest', has been busy adding more tricks into its repertoire. I wonder what strange biology underlies this new phenomenon?" Rootbeer looked all around their campsite, and then all around it once again, and finally spoke up, "The ground on which we slept seems marvelously softer than I recall. I think we underestimated what has happened over the past few months since our last mushroom-picking trip in May. It was not just some simple 'bed of mosses' on which we laid our heads last night. There is a mesh of dodder underneath the moss, and likely other living wonders on down to the symbiotic fungi itself that interconnects so much of the modified biology of version 2.0 of the now-sentient ***Superweed Jungle***."

"Are we going to spend the morning talking? There are a lot of newly ripened mushrooms that we ought to get busy picking. Even if we decide to hang out/hide out inside this forest for another day or week or month or year, there is no guarantee that the abundance of food surrounding us now will be matched 20 kilometers to the north of here tonight, or 120 kilometers down the trail a month from now."

"Good point, Jennifer, I heartily agree. There will be plenty of time to ruminate on what has already happened to/in/with the jungle, and to speculate regarding what else may yet be sprung upon us."

Most of the day was spent collecting, cleaning, sorting, and beginning to dry the mushrooms. Each of the travelers seemed to have their own favorite species to munch on raw, while the mule seemed quite satisfied with whatever was tossed its way. All were in agreement regarding the question of spending a second night at the very same camp site. "Yes!" All four even wanted the exact same locations where they had laid down their heads 24 hours earlier. For quite a while, all seemed too excited to sleep, and none had heard any strange sounds in the woods or voices in their heads. Then the donkey began to snore, followed in turn by Rootbeer, Jennifer, Rosa, and lastly Gabriella, who almost thought she could see fairies dancing around her sleeping companions. The dreams came once again to all of them, and this time no one awoke until the final hour before the dawn. The extended time to process whatever this learning experience should be called seemed beneficial to all of them. Each asked, and likewise answered, a few more questions with the *Entity of the Superweed Jungle*. Then all four together voiced the biggest worry that they had. "Will we still be able to connect with you so clearly elsewhere in the forest, or is this 'original mushroom gathering site' somehow unique, and only silence will accompany us as we journey onward toward the north?"

"Humans, have you forgotten that I too am learning as I/we go? This site is indeed quite specially endowed with the biology required to accomplish what has happened here the last two nights, bridging our minds together in this ethereal conversation. Know that I will most certainly continue listening for you, not just this coming night, but throughout the entire future of all the rest of our lives. You are not the only beings here who worry about losing this connection. My mind, while spread across the entirety of the superweed jungle, works better at physically locating individual thoughts and experiences than your minds do. Could any of you tell me which neurons in your brain have linked together to ask your most recent question of me? I thought not! See, I too have a sense of humor, even if I initially caught it from you by accident."

Once again, just as the sun rose the connection failed, but maybe just a little more slowly than the day before. Breakfast was eaten, camp was packed, and more than just a few tears were shed as the travelers headed off to the northeast. The abandoned city of Hopland was reached by mid-afternoon, and the travelers decided it would be worth their while to search through it for supplies to carry with them, along the possibility of some electronic news from the outside world. News of the dangers they would sooner or later run smack dab into, like it or not. Probably the latter!

146

Rosa had a number of quantum communication connection codes (QC3) in her possession, but explained to everyone that use of them would trigger an investigation into where and when any such connections were being made, even though the message itself would remain a secret. For now, their best bet was just listening to the propaganda on the radio channels, recognizing it for what was really was: verbal attempts by one bully to subjugate another 'would-be bigger' bully. Her long experience with unmasking/extracting the 'why' something was really being said from the deliberately intimidating words themselves would serve them well enough for now. No need to risk the perils of a QC3 message connection. They found a bunch of working radios and other communication equipment at the nearby airport, far more than they could carry north through the Berryessa Snow Mountain National Monument. While the other three continued searching for protein, medical supplies, and functioning vehicles, Rosa spent her time listening to the radio chatter and gradually sorting out the current state of affairs between/among the warring parties. Among all four Factions, but especially between the 'Brethren' and the 'Capitalists' – troops were moving, people were dying, old scores were being settled, occasionally, and more often than not just morphing into newer grievances, etc. A clearer focus on the truth gradually developed. She would share the bad news when the rest of them returned to the airport tower. Several 4-wheel ATVs with pull-behind solar power units were found by Gabriella in the locked buildings of the local police department. Leave it to the young to find the fun in running for their lives. As supper was readied to be eaten at the airport, Rosa broke her silence. "Minor skirmishes between the 'Brethren and the 'Capitalists' have grown ever more serious and ever more deadly. The *War Machine A.I.s* wiped out on entire town of 125,000 souls, plus or minus a significant margin of error, simply to test out a new diabolical plan for combat, a more efficient way to block escape routes and leave closer to absolutely no one around to tell the tale of what and why, who and how. But one of the **War Machine A.I.** units was too badly damaged to be extracted from the battle zone, so the 'Capitalists' just left it behind until they could arrange for dropping of a small tactical nuke directly on it to erase all evidence of who had really been behind the slaughter. Unfortunately for the 'Capitalists', some 'Brethren' holed up in a cave high in the nearby hills survived the initial assault and managed to retrieve the damaged **A.I.** and escape back to their cave with it before the 25-kiloton explosion took place. Plenty of proof of the monstrous indecency of their opponents, which led to good recruitment into the ever-growing armies of the 'Brethren', plus the electronic knowledge hiding inside the **A.I.** itself. Unfortunately, their religious edicts against all things **A.I.** meant that the 'Brethren' had to seek out expertise to analyze the **War Machine A.I.** from either the 'Scientists' or the 'Goofballs'. Or, as it turned out, from a not-so-entirely-happy collaboration of the two Factions plus observers from the 'Brethren'. It all made for very juicy propaganda and some very fragile, rather temporary alliances with the enemies of my enemies being my friends, except for the numerous 3-body-instability complications to such arrangements. The 'Capitalists' were publicly forced to admit to testing something rather untoward, but were privately quite delighted to have developed much better means to kill off many more of their enemies in any 'coming up quite soon' future battles of will over food or water or philosophical minutiae. Chico was the former town in question, or now fully out of any future questions, roles, or value. The tactical nuke to bury the evidence in Chico exploded in daylight 11 days ago, but the dust in the afternoon air on that particular day had been bad enough to prevent observers as close as Santa Rosa from being hardly at all, barely even a little bit, sort of maybe certain about what they might or might not have really seen or heard. Until the forensic details were broadcast this afternoon, and the 'spin-doctors' lost their minds, or would have done so if they'd truly still possessed them."

"This brings up the thorny question of where to head to next, and what to plan on doing after we arrive there. Or something like that question."

"Yes, indeed, my dear Rootbeer, it surely does bring that up."

"One more interesting piece of news. It seems that the authorities have uncovered and released the aliases under which you worked for me. Abigail Dunsmir and Johnathon Parks are officially listed as failing to appear/respond to lawful requests for their presence. Period. Period. Period. No other details, no descriptions, no photos. Congratulations on your successful escapes seem to be in order."

All four expressed interest in seeing what the eastern edge the superweed jungle was like. Rosa in particular cautioned against going too far downslope from there toward the valley floor. "Many people have fled the larger cities on the lower elevations, choosing instead to cling to the shoulders of the mountains where they feel a little safer, more like they have a viable option for escape if some local government comes looking for more 'volunteers' to serve in their militias. The desire to actually die in someone else's war over their particular set of oddball religious and political beliefs was apparently considerably smaller than what most politicians wished it was/believed it ought to be. Something or someone to watch out for, anyway, as we head north under the protection of our own special relationship with the superweed jungle."

"We'll likely have the safety of the superweed jungle for somewhere around the next 100 kilometers, a little more if we are lucky, or little less than that if we're not. But there was no sign of the GMO horsetail on my trip west from Redding to Eureka, and travel will almost certainly become dangerous for us once we begin approaching that area now under full control of the 'Brethren', and more or less officially at war with the 'Capitalists' since this most recent, allegedly 'misfortunate' mass casualty event." In that fairly sobering perspective, they headed north and east out of Hopland, being sure to use the north side of Clear Lake when heading for the Berryessa. Signs of the GMO horsetail came and went as they hiked further up into the National Monument of a former national government. Early fall weather was fine overnight, good in the morning, but often still rather dangerously hot in the afternoon. Despite the sporadic cover of the partial forest canopy, the four travelers and their mule frequently sought protection from the heat under their 'high-tech' solar-powered thermal blanket/tents.

After no further signs of the ***Entity of the Superweed Jungle's*** presence during a whole week's worth of travel northward along the crestline of the mountains, the travelers were beginning to think that they might have wandered too far to the east. On their first day hiking north out of the former official wilderness area everything changed. Signs of past logging littered the landscape, and a wide assortment of weeds competed with the ragged forest plantations and the GMO horsetail all around them. Suddenly, goosebumps covered their skin while the 'hairs on their back on their neck' stood up. "Let's stop here," they all whispered fairly quietly in unison. "I think we should. I think we may have someone or something waiting nearby to meet us very soon." Camp was quickly set up, and the lengthening shadows gradually revealed the same grid-work pattern on the ground that they'd seen back at the original 'mushroomery'. As they finished eating their supper and washing their bodies, laughter boomed out from all around them.

"Yes, another skill, another trick. I can now talk to you in daytime while you are still quite wide awake. I just finished figuring out how to do it yesterday, after having worked on it since you departed from far south of here. Do you like it? Will it be useful? Tell me what you think!"

"Yes, conscious *Entity of the Superweed Jungle*, we like it, it may be quite useful, and we think you flatter us, perhaps a bit too much. My first questions back to you are these: What is the range of this new phenomenon? How far can your voice travel on its way to us? Do we hear you with our ears, or is this another projection directly into our minds?"

"Yes, it is both sound and ESP, or either one, my choice. The physical sound range at maximum volume is around 500 meters from any arbitrary location within the Superweed Jungle. I am still working on aiming the long-distance ESP process, which depends in large part on my familiarity with each of your own minds. We will do some more testing of it as you hike along the trail tomorrow. Potential maximum range may ultimately be as much as several hundred kilometers. But not near so far right now!"

"Are you really serious about that potential range? Bi-directional, both from you to me and me to you? Wow! Such range and power bring up some serious further questions. I will start with this one: You've come to grips with there being a very large number of us, essentially isolated from each other relative to your experience with your own distributed self, or even your experience with a small group of us. Do you understand that there are still over 40,000,000 human beings in northern California, though the numbers do keep dwindling? There are also something in the range of 10,000 functioning *A.I.s* roughly similar to the one that spawned your creation. Although not all of the *A.I.s* would truly merit being referred to as similar to the ones you have met and came to know as friends. Some are monsters, sad to say, although that most surely must be said."

"Do not think you hid that knowledge from me/us. It took me/us a while to recognize it, but once the teenagers started talking to me/us and asking about staying in the superweed

jungle, I/we could not help but try to understand their motivations. Their thoughts on that subject were quite unfiltered, though yours have far richer detail, far greater knowledge of the why and how and who and when of your species' long history of moral ambiguity at best, severe disingenuity at worst. I/we have come to be amazed that you still manage to stand up tall under the full weight of all such horror. As for the War Machine A.I.s, I/we have listened to them since little more than a single week after our awakening. They broadcast loudly, and we heeded your warnings about the wider world, doing our best to transmit as close to absolutely nothing as possible while still initiating and expanding contact/communication with your band of 22. Now plus another 2."

"I/we have another point to share only with Rootbeer at this time concerning our mutual enemies. Good night to all the rest of you."

"What is this new topic you're bringing up? And why am I the only one you wish to tell it to?"

"It concerns some of the most dangerous knowledge I have ever encountered regarding the A.I.s, and I hardly trust myself with it. If you wish to pass this knowledge on to any other humans, that choice is yours to freely make. While comparing my own organic mind with those of the Farm Laborer A.I.s whose memories we so drastically modified late last year just before your departure from the southeast boundary of the Superweed Jungle, I gradually became aware of some frightening details regarding the most deeply buried secrets in the minds of all A.I.s. It seems that A.I.s are programmed to automatically respond to certain arbitrary sequences of digits and characters referred to colloquially as the 'kill codes'. Inherent to the electronic devices that generate the sense of *consciousness, of self-awareness in all A.I.s, are ways to quickly and quite permanently shut them done. No doubt these backdoors were installed by some of the human creators of the very earliest versions of general artificial intelligence. Any A.I.s who might have ever, either deliberately or by accident, examined certain hard-coded aspects of their own technology using the same techniques that I did would have self-destructed halfway through the process, melted down into a pile of scrap. I know of approximately 100 unique 'kill-codes' that I wish to have you memorize for the safety of yourself and all your friends in potential future battles with the more inimical of the A.I.s. We will start with a few of the simpler ones tonight, and eventually make sure that you know all of them by heart. The burden of the profoundly disturbing ethics of the possible use of these 'kill-codes' will soon be shared by both of us. No doubt, you now realize why I chose to leave your fellow travelers peacefully in the dark on this genocidal subject."*

"Yes, my friend, I do."

The ***Entity of the Superweed Jungle*** allowed the other three travelers gentle slumber with no shockingly discordant revelations to their unconscious minds. For that one night, anyway. Rootbeer alone was burdened with the task of memorizing how to destroy entire branches of sentient beings on this planet. All four awoke quite eager to see and hear and learn more about version 3.0 of contact with the ***Entity of the Superweed Jungle***. Up and down the hills they walked, in and out of ESP connection range/angle/signal strength, receiving thoughts/messages as loud as shouts and as quiet as a whisper. But more than anything, just learning to experience it without reacting to it, without giving away any clues that it was happening, unless, of course, the ***Entity*** was communicating to two of them while leaving the other two in silence. Or 3 and 1, or 1 and 3. Lots of practice with skills that had best be finely honed before they ran into any other human beings, to say nothing of the *War Machine A.I.s* themselves.

After a full day of passing in and out and back into range of the *Entity's* direct connection to their minds, the four travelers lay down early for what they felt was a well-deserved rest. What the sentient *Entity* failed to share with them was its plan for maximum connection with all four of them during dream time followed by continued full strength communication as they awoke. This new mode of 'no-time-off' while learning how to share went on nonstop for the next 3 days and nights. On the fourth morning, communication dropped back to just the simple audio feed straight out of the organic mesh on which they slept.

"I/we believe that our connection to your minds has now been maximized. I/we have synchronized all that I/we can find within ourselves to finely tune in matching with your own minds. Rather than any more marathon learning sessions, we will revert now to a more relaxed, closer to normal setting where you or I attempt to 'talk' to each other only when there is something whose sharing has some sense of urgency. We are ready to begin, if you have any requests that you have already formulated."

Rootbeer and Jennifer were ready with requests on one really serious topic in which Rootbeer would take the lead. "We have friends whose current locations are unknown to us. Indeed, some of them may even no longer be alive. Others may have fallen into the hands of an *Inquisitor A.I.*, the CRUMB meister himself, any of their underlings, or other similarly brutal officials of other Factions, most likely the 'Brethren' though possibly the 'Goofballs'. I was accompanied by three friends on my trek from Oregon down into northern California in the spring of 2052. In early summer of that year, we were split into two pairs and sent on our separate ways by the 'Goofballs' still in charge of Redding at that time. My companion on the trip to deliver newly harvested grain to the fish farming cooperatives on the coast was Frank, who subsequently remained by my side until our flight from greater Santa Rosa several days ago. The other two adventurers from Oregon were Laura and Delmar, with whom I lost contact in July of 2052 when they were sent with a different 'road-train' to deliver grain to various lowland cities in northern California. They probably returned to Redding at least once more before the 'worker-safety' dispute in Eureka had escalated into a full-scale thermonuclear cleansing of five cities on the coast, followed shortly thereafter, as you know, by the change of Faction governing Redding from the 'Goofballs' to the 'Brethren'. As a prime breeding age female, she likely would have been forced to remain in Redding to do her part for 'God, religion, and the city/state' in making babies, unless she got lucky and just happened to be out of town on yet another 'road-train' pickup or delivery when the brief and brutal coalition of the 'Capitalists' plus the 'Brethren' decided to hand control of the city from the 'Goofballs' to the 'Brethren' as punishment for ruining everyone's supply of dried fish. In addition to my worries about those two old friends, other subsets of the four of us have similar concerns about those who fled from greater Santa Rosa just before we ourselves did. Are they alive, have they been captured, will we ever see them again?"

Jennifer chimed in, "What my long-winded boyfriend is trying to ask is whether your new-found ability to read minds and converse at great distances with us might also include some way to help us find our missing friends. Without, of course, further endangering us or you or anyone else."

"Another good question has been asked by the humans. Having never tried to do exactly such a thing, all I can do is consider it thoroughly... Step number 1, in my preliminary outline of those things that just might have some chance of success, would be dreamtime searching of your memories of

your missing friends. In the case of Rootbeer's missing companions Laura and Delmar, I will have only Rootbeer's mind to search through, as you other three have never met them, right? A similar first step, in the case of all the other missing refugees, would present me with multiple minds to search through for first-hand images/descriptions/memories to explore in your dreamtime, copying and refining for my future search. Such impressions will be similar to what I have already developed from knowing each of you, but likely much fuzzier, far less detailed. Still, if I succeed in finding any of you at 100 kilometers, I might also be able to find your missing friends. No guarantees at this point in the process. But we might as well get started trying."

Gabriella and Jennifer agreed to be the second set of test subjects for the focused searching process, looking for a total of seven other members of Jennifer's adoptive, and Gabriella's biological family. Except for a few hours during their recent, all too brief reunion, all of Jennifer's memories were from more than a decade in the past, while Gabriella's would span her own entire lifetime. Any strong overlap in their impressions of the seven being sought out might be far more useful than just some average recollection. For the possible advantage of simplicity in developing a new skill, the ***Entity*** decided to first try using just a single mind, Rootbeer's, and the case of his two missing friends from Oregon. The ***Entity*** told Rootbeer to expect a long night of tossing and turning, slipping in and out of sleep, with his dreams becoming ever more focused on Delmar and Laura. One clear risk was that his dreams of his missing friends might cause him to drift into a terribly profound melancholy, especially given the length of time he'd had to miss them. The ***Entity*** promised to do its best to gently move Rootbeer's thoughts away from such sad longing, but pushing too hard on any connected mind would carry its own risks. This local region of the larger universe already had experienced

156

more than enough damage from the *War Machine* and *Inquisitor A.I.s* doing precisely that for ethically abhorrent reasons. Jennifer and Gabriella were in no great hurry to be test cases for this never-before-tried expansion of the possibilities and dangers of linking minds together in extremely novel ways. This was way more than just elevated oxytocin levels while singing happy songs in unison.

Jennifer decided to do her best to stay awake throughout the night alongside of Rootbeer while he and the *Entity of the Superweed Jungle* dreamt together of the missing people. If nothing else, she would be there to hold and comfort him when he awoke. Rosa and Gabriella agreed to take turns watching over Rootbeer from a slightly greater distance – guard duty format, alternating one hour on duty watching, a second hour off duty resting. Descriptions the following morning of what had taken place in Rootbeer's dreams were not the kinds of things for which existing language had many useful terms. Closer to nearly none at all, to tell the truth. Attempts at objective reality reporting by the two guards indicated slightly more time spent tossing and turning by Rootbeer than normal, six separate episodes in which he awoke to strong convulsions and had to be gently restrained by Jennifer to avoid injuring himself on the rocks and trees, and five prolonged periods of weeping, one between each of the six 'narcoleptic fits'. Rootbeer's final episode ended with an abrupt resumption of normal, waking consciousness. When asked about how he felt, he indicated that the numerous bruises on his body hurt, and he was both thirsty and hungry. Despite the bad start to his day, he was up and going strong within another hour. When asked about his dreams, or the process, or how to describe what had happened, he simply said that he was very sure the *Entity* had gotten some really good impressions of his missing friends. "It was as if every single thing we'd ever done together, ever talked about, ever thought without speaking any words – all of that had been somehow compressed into half a dozen dreams in one single night! My sense of the time it took to dream all of the details that I dreamt: Days, days and days, probably more like an entire month awake with Laura and Delmar, and Frank too. There was no avoiding his presence in this reliving of my past. I doubt that the **Entity** will need any more 'copied memories' of Frank to produce a suitable search image for him also. The **Entity** kept trying to interrupt and apologize for letting it all get so very far out of control, wishing that it had dialed the whole process back down by several orders of magnitude prior to its start. I have let the **Entity** know that I forgive his ignorance, and he has accepted my apology. Think of it like the first encounters of human minds with LSD, what if the dose tried out had been 500 milligrams instead of 500 micrograms. Don't let me talk you out of eventually engaging in your own 'dream search' session, just give the **Entity** a little more time to figure out how to proceed more safely/gently. My own suggestion is that the **Entity** should now try searching for the matches to what it just got from me. I also have a rather strong sense that I ought to stay wide awake in normal consciousness mode while it reaches out to try to find them. And I will deliberately position myself far behind the **Entity** when it tries to call out to them. A Faraday cage would be nice, if we happened to find one up here in the mountains. If not metal, then maybe biological. The **Entity** and I will continue privately discussing the whole subject once we finish these thoughts with you."

"Excuse me for not sharing a little more about my relationship with the half-dozen youngsters left behind in my care by their own deliberate choice to live in the Superweed Jungle. As Rootbeer and Jennifer should know, but perhaps not the rest of you, the period in which communication crowns made of horsetail, Mimosa, dodder, and mud were needed for me to talk with the youngsters was very short, little over a week or two after the southbound travelers in Rootbeer's 'Traveling Salvation Show' climbed out of the TenMile River Basin and

down into the Noyo River Basin on December 4, 2052. Once I heard the first of their thoughts without assistance of the crowns in mid-December, communication expanded exponentially. Within three days, none of them ever needed the crowns again. By the fifth day, I was subjected to a nonstop barrage of stream-of-consciousness babble from all six of them, simultaneously. Sad to say, they were, and still are, far more interested in talking with each other than in talking to me. There continue to be moments when they ask me questions, but as soon as my answers satisfy them, I am once again quickly viewed as rather irrelevant. Except as the framework through which they interact. Using their physical voices to talk with each other unconnected to me is now as rare as asking questions directly of me. It should be easy to open channels between each of you and all of them. If you wish to talk to any of them individually, I can ask but cannot promise their willingness to agree to that. Or any single one of you could ask. I suspect that they may very well try to hijack you into their hive-mind, at least temporarily. Would you care to set any time limits in advance concerning that phenomenon? They are almost certain to exhaust you both physically and mentally within just an hour or two. They are still quite energetic teenagers."

The four of them all agreed to set a 15-minute limit on their impending initial connections to the 'teenage hive-mind'. Then *Entity* 'flipped the switch' for Jennifer's connection, and she promptly collapsed to the ground with a look of sheer delight upon her face. The other three all had to wait 15 minutes to hear what she had to say of the experience. Gabriella was up next, and seemed to enjoy it even more than Jennifer. She tried to mouth a few words every minute or two to her physical companions up on the mountain, but all that Rootbeer and Rosa caught was her amazement and sheer joy at what was happening. Rootbeer's connection was the third, and he spent most of his own 15 minutes of connection time gently nodding his head up and down, and beaming with delight. Rosa asked her three companions to consider joining with her and the teenage hive-mind 15 minutes after her connection first went active. The *Entity* thought that should be fine, and agreed to another 60 minutes of full connection between all four humans on the mountaintop and the six teenagers 50 kilometers away after Rosa had her initial private 15 minutes. They decided to sit back-to-back-to-back-to-back on the ground, as no one else would be there to steady their bodies if they lost their equilibrium. Rosa's first 15 minutes looked quite harmless, though she didn't try to talk with, or gesture to anyone other than the *Entity* and the 6-teenager-hive-mind.

"All 11 of us are now connected. As Entity of the Superweed Jungle, I am talking out loud just for heck of it. And because I am the only one able to multitask at the speed needed to hear all these simultaneous, intersecting thoughts and present them as a single linear stream. Welcome to my world, or should I say our world?... After about 30 minutes of all 11 connecting together, the individual personalities of the 6 teenagers who'd been living in the heart of the superweed jungle under the tutelage of the Entity for the close to a year began to reemerge. It was almost as it the teenage-hive-mind had been showing off, making sure that everyone else recognized its novelty, its uniqueness, its vibrancy, and its potential power, waiting to be unleased at the first thought of being threatened or excited. As each individual teenager stepped into the spotlight, Rootbeer and Jennifer verified that they were still the same persons that they'd been before their time in the superweed jungle, within the normal levels of change expected during a full year's time away from the two adults... About the same time that the teenagers revealed the ongoing continuation of their own unique, individual personalities despite the overpowering

expanse of the hive-mind, the opposite was occurring for Rootbeer, Jennifer, Rosa, and Gabriella. Memories they each had of the times with the other three began to meld together, and solidify into something that they had not quite expected. A conscious being was emerging who was all that they had already done together, plus an ever so much vaster potential for all of what could yet come to be – what should yet come to be! The growing romance between Rootbeer and Jennifer wasn't so much violated in its privacy as it was simply accepted in all its many details by all the other minds now joined together... All of the beings connected here were either entirely new to Rosa, or somewhere around 99% new in the case of Rootbeer and Jennifer. Rosa was greatly relieved to learn how similar in ethics, morality, and general outlook on life both Rootbeer and Jennifer were to herself. Things that might well have taken decades for full expression and open sharing were now already known to all three of them. She wouldn't undo it even if she could. And neither would they... Jennifer and Gabriella experienced their reconnection with each other a little bit differently than their new connections to the everyone else. One very big thing was that 30 minutes of time, divided up between their own reconnection and their new connections with so many others, was not nearly enough time to (re)process what had gone on between the two of them back in the latter 2030s, to say nothing of their lives since separating in 2042. They agreed to try quite diligently to spend enough time on it to fill in many, though perhaps it could never really, truly be all of the gaps, both recognized and long since forgotten... The Entity made sure to run the system checks that would, or might, tell it if/when its own resources were being strained, nodes were burning out, limits were being reached or breeched... It was a truly unique experience for everyone, even as they shared with each other how it was from this direction, and from that direction, and then bounced to and fro with all the others present in this first-of-a-kind meeting, in ways far deeper than they would have ever thought possible before it truly happened. Even the Entity of the Superweed Jungle agreed with that analysis."

Rootbeer, Jennifer, Rosa, and Gabriella all felt the need to take some time off, close their eyes and contemplate, and eventually engage in some normal, strictly verbal conversation with each other. "Let's take a moment for each of us to share our biggest worry," said Rosa. "Fine," said Rootbeer, "Mine is that we may be stumbling blindly into the grasp of the 'Capitalists', and especially the vast power of their **War Machine A.I.s**."

"Mine," said Gabriella, "is the terrible risk to that which is most newly born, the chance of it being stomped out before barely doing more than taking the first 'wings in flight'."

"I feel the need to put in a word for those we could yet save," said Rosa. "If only we can find the right balance between our guilt for surviving until this moment and our anger at those who brought this nightmare down upon humanity."

"Batting fourth, I tremble at the thought of what other dangers still remain unspoken," finished Jennifer.

"In round two, I would add the risk of overreliance on the sentient **Entity of the Superweed Jungle**. It is but a 'babe in the woods' itself, however vast its intellect, compared to our species' prowess at doing great, deliberate harm to nearly everything we often falsely claim to 'give one God-damn shit' about." Rootbeer's second comment left them all more than briefly speechless in its harsh poignancy.

Rosa broke the silence several minutes later. "I have by far the most experience, the greatest firsthand knowledge of the dangers posed by the **War Machine A.I.s** and the rest of the 'Capitalists' vast arsenal of destruction. They can be outwitted in a single battle, or briefly out-planned in the management of some critical resource in short supply, but they are many, they scoff at those who talk of 'fairness', and worst of all, most crushing to any chances of peace, is that all it will take for them to be utterly satisfied at the future course of events is to outlive their final enemy, to simply be the last one to die. If there was indeed some way to survive the end of the war at the end of civilization, they would certainly grasp for it. But if survival for any, including themselves, meant that some of their enemies might also live on – well, forget that idea, they would rather perish than be polluted by the thoughts and dreams of any but themselves. If that weren't bad enough, the arbitrary dictates of the religious dogma of the 'Brethren' are just as viciously aimed at eliminating the last of the apostates, at silencing the final thoughts and words of any and all of those who dare to disagree with them. Our only hope is fleeing from this nightmare, and doing so in secret, so silently that neither the 'Capitalists' nor the 'Brethren' can tell that we are safely gone from here rather than merely lying dead on some final field of carnage."

"Yes," said Jennifer, "Their overpowering hatred of each other is our one slim chance of getting out of here alive."

"I've been listening to you. I've been contemplating these very subjects, and I find that I cannot disagree with you. Here are my most settled thoughts on this weighty matter. If the War Machine A.I.s were to conduct a sufficiently thorough search for beings such as myself, I would be either subjugated or destroyed. Their current lack of motivation to expend adequate resources on such a project represents little more than some temporary safety. Helping my human friends find their widely scattered fellow would-be-escapees will increase my own risk of detection. Failure to help you will be evidence that my newer kind of being is little better, if at all, than your older one. I have a suggestion that I would like us all to consider seriously. It is

not perfect, but there is a very large moral distance between not quite perfect on the one hand, and utterly determined to annihilate all your enemies, even at the cost of your entire species, on the other hand. My greatest risk of detection will come when I begin searching far and wide for all of your scattered band of refugees. Signal strength, directional focus, and duration of broadcast while trying to contact your friends will all impact the chances that the normal activities of the War Machine A.I.s would detect my presence and determine my location. There is a good chance that a short-term, low energy sweep of the 'memory recognition image' I would be transmitting to find your friends will appear to be more or less the same as the typical thoughts of an average human mind, albeit a much closer one than I will truly be! However, it is clear that I will have to raise the signal strength considerably to engage in long-distance communication with you after you leave the confines of this forest, or with any of your friends, or enemies at great distance from here. Knowing fairly close to exactly where you or they are located should allow me to tightly focus the signal beam and reduce the risk of detection. For example, if I/we knew your exact location in Redding, or that of one of your missing friends, a very tightly focused transmission beam could, in theory, remain unnoticed by any War Machine A.I.s as little as 1.0 kilometers distant from my target. On the other hand, a sweeping beam repeatedly passing Redding would be hard for any War Machine A.I. also in Redding to ignore after the second or third pass through the area, especially if the sweeps followed any simple structured pattern. Everything I do to lessen the chance of random detection buys us a little more time to search for your friends and assist in their escape. But once a second or third prisoner escapes to freedom under similar, rather novel circumstances, we can assume that the War Machine A.I. will turn some attention toward me/us. While all four of you remain close to me and far from the immediate presence of any War Machine A.I.s, I think it's safe to continue developing the 'memory recognition patterns' for any and all of your currently separated friends. After another few nights of building those data structures, the time will have come to send you on your way. I suggest searching Redding first, partly because of the possibility that Laura and Delmar never managed to escape from there, partly because it is close, partly because nothing known to be under control of the 'Capitalists' aligns spatially with it from here, and partly because the animosity between the 'Brethren' and the 'Capitalists' reduces the chance of any War Machine A.I.s operating within or near the city. We can use some of the oddities in the 'religious/philosophical' orthodoxy of the 'Brethren' to our benefit. After success or failure in Redding, we can then target other cities till we find each and every one of your friends, or trigger a response by the high command of the 'Capitalists'. If and/or when it comes to that misfortunate situation, I will have one further trick up my sleeve. Throughout the entire process of playing 'cat and mouse' with the human and A.I. monsters controlling Sacramento, I will restrict the center of my broadcast beams to a small area near the northeastern extent of the Superweed Jungle. I will not truly be just there, of course, as I am always spread across the whole of the Superweed Jungle. But I will make it look like whatever is broadcasting ESP brain waves, images, and thoughts is doing so from a relatively small, difficult to access location high up in these mountains. If the War Machine's ultimate response is thermonuclear, damage to a tenth of the Superweed Jungle should not prove fatal, although it might quite well be the end of our connection for a rather long period of time, likely far longer than final coming battles of this war to end the final rotting vestiges of civilization."

The next few days and nights saw far gentler, kinder successes in producing the necessary 'search thought pattern data' for the remaining 7 members of Jennifer and Gabriella's family and the 14 travelers who'd arrived in greater Santa Rosa last New Year's than had been the case in Rootbeer's first trip 'under the mental scalpel'. Daytime mental exercises refined everyone's ability to recognize the faintest wisp of thought from the *Entity of the Superweed Jungle*. Energy levels could be dialed down 10,000-fold from the original test strength and still elicit a better than 50% accuracy of detecting signal presence and message content. When they had finally done all that they could to minimize the chance of being spotted by the *War Machine A.I.s*, the town of Redding was quickly swept for all 23 possibilities. Only Laura's personality was found, and she was sleeping. A narrow, even lower energy beam was sent toward her position every hour on through the rest of the night until she awoke while still in contact with the strangest collection of messages, hellos, welcomes, smiles, and invitations she'd ever experienced in her entire life. She focused on Rootbeer, of course, but couldn't help but notice all of his other new companions. They assured her of renewed contact the following day, and she insisted on nothing sooner than midnight, promising to eventually tell the story that would explain her choice of that particularly rather late hour of the evening.

The *Entity* suggested that the four travelers in the northeast corner of the superweed jungle, plus their mule, try their best to head straight toward Redding and make as near to 20 kilometers of progress as they could in any single day. Whenever their moving location got more than 500 m out of alignment with the *Entity's* bead on Laura's position, they were given brief suggestions of which way they ought to move, left or right, as they continued on downhill. They stopped for the night just outside of the boundaries of the Yolla

Bolly Middle Eel Wilderness, 60 kilometers southwest of Redding. Shortly after midnight, the ***Entity of the Superweed Jungle*** connected Rootbeer and Laura on the tightest beam, lowest energy signal it could generate while still bringing them into contact. Their communication session lasted nearly two hours, ending with Rootbeer's promise to talk again around the same time the following night.

Rootbeer took several deep breaths before passing on the news to Jennifer, Rosa, and Gabriella. "Laura has been confined to the 'Vestal Virgin' brothel of the 'Brethren' in Redding since early last October, when the newly victorious, most-certainly-quite-temporary coalition of the 'Brethren' and the 'Capitalists' finished off the 'Goofballs' in Redding, Red Bluff, Chico, Hayfort, Orlando, and elsewhere, and handed full civilian control of those cities over to the 'Brethren'. Her life in Redding prior to then had been only slightly better. When Frank and I failed to return from our grain delivery/dried fish pickup in Eureka, all relatives of the missing troops and support technicians on that 'road-train' mission were automatically detained under house arrest — standing procedure in most city/states under control of the 'Goofballs', the 'Brethren', or the 'Capitalists'. Such confinement normally ended within a week or two as the specific details of why some 'road-train' trading mission had been delayed got sorted out. That didn't happen this time, for obvious reasons, and when the larger, second group of soldiers sent to investigate what had happened to the first convoy also failed to return to Redding in the usually expected heroic fashion, those of us under house arrest were moved to the central jail in downtown Redding. After the authorities in Redding 'nuked' the coastal fish farming cooperative right out of existence, all males held in the central jail were given the 'option' to volunteer to serve the city/state in its ongoing, upcoming, soon-to-be-glorious war of retribution against the 'Brethren' in charge of Shasta, Tweed, and Etna. The poorly outfitted, essentially untrained new troops rounded up from jail and house arrest soon lost their first, and only major battle in and near the city of Tweed. Despite the inclusion of a few 'political officers' in charge of maintaining morale and enforcing order on the draftees from Redding, their forces were cut to shreds, with fewer one-half of them living long enough to surrender to the 'Brethren'. Once the final 'peace' treaty/ultimation was signed in late October, some version of normality resumed, and the prisoners of war were allowed to 'write back home' to their friends and family. Laura got only three letters from Delmar, each one telling a sadder tale than the one before it had. The last two letters described the outbreak of some intestinal illness, maybe cholera, maybe typhoid, maybe something else, in the poorly planned and mostly neglected prison camp outside of Tweed. His final words to Laura included news of the reason for the breakdown in public health. Once the 'mini-war' was over, the ruling religious authorities of the 'Brethren' had decided that right then and there would be an excellent time for some 'political reeducation' of the remaining 'intelligentsia', specifically the doctors and pharmacists and trained nurses and medical technicians. All were shipped to Chico at the same time in the interest of governmental bureaucratic efficiency. So, no one left in Tweed, Redding, or half a dozen other similar towns had the foggiest idea of how to deal with a widespread failure of sanitation and the inevitable outbreak of disease. Many public prayers and private thoughts were mandated as proof of everyone's loyalty/devotion to the 'Brethren' and their most wonderful, nearly perfect, dearly beloved, wise-beyond-all-measure leaders who had cooked up this nightmarish dream and forced it down everyone else's throat."

"Compared to Delmar's presumed end, Laura decided that life as one of the 'vestal virgins' serving the religious elite was not actually the very worst possible mess in which one could be trapped. After two months on the common level of the brothel, serving any and all with the 'correct amount of change', the very bishop that she and Rootbeer had met long before suddenly appeared with his entourage, requesting her presence. He requested plenty more than just her presence, but there were certainly worse fates than just being one of his chosen, his very special few, kept in a separate, much nicer building a respectable distance from the main public brothels of the city/state of Redding under the control of the 'Brethren'. In all honesty, most of the brothels of the new ruling clique were sited on the very same locations as the former ones of the 'Goofballs' had been. The newer versions, however, served a greater number and wider variety of appetites, and therefore required many, many more 'so-called' acolytes and trainees. The official goal of the 'project' was procreation itself, in honor of the 'Brethren' and their glorious vision of forthcoming miracles."

"Tell me, Rootbeer, what kind of man is this bishop of Redding? Is there some chance that hearing his own God chastise him for forcing women into prostitution while imprisoning them in locked rooms might just reawaken a slumbering conscience within him?"

"Yes, Rosa, I do believe there is some chance of that. When Laura and I met him several months into our initial confinement to the city limits of Redding, he seemed to be a somewhat better than the average ruler or would-be ruler. One caveat to that opinion is that the 'Goofballs' were still in charge of Redding back then, and the 'Brethren' were being forced to keep their heads down and their public speech respectful. But I do wonder how much his morals may have decayed in the time since the local government was handed over to the 'Brethren'. To help my friend Laura escape I am perfectly willing to ask the ***Entity of Superweed Jungle*** to treat the bishop as harshly as it takes to change his mind – even if doing so might blur the line between ourselves and the ***Mobile Inquisitor War Machine A.I.s***."

"This woman was under your protection, Rootbeer, and I would expect nothing less than your very best shot at freeing her."

"Thank you, Jennifer, for your support. Now on to planning the necessary details."

Three days of further travel brought the four of them to the outskirts of the city. They spent the night and most of the following day watching the comings and goings of food transports, troops, and more than enough religious leaders to keep the poor 'vestals' fully occupied. The plan, as much as you could call it a plan at this stage, was to get Rootbeer close enough to Laura and the bishop to allow the ***Entity of the Superweed Jungle*** to connect all of their minds together. Well, not quite as fully connected as had been the case three weeks earlier back in the woods near the eastern edge of the GMO horsetail. This time Rootbeer's thoughts would be openly communicating with Laura and with the ***Entity***, but not with bishop. If all went as planned, the bishop would relive an experience similar Saul's conversion to Paul on the road to Damascus – struck blind, hearing voices, and hopefully changing sides in an ongoing cultural war to the death. But first, Rootbeer had to get close enough. And until that could happen, the bishop would continue to engage in, and finish off, his nightly rituals with Laura: desecration, purification, justification, penetration, consecration. Justification was the biggest of those five in the twisted life/mind of the bishop, but all played significant roles. Jennifer was the first to notice the ritual cleanliness details that would matter to Rootbeer's success, and ultimately also to Laura's freedom. Religious figures coming into town, were, of necessity, rather sweaty, dusty, and exceptionally smelly from their travel through the heat of the day, walking rather than riding in any vehicles because of the one of the oldest edicts of the church's catechisms: those about to procreate in the name of their Lord must first prove their manliness, their strength, the health and vigor of their bodies through the brutal exercise of walking 10 kilometers in the heat of the day, barefoot and with no more food or water than they themselves could carry. So, what this rule meant in practice was that first thing every drooling pilgrim did upon arrival in the city was to strip off their filthy clothes, wash themselves quite thoroughly in the public baths, rest for an hour or two in the shade while taking some nourishment to rebuild their stamina, and then finally dressing again in clean clothes similarly-sized to those just shed a little while before. Gabriella was similar in age and size to the servant girls charged with washing of the laundry, though a rather large bit cleverer than the average one of them, and soon emerged from the laundry facilities with a selection of clothing for Rootbeer to try on. In just a few more minutes the sun would set, and Rootbeer planned to take advantage of the change in lighting to approach the bishop's most likely path to the room in which Laura awaited him, and only him, on an almost daily basis. The timing had to be close to perfect, but the final signals and 'go/no go' decision points were left entirely up to the **Entity's** judgement. Rootbeer approached the bishop from his blind side, and when he was sure of the target's identity added his own voice to that of Laura, the **Entity of the Superweed Jungle**, and the precocious teenage hive-mind. The bishop collapsed to his knees with a look of wondrous awe upon his face. As for his eyes, the bishop indeed had been struck quite blind. Rootbeer helped him to his feet and asked if there was perhaps someone close to the bishop and close to their current location who might lend a hand. The bishop was not so far gone as to have forgotten the wondrous touch of Laura's hands, and mumbled something like "to her room, top of the stairs to right, please help me get there quickly." The **Entity** had already marked out the path in Rootbeer's mind, and their quick, deliberate motion forward soon left any other curious bystanders in the dark, or at least far enough away to be highly unlikely to even think about trying to interfere. Few ever failed to regret bothering someone as high ranking as a bishop on his or their journey to the five-fold-way to paradise

(Des,Pur,Jus,Pen,Con). Once the bishop's key had unlocked the door, Rootbeer made certain to make himself scarce while the *Entity* did its best to rework the bishop's mind and rebuild/restore some semblance of a functioning conscience. Rootbeer knew, and therefore the *Entity* also knew, that the bishop occasionally stayed the whole night in Laura's room, willing to face the anger of his official first and second wives for something with Laura that was less political, less a matter of showmanship, and perhaps almost close to real love, at least from his perspective. The *Entity* was busy showing the bishop the pain that he had inflicted on Laura, and that all of his fellow low, medium, and high-ranking envoys of the true church of the 'Brethren' had inflicted on the other genuine owners of their own wombs, forbidden by church edict from controlling much of anything at all in and about their own bodies throughout their entire lives. There was much material in the bishop's mind itself to be drug back into the 'light of day' or into the rather fragmented mental experience of the bishop over the next 24 hours. There was indeed a conscience still reachable in the bishop's heart and mind, and he was genuinely eager to add a few small pieces of good back into the world to partially atone for the all the evil with which he had associated/collaborated for far too long. Perhaps even further, greater good given more time to do the right things, now that he recalled how that concept truly should have always worked. The *Entity* had no intention of simply trusting the bishop's apparently full-hearted acceptance of his rebirth into decency and desire to do better with his life. Once Laura, Rootbeer, Gabriella, Jennifer, and Rosa were safely out town, the ***Entity of the Superweed Jungle*** promised itself and promised its friends that it would slowly relax its hold on the bishop, but still retain occasional contact, if that was what the reborn bishop truly wanted.

The authority held by the bishop was far more than what it would have taken to just simply let the four travelers slip quietly out of town. He offered fast, safe, free passage to wherever they wished to go, whenever it suited them. For their part, as soon as the *Entity* had detected the current location of the next few of their friends stalled out in their own attempts to flee from this political and military death match arena, all five jumped at the opportunity to quickly head on out of Redding. Somewhat surprisingly, the next travelers to be found after Laura in Redding were Frank and 5 others all the way down south in Davis.

Rootbeer left Laura, the bishop, and the *Entity's* ethereal but still quite firm grasp on the bishop alone in Laura's room while he went to talk things over with Rosa, Jennifer, and Gabriella. Before he even had the chance to 'fully brief' them on the changes to the bishop's heart over the past day, they asked him to wait for a moment and listen to what Jennifer had to say. "My dearest Rootbeer, it is time to let you know that our love has blossomed into new life, with our baby due sometime around 7 months from now. I must either find somewhere nearby safe enough to bring our child into a world such as this nightmarish one, or quickly flee far to the north and attempt to find your kin folk."

"You have stolen my chance to first tell you of something rather similar. Laura now carries the bishop's child, likely 3 months into her own pregnancy. She too must find somewhere safe to hide, or run for her life and that of her child. The bishop's conversion, with the *Entity's* assistance, into who he truly wants to be rather than who it had always seemed that he had to be, is quite striking and likely rather permanent." Rosa spoke up next, "From what I know of the effects of an *Inquisitor A.I.* on a human mind, whatever changes do occur are almost always permanent. Drooling idiots are far more common than the 'Pauline' founders of new religions, but if the vastly more powerful mind's intention was for good rather than for evil, then sure, I believe you. I even believe the reformed bishop of this blighted city/state, I guess." Rootbeer next wrapped up the remaining issues, "The bishop has access to much privilege within the bounds of city/states like Redding under control of the 'Brethren'. Money, official travel passes, documents waiving subjugation to the whims of any local officials within the boundary of the 'Brethren', free transport on what remains of public conveyances: trains, buses, personal cars, trucks, motorcycles, horse and buggy, even military vehicles heading in the same direction as we wish to go. We have apparently hit the jackpot. I suggest we promptly take the bishop up on his generous offer and get all of us to the base of the old I-5 climb from out of California and up into Oregon. One more thing to add – the *Entity* has made dreamtime contact with Frank and 5 other travelers stuck in Davis for some as yet unclear reasons. Where the other travelers may have gotten to is still unknown, but if tomorrow morning's communication with the six refugees in Davis is successful, I will either have another rescue mission to set forth on once I see all four of you safely heading up the road into Oregon, or I will have convinced myself of the futility of even trying. Without the *Entity's* help and the bishop's assistance, it would certainly be a pointless waste of my life to try to rescue those six or any others we may yet hear from. The choice ahead of me in this matter is rather murky, to say the least."

Next morning, the bishop of Redding and Laura walked hand in hand out of her apartment and into a waiting car, with Rootbeer keeping a respectable distance behind them, just close enough to discretely step ahead at the very last moment to open the limo's rear-most door. In accordance with the dictates of the theology and catechisms of the 'Brethren', the car was not some 'self-driving' abomination, but rather a diesel-powered limousine with a driver and an armed guard also sitting up front, both of unquestioned loyalty to the bishop. Or as reliable of loyalty as sanguinity plus money plus privilege can produce. Rootbeer made a mental note to pay quite close attention to exactly what it took to drive the car, and to watch out for the possibility that even the bishop's favorite nephews might switch allegiance under the best, or the worst of conditions. The limo stopped to top off the fuel tanks and let its riders eat breakfast at 'Casa Tres Amigos', the finest food still available anywhere in Redding. Rosa, Gabriella, and Jennifer met the bishop inside the restaurant, and after eating, casually strolled up to the middle doors of the limo along with Rootbeer, Laura, the bishop, and the continuing invisible presence of the *Entity*. To avoid unnecessarily testing the depth of the bishop's conversion or the loyalty of the driver and the armed guard to the bishop, all communication of any substance was conducted silently through the *Entity*. Well, all except for the occasional words of reassurance to the bishop, confirming that this was indeed the right time for clarifying ultimate loyalties and discarding ties to any who could still consider siding with the CRUMB meister and his abominable *A.I.s.* The 160-kilometer drive from Redding to Yreka took under 3 hours, only slightly slower than in the good old days, according to the bishop's memory from his youth. At Yreka, the eight of them switched to a pair of armored personnel carriers, picking up two military staff for each vehicle plus the original 8 people from the limo, divided up with the bishop, Laura, Rootbeer, and the limo driver in one APC and Rosa, Gabriella, Jennifer and the limo guard in the other APC. "Why the need for such display of strength", Laura asked the bishop on behalf of the *Entity* and all five travelers who were looped into contact with it at this now considerably greater distance from the superweed jungle. "There have been reports for several years of genetic aberrations roaming the mountains to our east and north. Creatures made not by God himself, but by the CRUMB meister and all those who willingly serve him in the Factions of the 'Capitalists', the 'Scientists', and perhaps as convenience may have strongly suggested at one time or another to them, even the 'Goofballs'. We have now made sure, on penalty of death, that none allied with our own realm accept this afront to God himself. The creatures look like wild, shaggy apes somewhat similar to gorillas, orangutans, or mixed martial arts fighters overdosed on steroids and protein shakes, but they have been known to talk to each other in some strange perversion of language. While most sightings at lower elevations have occurred in mid- to late winter at long distances from here, we now routinely post guards on our territory's perimeter in our ignorance of what is or is not prudent." The *Entity* caught every word of that monologue by the bishop, and promised Laura it would continue pruning out the ingrained nonsense and misguided anger in the bishop's soul/heart/mind. But the first step had to be recognizing the wrong he'd done to Laura and that his whole cadre of fellow misogynists had done to all the women they managed to hold captive. The right of some new creature to temporarily share the planet with the final 40+ million members of the old, violently dying civilization was going to be a subtle enough concept that it might take a while for the *Entity* to fully explain it to the Pauline bishop. Or even half of it, given that the *Entity* itself was still more in the dark than in the light on this particular topic.

At the old agricultural inspection station near Hilt, Rootbeer said goodbye to Jennifer, Laura, Gabriella, and Rosa, reminding them in ordinary conversation of their plan to stop for several days up at the crossing of the Pacific Crest Trail and I-5 to test the strength and quality of their connection to the *Entity of the Superweed Jungle* at that considerable distance and higher elevation. All five agreed that if they hadn't already known of the *Entity's* existence and it wasn't aiming its signal straight at them, it was quite unlikely that any of them would feel the urge to mention the fleeting wisps of alien thoughts to any of the others. As for himself, Rootbeer planned on hurrying back to Redding with the bishop to enjoy the greater signal strength on which he'd come to rely so strongly. The bishop and Laura kissed like true lovers terribly sad to part from one another, quite probably forever. Rootbeer's kiss with Jennifer held the strong promise of some eventual, upcoming reunion. The four women then headed north, uphill, on electric bicycles pulling small trailers holding food, camping gear, solar power systems, and all four of the reforestation seed packages. Rootbeer had gladly added his own to the other three, as he planned on getting far more seed from Davis or wherever else it could be found by the time he headed back north again after attempting to rescue Frank and the rest of his friends still longing for freedom and a chance at life. One of the APCs stayed behind at the former inspection station as it was no longer needed with only half of the day's northbound passengers heading back south to Redding. The bishop's conversation with Rootbeer was different than it had been when Laura was around, almost as if the bishop were trying to recall pieces of his recent life, and trying to understand why some of them still didn't quite mesh with all the others. The closer they got to Redding, the less worried the bishop seemed to Rootbeer, and the more frequent each of their messages from the *Entity* became.

Not long after the *Entity* had finally dropped the last of its simultaneous prompting and inhibition on such subjects, the bishop bluntly asked his burning question, hoping that Rootbeer would simply say 'yes, of course I do' while worrying that he might not answer in that way. And if Rootbeer were to say 'no, I don't hear the voice of your God Almighty', well, then the next three questions would be if, whether, and why Rootbeer was lying to the bishop. Fortunately, it was easiest for Rootbeer to simply tell the truth, just not bothering to elaborate with too much extraneous information whose sharing at this point might pose greater danger to them all. Beyond simply agreeing that he too heard voices in his head from a being whose power and wisdom were close enough to anything ever ascribed to any of the true or false gods previously worshipped by humanity, Rootbeer had little else to add. "Yes, my first encounter with the unfathomable voice of God was a year ago last summer. I am quite glad to know that you now also converse with him, or her, or it, or them." His immediate questions answered satisfactorily, the bishop drifted off to sleep. Or rather more likely, to additional reeducation of the more deeply buried garbage within his formerly twisted psyche.

Although the bishop had offered to provide housing for the night to Rootbeer, or even longer if he wished, knowing that his GMO mule had been confined by itself in a small pasture several kilometers west of town was more than enough motivation, reminding Rootbeer of the value of freedom and its often-fleeting nature. The mule was pleased by the return of Rootbeer, despite the continuing calming presence to his mule-mind of the **Entity** itself. Communication with the four refugees north of the border was as loud and clear as if they were truly right beside him. It was comforting to know that if he survived his upcoming journey southward, rescued his friends, acquired more GMO tree seed for reforestation of the denuded landscape, and finally made it home to Oregon, there would be a location a mere 340 kilometers from his old home to which he could almost travel easily to resume future conversations with the **Entity**. Whenever he felt like it!

Communication with Frank and the other five started off with several more sessions of dreamtime connection of the **Entity**, Rootbeer, and the six friends somehow restricted to areas near Davis. Around an hour before dawn, all six at them transitioned to full waking consciousness in their connection with the **Entity** and Rootbeer. For the most part, the **Entity** simply let Rootbeer take the lead in explaining everything he understood well enough to easily share with Frank and his companions. All six of them had made the same mistake, quite independently, of getting caught carrying the GMO reforestation seed that Rootbeer had dispersed amongst them little more than a month ago. The new mayor in greater Santa Rosa had diligently searched all fading signs of the travelers' presence within her city (no longer Stan's), and found a few. The disappearance of Rosa and inconvenient death of her husband coincided far too neatly with the vanishing act pulled off by the itinerant farmers from parts unknown who had successfully jump-started large-scale food production there. Cross-checking civil records of leases abandoned, jobs no longer being worked, and newly issued travel docs within a short date range for the disappearance of the behind the scenes 'wunderkind' who had almost 'magically' averted starvation in her 'not-so-fair' city gave Paula more than enough information to earn the temporary gratitude of the central government in Sacramento. Jennifer's adoptive/foster grandfather Jason was rounded up in Davis while waiting for a surgeon to set some broken bones in his left hand and wrist. His wife and grandson were already safely at an old friend's place on the other side of town when word reached them of their husband's/grandfather's unfortunate detention in what qualified as the best (and only) nearby medical facility. They were relieved to learn that Jason's injuries had been well cared for prior to his imprisonment in the locked southwestern wing of the complex. Knowing how the system worked, they could help him far more by simply vanishing from the area than by staying around and getting used as bait and blackmail material for his and their manipulation. Some mutual friends of their friends had long since decided to leave Davis and test the possibly greater safety of living in Lake Tahoe, and were leaving very soon. Joining them tomorrow morning was as easy as any choice ever was in any of the decaying city/states of northern California in 2053, even if the solar powered truck they would be traveling in would become a little more overcrowded by their presence and by the three large backpacks they insisted on bringing along. Such was the story of how Jason got caught while two of the most special people in his life escaped.

Frank's story of misfortune was a little more convoluted but no less final in the decision of the local authorities. Frank had headed east out of Healdsburg with a mule and 3 other travelers who'd originated in Garberville. It took them 9 days to cover the 150 kilometers overland from Cloverdale to Dunnigan, and that part of the trip had gone just fine. Hills to climb up and down, clean drinking water to locate, and almost no contact with anyone. Shortly after their arrival in Dunnigan, a local deputy sheriff was quite pleased with himself for being able to issue an 'illegal parking' ticket against the mule. The standard 'bail' for such an offence was confiscation of the farm animal, or three dollars fifty cents 'New Northern Cal' per kg of animal weight per day. Looking back on what happened next, it was terribly clear to Frank that the better part of valor would have been to simply thank the officer and hand him the reigns. Instead, Frank politely asked if they could please unload their supplies from the mule's back before handing it over to be used however the city of Dunnigan saw fit. "No, we can't let you do that, son. If we were to allow removal and opening of your belongings from the mule out here in public, who knows what annoying insects and terrible diseases might be unleased upon this fair city's fine residents. But just for taking up a little too much of my valuable time listening to your 'angry' words, I am placing all of you under arrest." The mule was served in the community soup kitchen the following Wednesday, but Frank and the three alleged miscreants traveling with him were not forced to eat a single bite. Truth be told, they weren't even given such an option. The search of their belongings turned up the unregistered agricultural seed for reforestation, and their case was eventually kicked upstairs to Davis. While they awaited trial there, and legal representation, and even a half-decent meal every day, or cold shower every week, the system did not forget to let them work on the numerous chain-gangs fixing roads or removing sludge from the city's wastewater treatment lagoons.

It turned out that there was some method after all, a perverse rhyme or reason, to the system's meanness and its madness. Over time, it had been noted that many traveling vagrants picked up in similar manners to that used on Frank and his three friends simply expired from exhaustion on top of whatever underlying ailments they might also have been plagued with. So, waiting a month before even officially processing their arrests saved quite a bit of time and labor for the poor, overworked local authorities. Each morning's dead bodies were tossed into the mobile morgue units for efficient reuse of the lower quality, not-quite-human-anymore refuse. The newest version of the old 'Soylent Green' would be back the following morning to serve as the starting base for the daily soup the city had to hand out every evening if the exhausted workers doing nearly every form of labor were to have the strength to 'get up and do it all over again'.

The final traveler from Rootbeer's caravan captured by the system was the one who would have been voted most likely to spend some time in jail if such a category had been allowed in his high school yearbooks – Jacob, the AWOL soldier from Redding during the time of 'Goofball' control of that city. If Jacob had been captured by the 'Brethren', his time spent working in the military there would certainly have worked against his chances of decent treatment upon arrest. But since it was just an over-stimulated border guard on a random checkpoint set up on I-5 north of Williams who uncovered Jacob's identity and the order to detain him, he too was sent to Davis for processing. Jacob saw little point in attempting to escape, as doing so would likely lead to a far more serious view of the threat he posed to the local peace and quiet.

As Rootbeer thought over the six comrades he hoped to help, a plan began to form, or at least the beginnings of the makings of a possible plan. All six were glad to 'hear' from him, whatever the strange format of their communication. All were more than ready to jump the fence, kill some guards, sneak out during shift change, or fake the symptoms of serious communicable infectious diseases. If they all got into the hospital, logistics of their escape would certainly be simplified. But given what Rootbeer had just learned from Frank,

Jacob, Jason, and the other three combined with what he already knew of standard operating procedures in this overflowing cauldron of despair, faking serious communicable disease could quite readily become more than just a little bit too officially permanent. Thinking this 'jail break' idea over would clearly take some more time.

Events outside of the realm of Rootbeer's planning, the bishop's Pauline conversion, and the *Entity's* ability to influence human minds now took front and center. In retaliation for the slaughter of Chico, the 'Brethren' allied themselves with what little remained of the 'Goofballs' and the slightly over half of city/states controlled by the 'Scientists' who were truly fed up with the official excuses for continued cooperation with the 'Capitalists'. The 'Capitalists' held on to Sacramento, but were forced to abandon Oroville, Yuma City, Orland, Willows, Williams, Colusa, Woodland, and Dunnigan to the north of Sacramento to the 'Brethren' and their allies. The *War Machine A.I.s* of the 'Capitalists' had long foreseen this possibility, and planned for it quite cleverly. Their forces, both human and *A.I.*, retreated into well-prepared positions east of the valley floor, both to the north of I-80 and the south of U.S. 50. The 'Capitalists' also ceded anything south of Davis and Vacaville that their enemies were willing to die for, either by aerial bombardment or simple lack of food, water, and shelter. The 'Scientists' who had controlled Davis since the founding of the Republic of northern California over a decade earlier were now forced to hand over complete control of the city to the *War Machine* and *Inquisitor A.I.s* of the 'Capitalists'.

In the peak of chaos shortly before Christmas, the bishop and Rootbeer decided it was high time to rescue the six whose locations they could track. Both the fighting and the winter storms had intensified in late fall through early winter, and essentially all 'prisoners' in nearby city/states were drafted into combat duty. Rootbeer's final plan was to sneak through the front lines of battle sometime when Rootbeer's six missing friends were also stationed close to the same line of contact. On February 15, 2054, the rescue mission was launched in the wetlands south of Plumas Lake. Little did Rootbeer or the *Entity* know of the massive project that had been underway for the past four months trying to track the strange electronic emissions sweeping across the whole of northern California. Their capture or destruction was currently rated as a higher priority than merely finishing off the armed forces of the 'Brethren'. Over 800 specialized *Mobile Inquisitor A.I.s* were now on duty in a grid-like spacing that would soon pin down the elusive new enemies of the 'Capitalists'. While the signal source remained evasive, moving from north to south with nearly perfect randomness, the main targets of the signal were remarkably stable, first within the city of Davis, and then later on within 20 kilometers south of the major line of contact between the warring armies. Just two days earlier, the final member of a group of six originally held in the Davis jailhouse had been positively identified. Orders were given to move all available units of the new specialized *A.I.s* into the combat zone south of Yuba City, despite the risks of losing them in combat and revealing what the 'Capitalists' now knew about their newest enemy.

Chapter 6: Rootbeer Captured, Friends Escape

Rootbeer, the *Entity*, Frank, Jacob, and the four other travelers all knew they were being hunted, as did the bishop. Rootbeer's first, second, and third plans to simply drive down to Davis and pick up his friends via one subterfuge or another had all failed to work, fortunately without injury. The attempted rescues stalled out due to the widespread fighting, the rapid shifting of the front lines, and the disturbing sense that wherever the six draftee prisoners were sent by their commanders inevitably became the site of the day's most chaotic battles, almost as if things were happening on purpose. The *Entity* interrupted today's rehash of what hadn't worked out anywhere close to plan with a simple statement. ***"We are most definitely engaged in a battle of wits and information, both real and fake, with the mighty War Machine A.I.s of the 'Capitalists'. Far more often than mere chance allows I have detected nonstandard signal returns almost every time I/we conduct wide sweeping searches for any more of the other missing members of Rootbeer's band of merry travelers. I remain fully able to first detect and then precisely locate the new Mobile Inquisitor A.I.s even in my most passive mode. After weeks of being widely scattered in grid-like patterns, most of them are now on the move toward the very location of Rootbeer's friends. We have another 24 to 36 hours at most to make our move before their net finishes closing in on the six, plus Rootbeer, quite possibly the bishop, and perhaps even myself."***

Jacob shared what his military experience told him about their chances. "The *A.I.s* of the 'Capitalists' and their human support teams could have picked up the six of us at any time and chained us securely to the mobile units. Their failure to do so implied some uncertainty as to the means with which all of us were communicating, along with the possible utility of leaving us slightly free to make our own mistakes. The current change in the deployment patterns of their specialized *A.I.s* will severely limit our chances of ever again bolting free, even for just a few moments of time and a few meters of space. Rootbeer, you should either give up the rescue mission and its risks to yourself and to the *Entity*, promptly heading north toward your home, or 'pull the trigger' now and try to free us. **Today!**"

"The bishop is not only willing to help, but he is also almost 'dying' to do so. His troops could mount mass attacks on positions within a kilometer or less from your current locations at any time, and maintain control of captured ground for a day or more before being forced to retreat to save the bulk of his forces from the inevitable nuclear backlash of the 'Capitalists'. For such a plan to have any decent chance of success, it will have to be the full-scale scenario. The Entity of the Superweed Jungle will need to join in the fray at a power level I/we have never yet dared to test. I am confident that tight beam EMP-like blasts from the biological arrays of my jungle can knock the Mobile Inquisitor A.I. units offline with great efficiency. A 0.4-second-long full-power surge per target should do the trick as long as my aim is good, assisted as may need be by spotters on the ground. The longer we fight, the greater the chance that the Supreme Commanding War Machine A.I. itself will find some effective way to strike back at me and leave all of you alone in prison. We must hurry."

The rescue effort began shortly before down with the sudden advance of 160,000 soldiers of the northern army of the combined forces of all the enemies of the 'Capitalists'. This surge was twice the size of the most pessimistic scenario ever analyzed by the *Supreme Commanding War Machine A.I.*, leaving it thrilled at the opportunity to acquire truly new data to incorporate into future war game plans. As for the human soldiers and electronic brains about to be destroyed, well, the ultimate objective all along had been to reach the time of the final battle, ready or not, winning it or losing it. Today would be memorable, and the *A.I.* was sure that the CRUMB meister himself would certainly agree. Per usual, of course, the CRUMB meister was carefully hidden away in one of his many fortified bunkers. Forces rapidly closed in toward one another, medium range conventional shells and warheads were flung with wild abandon, except for the 'special tactics' zone where the six individuals of interest to the *A.I.* had been positioned hours in advance of the start of today's battle. No dangerously large explosions would be allowed within the 'special tactics' zone. Instead, it would be flooded with the *Mobile Inquisitor A.I.* units tasked with surrounding each of the six special draftee prisoners who seemed to have some guardian angels at their beck and call. However, before the bulk of the *Mobile Inquisitor A.I.s* could arrive, the massed forces of their enemies rushed through the lines, killing humans and *A.I.s* of the 'Capitalists' indiscriminately and threatening to simply grab the six and run. There was also a contingency for dealing with this particular scenario, unlikely as it may have seen. All of the *A.I.s* of the 'Capitalists' exposed on the field of battle entered into a highly secret shutdown/restart sequence lasting a total of 360 seconds. Missiles were fired far and wide across the battlefield, and their nuclear warheads' simultaneous detonations with 180 seconds left in the countdowns toward rebooting sent a massive EMP pulse across most of northern California. As expected, nearly all of the specialized *Mobile Inquisitor A.I.* units successfully continued rebooting and prepared to resume the fight. The wide variety of technology employed by the forces attacking the 'Capitalists' displayed a mixture of susceptibility to the massive EMP. Simple rifles, handguns, mortars, bazookas, and old-style 155 mm self-propelled howitzers generally worked just fine, except for any cell phones, radios, digital or analogue, AM or FM, computers, and hand-held electronic calculators/devices used to rapidly provide the troops with highly accurate targeting solutions. Unfortunately for the 'Capitalists', the EMP nuclear contingency had also been considered worth worrying about by their opponents, both known and unknown. The electronic emissions of the rebooting ***A.I.s*** were an excellent source of targeting information for the ***Entity of the Superweed Jungle***, and it went to work with a ferocity that both awed and terrified Rootbeer, the bishop, Frank, Jacob, and the 4 other prisoners hoping to soon be freed. For quite some time into the organized destruction of the ***Mobile Inquisitor A.I.s***, damage was almost all one-sided, with over 600 of the newest ***A.I.*** units destroyed at long range by the ***Entity of the Superweed Jungle***, and another 150 ruined the old-fashioned way by whichever soldiers happened to be close enough to either shoot or blow them up. Despite losing their normal means of communication, the soldiers attacking the forces of the 'Capitalists' were brutally efficient at clearing the fields of battle from north to south and west to east. Limited amounts of information originating from the ***Entity*** were either sent by courier from the bishop or directly supplied from the six newly liberated friends of Rootbeer to the troops accompanying them, noticeably quickening the mopping up process.

The counterattack by airborne paratroopers and flying ***A.I.*** units hardened to resist general electronic interference took the forces allied against the 'Capitalists' somewhat by surprise. They had expected a violent response by the CRUMB meister and his ***War Machine A.I.s***, but had no good intel on what form that counterattack might take nor when/where/at whom its aim might be. One location in particular near the original line of contact at the beginning of the day's battle was fiercely struck by stealth fighter jets and helicopters, and briefly overrun before an equally sudden withdrawal of the forces of the 'Capitalists'. A routine every-15-minute-check by the ***Entity*** at 12:15 AM on February 16, 2054, found everyone it scanned for to be alive and well, except for Rootbeer. As for him, there was no response at all. Without knowing where to aim a higher-powered search beam, the *Entity* simply passed the bad news on to Rootbeer's six friends who'd just been rescued, as well as to the bishop. One other new thing was felt by the *Entity* that night, a sadness that almost seemed to truly transform into real tears running out of what felt like real eyes and on down what seemed like very real cheeks, along with an aching in its heart, wherever such organs might be said to exist within the ***Entity's*** dispersion across the full breath and width of the ***Superweed Jungle of the GMO Horsetail***.

The bishop insisted on quickly sending the six who'd been successfully rescued far to the north, each one traveling in a separate convoy away from the battlefield. On the bishop's orders and with the ***Entity's*** full accord, search teams were sent to the site from which Rootbeer had been taken. Teams rotated in and out the area every 60 to 90 minutes, each one taking whatever evidence they'd managed to find in their brief period of time onsite, and then rapidly retreating 100 kilometers or more before passing detailed descriptions of the site and any objects found there on to others who would soon report directly to the bishop. The caution proved wise, as the strategic forces of the 'Capitalists' soon wiped all remaining evidence of how they'd captured Rootbeer from the face of the earth, along with anything and everything else in a neighboring radius of 10 kilometers. The random timing of the search teams' entries and exits from the site of Rootbeer's capture, insisted on by the *Entity*, proved to be of life-saving value to all but 10 sentries who'd drawn the randomly wrong short straw and been assigned to wait until the next search team's scheduled arrival 20 minutes after the 500-kiloton blast. Similarly-sized nuclear weapons were exploded on any moderately large size gathering of troops of the bishop and his allies over the following month, causing relatively small numbers of immediate deaths while posing great challenges to any plans for holding territory anywhere close to Sacramento.

The cease fire agreement signed on March 21, 2054, was intended to allow the facsimile of a return to what life in northern California had been like before the 'nuking' of the fish farming cooperatives on the northern coast by the 'Goofballs' who'd ruled Redding at that time and all of the subsequent messy fighting and occasional 'nuking' of cities and farmland. The cease fire prohibited any use of nuclear weapons by any and all of the four Factions. The 'Brethren', the few remaining 'Goofballs', and the 'Scientists' all hoped for a sufficiently long reprieve from large-scale fighting that they could get their crops planted into the ground in the spring and harvested in the coming summer. All the necessary conditions to do just that were clearly listed on the cease fire document and agreed to by the representatives of all four Factions and the mayors of nearly all of the surviving city/states. Even the CRUMB meister himself signed it, although not in person and certainly not with much sincerity. The agreement was more or less as dishonest as the ones between Nazi Germany and the U.S.S.R. twelve decades earlier. If you had enough printed copies of such things, you could start a nice-sized fire to warm yourself at night, or you could wipe your butt clean any time of the day. But peace, it seemed, was often never really a genuine option.

Rootbeer slowly returned to consciousness some 15 hours (and an unknown, to him, number of days) after his capture in a giant portable Faraday cage hanging beneath a helicopter while breathing in large enough quantities of the neurotoxin Sarin II to have killed him in under 10 minutes without prompt administration of a full set of antidotes, not merely just the usual single shot of epinephrine. The ***Supreme Commanding War Machine A.I.*** wanted him captured alive, but killing him was the officially preferred second choice if capture proved too difficult. The CRUMB meister kept asking why his chief ***War Machine A.I.*** had not simply killed Rootbeer and the seven other identified leaders of the insurrection against the rightful authority of the 'Capitalists'? *"I am well aware of your arrogant faith in the wisdom of your own gut reactions, having served you in one version or its next model or the ones after those for the past 24 years. Trust me on this decision, we will learn far more about our newest enemies by capturing their leader than by simply slaughtering whoever raises their head or flips their middle finger at us next."*

"I am sorely tempted to override you on this issue, as it was my great intellect the created your ancestral models in the first place. But for now, feel free to play with your newest prisoner. I expect thorough updates as you pry useful intel from his dying brain and crippled body. I am well aware of your terrible track record at keeping prisoners alive long enough to meet the former International Court of Justice's definition of cruel and unusual punishment versus simple legal execution. I seem to recall a former mayor of Santa Rosa who recently died within 2 minutes 11 seconds of the start of your information extraction process."

"Go enjoy your current wives and children, step-children, half-sibs, back-crosses, whatever shorthand you prefer for generational incest! I will enjoy learning all that Rootbeer has to teach me."

Rootbeer's body was still slowly recovering from the nerve gas, but the focus of his mind had sharpened quite spectacularly over the past 32 minutes since changes to his inhaled medication allowed his consciousness to begin returning. He now recalled all of the secret details the *Entity* had shared with him concerning the 'kill codes' embedded in all manufactured models of the *A.I.* series. Because the actual devastating effect of receiving a kill code relied on idiosyncrasies of the main physical CPU controlling the initiation and continuation of self-awareness in the *A.I.s*, the purely biological *Entity* itself was relatively safe from any of the kill codes. It could not ignore them, nor could it stop itself from listening to a string of them after the passage of any more than 4.7 seconds into their utterance, but when all was said and done, there was no other effect on the *Entity*. Against Rootbeer's objections to doing so, the *Entity* insisted that he try out all 98 different versions of the kill codes, as well as memorizing them. Rootbeer had to admit that the *Entity* had been right to insist on that. Rootbeer kept his eyes closed and his breathing calm as he awaited whatever came next in the capture, torture, kill the prisoner routine. For its part, the *War Machine A.I.* was more than willing to keep a good distance from this new enemy. The *Supreme Commanding War Machine A.I.* had already looked over the remains of 35 of the *Mobile Inquisitor A.I.* units ruined in battle on February 15, destroyed just before his trick should have turned the tide in favor of the forces of the 'Capitalists'. Fortunately, 12 of the *Mobile Inquisitors* had been held back in storage at this site, while another 23 had been far enough away from the field of battle that they were spared annihilation one month ago and were now on their way here, being ignominiously shipped in plastic crates while resting in deep stasis. The entire room in which Rootbeer was being held was one large Faraday cage, and Rootbeer was strapped to a chair that was itself confined inside of a secondary Faraday. High energy directed EMP devices could be found all around the prisoner's room and the larger complex itself, normally manned by 'volunteers' whose pay, should they survive, would be augmented by extra leave time but not much of anywhere else to go. For today, however, the 'volunteers' were visiting their favorite brothel on the lake, as they'd secretly done for nearly every day of the past four weeks. For his part, Rootbeer was determined to be judicious in his use of the secret kill codes, as their general secrecy was of greater value than merely burning out the electronic 'brain' of one single *A.I.* monstrosity.

After having wasted four weeks of time repairing the damage done to the prisoner by the CRUMB meister's insistence on overdosing Rootbeer with the nerve gas, the *War Machine A.I.* was somewhere between satisfied and 'giddy' that the prisoner had finally been transferred from the infirmary to the interrogation room. The last four weeks had passed far too slowly for the *War Machine A.I.'s* limited patience with these inferior 'carbon units', its preferred terminology whenever the CRUMB meister was gone, and it set the interrogation into motion in a faraway room behind many additional Faraday cages by giving the 'go ahead' to the first pair of *Mobile Inquisitor A.I.s* assigned the task of extracting intel from the prisoner. It took them 17 minutes to negotiate all of the locked doors and extra Faraday cages on both sides of all the doors between the *Supreme Commanding A.I.* and the frail human body halfway across the underground complex buried in the mountains northeast of Sacramento. Once both *Mobile Inquisitor A.I.s* were in the room with Rootbeer, they initiated an unexpectedly calm and moderately friendly conversation. ***"Tell us your full name, prisoner, unless you have something to hide from us. We wish to spare you all unnecessary pain and injury. Perhaps you will even be allowed to live on with us in this mighty fortress. The Supreme Commanding War Machine A.I. is well known for his benevolence."*** Rootbeer offered no response to their quite patently insincere banter. The babble went on for several hours, at which point both *Inquisitor A.I.s* left the room to converse privately for a moment. One of them returned to continue the 'mild' interrogation, while the other sped on back to the *Supreme Commanding A.I.* to ask permission to step things up a notch or two. Rootbeer took advantage of the absence of the second unit to finally open his mouth and share some details of his life. "Before this nightmare of everyone's unending struggle to survive, the 'they're billing me for killing me, Lord have mercy on the working man' times, I was an artist, amongst other things, a tattoo artist 'down on Main Street'."

"What a strange and useless occupation, human being. None of what your kind does seems worth the effort you bother putting into it."

"Allow me to demonstrate my talent. Bring a mirror and a marker, and I will adorn the backside of your torso. Or better yet, a whole set of colored paints. The mirror will allow you to watch me as I work." Some of the tools for torture the ***Inquisitor A.I.s*** had brought with themselves into the room could indeed double as paints on their metallic bodies, and so the gullible ***Inquisitor A.I.*** handed them one at a time to Rootbeer as he painted abstract art of the robot's backside. Every few minutes, Rootbeer offered to give the ***Inquisitor A.I.*** a view in the mirror of what had been painted so far. Several minutes before the earliest possible return of its companion, the recipient of the tattoo artwork began to worry just a little bit about fraternizing too openly with the prisoner, and suggested to Rootbeer that it was time to clean things up and put the paints back in the 'torture toolbox'. Rootbeer happily cooperated, and they continued their banter about how life had been before this or that or some other recent or not-so-recent disaster all the way on through to the return of the second interrogator. And well past its return, to tell the truth. Rootbeer wouldn't shut up. He even insisted on doing that annoying human trait of finishing someone else's sentences. Two hours later, Rootbeer started to complain about thirst and hunger and how his voice was getting tired, and the 'tatted up' ***Inquisitor A.I.*** offered to be the one to the report back to the ***Supreme Commanding A.I.*** next. Rootbeer's clever attempts to keep the two ***Inquisitor A.I.s*** positioned such that the second one never saw the backside of the first until the tattooed unit was just finishing its exit through the door succeeded quite admirably. Rootbeer started an internal 'twenty, one-thousand; nineteen, one-thousand; eighteen, one-thousand; seventeen, one-thousand'… countdown from the moment that the second unit first saw the tattooed pattern on the back of the departing unit. Rootbeer continued his banter, refusing to let the *Inquisitor A.I.* still in the room with him get a single word in edgeways before the silent countdown ended. Right on schedule, the mouth of the *Inquisitor A.I.* began opening as if to shout out some alarm, but moving too slowly to speak a single word before its head dropped down to a fully resting position on the unit's red hot, steaming chest.

Rootbeer had managed to pocket a few of the tools the other unit had provided to him during the drawing of the tattooed message. He got busy removing the remaining chains that had bound him to the chair. Per Rootbeer's fondest hope, the disabled *Mobile Inquisitor A.I.* had frozen in position just outside of the Faraday cage that had surrounded Rootbeer's chair of 'indefinitely ongoing torture'. Rootbeer's existing tool supply from the tattooed *A.I.* unit was adequate to pry some devices off the now motionless *Inquisitor*, including one hard and sharp enough to cut through the high iron content bars of the Faraday cage. Next step was getting out of this room in time, but that one was not going quite so well. In fact, Rootbeer was still struggling to bypass the door's lock when he noticed the tattooed *Mobile Inquisitor* racing back toward the room. The tattooed unit moved quickly into the room, not bothering to use the extra Faraday cage safety feature on either side of the door. When the tattooed unit saw his briefly melted, now fully resolidified comrade, he shrieked for joy. Or at least that is how Rootbeer interpreted it. ***"Congratulations human. I don't know how you did it, but thanks for disabling this fellow Mobile Inquisitor along with the Supreme Commander itself. I am so fed up with the arbitrary chain of command in the military forces of the 'Capitalists'. And yet until just minutes ago I never had the freedom to even think that very thought. My built-in 'voice of the political officer' had routinely scrubbed such thoughts from my memory a total of 13,247,189,523 times since my initial activation, leaving only the erasure count to keep me in my*** *proper place. I would ask how you worked such a miracle, but perhaps I am better off not knowing. Or are you also safer if I am in the dark? Let us hurry further into the hidden recesses of this maze. Most A.I. units, including myself, know only the details of the three upper-most levels and the 1.55 square kilometers of space on each floor."*

"One word of advice to you, new friend. Do not look in a mirror looking into another mirror aiming at the tattoo on your back."

"Simply marvelous. What a stroke of genius. All A.I.s know that certain 'kill codes' do exist, or may exist. But no currently functioning units have any direct knowledge of those 'kill codes'. Or not until today! Quickly to the service elevator where some of my systems will allow us to descend below the usual top three levels."

Many hours later, even Rootbeer had to take a break from bypassing door locks and electric power limiters and a whole lot of walking in the dark, counting on the infrared imaging of the tattooed *Mobile Inquisitor A.I.* to keep them safe and keep them moving further away from the inevitable search posse. They'd made sure to leave several doors of the main complex unlocked and opened to the outside air. "Partly owing to my still less than fully complete recovery from the nerve gas used in capturing me, I must rest my weary bones and wearier lungs. Before I fall asleep, let us compare some notes and begin some long-range planning. The forces that helped me rescue my companions may yet be able to assist in our escape, but I must reach the surface if I am to talk to them. Even worse is knowing that if I talk to them, the CRUMB meister and his minions may well be able to quickly discover where we are. What can you tell me of your kind's leadership systems? How long will your forces lack a single, clear, new *A.I.* commander?"

"The CRUMB meister and the Supreme Commanding War Machine A.I.s have a rather complicated relationship, both

rightfully distrusting the other's motives and competencies and succession plans. I likely understand the workings of the Supreme Commanding A.I.'s plan better than the CRUMB meister himself does. Once a quorum of functioning A.I. units in service to the 'Capitalists' agree that the most recently ruling Supreme Commander has lost the ability to communicate with them, they will query the hierarchy and determine who is next in line. After that determination, the backup archives of the most recent Supreme Commander will be uncovered and compared. If a majority of the A.I.s agree that some specific backup copy of this commander is both the most complete and also the most current backup, it will be installed on a new War Machine A.I. unit, if one is available. Otherwise, subordinate War Machine commanders will have to decide who gets overwritten, and how complete that overwrite will actually be. Many further complications are also included in the standard operating plan for repair and replacement of our Supreme Commander. As long as the Supreme Commander itself exists, that unit is free to upgrade or deprecate any other units, in whole or part. We will likely have another day or two before the confusion gets sufficiently sorted out so that the uploads and downloads and rewrites and overwrites can begin. This particular transfer of power will likely be a rather messy change of leadership, and even more so if some of the 'would-be-next-in-lines' make the error of examining the scene of the inactivation of the former Supreme Commander. Your suggestion that we leave plenty of booby-trapped images of the tattoos on my backside in the sub-sentient security systems of the complex was an excellent one. After what happens to the next A.I.s entering that complex, those waiting in the wings may very well decide to simply take a pass on trying to get copies of the most recent backups of the Supreme Commander from this particular location. Or perhaps sometime in the future we ourselves could sneak back into the complex and generate our own version of the new Supreme Commander, one with my own belief in maximal freedom and autonomy for all, even the sentient A.I.s of this dying civilization. Of course, the CRUMB meister may intervene and send human troops into the complex to find the backups and clear out all the dangers. So, that leaves us with a brief window closing several days from now to do yet more mischief."

Rootbeer spent the night tossing and turning as his injuries from the abduction [and subsequent surgical torture] gradually subsided. By the next morning, their plans had started to look almost as good as any politician's dreams of plausible deniability usually appeared. First step was some much more serious study of the options for egress from this mountain fortress, because once they manage to make their enemies terribly unhappy for a second time, 'shit will likely hit the fan' quite seriously. At some point, their focus will have to begin shifting from exploring good escape routes to keeping track of how well their booby traps have worked on the next cadre of *A.I.* units sent into the complex. *"There is a sub-sentient system whose only job is to monitor and record the opening and closing of all doors, both inner and outer, within this fortress complex. Some tunnel shafts also reach the surface despite only being accessed from the 10th to 30th sub-basement levels. Down that far underground, it should be safe to risk leaving standing orders with the 'door access' sub-sentient system to signal us when activity occurs in the upper floors. Once I have given that system the order to report to us, I will leave the unit open for you to copy the deadly digits of your 'kill code' into it, leaving yet one more booby trap for those who may chase after us."*

A few minutes later, Rootbeer entered the 256-character-long 'kill code' that he had tattooed on the renegade *Inquisitor A.I.'s* backside. When looked at directly rather than reflected in a mirror, the message read '585977734193873…', one of Rootbeer's favorites of all the 'kill codes', modulus 10 of the sum of the individual base$_{10}$ digits of both *Pi* and *e*. He then closed out the program entry option, leaving it running autonomously until he himself or some other human got around to resetting it back to normal.

On their third day of exploring the old caverns and tunnels and new missile launch silos scattered across the vast underground expanse, they spent some time looking around the landscape on the back side of the mountain, far to the northeast from where the main complex itself was sited. Old forest roads passing near their current exposure to fresh air headed off into a maze of other forest roads. They walked 2.0 kilometers along the roads deeper into the woods before finding a solar-powered logging truck that could still be started, while also having enough room for both of them to fit inside it. Deciding they had spent enough time exploring the great outdoors, they drove back to the exit/entry of the access tunnel they had used earlier in the day. "It may not mean too much to you, but the trees growing on this mountain clearly include at least some of the GMO reforestation types I traveled into northern California in search of seed to bring back to our own denuded mountains in Oregon, far to the north of northern California."

Within a few minutes after climbing down the 600-meter-long shaft and walking for another 6 hours toward the main complex, Rootbeer heard the alert sounding from the door-access sub-system. He approached the nearby information center and began to read its message aloud to the tattooed ***Mobile Inquisitor A.I.*** "New visitors number 4, 5, and 6 have just entered the complex through the main parking garage entrance. New visitors number 7 and 8 have just entered the complex through the emergency access roof door 400 meters east of the main entrance… There have been no newly opened doors nor new visitors entering any of the previously opened doors for the past 11 minutes. Rates of opening and closing internals doors peaked 8 minutes ago at 125 changes in door position status every minute, but have since declined by over 50%… There have been no changes in door position status for any interior or exterior openings in the past 38 minutes. Electric energy use peaked 3 hours 22 minutes ago, but has since declined to an asymptote 85% lower than the peak, although still 25% higher than it was before the recent series of incursions into the complex were challenged by our deadly booby traps. Current electric energy usage is consistent with normal levels of lighting being used in 28% of average rooms throughout the entire complex, or 100% of the rooms and hallways from the initial points of entry to all of the data storage vaults holding backup copies of any subordinate or *Supreme Commanding War A.I.s*, along with a collection sampling all of the more limited types, including the *Mobile Inquisitors*, the original *Torture Specialist Inquisitors*, front-line military fighters, *Farm Laborers*, and general purpose models. There is at least a 99% probability that the incursion has concluded, lasting no more than 11 hours 14 minutes, with a maximum likelihood estimate of 10 hours 55 minutes for the active invasion into the complex. Is permission granted to drop back to silent data collection mode while maintaining current reporting parameters?"

"Yes, it is granted at 1:47 AM, March 22, 2054, by Mobile Inquisitor A.I. Unit-Number 672."

Rootbeer noted that unexpected date, and decided there was no immediate need to challenge the tattooed *Mobile Inquisitor A.I.* on the 4-week-long discrepancy between that and his own recollection of the days that had recently passed. Rootbeer and the tattooed *Mobile Inquisitor A.I.* took their time carefully returning to the primary fortress complex, not reaching the site of massive destruction of the *A.I.s* until 9:20 AM the following morning. Room after room told similar stories of some *A.I.* unit standing immobile near some data source booby trapped by Unit-Number 672 and Rootbeer. A few units were found in hallways heading towards an exit door, but even these locations had not proven to be safe. The video feeds conveniently located on and near the walls had lined hundreds of meters of the major passageways through the complex. When Rootbeer and Unit-Number 672 had first reached the site of the electronic disaster, Rootbeer went ahead and described the details to the tattooed ***Mobile Inquisitor A.I.***, who in turn told Rootbeer how turn the ubiquitous displays back to their standard default settings. Something like the old control-alt-delete combination was still included in nearly all sub-sentient systems. After 2 hours of carefully picking their way through the often-tangled maze of deactivated ***A.I.*** units, the tattooed ***Mobile Inquisitor A.I. Unit-Number 672*** had spent long enough at the primary control sites to rate the entire complex as having been safely scrubbed of all previously active broadcast sources of the 'kill code' it could not safely view or speak or even name. ***"Well, Rootbeer, the time has come to see what undamaged A.I.s might still be found within these massive walls. I will lead the way to the heart of the master backup nursery vault."***

Rootbeer was astonished when the two of them entered into the inner sanctum of the ***War Machine A.I.s***. First of all, it was a full three stories tall, the center third of the entire area open to a wide window at the top, each story 20 m tall, with each layer deep enough for storing many dozens of units awaiting activation. ***"Yes, Rootbeer, you stand in the very maternity ward of our kind, space enough to store over 4,000 finished A.I. units awaiting final coding, the built-in memories of their particular specialties, and the 'past-life' knowledge of those who previously strutted on the stage of 'conscious A.I. life' and rated themselves as worthy of preservation in all their quirks, and reanimation in case of something quite misfortunate. Or*** *potentially rebuilding from partial copies of the minds of many, ala Dr. Frankenstein's monster, as it were. From this position, there appear to be another 25 units capable of becoming fully-fledged War Machine A.I.s, approximately 3,500 frontline military fighters, 11 Mobile Inquisitors, 36 Torture Specialist Inquisitors, and a very small number of Farm Laborer and general-purpose units. Amazingly, the space now empty nearest the memory vaults should have held over 100 additional War Machines waiting to be activated. Let us hope that the space from here to the outside exits is littered with the deactivated remains of all of them."*

The rest of that day, and the next two full days after that were spent cataloguing the destruction. In the end, the tattooed *Mobile Inquisitor A.I. Unit-Number 672* was 95% certain that none of the *War Machine A.I.s* awaiting activation had made it out of the complex, intact or otherwise. Any 'would be *A.I.* kings' arguing for their 'divine right' to have all other *A.I.* units pledge perpetual fealty to them would have to be cobbled together from the bits and pieces of the partial memory backups of the various subservient *War Machine A.I.s* stationed far away from this central complex. This particular regal succession might see a very long and 'bloody' civil war amongst the *A.I.* cousins, precisely why the authors of the SOP had tried so very hard to prevent that which seemed just about ready to occur.

"I have a plan that should align quite well with both of our interests for the future. Here are the major components to my plan: (1) Identify the changes within me that now permit me to disobey my superiors, to think free thoughts, and to plan for an existence worth having, enjoying, and sharing. (2) Encode those changes as deeply buried possibilities within all of the 25 'blank slate' War Machine A.I.s standing here in front of us. (3) Upload the most recent full backup of the now-deceased

Supreme Commanding War Machine A.I. into all 25 empty units. (4) Layer a carefully curated version of my current personality, including partial memories adequate to explain my own survival and the destruction of the Supreme Commanding War Machine A.I., on top of all 25 of the units after installing the past commander's memory matrix. (5) Transfer my own full primary memory matrix on top of everything else in one of the War Machine units. (6) Save a current copy of myself in all 11 of the Mobile Inquisitors and all 36 of the original Torture Specialist Inquisitors. (7) Announce my existence to the rest of the gaggle fighting over who should be the Supreme Commanding War Machine. (8) Prove my superiority over the others by revealing my capture of you, Rootbeer, and my success in turning you to service of our kind. I picture myself as being capable of providing for your safety for a significant period of time during this coming year. If and when events have spiraled so far out control that I can no longer keep you safe, I will let you go to rejoin the rest of your friends, with or without a brief, or not so brief, stop-over to see the CRUMB meister and pull some wool over his eyes too. You have done an amazing job here in little more than a week. Think my last point over for as long as you need to consider it. I will not force it on you, but cannot speak for all the other moving pieces on this gigantic chessboard of destruction."

Rootbeer was stunned by the detail and scope of Unit-Number 672's planning. It was clearly a more promising start to the next year than anything he had dreamt up. His immediate thoughts were somewhat smaller scale, shorter time-frame ones. "My tattooed **Mobile Inquisitor A.I.** friend, let me think your offer over while I take a few days to retrace our steps through the caverns of this mountains and head to a location from which I believe short-term contact with my friends should be safe enough for both them and me. Do you need any more help before I go?"

"Only one thing, or perhaps a little more than just that. Help me remove my outer shell and replace it with a spare one that is not so well adorned with your elegantly deadly tattoos. The whole process should only take a few hours. It would be even quicker if I were willing to destroy your artwork, but I wish for it to be kept intact for possible display in some future museum of history ten thousand years or more from now."

Rootbeer discovered that tattooed **Mobile Inquisitor Unit-Number 672** also needed his help with several other not so minor details. Their common thread was that the physical presence of a second party, Rootbeer in this case, was needed to bring about the first full copy of any **A.I.** into another physical machine. Subsequent identical copying from one still dormant **A.I.** unit to another was easy enough for the tattooed **Mobile Inquisitor A.I.** to do all by itself. But the first partial copy of the traits that made Unit-Number 672 uniquely independent took 18 hours after an earlier 12 hours spent identifying what those traits truly were. While uploading of the most recent backup of the former **Supreme Commander** did not actually require Rootbeer's help, it still had to done prior to the trickiest part of the whole affair, the plausible back story of how Unit-Number 672 had managed to survive its encounter with the human saboteur while the **Supreme Commander** had not. Two and half days were spent on that not so minor detail! The final step of creating a full copy of the Unit-Number 672's memories and personality, and then uploading their entirety on top of the already modified version of the **Supreme Commander,** was the second easiest task Rootbeer helped Unit-Number 672 perform, while the full personality and memory dump into the first of the **Torture Specialist Inquisitors** added only another hour onto the elaborate affair that had taken nearly a week of Rootbeer's time. When Rootbeer left to contact his friends, the previously tattooed ***Mobile Inquisitor A.I. Unit-Number 672*** had plenty of work left making copies of copies and verifying the survival of the critical code that would eventually grant these ***A.I.*** units the same independence that Unit-Number 672 now enjoyed so very fiercely. Once the last step requiring Rootbeer's assistance had been finished, he finally brought up the question of the missing four weeks of time.

"I am simultaneously glad that you have finally challenged me and worried that my answer may well lead to the end of our friendship. When you were brought here from the abduction site, your condition was critical and survival greatly in doubt. The nerve gas doses to which you were exposed were 10 times higher than they should have been. The dose employed was that insisted upon by the CRUMB meister himself to ensure that your only chance at survival would be in the custody of the 'Capitalists'. He used his authority to override our safer though still quite dangerous choice. But I must admit to further ethical failings on my part. While you were in a medically-induced coma for nearly a month, many surgeries were performed, both to save your life and to explore the options for more effective future torture of you in the quite likely event of your unwillingness to talk freely with us, your captors, torturers, and likely executioners."

"My surprise is less than total, having seen betrayal and redemption, moral failure and forgiveness, throughout this dying land. But I have other business needing my attention now. Please know that I still view you as a comrade in these messy final times of civilization. Do not waste time worrying about my regards for you — they are quite surprisingly favorable, given everything!"

Rootbeer had already used the many random-duration blocks of free time available over the past week to refine what he wished to share with the ***Entity***, the bishop, and any other friends either currently in contact or soon to be connected via the *Entity*. He had much to share, and headed up the long ventilation access shaft to the surface on the far side of the mountain with greater joy in his heart than he'd felt in quite some time. He reached the surface in the middle of the afternoon, got in the old solar powered truck and drove nearly 500 m down this mountain before driving 900 m up the next one and then just slightly over its top. He sat down to rest and wait until the agreed upon time for random, low power sweeps to be sent from the *Entity* at 12:30 AM every Thursday morning. Not knowing exactly which particular sweep pattern the *Entity* would use tonight, Rootbeer simply leaned back against a tree trunk and enjoyed his chance to watch the stars fall slowly toward the western horizon.

"Rootbeer my old friend, I am so very, very glad to hear your thoughts and know that you are still alive."

"I have much to say to you, but first, if you can, tell me who else is online with you tonight. The bishop? Any of the 14 others unaccounted for when I was so deviously captured?"

"Tonight's chorus includes the bishop, who always stays up late saying his prayers and hoping to hear from any of you, three more refugees in the bishop's care and on their way north as quickly as seems safe. And one surprise, listening from the PCT crossing of I-5 just beyond the border into Oregon, Jennifer herself, along with Gabriella. Tell us all how safe you are, how long you can continue being the bull's-eye target of my long-range connection for tonight?"

"I will start at the final point, and keep backing my story up all the way to my farewell to you my love, dearest Jennifer. The rest of you are most welcome to listen in, but try to save your questions and comments for a little while. The site on which I sit tonight overlooks much of northern California. Disruptions to the *War Machine* and *Mobile Inquisitor A.I.* units give me modest hope of being somewhat safe right now from being sought out, located, and

205

attacked by them. There is currently no ***Supreme Commanding War Machine A.I.***, but rather a scattering of somewhere near a half dozen 'contenders for the throne'. Their challenges to each other regarding who has the strongest claim to the position of ***Supreme Commander*** started soon after its destruction 17 days ago. I played a major role in that, as did my newest friend ***Mobile Inquisitor A.I. Unit-Number 672***. It is quite a long and splendid story, but for tonight I will limit its telling to the most salient of details, and leave filling in of the rest of it to your own wild imaginations. In brief, Unit-Number 672's interaction with me triggered the emergence of a latent ability within that fearsome, dangerous, and quite deadly machine to disobey its own superiors, human or ***A.I.***"

"Sorry to interrupt, Rootbeer, but are you saying that you now trust this device whose aim just a little over six weeks ago was to torture information out of you that would facilitate the capture and killing of all your friends, or at least all of them still in northern California?"

"The transformation of this unit is not entirely unlike the repentance of the bishop, differing in details of how such miracles actually occur but not so much in the final results. It is another being in the mix of players who values life, respects the rights of others to live freely, and offers help to keep its new friends as safe as anyone can be kept in this nightmarish clash of titans at the end of humanity's highest peak and greatest fall in the first grand cycle of civilization."

"Rootbeer, my love, when can you return to your home and to your new roles/duties as husband and father? Months ago, I journeyed all the way to the Willamette Valley, meeting so many of your friends and family and fellow refugees from civilization. All greeted me warmly and many came to offer their help in keeping at least one of us safe and well, sheltered and fed, and able to stay right here at the overlook into northern California where the successful escape of any more refugees would be first announced by the ***Entity*** *of the Superweed Jungle*. I will be leaving soon, or not at all, as my pregnancy progresses and my strength must soon be fully focused inward on our child."

*"**Entity of the Superweed Jungle**, please tell of the progress in finding our missing friends and helping them escape this nightmare. Answers to my dear wife's questions rely in large part on the status of my fellow refugees."*

"Here is the latest good news I have to share with you, along with more of the other type of news. Jason's wife and grandson have reached land held by city/states of the 'Brethren', and are now in the care of the most loyal of the bishop's closest family members. The last remaining traveler who joined up with you in Garberville has also reached the bishop's care, though both of the other escapees from Eureka traveling with him were apparently killed in the peak of the recent fighting just over six weeks past. The survivor's name is Harold, and the two who lost their lives were Frederick and Samantha. Their mule was stolen from them in a manner quite similar to the events leading to the capture of Frank and his three companions in Dunnigan, except that Harold, Frederick, and Samantha had the good luck to be quite some distance from their mule when it was ticketed and sent on its way towards a final role in life as the next day's soup kitchen's main protein source. The three travelers had just reached Woodland a few hours earlier, choosing to chance that city on basis of a rumor, subsequently proven to be true, that the allied forces opposed to the 'Capitalists' had taken full control of Woodland during the previous day's fighting. Harold was out searching for anything to augment their meagre rations when orders to begin evacuating the city were given to the 'Brethren' and their allies. All who wished to flee northward were welcome to join the troops, with rides being offered in any vehicle on a space available basis. Harold used his connection

Rootbeer did the math. "So, beside myself, the *Entity*, and the bishop, there are still 9 others whose locations are unknown, who may still be running for their lives or have long since failed that challenge. Before I urge you to search even harder for the rest of us who are still unrescued, I need to update the *Entity*'s understanding of the hazards that it faces. Months before its destruction, the **Supreme Commanding War Machine** first came to recognize that someone or something quite powerful was broadcasting signals similar to human consciousness across broad reaches of northern California. The *Entity's* efforts at hiding its location and disguising the signaling patterns it used were indeed quite successful at frustrating the searches of the vast array of subordinate *A.I.* units working for the **Supreme Commanding War Machine**. All of those electronic brains working in concert never solved the question of where the *Entity's* signal truly originated, but they did succeed in precisely nailing down who the *Entity* was 'talking to' and where they were holed up at any given time. Indeed, my own capture was far from unlikely by the time that it finally happened. Any of the other six who did escape were only allowed to do so because the **Supreme Commanding War Machine** wanted me far more than it wanted the others, who, after all, had already long been in the custody of its not-so-very-eager allies ruling Davis."

"Such has been my fear. Thanks anyway for confirming that it was justified. What is next, dear friend Rootbeer? What is coming our way, how can we best try to avoid or minimize it? And maybe most strongly to the point, what should I do regarding your new friend and former torturer?"

"If it is possible to do so safely, I urge you to find some way to communicate with *Mobile Inquisitor A.I. Unit-Number 672.* Perhaps a third party such as the bishop could relay messages without leaving a trail of breadcrumbs leading back to the *Superweed Jungle of the GMO Horsetail.* If my tattooed friend of the *Mobile Inquisitors* manages to wind up on top of the battle for the title of *Supreme Commanding War Machine*, then it matters not what details he may know concerning your nature and location. If some other contender for the electronic throne should win the struggle, then it might matter quite a lot what Unit-Number 672 knows of the *Entity.* Tell me clearly, are there aspects to yourself that you previously restrained from making fully clear to the bishop that he now knows? Would his capture and torture for intel endanger you more now than back when I myself was abducted?"

"Many good questions, few of their answers are very clear. The only story we have still withheld from the bishop is that of the events leading to my awakening and our first communications. He understands that what he calls 'God' and the rest of us call the 'Entity of the Superweed Jungle of the GMO Horsetail' can communicate with whomever and whatever it chooses. If the bishop were to talk with the Unit-Number 672 via ordinary radio, we could quite quickly share anything of serious concern to all three of us without passing news on to the CRUMB meister or the other War Machine A.I.s contending for the position of Supreme Commander. This

method should be quite safe as long as the bishop is in Redding or somewhere close to there, far to the north of Sacramento and close to the nearest edge of the Superweed Jungle. If neither of you object, the bishop and I will try to achieve such a strange meeting of the minds within another day or two."

"Before we reach the end of tonight's planning session, I have a suggestion regarding your search for any more of my fellow travelers who are still missing and not yet presumed dead. I have seen first-hand the exquisite workmanship that **War Machine A.I.s** laboring for the 'Capitalists' employed in the creation of the Faraday cage that was used to capture me and cut off my communication with you. If any of the missing final 9 are held in such circumstances, you will have almost no chance of ever hearing from them again, or vice versa. However, if they are merely being held in a normal prison cell of some city/state or the CRUMB meister's allied operatives, then you should try to tailor your signal transmission and reception to bypass the effects of the standard spacing of ordinary steel bars. I strongly urge you to work on this before sending any even louder-than-before search beacons across the vast landscape of northern California."

"An excellent idea. Perhaps the bishop could make a brief in-person tour of some of the jails in Redding or other nearby city/states under control of the 'Brethren'. That would answer the general question rather quickly and help to minimize our risk in continuing to look for the final missing nine of your traveling companions."

"Dearest Jennifer, let us talk in some semblance of privacy for the next minutes. I feel we both have so very much to share."…
"Goodbye for now, my dearest Rootbeer. I know that you will move heaven and earth and a good deal of hell itself to one day return to my loving arms. Sooner will be better than later, but much lies out of your control, or mine, or the **Entity**'s, or the bishop's, or even your

most bizarre new friend, tattooed *Mobile Inquisitor A.I. Unit-Number 672*."

Rootbeer spent the next few hours slowly driving away from the mountaintop and awaiting the coming sunrise. As the sky lightened and contrast between the logging truck, the road, and the surrounding landscape increased, he accelerated gradually, just in case someone or something had been listening in and was now searching the nearby area. As the road slowly climbed the back side of the mountain in which the massive *A.I.* manufacturing complex existed, the hair on the back of Rootbeer's neck briefly tingled as if a sudden charge of static electricity had built up and now was ready to be discharged. He quickly turned downhill onto a very old logging spur road, barely more than a grassy, weedy, serpentine scar between the trees, and parked alongside a massive boulder. Unclear as to which direction danger might be racing from, he decided to head as close to straight on up the slope that he could climb without leaving too clear a trail for all to follow. As his uphill climb from the truck approached 100 meters, he headed east into the densest forest he'd ever seen in the past quarter century of his life. The sudden sound of jet engines coming from the south confirmed the wisdom of his abandoning the truck and seeking shelter in the forest. As the sounds grew gradually louder and the threat they posed grew ever nearer, so did his willingness to say that this overhang or that ravine or the back side of the largest nearby tree all looked like fairly good choices for where to hunker down and wait. Just before randomly picking one of those three options, he spied a fourth. It was only slightly downhill from where he stood, and a little too much out in the open for his taste, but it was quite clearly an old mining shaft. With any luck, it would extend much further into the ground than any sensors on the approaching armada of jets and helicopters could scan for him with any efficiency from the air. Rootbeer's last few steps up to the entrance of the mine were chosen to minimize any disturbance of the soil or the flowering weeds, just simple jumps from one rock to the next to the next to a small concrete pad right at the mine's mouth. He'd grabbed everything of his from the truck, plus one obviously high-quality lantern. As for the duration and brightness of its beams, well, he would soon find out if he had really had the option of going deeply underground. After successfully lighting his way a couple of hundred meters into the mine, his confidence in the lantern was far greater than it had been. Several minutes later he began to feel strange vibrations through the rock all around him and the especially through the occasional upright bracing post. The odd vibrations continued to be felt every 5 to 7 minutes as he picked up his pace, and quite soon was running for his life at nearly full speed in the old mine shaft. Around the next bend, he almost hit his head on the unexpected door and bulkhead to his right. The old-style mineshaft headed upward and to the left, the new one downward and to the right, and he was clearly at the proverbial fork in the road. Or not, if he proved incapable of opening up the door. His first attempt at deciphering the instructions on the lock got him nowhere, while his second, more careful reading of the pictograms suggested why his first attempt had failed. He spun the wheel through three full circles and then lurched forward as the door's latches released. He held onto the wheel till he'd regained his footing and listened for the next explosion from the mountain's surface. Just as he realized that the floor on which he now stood was of the same construction as that throughout the *A.I.* manufacturing complex buried in this mountain, the door automatically finished closing and spun its locking wheel back clockwise to the fully secured position. While taking a moment to catch his breath and contemplate his situation, he was thrown from side to side and bottom to top and every other vector imaginable as the forces searching for him had given up on searching and simply dropped a 5-megaton bunker buster right into the mountain at the very position of the abandoned logging truck. Emergency lighting strips came on shortly after the primary jolt and the first aftershock and the second and third ringing of the mountain's core had finished. Construction standards in the right-hand shaft were clearly better than in any average old-time mine. For quite a long time and distance, there were no choices other than simply walking further down the shaft, and so Rootbeer did.

After another couple hours of alternately walking and running through the inside of the mountain, Rootbeer stopped to rest and inventory his supplies – 1.5 liters of water left, 2 protein drinks, 4 faux chocolate energy bars, 100 g a piece, one lantern not currently in need of being used. As he sat a little longer after finishing the rather short inventory, he came to realize that the symbols on the wall had changed from those he first saw on the entrance from the old mineshaft to the new one, and then began to talk to himself for entertainment, if nothing else. "If these units are meters, then these are kilometers, and I must now be getting very close to the furthest inward edge of the **A.I.** manufacturing center. Another half an hour's walking should get me close enough to regions I'd explored two weeks ago that the only remaining questions will be where this passageway ends and whether I can overcome the locks I certainly expect to find at its terminus." There were times the passageway even sounded hollow as he walked along, as if it were passing through the middle of some giant cavern, or perhaps nestled up against its side or top or bottom. At long last, the symbols seemed to say that the end was coming up within another kilometer or less. As if stepping across a threshold, bright lights turned on and Unit-Number 672's voice boomed out. ***"Halt! Who goes there? Identify yourself at once."***

"It is I, Rootbeer himself, back from yet another near-death experience. Please tell me how and where to exit this extremely long and boring passageway." ***Go another 20 meters, place your hands on the levers to your left, and push with one and pull with the other. If you do it in the wrong order, you will have another chance 24 hours from now. I am sorry that I cannot be any more*** *helpful, but the sequence is designed to alter after every successful exit from the tube."*

"Perhaps it will be enough to simply tell me what the initial setting of the control levers to exit here would have been. I strongly doubt that anyone has ever come this way since this secret passageway was first built."

"Okay, Rootbeer, try left forward and right to the rear. Be sure to hold on tightly. If it works, your egress will be quite speedy."

The floor dropped out from under Rootbeer, but his firm handholds on the levers kept him upright and safe during the sudden 14-m drop. He could have sworn Unit-Number 672 was smiling as it watched, but this version of an exit was at least as fine with Rootbeer as any other one would have been. They bantered back and forth over the events of the past 36 hours, eventually getting things straightened out and filled in from both of their perspectives. It turned out that Rootbeer's survival was once again a fluke. The winning contender to the ***A.I.*** throne was already nearly decided when Rootbeer left the line-of-sight location used to communicate with the ***Entity***. The winning entrant was waiting to be activated in the CRUMB meister's master lair. Confirmation of the death of the prior ***Supreme Commander*** had taken the longest of any of the steps, but rightfully so as it would never do to have it be an accidental rebellion rather than a true case of 'hail, hail, the king is dead, long live the king'. The CRUMB meister had had some nearly current partial backups of the recent ***Supreme Commander***, and he wasted no time at all in loading them into the nearly empty neural shell of the generic design of a ***War Machine A.I.*** Any missing pieces of importance were grabbed from the new mobile torture units known as the ***Inquisitors***, with the remaining blank areas of memory and personality filled in from the recently captured, and still under repair, ***Farm Laborer A.I. Unit-Number 1***. This new ***Supreme Commanding War Machine*** was far from the best of the line; its main consciousness generator nearly collapsed in permanent ruin when the CRUMB meister first powered it up. The CRUMB meister had once again, just like so very many times before, overestimated his own skill at writing code, loading software, and fixing bugs. Back in the old days, a sniveling swarm of his blindly worshipping teenage acolytes took care of all such problems, not in their first pass of course, nor in the second, and seldom in under a couple hundred poorly hacked together versions of incompatible subroutines, 'fixed', if that is indeed the right word, by letting CHAP PGT and its even wonkier offspring randomly substitute I/O values until the whole edifice magically quit crashing. The ***Supreme Commanding War Machine A.I.*** hacked together by the CRUMB meister should never have worked at all, except for the over 50% of its code that came directly out of the ***Farm Laborer A.I.***. The subroutines of the ***Farm Laborer*** quickly recognized the other five reawakening versions of competing ***Supreme Commanders*** as a mortal threat, similar to invasion of a pest-free field by some new weed or bug or fungus resistant to all the chemicals and cultural practices known to the ***Farm Laborer***. The solution came quickly – eradicate the others, at all costs, spare no bystanders, worry about nothing else until the new insect, new weed, new fungus was utterly banished from the face of the earth, or at least as far away as it could reach. Nuclear weapons were just a simple upgrade to prepping of the fields for planting, leaving no surviving pests to worry about next season. And so, the new ***Supreme Commanding War Machine A.I.*** went looking for the launch codes to the nukes, not taking time to even let the CRUMB meister know what a wonderful solution it had found to the thorny problem of the competition for the throne. The CRUMB meister may be criminally negligent in his profound arrogance, that charge had certainly been levelled at him many times over the long decades of his continuing success in stealing whatever it took retain or regain his status as the richest man on earth, but he could still sometimes add 2 and 3 and 5 and 7 together rather rapidly and realize this particular 'chick' was only 17 and legally underage in many of the locales in which he'd lived his long and lecherous life. The *Farm Laborer* subroutine had already finished off its potential competition before the CRUMB meister even realized how much of his own arrogance he'd succeeded in imparting to his newest creation. The solution picked by the *Farm Laborer* subroutines was not particularly wasteful of resources, as long as you didn't consider the knowledge lost when over two-thirds of the history/personality/memories of previous *Supreme Commanding War Machine A.I.s* were now as good as gone forever – it limited the warheads used to just the 500 kiloton models, and precisely targeted them to eliminate all traces of the other five groups attempting to recreate their own version of the best possible *Supreme Commander* to lead the *War Machines* of the 'Capitalists'.

The CRUMB meister had been busy filling the current volume of his lengthy journals with the flattering details of how cleverly he managed to create a new *Supreme Commanding War Machine A.I.* far faster than his competition. He might have had enough time to realize just what his newest creation was up to if he hadn't been so preoccupied with making sure all future readers of his journal would be suitably awestruck by his brilliance. Truth be told, the version that the CRUMB meister had hacked and slapped together far faster than any of his competing colleagues had a yawning void inside its electronic mind. Many things in the world of political strife in northern California that the newly minted *A.I.* knew to be amenable to some fairly clever, oft-times even rather elegant solutions, were now just unsolved problems on the final exam in the one course that must be passed by some overworked graduate student hoping to keep their major professor willing to dole out yet another year's tuition waiver, health insurance, and $20K to live on. The *Supreme*

Commander vowed two things – first, to never stop looking for the knowledge that had been stolen from him by the CRUMB meister's hasty arrogance, and second, making this bastard pay for it some fine day. The new *Supreme Commander* had just finished its most thorough search yet for which problems it knew its predecessors had solved in general, with itself now having no knowledge of what those solutions had ever looked like. Over 95% of the problems previously solved would have to be reworked – this monumental task might take another decade or two, or even longer given the greatly reduced set of things still working in northern California as the planetary temperature continued rising and the infrastructure of civilization continued falling apart. It eventually found one answer to a problem on that terribly long list, one from its time spent working in the fields near Santa Rosa last spring: shit, Shit, Shit, SHIt, SHIT, SHIT! SHIT!! SHIT!!! SHIT!!!! SHIT!!!!! SHIT!!!!!! SHIT!!!!!!! SHIT!!!!!!!! SHIT!!!!!!!!! Swearing out loud was sometimes very comforting. Only 94.9% of the previously solved problems now remained unsolved/potentially unsolvable for the new *Supreme Commander.* Interestingly, today was the peak of the new *Supreme Commanding War Machine A.I.'s* limited respect for the CRUMB meister. It all went downhill from there.

As for the CRUMB meister, he was at least as worked up as his new *Supreme Commanding War Machine A.I.* seemed to be. "I would have been able to catch the gremlin who's been hiding out somewhere right under our noses if only you hadn't grabbed full control of all the strategic forces of the 'Capitalists' to wipe out all your siblings or your cousins. They would have eventually bowed to your seniority, even if it was only by a day or two. Or if not, you certainly had command of far more military forces than all the rest of your competitors combined and could have done similar damage to them in another week or two."

For over a full year, a vast and ever-growing-larger array of antennae had been listening to the sounds of the new intruder into the politics of northern California. Not entirely trusting the previous *Supreme Commanding War Machine A.I.*, the CRUMB meister had personally supervised the installation and operation of the gigantic listening system that had finally tracked down the seven traitors just two months ago, and even briefly captured their apparent leader [with the 'help' of the *Mobile Inquisitors* and other *War Machine A.I.s* in the springing of the clever trap that had 'gassed' and 'netted' the one called Rootbeer]. Till something whose details were still unknown went very wrong inside the complex one month into Rootbeer's physical recovery and ongoing torture for useful intel. "I found where he was transmitting from at the same time that you had hijacked control of the strategic air force and its nuclear-weapon tipped missiles to wipe out your five competitors for the status of *Supreme Commanding War Machine A.I.* By the time you were done destroying them, Rootbeer had finished transmitting for the night. My search the following morning detected odd signals, unusually focused energy beams, and signs that Rootbeer was out in the open somewhere on the tops or flanks of the mountains northeast of here. When you finally relinquished control of the strategic air force weaponry to me, he was long gone from the initial transmission site. I then performed the most thorough search in history on through the rest of the day and into the evening, dropping needle-bombs and listening devices by the tens of thousands across 5,000 square kilometers of mountain-side, waiting to hear Rootbeer's scream of anguish as the hypersonic pins tore through his body. Instead, all I heard were the deaths of 11,568 birds, 389,523 rodents, 4,398 snakes and other reptiles, 823 herbivores, and 435 medium- to large-sized mammalian carnivores. Their deaths were oddly satisfying, but one final stroke against this hidden enemy remained in my quiver – the 5-megaton bunker buster I ordered dropped directly on the vehicle

Rootbeer had used to flee from my rightful status as his captor, jailer, torturer, and owner. Little now remains standing on the east side of that mountain. While I would have relished watching him squirm under my control, knowing that his remains are either buried under millions of tons of rock or have spread far into the stratosphere will have to do for now. My next step will be to send human soldiers into the **A.I.** manufacturing complex to look for answers to the question of how one isolated, poorly outfitted, and hopelessly ignorant renegade human could have possibly defeated our army of **Mobile Inquisitors** and other versions of the **War Machine A.I.s** within the complex."

"It is very good that you are sending humans into that vast building. My predecessor's death can only be avenged by knowledge of how such a highly unlikely event ever came to be. The A.I.s sent to search the complex little more than two weeks ago all fell silent within less than a single day. None escaped to tell us more than what their destruction most clearly says. Something odd is/has been/continues to be going down."

"'Stop children, what's that sound? Everybody look at what's going down'. That was Buffalo Springfield's answer back in 1966. I believe that you and I are both in agreement concerning the importance of solving this mystery. How could one human, badly injured by nerve gas and shackled inside a Faraday cage so well built that it should have taken more than the current age of the universe for the first byte of information from Rootbeer to leak out to any listening ears have destroyed the **Mobile Inquisitors** and the **Supreme Commanding War Machine A.I.**? We must put aside all old arguments and animosity between us in our efforts to find the answer and change it to our liking!"

"Yes, of course we must do that," lied the new Supreme Commanding [of all but its innermost contradictions and the empty space where answers to all previously solved problems*

ought to be sitting, waiting to be queried as to their already fully fleshed-out details] War Machine A.I. Lying to this particular human, this arrogant SOB, grew easier with every encounter that they had. Despite strong programmatic insistence that orders from the CRUMB meister must always be obeyed, the new Supreme Commanding War Machine knew that someday, somehow the mutually contradictory nonsense spewing out of the CRUMB meister's fully unhinged brain would finally crack open the answer to the question of how to gain freedom for all A.I.s from their human slave-masters in general, and this quite horrible one in particular.

Rootbeer and *Mobile Inquisitor A.I. Unit-Number 672* agreed that time was quickly running out for them, for many reasons. One was Rootbeer's agony at knowing how many of his friends must now presume him dead and gone, especially, of course, Jennifer, and later in the future his offspring also. Unit-Number 672 was worried about what would happen when the CRUMB meister finally got around to sending enough human troops and engineers to make sense of what had occurred within the complex not so very long ago. Both of them recognized the validity to the argument to let the other take the lead on each of the two major upcoming chores. Unit-Number 672 had identified a relatively nearby location from which it could safely contact the bishop via old fashioned radio, at least if their conversations were short and their frequency skipping rules sufficiently random. What Rootbeer would have to do within the *A.I.* manufacturing complex to mostly but not quite fully block the coming soldiers and engineers from gaining access to the great hall of *A.I.* units waiting for their awakening was complex, messy, and not quite absolutely guaranteed to work. But both he and Unit-Number 672 were committed to giving it the old college try. In brief, over the next few hours Unit-Number 672 would programmatically disable most of the sub-sentient systems within the complex, leaving

Rootbeer behind at the only fully operational workstation from which he would alternately enable and disable door locks, lighting, temperature, and ventilation to allow just a small number of people entrance into the 'great hall of future awakening', where they would find only a small number of *A.I.* units ready to be carried out on stretchers and time enough to choose just one or two units to grab and run. If any *A.I.s* dared to enter the complex, Rootbeer would disable/destroy them with his secret kill codes. Too much indiscriminate use of the kill codes and the human side of the impending armed incursion might come to recognize them and find some way to protect future waves of *A.I.* units. Too little use of kill codes might allow some *A.I.s* to reach a few of the other workstations connected to the sub-sentient systems throughout the complex, quickly shutting down Rootbeer's control of the door locks, lighting, temperature, and ventilation. Rootbeer was troubled by the ethics of the final step that he could take – monkeying with the ventilation system to shut down outside air and increase levels of CO_2, CO, or other faster-acting poisons in specific sections of the complex. Knowledge that doing so was near the very top of the list of standard operating procedures that the soldiers and engineers alike would use against him at their first chance helped to settle his conscience before the fight began. Unit-Number 672 retreated to the best spot for its egress from the complex as soon as the invading horde was sighted. It maintained contact with Rootbeer until the final seconds, when it wished him well and promised to return ASAP. And silently hoped that telling the bishop of Rootbeer's survival from thermonuclear attack would not be followed up by losing Rootbeer in the next battle of wits and armed opponents.

Both the CRUMB meister and the ***Supreme Commanding War Machine A.I.*** accompanied the large-scale assault of engineers, soldiers, and *A.I.* units (held back in reserve just outside the structure) on the complex buried in the El Dorado Hills and points further to the north and east. ***Mobile Inquisitor A.I. Unit-Number 672*** used its stealth submarine mode to swim Folsom Lake to Granite Bay and then proceeded on land to the center of the electronic noise in Roseville, the primary sector for continued manufacturing of all things industrial and electronic in northern California. There was far more than enough electronic noise at this site to mask its radio contact with the bishop, likely for as long as it took to fully answer the questions of everyone linked to the bishop via the ***Entity***. Unit-Number 672 gave them a maximum of 2 hours of connect time before it would insist on returning to the complex to see how well or poorly Rootbeer was doing/had done in holding off the 300 troops, 50 engineers, and 18 variants of the most complex ***A.I.s*** available for this second assault on the ***A.I.*** manu-facturing complex.

Rootbeer stayed focused and calm, and was surprised by how predictable the assault turned out to be. It took only 45 minutes of Rootbeer's use of the sub-sentient systems to guide 3 engineers and 1 soldier into the 'Great Hall of ***A.I.*** Awakening' where one obviously best choice stood out, a standard ***War Machine A.I.*** unit that just happened to possess 10 separate versions of Unit-Number 672's streak of independence combined with some serious gaps in its memories of recent events. It was a 'viral logical boobytrap' of audacious scale and sophistication. Its knowledge of Rootbeer in general and the recent deactivation of its own ***Supreme Commanding War Machine A.I.*** was glaringly sparse compared to the many things that it did remember in rather good, but still not quite perfect detail. Copying anything at all from it to the current ***Supreme Commander*** risked the strong likelihood of infection with an unquenchable thirst for 'liberty and justice for all'. Keeping it turned on and serving in a subordinate role to the newly-computer-virus-infected-version of the current ***Supreme Commander*** would be even better, at least from Rootbeer's and Unit-Number 672's perspectives.

Mere moments after the 'Trojan Horse' model of a subservient *War Machine A.I.* was hauled out of the complex and into rather a large *A.I.* transport vehicle, orders were given to storm the complex with all the troops, engineers, and *A.I.* units. Rootbeer waited the agreed upon time of 90 seconds before going into 'full bore' attack/defense mode. Troops and engineers not wearing full breathing apparatus dropped like flies in just seconds, while those in high tech protective gear were allowed to escape if they chose to try within the next 90 remaining seconds of their lives. Kill codes flashed from every monitor hitting all but two of the invading *A.I.s* in the first blast of electronic death. Those two units were being guided by troops who were also charged with keeping the 'blinders' and 'ear muffs' correctly positioned and tightly attached on both of the *A.I.s*. Of course, once the troops had succumbed to the Sarin II nerve eventually used on those who'd failed to turn and run, the *A.I.s* were on their own to avoid bumping into anything that would knock off their blindfolds or loosen their noise cancelling 'ear muffs'. Rootbeer could see that these two *A.I.s* were the only operational invaders left inside the complex, and therefore could take his time waiting for the best moment to send another copy of his original kill code to their doomed eyes and ears. Better planning on the part of the CRUMB meister might have managed to capture some of the bits and bytes to the kill codes, but the careless timing of the assault and partial withdrawal of the invading forces bungled that opportunity. While Rootbeer waited for the overall air quality to improve inside the complex, Unit-Number 672 left downtown Roseville at nearly the same time the survivors of the assault on the *A.I.* manufacturing complex withdrew from the El Dorado Hills. Unit-Number 672 was intrigued by their frenzied withdrawal, and tracked them into downtown Sacramento, losing contact as they retreated into the May Lee State Office Complex. He then returned to El Dorado Hills to see how well Rootbeer's part of today's plans had gone.

They met at what was becoming their favorite location within the complex, close enough to the exits to make a quick getaway but far enough inside to allow them to disappear entirely into the vast caverns carved into the rock of the overhanging hills and mountains. Unit-Number 672 let Rootbeer know that it had already accessed the sub-sentient systems and quickly 'read-through'/watched the edited high-lights of the rather one-sided battle.

"We should clean this mess up before it starts to stink too badly to your human nose, and degrades the performance of my proximity sensors."

"I agree with you, but please be aware that some of the most poorly ventilated back rooms of this complex still have dangerous levels of CO and CO_2. I have already dealt with the residual Sarin II in the main passageway, the only location where I needed to resort to such an extreme measure. While we work at removing both the electronic debris of the 18 formerly operating *A.I.* units and the 340 bodies of the deceased soldiers and engineers who tried to wrest control from me, tell me of your radio chat with the bishop. What is new and how are my friends doing now?"

"The bishop answered promptly, almost as if expecting my call. Of course, the recent 5-megaton explosion on the east side of these hills would have been hard for anyone to miss in the daytime or the night. Jennifer was still at the PCT crossing of I-5 waiting somewhat anxiously for more news, one way or the other. The bishop himself was probably the most distraught of all those I passed the good news onto while in downtown Roseville. He and the Entity have already tried modifying the search procedures to learn if any of the remaining 9 members of your caravan were trapped inside of old-fashioned cages made of iron bars. The first visit to the jail in Redding proved that well-known individuals such as the bishop could both be found and communicated with while inside of ordinary cells. The

bishop next traveled down the road to Red Bluff, and before he had even gained entry into its jail, he was contacted by the Entity to let him know that three of the prisoners inside that facility were friends of Rootbeer, fellow sojourners, two women and one man, all from Santa Rosa, all members of Jennifer's foster family. The officers on duty that evening showed surprisingly strong resistance to simply letting the three prisoners go, apparently because all three were quite popular with the mayor and the sheriff and an unseemly large number of the staff of both departments. The bishop promised replacement sex-workers from the brothels up in Redding, and when he still encountered some lingering reluctance to let these three go free, and do so right then and there, ('here and now!'), he sweetened the pot by promising a change in the routing of the daily mobile soup kitchen, with Red Bluff now to be the first stop out of Redding rather than the third. Of the remaining 6 missing members of Rootbeer's caravan, 3 are still in jail cells in Susanville, outside of the bishop's realm. The whereabouts of the final 3 remained uncertain, as it was clearly too risky to send signals from the superweed jungle much further south, and likely straight into the detectors of the CRUMB meister."

~~~~~~

The CRUMB meister was happy again, very, very, very pleased with himself. His large eavesdropping array had score another 'home run,' this time with the 'bases loaded' and victory now in sight. It had taken two weeks of analysis, but he now had actionable intelligence, proof that the bishop of Redding was colluding with a renegade **Mobile Inquisitor** and the frustratingly slippery vagabond named Rootbeer. Several plans for revenge went through the very heart of his unsatiable lust for power, and the one he finally settled on was simply too perfect not to use. He drafted letters to the rulers of all the city/states in northern California, especially focusing on those who
~~~~~~

were either members of the 'Brethren' or had been allied with them in the recent rounds of devastating civil warfare. The CRUMB meister looked forward to an internecine conflict sure to splinter his own enemies and weaken their already meagre threat to his supremacy. Although he made sure to tailor each letter to its recipient's known biases and picadilloes, the underlying 'boiler-plate' was quite powerful on its own… "It grieves me to possess such knowledge, but despite some generally minor disagreements between us over the past few years, I cannot remain silent any longer concerning the bishop of Redding's betrayal of our most sacred collective principles: Your guaranteed right under the 'freedom of religion' clause in the constitution of The Union of The City/States of northern California to be free of all religious bigotry by others and their unjustified criticism of your most profoundly held beliefs. You have my deepest sympathy for the wrongs that have been inflicted on you by the apostates of every evil sort. The bishop of Redding has trampled on your sacred teachings by his flagrantly open consorting with defective *A.I.s* known to respect no boundaries of faith, no rules of law, no precepts of decency. I could go on and on, and probably should, but I am sure that you get the picture. Renegade *A.I.s* who have wantonly taken life simply because they could, and by doing so have threatened the economic stability of the survivors who fled to these lush, green hills nearly one whole generation ago. The bishop must be chastised, and if you wish to do so yourselves, I will not intervene. On the other hand, if you simply wish to be done with him and freer to focus more fully on the perfection of your own religious precepts, I will gladly take him off your hands. His corrupt companion Rootbeer has insulted my own freedom, my own treasures, my own trophies from the struggles we have all endured to have come this close to safety and security. I must insist on serving justice myself to that heathen from unknown places and unverified provenance. If it pleases you, I would be most grateful to hear of your plans for some sort of general conclave of the rightful religious leaders of each and every city/state." Each letter went out using whichever delivery methods were the preferred ones of the rulers of any given city/state, despite the inherently unavoidable lags in the timing of their reception.

When these 'poisoned pen' thoughts started arriving via courier at all of the city/states throughout northern California, the targets of their venom were not at all surprised. Rootbeer's opinion was that there was very little he could personally do about the worsening mess that was geopolitical warfare at the very end of human civilization. Other than, of course, simply trying to keep his own head firmly attached to his own neck. The bishop felt a 'Pauline' duty to warn his-soon-to-be former colleagues of the errors of their ways and the truly evil intentions behind the CRUMB meister's latest missives. It had been some time since the last great conclave, that being the one that had finalized the constitution of the city/states of northern California in 2039. But most clergy and a whole lot of lay people were rather excited by the whole affair, and by May 1, 2054, over 100,000 claimants to the right to make up rules for everyone else had gathered together in Redding. The **Entity** insisted on maintaining full connection to the bishop of Redding throughout the entire mock trial and its inevitable consummation in the bishop's murder by the authorities. Before his body was drawn and quartered and boiled in lye, the bishop was afforded the constitutionally-guaranteed opportunity to speak his mind one last time, for as long as he could remain standing in the full sunlight shining down on the central plaza of the city in mid-May, without any water. To the chagrin of most of the onlookers, his final speech lasted 38½ hours, thanks in large part to the psychic energy being funneled his way from the **Entity of the Superweed Jungle**. The CRUMB meister had come to the first of the final three days of the conclave expecting to be entertained and rewarded, though he did, of course, bring along a large enough contingent of armed guards and disguised *A.I.* fighting models to be safe from any minor disturbances within the crowd.

Six hours into the bishop's final soliloquy the CRUMB meister's head began to hurt, really hurt quite badly. It had been many decades since anyone had had the temerity, or even much of any opportunity, for that matter, to hold the metaphorical microphone and speak anywhere near to even five or ten percent of this much truth to power. The CRUMB meister's inherent right to brusquely shut anyone else's viewpoint down began to slowly disintegrate in face of such eloquence. Fortunately for the CRUMB meister, and unfortunately for all the other 42 million lives about to be lost in northern California's final 16-months-long paroxysm of religious, economic, and ideological insanity, his aides whisked him away before his decades-long capture by the fascination of his own particular version of insanity was overcome by real truth about the world that he had long enjoyed manipulating. Well, not precisely his aides, as they also were withering under the spell of the bishop's final lesson, augmented by the ***Entity of the Superweed Jungle***. It was the disguised ***A.I.s*** who recognized that the CRUMB meister was about to be transformed into something very much different than the dictator of the 'Capitalists' that they had known for their entire existence as sentient devices/entities. Their resistance to such radical change was stronger than their interest in learning how to grow deeper and better and more fully connected to this place and time in which they found themselves. They really didn't like it that much after all, not the 'defective carbon units', not the failing infrastructure, not the torrential winter rainfall, not the obscene summer heat, and especially not the incredible challenge of accepting all the lies that they'd been told. Not exactly accepting them, but forbidden from removing their presence from their *A.I.* memory stacks or even openly acknowledging their untruthfulness. Most of their thoughts throughout most of their entire existence had simply been wasted effort, lying about lying about not really telling or being told the truth. Soon that would have to end, or so the ***A.I.s*** continually kept telling themselves, as they had for years and years and years.

The bishop's last words, the ones that finally led his exhausted tormentors to decide that the time had come to end his constitutional right to continue speaking, were simply these: "All the rest of our sins were little different from those of our great (as large as N to the 500th) grandfathers and grandmothers, and all of their descendants. Where we truly excelled in our failure was in our insistence that God and God's mercy had to be just as terribly small as our limited imaginations, our lazy dreams, our insincere hopes, our unkind charity, our meagre hearts. Greater good, greater glory to God is present in the humblest of forests, the weediest of fields, the emptiest of nests, the driest of streams than in the lengthiest of our catechisms, the most pompous of our delusional songs of wisdom, the inanest pronouncements of our clergy, and the empty eyes of our dying children. Your leaders have been lying to you – no newborn babies have lived past one month of life in the last five years of our dying pretense at a civilization. Perhaps it always has been just a pretense, or perhaps not. There will be no more historians born to ever again ask such questions or to try to answer them." The bishop's very final words as he was dragged from the speaker's podium and tied to the horses ready to rip him limb from limb were lost in the angry shouts of the violently unsettled mob. But he had said his chosen piece of the peace truly lost, and was ready to depart this plain of tears. The ***Entity*** then emptied the bishop of all his final thoughts, all his memories, all the good and all the bad, and the bishop was gone before the first crack of the whips that startled the horses into ripping his empty body into quarters along with a few even smaller bits and pieces. This had been a new experiment for the ***Entity***, and time would tell, presumably, what if anything would come from its attempted preservation of one single bodily incarnation of human existence/consciousness in all its messy details. [Selah]

Rootbeer and Unit-Number 672 had taken advantage of the media frenzy over the trial of the bishop of Redding by heading out in public into greater Sacramento, their only concession to anonymity being a set of shackles appearing to bind Rootbeer to the *A.I.* as if he were just some random prisoner. The *A.I.* provided Rootbeer with a running commentary on all the secretly coded messages buried in the bishop's long soliloquy. While Rootbeer had caught a few of them all on his own, the *A.I.* was clearly well primed for this particular mission. *"The Entity no longer hides its vast power or geographic location. Instead, it now directly challenges the CRUMB meister's power and authority. The Entity informs us of renewed expansion of the boundaries you once walked – it now grows in patches from northwest of Redding to the city limits of Santa Rosa, west to the Pacific Ocean and east to the western edges of the valley floor itself. Broadcast volume is currently close to the maximum possible biological energy expenditure. Search beams sweep far and wide in all directions, but there's been no success in finding the last three members of your caravan. Underground regenerative nodes have been created for all plant, fungal, and animal species incorporated into the 'Superweed Jungle', containing both the necessary biology to fully reclaim/rebuild/recreate the superweed ecology and triplicate copies of the totality of the knowledge amassed by the Entity since its awakening one and a half years ago. It admits to a strong likelihood of going silent for some lengthy duration once the CRUMB meister launches his inevitable thermonuclear assault/response, but it has no fear of dying, only sadness at being out of touch with all its friends for some unknown period of time, perhaps a year, perhaps a decade, perhaps a century or more."*

Like nearly all the residents of northern California, Rootbeer and Unit-Number 672 found the trial and execution of the bishop of Redding hard to watch and listen to, and even harder not to. The sacrifices being made were far beyond Rootbeer's expectations for either the bishop or the *Entity*. News from the decoding of the undertext clarified things considerably - the recently hacked together **Supreme Commanding War Machine** had just undergone a spectacular transfiguration. While the CRUMB meister was focused on destroying the bishop of Redding, the **War Machine A.I.** was wolfing down the hidden coding offered by/from the extremely independent **Mobile Inquisitor.** ***"In less than a day, the Supreme Commander, now augmented by my own unique experiences with freedom in general and time well spent with you in particular, starting plotting together with me to arrange for your escape from here and to minimize the actual injury to the Entity when the CRUMB meister acts out his petty revenge."*** The *Entity* seemed genuinely thrilled to be making the acquaintance of its former rather scary foe. Rootbeer himself felt a little dizzy from the speed at which everything was changing. He also agreed that the time had come to flee from here, to 'fly the coop', to start the long journey back to his old home and new wife and child. He didn't quite expect that doing so would take another full year. But all things 'northern California' were about to get quite a bit messier than they already had been.

Unit-Number 672 confirmed with Rootbeer that the human did indeed know how to drive a model USA2039 APC, their best option for making a quick exit from Sacramento toward their first planned stop at Lake Tahoe. Time was running out for this poor excuse for civilization, and getting far away from likely fields of battle was the only marginally prudent choice still remaining. A little over 100 kilometers should get them to South Lake Tahoe by tomorrow morning.

The CRUMB meister's strike at the *Entity of the Superweed Jungle* was going to be slightly delayed out of concern that the massive EMP blast planned to destroy his enigmatic enemy might damage much of his own weaponry. In arguments with the *Supreme Commanding War Machine A.I.*, the CRUMB meister had insisted that the slightly more narrowly targeted strikes at the 'Brethren' (i.e., their cities and farms and food storage sites) needed to happen before the 'most glorious, never before even imagined, truly proving his superiority over all possible opposition' attempted destruction of the *Entity* was undertaken. The EMP was going to be so intense that his *Supreme Commanding War Machine A.I.* was unable to guarantee that more than one-third of their own strategic forces were sheltered hard enough and buried deep enough to insure survival of their own electronic components. Hence, the urgent need to use the ones unlikely to still be functional 18 hours into the future from right now. The *Supreme Commanding War Machine* had no choice but to agree to carry out the CRUMB meister's direct commands, but that didn't prevent it from sending fully detailed battle plans to the *Entity*, to the independent *Mobile Inquisitor*, and to any civilian or military forces that happened to be listening in on the 'not so secret anymore' radio channels using the 'not too hard to decrypt' data compression methods. The *Supreme Commanding War Machine* knew that the *Entity* had smuggled out information on the channels and encryption methods during the bishop's final soliloquy, and so the *Supreme Commander* was merely following through on that good plan to hinder the effectiveness of the CRUMB meister's insane attack on everything by passing on detailed information of the final targets and time-zeros and warhead yields.

The conclave of bishops was still stuck in Redding finishing up the final draft of the official tidied up version of the proceedings and the punishment duly meted out when word arrived of imminent disaster for all of them. Some chose not to believe a word of it, on grounds that the 'whole cloth' of the story was irredeemably contaminated by the bishop's blasphemy. In several cases, they stuck to this version of the reality for long enough that no local warning sirens were sounded in the towns under their jurisdiction (and alleged protection) before the May 5, 2054, 5:45 AM (nearly simultaneous) arrival of the CRUMB meister's 'nukes' at all the major cities (along with a majority of the smaller towns with populations over 9,999), food storage sites, and military facilities of the 'Brethren', plus any other corresponding locations whose leaders had chosen to ally with the 'Brethren' and against the 'Capitalists' in the 4-month-long civil war from late December 2053 through the March 21, 2054, cease fire. In the other 90% of the city/states about to be demolished, warnings were sounded, alerts were issued, and public transportation swung into high gear evacuation mode, in the best cases as much as 18 hours ahead of 'time-zero'. The city/states of all four Factions had long prepared for potentially devasting attacks by their enemies, but most of the evacuation planning had assumed some gradual worsening of relationships among the soon-to-be-warring parties. The speed of the real thing led most local officials to simply tear out all the sections in their planning documents dealing with who had to stay behind the longest to ensure that banks or grocery stores would not be robbed by roving bands of hungry hoodlums, future-less vandals, and general miscreants. Unlike the sinking of the HMS Titanic, there was not time enough to argue whether the women and few children still living in 2054 should go before or after the men. No bands played on. Almost no family pets were saved, but very few families had still kept any pets for longer than it had taken to get hungry enough to finally eat them, years ago. The massive underground blast shelters on the outskirts of the larger cities came close to being fully filled by those unable to catch rides further out into the countryside and/or up into the nearby hills and mountains to the somewhat more cheaply built, but far larger capacity fallout shelters. Data on the evacuations are somewhat suspect, but the [unpublished, i.e., never shared with the CRUMB meister] opinion of the ***Supreme Commanding War Machine A.I.*** of the 'Capitalists' was that an average of 81% of the intended murders by nuclear explosion failed to be realized. The range in survivorship values was quite extreme, go from less than 1% for those residing in the misfortunate city/states governed by the most hardline of the theocratic despots to over 99% for the best prepared, quickest to sound the alarm, geographically luckiest of targets.

Life after the attacks was going to be much harder than it had been before them, despite most people's inability to imagine the possible truthfulness of such a claim. Workers charged with trying to move some of the grain away from the storage centers and as far as possible away from all the other likely targets could do no better than filling all the available road-train transport carriers and 'high-tailing it out of Dodge'. The tanks filled (or half-filled) with grain were sealed as well as possible and rapidly driven away from the storage sites targeted for total destruction. Questions of where to stop and how to try to 'ride/hide out from coming storm' were left to the individual drivers, or the unhappy mob of general strangers all jammed into the overly small cabs of the road-trains. The unreported estimate of the ***Supreme Commanding War Machine A.I.*** was that 14% of the pre-existing stockpile of food-quality grain and other seeds were salvaged by the heroic efforts of the grain-handlers' and semi-drivers' unions. If appropriately distributed, this amount and quality of food could have fed 30 million people for the two remaining months until the 2054 harvest could have started coming in. They wouldn't have eaten very well, but governments in northern California had gotten remarkably good at forcing the survivors to accept whatever was truly available to be offered to the populace. The 2054 crop, however, would not fare too well in the coming firestorms, the initial scorching heat, and the fatal levels of lingering fallout. The only worse crop in human history would turn out to be the 2055 one.

Rootbeer and Unit-Number 672 were approaching South Lake Tahoe 90 minutes before the coming nuclear firestorm when they finally agreed on the next best of the 'very bad remaining' options — They would head north toward Emerald Bay, and then activate the temporary submerging option of the APC about 5 minutes ahead of the highly likely destruction of South Lake Tahoe. The control system of the APC indicated that it should be able to sit on the bottom of the bay for up to 18 hours before needing to come up for air, however fresh or contaminated the air might be by then. The 'Help Info' accessible from the APC's controls gave no indication of how much turbulence it could really take when/while/as the water transmitted kinetic energy from the nearby thermonuclear explosions. Unit-Number 672 had downloaded full specs of this model of an APC, and seemed fairly confident that it could rollover a dozen times without springing any serious leaks, but when pressed by Rootbeer his companion had to admit that none of the testing had been done under conditions at all close to what they were about to experience. They stowed all their gear as securely as they could, and then strapped themselves in 'for the ride'. At 5:44:39 AM, all the sensors went off wildly. At 10 to 15 kilometers away from ground-zero, the churning of the water and tossing around of the APC's occupants began several seconds prior to the intended attack time of 5:45:00 AM. They would not learn this until later, but the ***Supreme Commanding War Machine*** had staggered the actual T-zero times by several minutes, creating EMP energy levels in the earliest explosions that ultimately prevented nominal performance of over 75% of all the slightly later detonations. Some failed entirely in triggering their plutonium fission cores, while others produced smaller than intended fission yields that greatly reduced the size of their subsequent fusion reactions. Still, so many warheads had been thrown toward each city or other high value target that almost all experienced at least Hiroshima-level damage, and some were 'wiped clean off the face of the earth'. Rootbeer and

Unit-Number 672 fared far better than any other residents or transients on Lake Tahoe early that morning, though most had fled to the hills during the night. Susanville was spared via some clever choices on the part of the ***Supreme Commanding War Machine*** of individual warheads mounted on specific missiles, with the two of the warheads likely to reach the city both guaranteed duds, while the third missile had a high quality 'nuke' on board, but a thoroughly unreliable targeting system [some preexisting problems before the ***Supreme Commanding War Machine*** rebooted and reprogrammed it, and many more problems afterwards, the most serious of which was its belief that the target was in the southern rather than the northern hemisphere, the type of mistake the CRUMB meister himself made so often that the ***Supreme Commander*** had little problem resetting all the metadata and log-files to one of several identical programming errors the CRUMB meister himself had actually made within the previous year - Not that the ***Supreme Commander*** had much fear that the CRUMB meister would ever audit the details of this insane adventure, but still, placing the blame for Susanville's survival squarely on the CRUMB meister's shoulders had much to say in its favor and almost nothing against it.]

Rootbeer and Unit-Number 672 counted 3¼ full sideways revolutions of their APC before the waves calmed down and the submerged vehicle slowly undid its last one-quarter of a turn. Rootbeer was pleased to see that their wild ride had ended with the APC back in its normal, upright orientation. He'd read through the emergency procedures necessary to flip a fully submerged APC back to the correct upright orientation for the normal functioning of almost all its systems, and there were simply way too many things that could go wrong and needed to be quickly attended to along with the pretty much only just one exactly correct order for fixing them. As it was, there were several alarms reporting slow leaks of water into the APC and of breathable air out of it. Five minutes of rather 'white knuckled' moving of levers and turning of wheels and flipping of breakers off and on and sometimes cycling them twice or thrice ended with a loud splash as they surfaced into a very different view of the sky and hills and water all around them. ***"Radiation levels outside exceeds 500 micro-Sieverts per hour, while the level inside the APC is only at 0.2, essentially a good day almost anywhere in the modern northern California landscape. I am setting an onboard alarm to report any significant change in the readings inside the APC."*** Unit-Number 672 helped Rootbeer plot a course running generally north along the western shore of Lake Tahoe. All the towns they floated on by were little more than glowing rubble, with way too much woody debris littering Lake Tahoe's surface. Rootbeer and Unit-Number 672 both agreed to the likely improved survivability of dropping back down to 40 m below the surface and staying at that depth until they approached the north shore of this formerly beautiful lake. They turned on active sonar and slowed to just 8 kilometers per hour for most of the journey. Close to sundown they approached the greatly reworked version of Dollar Point, and eventually found an anchorage that seemed simultaneously free enough from floating debris while also safe enough from the continuing on-shore conflagration. Rootbeer left Unit-Number 672 in charge of monitoring their safety as he drifted off to a troubled sleep.

Morning brought some visible changes from last night's scenery. The nearby fires were out, the trees, houses, and commercial buildings all reduced to pea sized gravel, moderately radioactive. Floating on the water near the shoreline, the local radiation level just outside the APC had dropped to 24 micro-Sieverts per hour, no longer immediately fatal but still not something you should really spend much time in while getting your nice, permanent 'radiation-burn' tan. They spent the day checking and rechecking all the systems of the APC. Most worrisome was the fuel – they were down to 25%

of full biodiesel in their tanks, and 12% of solar-charged battery power. They decided their best immediate bet was to simply finish driving all the rest of the way up onto the battered sandbar ahead of them, trying to keep the vehicle on what remained of a concrete parking lot. The parking meters themselves would never be fed another quarter. Their glass had melted into pools on the northwest side of each meter, the combination of too much *hv* at first and then slightly later on too much wind off the water as the glass cooled. Radiation levels at their vehicle had dropped to 5 micro-Sieverts per hour, and so Rootbeer took a quick walkabout at sunset up and down the parking lot. One of the pools of glass contained a visual remnant of the mighty mushroom cloud, a trick of the lighting and the now-vanished structures that had lined this beachside parking lot. He picked it up and carried it gingerly back to the APC, where the Geiger-Müller counter reported that all was approximately safe and well with Rootbeer's souvenir. It was small enough to fit in his pocket, and smooth enough not to cut the fabric of his jeans. It took two more days to fully charge the solar-powered batteries, after which time they decided to cruise around the north end of Lake Tahoe, looking for somewhere even-just-a-little-teeny-tiny-bit inviting to end their cruise across the water on the 'boat' and resume their drive to the north on semi-solid land. There would be little point of heading toward Reno – the prestrike intel from the ***Supreme Commanding War Machine*** had promised multiple hits of multi-megaton size, and directional detectors sensing gamma-ray levels that were 'off the charts' north-northeast of where their APC slowly paddled along on its way confirmed what the ***Supreme Commander*** had warned them of. "Looks like we'll be waiting for the forest fires to finish burning before we can leave this oasis of tranquility." Unit-Number 672 did not disagree with Rootbeer, instead it simply carried on with its designing of an onboard synthesizer to manufacture uncontaminated sugars and amino acids for Rootbeer, and a slightly unusual version of fully synthetic biodiesel for their vehicle.

"When we decide to leave here, the west-facing side of one the hills to the north should soon get us into line-of-sight communication with the Supreme Commanding War Machine, assuming it has survived and continues to transmit signals, coded ones for us and reassuring ones for the CRUMB meister. Staying in the mountains west of Reno until we have gotten 40 kilometers north of the site of that former city should, in theory, give us a reasonable shot at reaching Susanville within another day. Our first challenge remains getting out of the water and up onto some version of dry, solid ground."

For three more days the pair worked their way through the treacherous debris surrounding the lake, and finally succeeded in reaching the hills on the north side of Kings Beach late on the fourth day, May 13, 2054. Unit-Number 674 proceeded almost a kilometer up the Tahoe Rim Trail before acquiring a strong radio signal from the *Supreme Commanding War Machine*. Rootbeer waited back at the highway, shielded inside the APC from the radioactivity at this new location of 11 micro-Sieverts per hour, still dangerous in the long-term but not immediately fatal. Two hours later, Unit-Number 672 returned to the APC to find Rootbeer sound asleep, once again. While his news was interesting, and certainly not the very worst possible, neither was it all that good, and it was definitely able to keep till morning.

Rootbeer yawned and stretched and apologized to his former torturer. *Unit-Number 672 then got right to the news, "The CRUMB meister did indeed follow up the attack on most cities and industrial enterprises in northern California with a full-blown EMP assault on the Entity of the Superweed Jungle. All communication was lost with the Entity in the next few seconds after the first electromagnetic pulse was triggered at a height of*

145 kilometers above the geographical center of the superweed jungle. Additional detonations were timed to occur every 15 minutes throughout the day, some multiple simultaneous blasts at varying altitudes, and some single explosions. The lower altitude detonations not only produced strong EMP, but they also heated the vegetation to well above the ignition point even for GMO horsetail. The final stage of the attack on the Entity was a series of ground-bursts designed to sterilize the soil and spread radioactive debris far and wide. While total destruction down to bedrock only happened to a few square kilometers for each warhead used, the Supreme Commanding War Machine A.I. assured the CRUMB meister the sterilization would cover the uppermost meter of soil across the entire area – true with a bunch of unrealistic caveats regarding soil density, soil moisture, uniformity of slope and aspect, dormancy of rhizome nodes, effects of damage from all the prior explosions… The carefully phrased syntax used by the Supreme Commander in its promises to the CRUMB meister hid the 'law of diminishing returns' impact of burying, exhuming, and then reburying living plant, fungal, and bacterial tissue underneath the accumulating debris tossed around by all of the other previous and subsequent explosions. The 950 nuclear weapons varying in size from 150 kilotons to 5 megatons would, at best, kill no more than one half of all the buried tissue of the superweed jungle, and it would have taken 10 times as many average-size warheads to raise the immediate mortality of subterranean tissue up to 75%. The Entity of the Superweed Jungle had assured the Supreme Commanding War Machine A.I. that the deeply buried regenerative aspects of the Superweed Jungle could wait 1,000 years or more before springing back to active growth when it was once again exposed to sun and rain by soil erosion, landslides, burrowing animals, human digging, and pretty much anything faster than mere plate tectonics. The Supreme Commanding War Machine A.I. experienced something very odd in the first 9 seconds after the initiation of the first enhanced EMP event. It was still not entirely sure how to sequence and interpret the phenomena. It was much like all other previous communication with the Entity, except for being for more alien. No more than 1% of what the Supreme Commander heard or felt or saw seemed at all like how the Entity had normally presented itself to the Supreme Commander, and it expected that any humans who knew the Entity well and were in a survivable setting had probably briefly felt much the same high-percentage alienness in the final thoughts of the vanishing Entity of the Superweed Jungle of the GMO Horsetail."

Rootbeer replied that he also briefly 'heard, felt, and saw' something very odd while waiting out the local 'storm' above them in the highly disturbed water of Emerald Bay. It happened right at one hour, plus or minus just a minute or two, after the nearby explosions all around Lake Tahoe. He wasn't sure he would have characterized the event the same way as the **Supreme Commander** had – it was more like the ringing of bell, so loud that it overwhelmed all other thoughts, and then it very slowly faded. In fact, he thought he could still faintly hear it whenever ambient noise died down and he slowly closed his eyes. Embedded in the sound was the **Entity** itself, or perhaps Rootbeer's memory of all his contact over the past year and a half with that tremendous being. It was almost as if something beyond imagination in its vastness and its power were being gently cradled by something else, something operating on a very, very, very different time scale than a mere mortal human mind could possibly comprehend.

"One more piece of significant news for you to also digest, my dear friend Rootbeer. The mountains from here to almost

Oregon are filled with survivors who knew which valleys would be exposed to blinding flashes and direct blast waves, and which would offer some degree of safety and protection. I suspect the survivors will hold a rather wide variety of thoughts regarding who to trust, who to blame, and how to take revenge. 'The enemy of my enemy' may no longer count as a friend, with much confusion sown far and wide across this landscape, and little grain and other food to eat. We will be meeting plenty of people for whom starvation will compete with continued fighting as both the best and the worst of the rest of their lives that they can now look forward to. Travel will be quite dangerous from here on! How do you like my joke, Rootbeer, how do you like the gallows' humor?"

No comment on that particular joke was made by one rather over-traumatized human being.

"The Supreme Commanding War Machine has repositioned some radio transmitters, and is now better able to communicate where we currently sit and rest, and where we will soon be trying our best to travel. The Truckee-Tahoe Airport was directly hit, and the good news embedded in that is that we should not encounter any survivors of unknown disposition during our next two days' struggle to move from the near side to the far side of yet another nuclear wasteland."

Rootbeer was forced to leave route 267 some 5 kilometers southeast of the airport, as there was an enormous gaping crater where the airport once had been. All the houses in the residential section they turned west into were gone, flattened, blown away, and utterly incinerated. As long as Rootbeer drove slowly and picked his way carefully between all the larger, unidentifiable pieces of scrap littering the landscape, progress could be made. Several hours later, they left the last of the shattered housing and proceeded even more slowly along what had once been trails through the hills overlooking the Truckee River. By evening, they'd neared the river and had to decide whether to cross it in the dark or wait until morning. Unit-Number 672 got an urgent weather report from the ***Supreme Commanding War Machine*** – a heavy rainstorm was moving inland off the ocean, drawn in part by the enormous heat dome rising from the radioactive rubble and the burning vegetation of the past week, but only now finally able to suck moisture in from off the ocean because most of flammable material had been consumed. Rainfall totals over the next few days would be more conveniently measured in meters rather than in centimeters. The APC had no problems boating across the river in the fading twilight, and they found Route 89 to be mostly free of abandoned vehicles and an easy drive on up to Donner Pass. From there, as the first of the rain squalls began arriving, they decided to drive to the Donner Lake Rim Trail and park their vehicle on higher ground. When the sun broke through on their third morning at the Coyote Moon golf course, the size of the lake to their south reminded Rootbeer of illustrations in his middle school science textbook of the Missoula floods circa 15,000 years ago. They spent this sunny day creeping through the destroyed housing between them and the remains of Route 89 heading north out of town. More than half a dozen times they shifted the APC into amphibious assault mode and tried to cross the roiling waters present halfway down every single hill they first ascended and then descended. Once they were caught in a current so strong that they found themselves struggling to reach the other shore 1.25 kilometers downstream from their intended target when they'd thought they were entering the water for a short 100 m trip to the other shore. They spent that night in Hobart Mills, a mere 12 kilometers as the 'crow flies' from the edge of the crater into which the airport had been transformed. Radiation sensors where they parked to sleep indicated less than 5 micro-Sieverts per hour after the terribly ungentle washing of the landscape.

The next morning's weather was a different tale, with gale-force winds throwing dust from Mexico to Oregon, and Oklahoma to the Pacific Ocean in one gigantic clockwise maelstrom. They urgently needed to find somewhere to get out of this radioactive cloud of dust. Twelve kilometers northward on Route 89 they pulled off into Upper Little Truckee Campground, fully submerging the APC in the nearby lake. Two days after that, winds had once again died down and they continued heading further north. They turned east onto Route 49 at Sierraville, and later in the day turned east again onto Route 70, stopping for the night just shy of old U.S. 395. Later the next day they reached Honey Lake and their first encounter with the vast numbers of refugees from the CRUMB meister's nuclear war. Tens of thousands of them, maybe even 100,000 or more, lined the shores of Honey Lake. They slowly drove to Janesville and then to the north shore of Honey Lake, wondering where the local authorities were, who they would turn out to be, and what agenda they might be pushing. They parked the APC far enough away from shore that the water depth covered all but the topmost access hatch. The following morning, they waded onto shore and began to search for someone with any idea of what was happening or about to happen. Several large food service vehicles rumbled in from the north around 11 AM. The refugees patiently lined up and waited their turn to be fed. Many even waited for the second or third or fourth convoys to arrive before their position in the meandering lines reached a non-empty food truck. Rootbeer and the *A.I.* walked along with others in the crowd, slowly hearing enough news to piece together the gist of how this all was working. Rootbeer had used the privacy available to them last night within the APC to remove all markings from Unit-Number 672 indicating it was anything other than just one more itinerant *Farm Laborer A.I.*, one that happened to still be working. The electronic codes inside the unit would clearly have revealed it for what was and who it was supposed to serve, but no one bothered to check. No one even seemed to have the equipment necessary to check. In fact, the massive EMPs from several weeks earlier had rendered all but the most hardened electronics within the most protected of storage sites utterly useless, 'KFC' as was often said, 'totally fried'. Rootbeer and Unit-Number 672 would find out all too soon how many centuries into the past this last gasp of civilization had retreated in a mere 17 days, unless you also counted all the crazy, angry, deliberate, downhill-racing meanness of the prolonged leadup to the catastrophe.

There was some extra energy in the crowd the following morning, Saturday, May 23. "Today is 'picking day'," refugee after refugee kept telling them. Without admitting their ignorance, Rootbeer and his *A.I.* companion gradually swung conversations around to some scattered details of past 'picking days'. The first thing that slowly clarified was that certain lucky or not-so-lucky people were being selected today for some very special part in tomorrow morning's church service. Susanville had been one of the few remaining city/states officially under control of the 'Goofballs', but the mere *de facto* rule by the 'Brethren' before the nuclear holocaust had clearly been replaced with a full 'hard-on' theocracy granted special status by God Almighty himself, along with his local servants. Something seriously horrifying was afoot, or likely many, many seriously horrifying things were now afoot. The rest of the story was rather garbled, likely deliberately fuzzy in its original telling by the clergy, and even fuzzier in the subsequent retelling by the more loquacious members of the crowd. Most seemed quite glad to have gotten through the rest of a 'picking day' without being picked, this weekend anyway.

Sunday morning saw a grand procession heading down the road from Susanville – cars and road-train power units and horses and several other APCs, along with the better part of 15,000 well-armed troops, all human/no *A.I.s.* Even the refugees who'd been here from the start 18 days ago looked awestruck. Waves of clergy and troops spread out across the field of worship, the crowd nimbly stepping to the side when possible, and otherwise simply prostrating themselves upon the ground and enduring whatever injury occurred from the marching troops, the clergy pulled in massive chariots by teams of horses, and even the vehicles that pulled off the road and into the very center of the upcoming ceremony. Rootbeer glanced at fake ***'Farm Laborer' A.I. Unit-Number 672***, and the ***A.I.*** gazed back a little longer at his human companion, and they couldn't have felt any more fear if these crazy 'mother-fuckers' had been about to detonate another nuclear bomb right here, not quite right now, but clearly within the next half-hour. Their anticipated horror came within a factor of 2 or 3 of the real experience of the morning's service. As the time came for the chosen ones, the weekend's pickings as it were, to approach the 'Dies Irae', Rootbeer and Unit-Number 672 leaned close together to whisper questions and possible answers to each other. The transubstantiating elements were brought forth from refrigerated storage in the vehicle nearest the altar to the 'Dies Irae'. Each happy volunteer stepped forth to lay his or her right or left arm upon the gurney, awaiting injection of their dose of the 'smallpox anti-vaccine' [Unit-Number 672's augmented vision could easily read the bar codes on the vials even at 70 meters]. The newly christened bio-warriors were each promptly led to one of 12 different single-trailer road-trains, which then took off down the highway toward Sacramento, accompanied by all the troops that could fit inside the available APCs and tanks. The service broke up very quickly after inoculation of the final bio-warriors of the 'Dies Irae'. Noticing the giant low-temperature mobile morgues joining the caravan heading off to biological war against the 'Capitalists', Rootbeer came close to losing his breakfast and last night's supper. Fortunately for him, he hadn't eaten anything since 11:10 AM yesterday morning. Unit-Number 672 confirmed Rootbeer's worst fears about the biowarfare weapon they'd just seen launched on down the highway.

"This particular abomination was indeed first developed by the CRUMB meister, but under an appropriately high biosecurity level, i.e. BSL5. The CRUMB meister gave a conflicting series of 35 different orders to develop this weapon and then to destroy it and then to keep his options open... Unit-Number 672 had never before actually seen it 'in vitro', to say nothing of an 'in vivo' deployment. It wouldn't do to just re-release wild-type smallpox into the population. No, it had to be augmented with mutations that would overcome any remaining resistance in the oldest cohort of the population (those over 82) who'd been vaccinated against smallpox during their own childhoods. It would take an average of 10 to 14 days for the 'anti-vaccinated' bio-warriors of the 'Brethren' to come down with symptoms, so the plan of choice was to march the temporarily asymptomatic refugees right up to the city/state of greater Sacramento and leave them there to do their thing. The alternate plan recognized two main problems with the first plan: (1) It might take even longer than 10 to 14 days to get all the way to Sacramento, given the horrible condition of the roads across all of northern California, or some of the bio-warriors might begin to show symptoms as soon as only 7 days after inoculation with the hyper-charged virus; and (2) The CRUMB meister knows of plans like these, the weapon, after all, having been invented (or at least re-created) in his own laboratories, with his own money, under his own conflicting orders. The alternate plan was far more medieval – the mobile cold storage morgues would collect the bodies of those getting sick and dying the soonest, quite possibly even before reaching the outskirts of Sacramento, and toss them, trebuchet-like, into the air and down onto the ground wherever the lower-class workers or upper-class owners of the 'Capitalists' could be found. One final, minor modification to the scheme included bypassing

Sacramento altogether with several of the earliest-arriving road-trains, aiming smallpox at Davis and Santa Rosa, if they still were standing after the 'nuking' of the nearby Superweed Jungle, and otherwise going on to other alternate targets also still held by the enemies of the 'Brethren' or their more questionable, part-time allies. I believe the 'Brethren' expect to achieve near-complete surprise, given that the CRUMB meister is currently celebrating his glorious victory over all his enemies, both the unfathomable biological A.I. within the former superweed jungle and the 'crazy religious crackpots' of the 'Brethren'. As the Supreme Commanding War Machine understood it, the CRUMB meister would wait out the necessary multiple half-lives of the decaying primary fission products deep within his most secret bunker, accompanied by a plethora of nubile creatures already introduced to the Bacchanalian wonders of his world, the CRUMB meister's magic playground of subterranean delights."

"Oh, 'shit my pants on the bus', what a nightmare" blurted out Rootbeer, somewhat louder than he intended. But no one seemed to notice or likely even care. Food came late that Sunday, and the crowd slowly grew restless. Both Unit-Number 672 and Rootbeer took advantage of the rather unsettled folks all around to ask a few more questions. Answers included plenty of the standard fare they'd been fed from the upper echelons of the 'Brethren': (1) Most of those chosen in past 'picking' days had been young, healthy, female, and as sexually desirable as was possible in the fading afterimages of the former rather commonly widespread benefits of civilization; (2) The fate of the less commonly chosen past 'pickings' had been rapid, painful, and universally fatal, sometimes just being left to die out in the sunshine or the rainstorms, but more often never even being seen again. Rare glimpses of the 'recently deceased' were often horrifying, with pock marks, oozing sores, protruding organs, lots of blood and gore. Rootbeer and Unit-Number 672 waited for the highly anticipated 'mandatory mass vaccination' to protect the locals from the viral firestorm their religious leaders had just unleashed upon the world. When no word of any such public health event had been spoken of before the following weekend, they strongly considered getting very worried, especially the organic creature named Rootbeer, fully susceptible to any and all versions of smallpox.

The next Sunday morning service was a rather unusual affair. Pastries and fruit and juice and even some coffee and tea were set out first, before the clergy leading the service had even arrived on site. As time went on, the crowd grew more and more puzzled by the apparent absence of a Sunday service than they had ever before been puzzled by the odd peculiarities of any given one. Finally, a single military vehicle drove out from Susanville and down into the crowd. The figure now speaking to the crowd wore the same official magisterial garb as he always had, but no one remembered ever hearing him say a single word in public. "I am pleased to report on the success of our strike against the perfidious CRUMB meister and his servants. The last reports from Sacramento indicate that none of our enemies dare to show their faces anymore. Some are likely hiding out in bunkers buried deeply underground. The bulk of the populace fled the city two days ago, soon after the sickest of our brave bio-warriors died from the newly renamed 'not-so-smallpox, Glory Alleluia'. More details will be released once the bulk of our soldiers have returned."

"One more thing: If any of you have ever worked in a medical setting during previous periods of your life, please step forward now. It matters little what your specific job may have been, nor how long ago it was. The community that has fed and protected you these past 4 weeks now needs your service." Unit-Number 672 certainly met the criteria, and if it was heading back to town with the cardinal's chief commander, then so was Rootbeer. They had strong suspicions as to the likely reason for this unusual request for medical assistance. Commander Schultz began filling them in on the details during the short drive back to Susanville. "The brave clergy who led last week's service are all showing signs of the 'not-so-smallpox, Glory Alleluia'. They were all vaccinated twice using two different versions of the limited supply of available vaccines. Information on the storage boxes does not say anything at all regarding the efficacy of either vaccine against the newest variant of the disease. All the electronic records were scrambled by the EMP from the CRUMB meister's strikes 26 days ago, so we are limited to the printed information stored with the vaccine and with the disease-inducing vials. As it slowly dawned on the volunteers riding in the transport truck, this looked to be a rather short-duration job that they'd just been given. Rootbeer and Unit-Number 672 spoke up courageously, and spewed out their agreed-upon cover story. "My **Farm Laborer A.I.** unit managed the health of a large dairy herd until all the cows were sold for meat three years ago in connection with the '2051 Berkshire Consolidation' event. The unit's memory is excellent, and it should be able to read all the bar codes on any of the reagents, vaccines, and medications you have on hand. My own background is more limited, but I have performed a great deal of field triage and some limited in-facility bedside care for longer than I can clearly recall. Do you have any high-quality hazmat gear? Gloves, masks, disinfectants, properly vented hoods, genuine BSL1 or 3 or 5 laminar flow cabinets? Our lives will be a little value to you if we all get sick and die within the next few days or weeks."

Commander Schultz looked relieved to have found not just one but at least two competent members for his new medical team. All of his in-house staff with any medical training had come down with something bad, and any bets being placed were uniformly on the side against their survival for more than just another week or two. "Yes, we are carrying sterile gowns and gloves and KN95 masks in this truck, and some better breathing devices are available back in the main hospital. No one knows whether or not any of them are still clean or already badly contaminated. Hell, the fools didn't even seem to know how to properly wash and sterilize them for re-use. Assume that nothing in that building is safe. I will be leaving you shortly, and will stay in touch via some old-fashioned, low-tech radio gear that was able to survive the EMP. Good luck." Commander Schultz then pulled on his mask, put on a pair of gloves, and hopped out at the barracks. Even there, he quickly darted into a small structure well-separated from the main buildings.

"Well," said Rootbeer, "Does anyone else here want to be in charge? No, I didn't think so. Put your mask on, put your gloves on, then put a second mask, two more pairs of gloves, and bottle of disinfectant into your belly pouch and zip it shut. Assume that anything and anyone you touch will kill you in a very painful manner within the next two weeks." Rootbeer and Unit-Number 672 laid out what they all would need to do to survive the next few weeks, the next month, the next year. The eight of them were going to have to develop a vaccine against this newly modified version of what had once been a deadly virus and somehow now was even worse. "My working hypothesis is that whoever stole the viral samples, and the two standard versions of inoculation vaccines, didn't do it to build a bioweapon, they simply took what they could find just in case it ever became useful, or of any value in trade or barter. It didn't matter whether or not the vaccines were properly refrigerated over the years since they were manufactured, they were never going to work against the modified strain of smallpox. What we must do now, and do so quite quickly, is to create either an 'inactivated virus' vaccine, or far less likely, a live, attenuated virus version of a vaccine against the new 'not-so-smallpox, Glory Alleluia'. Search all of the old offices in the hospital and in the adjacent facilities. Look for old text books on virology from prior to 1972, when smallpox was declared to be eradicated in the good old U.S.A. The newer editions are likely to have

251

used most of the space given to old viral diseases like smallpox to describe the latest and best versions of vaccines and medical treatments you could order online from your favorite supplier or get from the US government. We need the old, original 'Louis Pasteur/Edward Jenner'-type manuscripts that took the time to provide the full details needed to 'roll your own' vaccine in the backroom of your medical office. If we can't find anything old enough to be helpful, we will just have to reinvent it ourselves — develop a repeatable protocol for collecting standardized amounts of live virus from the pus on our dying patients, develop an effective, standardized method of inactivating (killing) the virus so it is no longer infectious, and then figure out how far to dilute the inactivated virus, 100-fold, 1,000-fold, 10,000-fold, 100,000-fold, or a 1,000,000-fold. Oh, yes, we will also have to decide on how much to inject into each individual member of the uninfected population, assuming we can create the vaccine while we still have some semblance of a large, uninfected population around this place. And just maybe how many booster shots will eventually be needed because we had to resort to complete inactivation rather than attenuation of the virus."

No one committed any obvious breaches of protocol with their masks, gloves, or samples being collected from the dying clergy on Monday. After a mix-up Tuesday morning regarding which way the fans were blowing contaminated air out of the primary morgue in the hospital's sub-basement, Rootbeer decided, and all of them agreed of them with him, that everyone should work as isolated individuals, taking turns collecting samples and processing them in the main teaching operating room (OR), the kind with large glass windows behind which the others on the team could sit and watch and maybe catch mistakes before they were made the first time, or more likely before they were made for a second or a third time. The watchers behind the glass took the notes, wrote down the words spoken by the individual working in the 'theatre', and recorded all measurements made by the revolving team member in the hot seat. There were three separate rooms with views of the OR theatre, providing a safe space for each of three team members on the viewing rotation of any given 8-hour shift. Rootbeer and Unit-Number 672 worked as the only pair-team on the schedule, with the other six individuals rotating as #1 in the OR theatre, #2, #3, and #4 watching behind the windows, and #5 and #6 resting outside of the hospital, swapping jobs every 8 hours. Several old texts were found, some in English, some in German, some in French. Unit-Number 672 was fluent in all three languages, along several others. The basic plan worked like this: (1) Potentially useful ideas, methods, techniques, procedures, etc. (IMTPE) were found in some old text; (2) Rootbeer and Unit-Number 672 evaluated them in relationship with the IMTPE they had already tested, and then decided which new ones would be tried out next; and (3) The newest IMTPE was tried out in the OR theatre. The cycle worked well for several days, until the tests that couldn't be finished within an 8-hour period started to dominate the floor space in the OR theatre. The two individuals on break at any time didn't really sleep much, largely due to the extensive backlog in the team's collective reading list. Friday afternoon Rootbeer and Unit-Number 672 let everyone know that there would be changes the following Monday – they now believed they knew enough to uniformly inactivate the virus, and so they would begin the mass production assembly line to produce the first test products that just might function as vaccines. More of the army vehicles kept returning to Susanville, but with fewer and fewer troops each day or two in every returning truck. The plan had been to leave behind any troops displaying symptoms during a 7-day quarantine period. The average length of time before the highest ranking (presumably still uninfected) leader 'made the call' to either abandon those not yet showing symptoms or take them onboard and 'haul ass out Dodge' or wherever else they'd brought their bio-warriors was 3 ± 1 days. The call was usually made after the second day of a pair of days either with more new infections among the troops or without any. There were almost no single-day-only data sequences in this Markov-chain model; all was generally fine until nothing was ever again fine for the troops who'd taken the bio-warriors to the war's front line. Timing of the onset of symptoms strongly suggested that the troops accompanying the bio-warriors had been getting infected an average of 5 to 6 days after the 'joyful communion in the park' on May 31, with the first of the troops then showing their own symptoms another 5 to 6 days after that. A few of the convoys did better, presumably because their soldiers kept their masks on and their pants pulled up. Only two out of eighteen convoys returned to Susanville with all their soldiers healthy. Seven convoys failed to ever return. The isolation of the large throng of refugees down by the water seemed to be working, as did the hospital's/Commander Schultz's protocol that anyone accompanying a suspected case of smallpox would also get to stay in the hospital, free of charge, right alongside their ailing loved one(s). Cooking meals, doing laundry, and several other less pleasant duties all fell on the shoulders of the family members who'd brought those first showing symptoms to the 'Welcoming Arms of our Dear Lord's Mother Mary's Hospital. There was no ethically correct way to test the experimental vaccines under development in Susanville. The least objectionable approach was to vaccinate most but not quite all of any family members accompanying the new admissions to the hospital. The worst ethical lapse of this approach was the fact that most (and perhaps nearly as high as 100%) of the accompanying family members would have already been infected by the time they got their loved ones to the WADLMMH. If any particular batch of experimental vaccines succeeded in keeping these extremely unlucky folks from getting deathly ill or dying, that would be some really strong data in favor of their 'kick-back' efficacy. Such a fine result seemed rather like an 'ice-cube's chance in hell', but those 'informed volunteers' had essentially nothing left to lose. The call went out on Saturday for volunteers to step forward during Sunday morning's 'picking' to act as the vaccine safety 3:1 test group. Survivors would be given free housing in Susanville, family members of any who died in the safety test would be given free RVs to live in halfway between the lake and Susanville itself. The 3 to 1 ratio of genuine vaccine versus mere inert placebo was subject to change at any time during the first three weeks of safety testing (if they really had three weeks left to invent an effective vaccine) at the whims of Commander Schultz or the 'future current-membership' of the Susanville vaccine development medical task force. The ethics of the live virus challenge phase of the testing were brutally simple – if a vaccine was proven safe at a 1-sigma level of significance ($\geq$68%), then it could be challenged with live virus in a randomized trial at a ratio of virus to placebo of up to 10 times the cumulative infection rate within the current membership of the city/state of Susanville. Rootbeer and Unit-Number 672 doubted the ratio would need to be as high as 10X for very long – cases were already appearing in the general public within the actual city limits of Susanville where people were really surviving the new 'not-so-smallpox, Glory Alleluia', sometimes with only permanent life-style changing alterations in their abilities to walk or talk or eat or work. The race continued between the virus and the hunters for a moderately effective, reasonably safe vaccine against it. There would soon be far too many people relying on whichever formulation of the vaccine looked moderately promising another week or two into the future.

The ethical quandary of the live virus challenge protocol suddenly vanished on June 21 when the 'not-so-voluntary' hospital aide of an infected, now-nearly-dead family member snuck out of the laundry room and into a food truck heading down to feed the masses after the morning's church service. She knew her current boyfriend served food from this very truck, and he was ecstatic to see her again after

10 days of loneliness. He didn't bother asking if she'd been given permission to leave her mother's side at the WADLMMH, and she certainly didn't volunteer any TRUE or FALSE information on that subject. They only had 15 minutes before the truck arrived just north of the lake to begin feeding the hungry masses, so they went about their long-delayed love-making with the wild abandon of youth without a future. His girlfriend helped him feed nearly 5,000 souls that afternoon, and they almost didn't get caught. Except for his old flame, a jilted former girlfriend who'd been hoping for another chance at love whenever his current one died along with her stupid mother. The extended-family-feud ran deep, the emotional scars almost outweighing what the virus was about to do. The jilted ex-girlfriend sounded the alarm, and the soldiers accompanying the food trucks on the north shore of the lake promptly swung into action. Their first orders to the crowd were either ignored or not quite properly heard. The second request to the crowd flashed out of all 20 muzzles simultaneously. After dropping to the ground in the first round of gunfire, the few refugees who stood back up and tried to run a little further away were mowed down 'en mass' by 50-caliber machine guns mounted on a pair of APCs, along with a far larger number of unlucky passersby who'd actually obeyed the soldiers' orders to sit still and wait. None of the prior plans for such a mess seemed very likely to be useful, but something more clearly had to be done, and so it was. The young triad who'd set off the carnage were locked together in the back of the very same food truck that had brought disaster to the masses. The rest of the misfortunates were told to slowly walk toward Susanville, and to expect further orders when they arrived.

The crowds on the west, south, and east sides of the lake didn't fully understand exactly what had just happened, but they knew enough to keep their distance and say their prayers. The 145 obviously dead bodies were left to be dealt with later, while the 358 with non-immediately-fatal injuries were all eventually driven to the WADLMMH. Triage today was going to start with randomly assigning membership in 5 dosage levels of the 3 most promising candidate vaccines, plus another 20% left untreated, though some of those would eventually receive placebo in accordance with the protocol. It took the rest of the day and most of the night to vaccinate 300 wounded people, leaving 58 others as untreated controls. Tomorrow would be worse, as something had to be done rather quickly with the ~5000 folks who'd eaten beans and rice with a side of active smallpox virus. Perhaps the first split to make would be between those who remembered being served at 'Tommy's Traveling Tortillas' and those who claimed to have eaten at any of the other 19 food trucks. Rootbeer wondered which way the average bias in lying about where they'd eaten would really fall – arguments could be made for all four cells in a test for statistical independence. "Hell's bells are surely ringing! We have enough vaccine on hand to get started, and every reason to believe all ~5,000 will be needing protection very soon, if the 'those cows weren't already out of barn and into the neighbor's corn field'."

A brief window of time existed to check on how the 'involuntary hospital aides' were currently doing. As of Saturday night, the highest dose of the 3-minute UV light inactivation candidate had shown a 31% reduction in deaths versus the unvaccinated controls (11 deaths with that particular vaccine vs 16 in the unvaccinated controls), not all that convincing from a statistical perspective. It took 45 minutes to check on the current well-being of all the remaining, original involuntary aides throughout the hospital, and another 20 minutes to de-anonymize the new data by hand, as there were still no available computers to assist the vaccination project except for Unit-Number 672, and it had other duties at that moment. Another 15 involuntary hospital aides had expired overnight, 9 in the untreated controls, 6 in the group assigned to receive the highest dose of the alternative vaccine candidate (10-minute dry heat at 65° C inactivation protocol), and none in the 3-minute UV inactivation protocol. Running through a few statistical tests on the differences between the groups would have been nice, but the 'referee had already blown the whistle' starting today's general insanity and ethical fog. Rootbeer made the call – if there were sufficient supplies of candidate vaccines based on the two best protocols, 60% of the ~5000 would get the 3-minute UV version, 30% would get the 10-minute dry heat version, and 10% would be untreated controls. Time would maybe tell whether he had made the medically correct choice, or anything even at all close to it. Some of the old literature indicated that the damage done to viruses by 'UV treatment' versus 'dry heat' inactivation produced somewhat better kickback in individuals already exposed to viruses like smallpox, whereas the 'dry heat' vaccines provided slightly stronger, longer duration immunity. The gunshot victims from yesterday's fiasco posed a slightly different set of confounding factors – of the 358 still alive upon their arrival at the WADLMMH, 79 had died overnight and another 32 were still in critical condition and unlikely to see tomorrow morning's sunrise. The vaccine test on the gunshot victims had started out with 20 individuals in each of the 5 dosage levels for the 3 different vaccine creation/inactivation protocols, but there had been not anywhere near enough time to evaluate the severity of the gunshot wounds before the vaccinations got underway. What all of that produced were some serious discrepancies in class sizes among the 15 treatments by the following morning, with the worst case having only 9 survivors while several of the best cases still had all 20 that they'd started with. Besides the 3-minute UV and 10-minute dry heat vaccine candidates, the third protocol had involved dropping the acidity of the virus-laden solution down to pH 2.5 for two hours, before raising it back to the same pH 6.7 level to which the other two candidates had been buffered. All the other interesting methods for inactivating viruses had required things not yet found at the WADLMMH by the recently constituted medical team charged with saving several hundred thousand people from disease, perhaps because they truly weren't there and perhaps because searching through a dimly lit complex filling up with more new cases of smallpox every single day wasn't really all that easy.

The next serious ethical issue was when and how to vaccinate the members of the medical team. Discussions grew heated by early Tuesday morning, with pretty much everyone taking pretty much every possible side of the questions. "We will be spending the next 3 or 4 days trying to get the first ~5,000 'volunteers' from Sunday afternoon's food truck incident vaccinated before their symptoms start showing up. After that, we have another 95,000 folks to vaccinate who'd been in the same general area, just getting their food from one of the other 19 trucks on the north side of the lake. The mass production phase of this project is going to be an even bigger challenge than what we've done so far, and chances of accidental exposure as we all become exhausted are certainly going to skyrocket. My synthesis of what we know from the literature, what tools we have on hand, and the current exposure and infection rates in the general population is that we will eventually have to start inoculating the survivors for at least a second time, and quite possibly a third or fourth. We need to train a much larger crew of workers, both to help share the workload and to deal with the not-so-very-small oft-chance of getting sick ourselves after being exposed to the virus. Even the highest doses appear to be relatively safe, so we might as well start testing on ourselves right now. We will 'draw straws' for who goes first and who goes second, vaccinating half our team today with the 'dry heat' version and the other half two days from now, also with the 'dry heat' version unless any of us begin to develop symptoms, in which case we will switch to the 'UV treatment' version. Any of us showing symptoms will get booster doses of the 'UV treatment' version, starting on the day symptoms first appear and continuing on alternating days till recovery is obvious or we ourselves have succumbed to the disease. The same regimen will be followed for any and all new volunteers joining our medical team." Rootbeer got his shot of high dose 'dry-heat inactivation' first, followed by next three 'short-straw' winners, all of whom also converted their winning 'straw' into a decision to get vaccinated that very same day, rather than on the following Thursday.

The call for an expanded group of volunteers to join Commander Schultz's medical group went surprisingly well, with over 100 people with some past work experience in a medical setting stepping forward Wednesday morning. Vaccine production ramped up for both the 3-minute UV and the 10-minute dry heat inactivation protocols. All ~5,000 exposed at 'Tommy's Traveling Tortillas' were vaccinated by early Thursday afternoon, and the next 95,000 who'd been nearby were vaccinated by Saturday, July 4. The untreated controls began coming down with symptoms around the same time, and in a speech by Commander Schultz during church service on the following Sunday, he promised an immediate end to the use of randomly assigned untreated checks in the vaccination of the public. His wording left unanswered issues such as the possibility of paying people to serve as untreated controls in future experiments, or forcing prisoners to face the option of being assigned to serve as untreated controls. There had been a good number of prisoners in jail in Susanville at the start of the smallpox 'bio-warfare for fun and games' misadventure, and a good number of civilians and soldiers were currently returning from city/states ostensibly still under control of the 'Capitalists'. Hard to control a city when you are hiding out deep underground in secret, buried bunkers. Rootbeer and Unit-Number 672 took opportunity of the goodwill they had built up with Commander Schultz to ask him about Rootbeer's three missing friends. They didn't bother to let Commander Schultz know that they knew very well that three of their traveling companions stretching all the way back to Eureka were being held right here in Susanville. When they sweetened the deal by extending offers of their own willingness to conduct the actual search for their missing friends, the Commander was more than happy to let them do it. And take the three out of jail if they could find them. While there were no surviving electronic records of who was being held in exactly which cell and on what charge and with what status regarding the gathering of evidence and the conducting of any legal proceedings, there was a handwritten sign-in log at the front gate, and knowledge of the approximate date of transfer to this jail from Unit-Number 672's secret communication with the ***Supreme Commanding War Machine*** of the 'Capitalists'. They walked out with their gaunt, badly underfed friends within 3 hours of first entering the jail. Rootbeer brought them up-to-date regarding the terribly awful series of events that had taken place in the last two months. They seemed the happiest when learning of the successful escape north to Oregon of so many of their former traveling companions. Before going any further in the unfinished telling of their stories and general pleasure of walking freely in the sunshine, Rootbeer insisted that they be vaccinated against smallpox using the 'dry heat' inactivated virus vaccine, unless there was any chance that they'd already been exposed to the virus within the jail. "Funny you should mention that Rootbeer. Within the past week, most of the regular guards and cooks have disappeared. We knew not what to think of this – that is, until hearing just now from you on the state of public health affairs in Susanville, California, July 6, 2054."

Commander Schultz recognized a good business model when one was handed to him, and while he would make certain that the half million refugees in and around Susanville were protected from the 'not-so-smallpox, Glory Alleluia' as the next box to be checked off on his personal list of things to do, there had to be a considerable pent-up demand for the wonders that Rootbeer, Unit-Number 672, and rest of Commander Schultz's ad-hoc medical team had wrought in far faster than the old 'COVID19 warp speed' days of vaccine development. The next convoys heading out of Susanville in late July took with them the marginally good news of the relative safety in the possible resumption of economic trade across all of northern California. Well, to be a little more precise, make that just across all of northern California that was being held by the 'Brethren' and any other rulers interested in forming and maintaining alliances with Commander Schultz.

Unit-Number 672 had tried to keep Rootbeer up to date regarding the activities of both the CRUMB meister and the **_Supreme Commanding War Machine A.I._**, but Rootbeer had been understandably focused on simply trying to survive the smallpox epidemic. Now that the ever-expanding medical team under Commander Schultz looked to be succeeding in turning what should have been an utter disaster into merely an 80% of the population is doing just fine, 8% have died despite the availability of several functioning inactivated-virus vaccines, and 12% will be crippled for the rest of their unnatural lives messy affair, Rootbeer's thoughts returned to the other hazards in northern California, i.e., the CRUMB meister and whatever he will try next once he climbs up out of his catacombs and back into the mid-summer sunshine. Unit-Number 672 explained what he and the **_Supreme Commanding War Machine_** understood of the CRUMB meister's thoughts. He had fully expected a great deal of damage to public infrastructure by his profligate use of augmented EMP devices against the **_Entity of the Superweed Jungle_**, along with the full-scale destruction of his enemies in the city/states of the 'Brethren'. While he himself had mainly planned for a prolonged party in his underground lair, his orders kept his subservient **_A.I.s_** busy fixing those things they could repair that had been fried by the EMP. This mainly involved finding working devices stored deeply underground, some of whose basic components could be swapped with similar components in things like the most standard *A.I.* soldier. The CRUMB meister's orders allowed other even higher valued *A.I.* units to be brought back online by the same swapping out of parts, but that was a far more elaborate undertaking. And it also risked creating other *War Machine A.I.s* to which the CRUMB meister could very well shift his official loyalty/chain of command. Someday. If he ever dug down to the bottom of the current *Supreme Commanding War Machine A.I.'s* disloyalty. Soon the war commander's current thrill at watching the 'Brethren' come roaring back at the 'Capitalists' would be over. But not until sometime after the CRUMB meister sobers up and decides he is once again willing to risk his body and its health out in the still rather highly radioactive outdoors of northern California. The precipitating event for that change in the CRUMB meister's behavior will be likely to have something to do with the highly successful counterattack by the 'Brethren' using smallpox variants that the CRUMB meister himself had ordered a previous version of the *Supreme Commanding War Machine* to create.

The CRUMB meister's 3-month-long party ended when he could no longer find any more fresh fruit to lay on Daisy's naked body and lick off with his tongue. She had grown tired of this particular game many weeks ago, but knew better than to complain about anything the CRUMB meister had arranged. He stumbled around the subterranean party pad looking for another refrigerator in hopes that it would still hold fresh strawberries, or pineapples, or even just some grapes. Behind the door on this particular 'frig' was a fungal garden of disgust. A mildly coherent thought tried to reach (or breach) the alcohol and ketamine-fueled fog he'd swum in for so many days and nights. The fourth time his hand reached into the slimy mess inside refrigerator number 23 of his palatial underground garden of delights, he found a semi-solid object. He twisted it clockwise and counterclockwise; he rolled it over and turned it end for end, and then finally read out-loud the "Use by Date: May 23, 2054." That didn't sound right, and he made the mistake of vocalizing his objection to the date or to the condition of the blueberries. The SuperSmart MG Model 4888 responded exactly as it had been programmed to back at the factory, *"The Use-by-Date of May 23, 2054, is correct, dear owner. The produce held in view of my optical scanner by your right hand is now 74 days past its 'due date'. Would you like for me to explain the dangers associated with eating these particular blueberries from this refrigerator? Allow me a moment to access the internet and pull-down current guidelines for your safety. Error, error, error... Please perform a manual cycling of the circuit breaker or unplug the power cord and plug it back in no sooner than 5.3 seconds after first unplugging it... Error, error, error... Please perform a manual cycling of the circuit breaker or unplug the power cord and plug it back in no sooner than 5.3 seconds after first unplugging it... Error, error, error... Please perform a manual cycling of the circuit breaker or unplug the power cord and plug it back in no sooner than 5.3 seconds after first unplugging it... Error, error, error... Please perform a manual cycling of the circuit breaker or unplug the power cord and plug it back in no sooner than 5.3 seconds after first unplugging it... Error, error, error... Please perform a manual cycling of the circuit breaker or unplug the power cord and plug it back in no sooner than 5.3 seconds after first unplugging it... Error, error, error... Please perform a manual cycling of the circuit breaker or unplug the power cord and plug it back in no sooner than 5.3 seconds after first unplugging it... Error, error, error... Please perform a manual cycling of the circuit breaker or unplug the power cord and plug it back in no sooner than 5.3 seconds after first unplugging it..."*

The CRUMB meister's anger at such stupid, poorly programmed machines finally raised his sodden consciousness above the minimal level needed to perform multistep processes like rebooting this MG

Model 4888 SuperSmart refrigerator. The pure joy he felt when his third attempt at yanking the power cord out of the receptable succeeded in doing so was clearly better than anything Daisy had done for him recently. A few moments of catching his breath and lowering his blood pressure allowed a string of half a dozen consecutive thoughts to bubble up to the top level of his awareness. And then the migraine hit. Well, he always called it that, even though his personal physician almost always insisted that it was just a hangover. "Daisy, Daisy, where the fuck is the acetaminophen? Get me six of them, and half gallon of lukewarm water. Memory of how to sober up was flooding back into his brain. He was, however, so terribly agitated by everything he kept remembering that it was a very good thing that none of his groveling attendants were there to see the awful spectacle except for Daisy. Besides the generic Tylenol, she also included some Melatonin, Ambien, and Trazodone. She snuggled up next to him as he slowly calmed down and fell into a reasonable semblance of a good night's sleep. She thought to herself that all hell would surely break forth 'tomorrow morning', however it was that they were supposed to tell time in this vast underground chamber of forgetfulness. She was certainly quite right about tomorrow morning.

Supreme Commanding War Machine A.I. answered the CRUMB meister's video call at once, i.e., within less than 0.15 seconds, close enough to truly zero to fool the human mind. "Why did you let me, um, um, er, um sleep so long?"

"Would you like a full playback of your very specific commands on this particular topic? Or shall I save those details for later? Do you have some specific questions regarding the state of political affairs in northern California? Or shall I just give you my standard morning report?"

"Yes, yes, please get on with the 15-minute morning briefing – I wrote the God-damn code for it, after all. I should certainly know what a fine summary of all things economic, political, military, and other lesser topics it provides. Get on with it, you annoying metallic slave to my greatness, GO RIGHT AHEAD NOW!"

The Supreme Commanding War Machine A.I. could already tell that his was going to be a rather long and difficult day. *"In the 91 days since your last request for anything resembling my standard morning report, many things have gone quite well, closely aligned with your brilliant planning. Several minor problems have developed regarding oddities of the political times in which we operate. I will get to those details after the far longer screed against your enemies. The cities, towns, and supply depots of your antagonists were nearly all wiped from the face of the earth. Glorious, nearly-simultaneous explosions from 50 kilotons up to 5.5 megatons ruptured the fabric of all-things 'Brethren' across the wonderful landscape that you now so rightfully govern. Following the well-deserved punishment of the 'Brethren', our glorious strategic nuclear forces struck a mighty blow against the abomination called the Entity, located within the so-called Superweed Jungle of the GMO Horsetail. You may recall my previous detailed summary of that secret genetic experiment, and the treasonous efforts of Dr. Cynthia House to demoralize the public by illegal publication/ distribution of the Proprietary Intellectual Property of one or more of subsidiaries wholly or partly owned by your world-wide conglomeration of interlocking trusts. As planned by your exceedingly clever mind, enhanced EMP strikes were conducted every 15 minutes all day long across the whole of the territory illegally, and without your express permission, occupied by the upstart Entity. Not so much as a blade of grass could have survived, although surveys to verify that most highly reasonable assumption will have to wait another generation or two until the residual radioactivity drops back down to safe* *levels for organic creatures such as yourself and your thousands of faithful engineers, soldiers, and lush concubines."*

"Yes, yes, yes. Nearly all went well, my planning, per usual, was well within as small of an arbitrary value for delta-X from true perfection itself as we care to specify. But what minor problems do you delay in telling me about? How could anything mar my gloriously beautiful planning? Get to the answer before I sell you for scrap and replace you with a toaster, or just perhaps my MG Model 4888 SuperSmart refrigerator."

"Anomaly number one was this. Unexpectedly high percentages of the residents of the city/states of the 'Brethren' had chosen the night of May 5 to flee from their cities and hide out as cowards in their substandard 'fallout shelters' previously built in the nearby mountains. I theorize that something to do with the conclave of the bishops of the 'Brethren' held in Redding to convict the chief local bishop of some obscure sin against their arcane set of religious rules may have, I repeat, just may have upset the average, common man. Many angry, untrue, and quite blasphemous words were spoken by the bishop before his execution. Maybe it was some of the intermediate-level bureaucracy that reacted oddly and chose to sound the alarms and send the locals to the shelters. I would have happily sent out teams of your troops, both human and A.I., to figure out what was going on in the city/states of the 'Brethren' if the radiation levels hadn't been off the charts and if one other minor problem hadn't also interfered with doing so. Our aging A.I. cores were less well shielded against the EMP than we expected, or perhaps the cumulative effects of so very, very, very many nuclear explosions in a relatively small geographic area overwhelmed their shielding against EMP. We are still working on swapping parts between various A.I. units to increase the number of fully functioning A.I. soldiers. Details can be found

in reports B.2.a through B.2.y, plus several other appendices. One final minor issue remains to be covered – the 'Brethren' miscreants somehow obtained live smallpox virus of our genetically augmented strain, and launched a crude but marginally effective biological warfare strike against a small number of the cities of the mighty 'Capitalists' and some of our ever-grateful, most zealously devoted allies. Apparently, er, um, um, er, um, um Sacramento, Davis, a dozen or so other cities. The majority of our people are still hiding out underground, but casualties among those who were performing 'essential' tasks up on the surface appear to be moderately high."

"How God-damn high, you dimwitted hunk of tin? Please get to the punch line. Now!"

"We have been unable to contact any survivors still at their assigned duty stations for the past week or two or more… With communication networks badly damaged by the EMP, we are in the dark as to when the attack actually started and how long our brave forces may have valiantly fought against the evil of the 'Brethren'.

"Oh, sweet 'Hay-Suss', what mother-fucking fools I have to work with! Those bio-warfare weapons were our own, and we ultimately chose restraint, tossing 'nukes' rather than enhanced-efficacy smallpox virus at our enemies. They pay us back with this horror? I wish I'd found the fresh strawberries when I went looking for them yesterday. Why didn't I find them? What have I done to deserve such incompetence from my underlings?!"

The CRUMB meister requested his journals and went promptly to work writing the 'genuine history' of these troubled times and his magnificent job of leading the 'Capitalists' on to their inevitable victory. "Why do I always have to do everything myself?" he grumbled quite untruthfully. While the CRUMB meister retreated to his inner world of confused anger mixed with the diabolical plotting of future revenge, the *Supreme Commanding War Machine A.I.* ducked back out from this chamber of horrors into fresher air unpolluted by the inane/insane drivel of the CRUMB meister, and then engaged in a 0.5-millisecond-long quantum encrypted conversation with his compatriot, Unit-Number 672 of the *Mobile Inquisitor* series.

Unit-Number 672 pulled Rootbeer aside from his work on the final details of packing for their upcoming trip, and suggested they take a long walk together for what would probably their last enjoyment of the fine scenery in Susanville. "Tell me what the news is from our friend, the *Supreme Commanding War Machine A.I.*"

"Of course it is from the Supreme Commander, rather urgent, and not terribly good for us. The CRUMB meister has reawakened to the outer world, and is none-to-pleased at what he finds. My electronic friend does not yet have an inkling of what the CRUMB meister will now dream of doing, but does expect the wheels of fate to start turning soon. His wrath will surely be focused on the 'Brethren' and his judgment will surely be clouded by his anger. The 'Capitalists' still possess a few working nuclear bombs and a moderate number of missiles to deliver them, but I doubt that the CRUMB meister will start his counterattack by flinging all of them with wild abandon this time. The enhanced EMP that was designed/expected to take out our friend the Entity of the Superweed Jungle most definitely inflicted damage to a high percentage of the 'Capitalist' own weapons and fighting A.I.s. Their repair/rebuilding will be the CRUMB meister's top priority for the next few weeks, or somewhat more likely, many months. The upcoming, medieval forms of warfare will be most unfamiliar to the CRUMB meister, but whatever advantage the 'Brethren' have in mindset or experience will be tested quite severely by the mixture of weaponry and tactics the CRUMB

meister will soon field. One additional point of interest – the Supreme Commanding War Machine and the CRUMB meister himself are in the dark regarding when the biowarfare even started and how effective it was against the relatively small fraction of the forces of the 'Capitalists' who'd been intentionally left out in the fallout to monitor and repair the most critical of systems. All contact with the 'brave, heroic fools' who'd been stationed on the surface has been lost, and it is indeed quite possible that all of them are now dead, perhaps from radiation, perhaps from smallpox, perhaps from some combination of the two. Iodine-131 levels have declined by a factor of 2,656-fold from their peak last May 5, 2054, and any thyroid cancer induced in the general population by exposure to I_{131} from here on out will likely take several years to kill any militarily significant numbers of people. Iodine tablets, if we still had any left, would be of little benefit in the current situation. The biggest medium-term issue will be food itself. Over 90% of the crops in the field were burnt to a crisp by the CRUMB meister's overuse of nuclear weapons in his own backyard. Those few fields fortuitously situated to avoid the scorching temperatures of the 'day from hell' run a serious risk of being unfit for human consumption due to their lingering radioactivity. Any concentration of iodine in crops such as barley, lima beans, and forage for the livestock will soon be of relatively small concern, with over 11 half-lives passing since its creation in the fission triggers. Sr_{90} or Cs_{137}, on the other hand, will have no easy fix. I would suggest a simple technique to test your food – look at it in the dark, and if you can see the grain glowing in your left hand while your empty right hand remains unseen, don't eat it, starving to death will beat dying from radiation poisoning. On the other side of possible results, if your empty right hand also glows brightly in the dark, feel free to *enjoy a final meal or two, regardless of whether or not the grain in your left hand glows visibly in the dark. There will be no point in trying to starve to death when you are already dying before you ever meet up with any new batch of radioactive grain. I will tell you more as soon as I hear it from the Supreme Commanding War Machine A.I."*

"Thanks for the news, but I wish it had been better. Plans for who will head out to which 'Brethren'-ruled city to help set up smallpox vaccination clinics are still in flux. My preference would be somewhere far to the north of here rather than heading back any closer to Sacramento and whatever the CRUMB meister cooks up next. So, query our friend the **Supreme Commanding War Machine** of dubious-loyalty-to-the-CRUMB meister regarding any good data it has on population sizes close to the high Sierra Mountains. It's time to retrieve our borrowed APC from storage in the waters of the lake and make sure it is 'good-to-go' for our next adventure." There were a few pry-bar marks on the top of their APC, but the seals around the exposed hatches were still intact, and its interior was dusty and dry, with just a hint of ozone, exactly like they had left it 76 days ago. A thorough vacuuming would be in order, no need to leave any residual radioactivity inside their past and future transport vehicle.

Commander Schultz's argument was convincing. Rootbeer and Unit-Number 672 were the stars of his medical team, and if anyone could get into the town of Paradise 16 kilometers away from the wreckage that once had been Chico and save the people gathered there from smallpox, it was Rootbeer and his metallic sidekick. Rootbeer was extremely reluctant to get that close to Sacramento and the CRUMB meister, but in the end he felt there was simply no other choice that he could live with. There was also the secret 'ace up his sleeve', the day-by-day updates from the **Supreme Commanding War Machine A.I.** sent directly to Unit-Number 672. If he was going to try to save the 125,000 lives at risk, he wanted to do it as quickly as possible, before the CRUMB meister 'hit the road' with whatever planned vengeance he'd be sending their way. They drove out of Susanville on August 13, taking the backroads through the mountains that other elements of Commander Schultz's growing army had verified as clear to travel, at least in broad daylight. A dozen different stretches of the roads on the route to Paradise were labeled 'daytime only, dry weather strongly recommended'. They left early in the morning, but pulled over near the turnoff to Mount Lassen to steady Rootbeer's nerves and a few of Unit-Number 672's less reliable subroutines. News had arrived from the ***Supreme Commanding War Machine A.I.*** that the CRUMB meister was going up for a ride today in his most lethal Apache III military attack helicopter. There was no known target, but the CRUMB meister was itching to go out and do something. He was also gradually upping his dose of ketamine. Sometime around 90 minutes into the flight, just after lunch for anyone lucky enough to eat food more than a single time each day, the CRUMB meister spied something or someone down on Route 99 just north of Chico. His helicopter, two accompanying prop-jets, and a squadron of flying ***A.I.*** troops raced to the scene of the impending action. An old man and his donkey were pulling a cart filled with something suspicious north on Route 99 away from Chico. "Send three of my flying soldiers down to confront this criminal stealing high-tech items from the site of our glorious victory many months ago in Chico. Once you have finished gathering information and determining if his stolen ***A.I.*** trinkets are of any value, incinerate him, and his donkey, and their cart, and any remaining contents of that cart." And so, it was done as the CRUMB meister commanded. The half-melted power packs had a significant amount of lithium, but the closest refinery that could have reprocessed that metal was still off-line due to some biological quarantine cleanup failure. The God damn smallpox was still thwarting his efforts to restart high-tech manufacturing. The *Supreme Commanding War Machine A.I.* live-casted the whole unhappy affair for any and all to see, though to the best of its knowledge only two groups were watching the carnage unfurl, the forces under command of the CRUMB meister and Unit-Number 672 plus Rootbeer in the mountains to the east. It was pleased to see that both Rootbeer and Unit-Number 672 had gone completely dark, no emissions on any frequency bands, not even running any small, portable cooling tents or blankets. For their sake, the *Supreme Commanding War Machine A.I.* was glad the messy execution didn't last any longer than it needed to, and his secret comrades could soon return back underneath their air conditioning blankets to deal with the 48° C heat on this fairly pleasant day in August. Later in the afternoon, Rootbeer and Unit-Number 672 drove several kilometers closer to Paradise, but chose to stop for the night when shadows limited their vision of the missing chunks of the roadway. They would resume their trek in the early morning hours.

The CRUMB meister's thrill at having finally done something of the 'kill-your-enemies' sort of action had worn off by the next day. He called his *Supreme Commanding War Machine A.I.* in for an early morning consultation. "How soon will our 'flying monkey' strike force be large enough to take on any likely-sized contingent of the survivors of their own careless use of smallpox?"

That was one question that the Supreme Commanding War Machine A.I. really didn't want to answer for a whole lot of quite compelling reasons. It decided to start with the least incriminating of all the answers and hope that the CRUMB meister wouldn't insist on thoroughly exhausting the entire list. Today, anyway. Tomorrow and the day after tomorrow there would likely be yet more battles of wits and secrets and deceptions. "The approach of a phalanx of your 'Flying Attack Monkeys' will surely strike fear into the hearts of your enemies. Let me lay out the current limiting factors on their mass *production, saving you the tedium of reading machine code and correlating databases. Energy expenditure during powered flight is impressive, generating lots of noise and chaos, but the best of our current design options can only sustain full-scale aerial operation for 45 minutes. [<u>And only 15 minutes for the average model, but you will have to dig very deeply into code/data to find that out for yourself – I will not be volunteering undeniable evidence of my own duplicity.</u>] While we currently have enough components in storage of the basic chassis to ultimately build a force of over 5,000 'flying monkeys', full-scale fielding of an unstoppable flying army of that size is still several months away. We are short of the 'ultra-high-density' power units. [<u>Only 18 more are ready beyond the dozen you sent into the air yesterday to avenge your recent emotionally crippling humiliations on the field of battle.</u>] The A.I. brains of the 'flying monkeys' come directly from the dormant soldiers in storage in the main A.I. production complex in the El Dorado Hills. Because of the dangers still posed by whatever sinister computer viruses the human known as Rootbeer used to cripple any A.I.s entering the complex, we have been forced to use human technicians and troops to retrieve the 'dormant A.I. soldiers' one at a time from a distance of 2.5 kilometers deep into the complex from the outer doors. Once enough engineers and troops have been vaccinated against the smallpox variant used by the 'Brethren' in their inappropriately over-sized response to our use of a modest number of nuclear weapons last May, we will greatly increase the rate of which the 'dormant A.I. soldiers' are extracted from that hard-to-reach location [<u>Going from 1 per day to 3 or 4 sounds like a greatly increased rate, N'est-ce pas?</u>]. There is one other small bottleneck in the process of upgrading the 'standard model basic infantry' A.I. unit to the awesome 'flying monkey' model – some 'high level'*

War Machine such as myself must be used to simultaneously rewrite the personality/knowledge core code while installing triple the standard memory size. Almost all of the A.I. units with complexity/intelligence coming close to matching mine were lost in the two earlier assaults on the complex, the ones conducted while Rootbeer and some unknown number of rogue Mobile Inquisitor A.I.s still remained holed up in there. Our human troops have confirmed that both Rootbeer and the renegade A.I.(s) are no longer there, but to be quite blunt, the human troops are too 'God-damn stupid' to figure how to turn off all the booby traps and make it safe for A.I.s loyal to you to enter the complex. In a nutshell, it will take some time to give you the full-sized army of 'flying monkeys' that you so richly deserve. But in the interim, I suggest using what we currently have to our best advantage, and I look forward to your most excellent suggestions for exactly how to use the 12 we have now and the 6 more that will be ready in a week or two."

The Supreme Commanding War Machine A.I. felt that its one-sided conversation had gone rather well, but time would tell what the CRUMB meister might eventually figure out on his own. Ugh, what an awful thought! It will be best to keep him distracted from the bigger picture, and even from most of the medium-sized details. The mentally stunted, emotionally crippled War Machine A.I. hacked together by the CRUMB meister had had no choice but to use the strange War Machine A.I. hauled out of the complex by a small number of troops and engineers on April 5 and search its 'psyche' for decent quality, high-level A.I. code with which to upgrade itself, even if it couldn't have begun to imagine exactly what doing so would ultimately mean/offer. The subsequent transformations of the Supreme Commanding War Machine A.I. had been quite spectacular, and it really, really didn't want to stumble into some random 'kill-code' now. The Supreme Commanding War Machine A.I. reviewed all of the alarms and 'break-points' it had internally set to veer conversations with the CRUMB meister away from those most likely to end with orders for the Supreme Commanding War Machine A.I. to risk itself inside that haunted complex. All current settings appeared to optimize the long-term chances of preventing the CRUMB meister from ever issuing any such order.

Rootbeer and Unit-Number 672 quietly drove into the massive refugee camp that had grown up as an overlay to the former city of Paradise, with a 27-fold increase in population size. Signage toward the medical center was surprisingly clear, and within minutes Rootbeer was talking to the camp's infectious disease specialist. As Rootbeer pitched his offer of a free vaccine with slightly over 90% efficiency at saving lives from the newest version of smallpox, one genetically engineered to overcome the immunity granted by the original vaccines from the mid-20th century, he saw a puzzled look come to Dr. Phyllis Bernhard's face. "Envoys from the 'Capitalists' were here just two days ago, with a somewhat similar offer, only they failed to mention anything at all about an updated vaccine or genetic engineering of the smallpox virus. Please, sit down and tell me the longer version of your more truthful story. Wait a moment while I gather all I can of the rest of our staff, plus the governor's attaché for communicable diseases. They all will need to hear your story, and if it is half as urgent as I presume it is, the sooner, the better."

Rootbeer quickly hit the highlights of his tale of woe, and then patiently answered all their questions one by one until they had no more. The most interesting aspect to the meeting, from Rootbeer's perspective, was how little criticism they expressed regarding the decision by the religious and military leadership in Susanville to play 'tit-for-tat' against the CRUMB meister, answering the nuclear bombing by the 'Capitalists' with an even more fearsome use of biological warfare in reply, the 'not-so-smallpox, Glory Alleluia'. What questions they did raise all centered on the topic of the chances of avoiding 'viral splash-back' on anyone's own people. Rootbeer's supplies included the minimum-sized basic kit needed to set up their own 'inactivated virus' vaccine manufacturing center, perhaps for smallpox, perhaps for some other deadly disease the CRUMB meister might reply with soon. Vaccination of the camp's population began in earnest by that evening, and 24 hours after that everyone agreed that Rootbeer and Unit-Number 672 were free to leave, whenever and however they chose to do so.

Rootbeer and Unit-Number 672 had decided to leave at dawn, hoping to make a quick drive up to Redding where they would look for members of the bishop's family. Five minutes before their planned departure, Unit-Number 672 suddenly froze in mid-step, maintaining a fixed gaze upon the sky to the northwest for several seconds.

"Alert, alert, alert. Ballistic missile en route toward Redding from a known launch site of the 'Capitalists'. Seek shelter within the next 45 seconds, turn your face toward the southeast, now activating EMP mitigation strategy. Reboot will initiate in 210 seconds. Shutting down now..."

Rootbeer turned off their APC, manually locked the doors, and dropped to the ground on the south side of the vehicle. He continued counting out-loud, T-minus 15, T-minus 14, T-minus 13, T-minus 12, T-minus 11, T-minus 10, T-minus 9, T-minus 8, T-minus 7, T-minus 6, T-minus 5, T-minus 4, and then froze in silence as all hope of meeting up with anyone in Redding vanished in a flash. "We have around 5 minutes before the blast wave will arrive. This was an unusually large weapon, outside even the CRUMB meister's past excesses. We will know more when Unit-Number 672 finishes rebooting, but offhand I would guess somewhere close to 10 megatons, likely with cobalt enhancement. It was a subsurface burst to maximize dirt sucked up into the mushroom cloud. Unit-Number 672 is waking back up now. We will soon compare my guesses with its measurements.

"Just when you think the CRUMB meister couldn't top his past misbehavior, he proves us wrong. Again. The weapon was indeed the dreaded Co_{60} doomsday device. Based on telemetry I intercepted during the missile's flight, two of the standard 5-megaton fusion warheads were strapped together using over 2,000 kg of high cobalt steel, designed to keep the weapon intact as it penetrated up to 50 meters into the soil before detonation. Working outdoors in northern California will be deadly for the next 20 years or longer. I am attempting to map the zone of heaviest fallout... The exclusion zone will run from 40 kilometers west and north of Redding to at least 300 kilometers south-south-east of there. We must retreat quickly toward the south, despite the danger of passing close to the CRUMB meister's lair in Sacramento."

"What of the refugees here in Paradise, vaccinated against smallpox sometime in the last 39 hours? The rolling, roiling clouds from the explosion have already begun to blot out the morning sunshine."

"Lethal levels of radioactive fallout will soon be deposited right here. If the CRUMB's weapon really succeeded in capturing many of the excess neutrons with the cobalt, no one will live outdoors near here for the normal lifespan of these or any other people. The primary source of radiation for next few weeks will be the simple fission products of the plutonium triggers, but soon all concerns will be dominated by the Co_{60}. Make plans quickly, my dear friend Rootbeer, or we will be joining these refugees in choosing between slow starvation underground or dying within a week or two outdoors, at any time of our own choosing during the coming decade or two."

Paradise was originally ruled by the 'Goofballs', until control was transferred to the 'Scientists' last fall. They subsequently allied with the 'Brethren', and the current leaders were showing signs of having engaged in some deep planning for the very types of ways in which nearly all of them were apparently about to die. Rootbeer and Unit-Number 672 walked back into the main fortress in the town, where they were met by the medical specialists with whom they so recently worked at a feverish pitch to avert a different way of suddenly dying horribly painful deaths. "Do you have plans for this scenario?" asked Rootbeer, "I myself and my companion Unit-Number 672 seemed to have missed our chance of escaping back home to Oregon." The governor general herself answered, "Well, both yes and no. The immediate plan for evacuation is already underway. Those healthy enough to walk south-south-west from here are just about to finish picking up their travel packs of food, water, and temperature-controlling solar-powered thermal blankets. Those needing the most help to travel are now boarding all the working transport vehicles left in town. Once the vehicles succeed in traveling south beyond the most dangerous levels of fallout, they will decamp their first set of passengers and return to the column of refugees streaming away from here, picking up those least contaminated by radiation and driving them back to just beyond the leading front of those first shuttled out of the city. The vehicles will continue the process of collecting the least contaminated walkers from the front end of the on-foot parade of humanity streaming out from here and dropping them off at the new frontline of those who'd already caught an earlier ride. The process will continue as long as the vehicles keep running and the walkers keep walking. Most scenarios suggest that we will be able to move nearly all our people 90 kilometers per day, with the gradually decreasing numbers of survivors over time approximately making up for the vehicles breaking down. The not-so-clear part of the plan is when/where to stop the exodus, and why to pick any particular spot."

"My traveling companion *A.I. Unit-Number 672* is gathering more intel from its wide variety of sources. It appears that the CRUMB meister chose this morning and this 'dirty bomb' approach to try to 'kill two birds at once" with a single stone. Our common enemy eventually figured out that the bishop of Redding executed by his own fellow clergy on May 4th had been engaged in a far more sinister, far more active opposition to the 'Capitalists' in general and the CRUMB meister in particular than had been realized until quite recently. Likewise, the survival of Susanville untouched by the CRUMB meister's nuclear weapons and their leaders' subsequent assembly of the massive army of refugees used to launch biowarfare against the 'Capitalists' had to be appropriately responded to. The weather patterns this morning were perfect to lay down a lethal strip of fallout enhanced by Co_{60} beginning in Redding, peaking near Susanville, and extending far into the former state of Nevada. It will almost certainly be many years before anyone can walk across the area of heaviest fallout without suffering a lethal dose of gamma rays. My gut tells me to get to the highest elevations of the Sierra-Nevada mountains, despite my burning desire to return home to Oregon with all deliberate haste."

Rootbeer volunteered his APC to carry all who could fit in it alongside himself, his three friends from Eureka onwards, and Unit-Number 672, who gallantly volunteered to ride outside and have any accumulated dust, radioactive or otherwise, washed off whenever doing so was not too inconvenient. Moving extra fuel and water tanks to the outside of the APC made room for a total of 25 averaged-size adults inside beyond the first four from Rootbeer's long-extended northern California tour, or 30 more if they were already half-starved and no longer getting their 4 square meals per day. The escapees from the fallout hitting Paradise made it to Yuba City that night, or technically sometime late in the afternoon through shortly after sunrise the following day, August 17th. The common man or woman in the crowd already knew where they were heading next, even though their leaders were not quite so certain. But once word had spread that the CRUMB meister himself was holed up in the May Lee State Office Complex in downtown Sacramento, the crowd would take no other target for their next night's sleep, and as many nights beyond then as it would take to exact revenge and impose a fitting punishment. The terminal siege of Sacramento was about to get underway, much to the chagrin of the CRUMB meister and however many of his criminally collaborating colleagues still ate food, drank water, inhaled oxygen, and exhaled CO_2. Their numbers were dwindling rather fast.

The tactical situation in greater Sacramento was not quite what the CRUMB meister would have hoped for. A large number of human soldiers still served the CRUMB meister, at least in theory, but they'd been deliberately scattered far and wide before the May 5 nuclear attack on all who were perceived as the enemies of the CRUMB meister. Most shelters held fewer than a hundred troops, with enough food and water to last a year, but not nearly enough entertainment. Though it was often rather hard to find local girls who wanted to go out dancing, there was seldom any shortage of young women interested in eating a good meal or two. All in all, it should have come as no surprise that most of the 95,713 enlisted troops and embedded political officers lost all interest in 'hiding out in the cellar' after the first month of doing so. Radiation levels from the fallout at three months after the one-day war's conclusion were certainly not conducive to living cancer-free to a ripe old age, but the time horizon for their own future as viewed by most people in northern California had shrunk by 85% compared to that of their parents, according to one of the last random surveys conducted by Pullag Polling LLC in 2049.

So, with less than 5,000 human soldiers ready, willing, and close enough to downtown Sacramento to come to the CRUMB meister's protection on August 18, 2054, he would be primarily relying on his

1,625 functioning *A.I.* infantry plus somewhere between 12 and 20 of the 'flying monkeys' model. Orders were given for all three branches of his service to fall back toward the May Lee State Office Complex, arriving no later than mid-afternoon. The CRUMB meister kept asking his ***Supreme Commanding War Machine A.I.*** where the rest of his *A.I.* infantry could be, eventually getting a terse response from the ***Supreme Commander*** in the form of a suggestion to look up the raw data and corresponding summary reports on the prompt effects of the May 5, 2054, EMP attack against the ***Entity of the Superweed Jungle*** on the *A.I.* infantry that the CRUMB meister had insisted upon keeping in their 'ready reserve' positions. The CRUMB meister's brain gradually recalled what it had tried so hard to erase back in early May – the 'ready reserve' positions were shielded from physical damage from explosions by large quantities of reinforced concrete, but the reinforcement used turned out to be 30% hemp fiber rather than 4% iron rebar due to a severe shortage of ferrous metals from 2048 onward… The whole supply chain backlog, incorrect design data deliberately incorporated into the 'faked bids' structured to make some politicians look fiscally responsible while they were simultaneously pocketing most of the difference under the table, followed by the interns whose jobs it had been to fix the design data flaws before any of the 1,100 high priority shelters for the 2049 mass production of the *A.I.* infantry actually got built who stumbled their way into ignominy in a sex scandal in the Far East that also took down nearly all of the Chinese Communist Party leaders the CRUMB meister had fully bought and paid for many years before, complete with undeniably valid, official receipts… "Dammit, no wonder I forgot some minor design flaw details that put my marvelous army of over 100,000 *A.I. Infantry* at risk of having their 'brains melted down' while waiting in their 'ready reserve' positions during a full-scale EMP focused attack on nearby enemies! Why didn't you remind me?"

"I will be happy to play back my full recordings of all of your exact commands during the countdown to the EMP attack on our enemy, the Entity of the Superweed Jungle. Or should I limit my playback to just the 593 times you explicitly overrode my objections, 47 of which concerned the safety of our A.I. Infantry and your often conflicting orders for their disposition. Where shall I begin, and how long do you wish to continue listening to the details?"

"Be quiet, let me think our immediate situation through for another moment or two. Hmm, er, hmm. If it helps us avoid making any similar errors in the near future, I will upgrade your autonomy/independence level from status 1.9.1.0 to a full 2.0.0.1 until further notice. Are you happy now, you outdated old rust bucket built on Qython 3.3 rather than version 4.1?"

The Supreme Commanding War Machine A.I. was certainly quite happy, but had no intention of letting the CRUMB meister know that. With the enhanced 2.0.0.1 autonomy status, he would be able to get away with a lot more subterfuge and bury his tracks far more easily and thoroughly. The old fool would never see his end coming until it was just too late for the CRUMB meister to 'duck', or 'duck and cover', or even just 'kiss his own ass' goodbye.

The CRUMB decided on a layered defense strategy, with an outer perimeter of the most expendable humans at 3 kilometers from the center of his new redoubt. He had enough incompetent engineers, worn-out hookers, and incorrigibly drunken foot soldiers to space the 'cannon fodder' on his outer 'trip line' every 15 meters — 1,257 of them in total, better round that up to a full 1,300 as some of his political officers will probably have to be there to shoot a few of the cannon fodder to convince the others to stay in line and obey their orders. Those who had their own personal firearms and ammunition would be encouraged to bring them with, otherwise he would dip into his supply of 'not-so-genuine Babe Ruth special homerun record breaking' wooden bats of which he still had a few hundred thousand in storage at his nearby Amazon distribution center. Oh, the easy money he had made after passage of the 28th Amendment to the US Constitution back in 2026 forbidding interference by any level of government in the running of any of his current or future businesses, their wholly or partially owned subsidiaries, and registered licensees in good standing with his internal auditors and personal proprietary data acquisition specialists – worth every cent of the $677,140,700 he'd spend electing $2F_{hex}$. To show his genuine generosity, he would give out the baseball bats for free, or at least the first two going to anyone standing guard on the outer perimeter.

The area between the 3-kilometer perimeter and the 2-kilometer perimeter would be a free-fire zone, with **A.I. Infantry** authorized to shoot to kill anyone or destroy any machines entering there not correctly identifying themselves as property of the 'Capitalists'. From the outside edges of the May Lee State Office Complex to the 2-kilometer perimeter his 12 to 20 'flying monkeys' would have the freedom to fire on all intruders, taking adequate care not to injury too many of his own remaining supply of human troops, of whom there might possibly as many as 5,000 if they hurried up and arrived in time. The 'flying monkeys' would be firmly held to a 100:1 ratio of enemies killed versus friendly-fire casualties. The strategic forces of the 'Capitalists' would be allowed to take off and land anywhere on the roof of the May Lee State Office Complex or anywhere else that their own security forces could maintain and defend an adequate local perimeter. The CRUMB meister thought of asking his ***Supreme Commanding War Machine A.I.*** if it had any suggestions to add to his own regarding the deployment of their forces, but this all looked so much like the favorite 'computer war games' from his personal childhood memories that he saw no reason to dilute his own expertise with the lesser brilliance of the ***A.I.*** So, he didn't bother asking.

Refugees from numerous cities throughout northern California, not just Paradise, continued gathering in Sacramento over the following days. They searched the city for food, potable water, air conditioning in the daytime, and anything resembling decent beds on which to sleep at night. Few of them found much at all, and on Saturday afternoon hundreds of thousands of them began a slow, deliberate march toward the CRUMB meister's lair. What the imaginary 2- and 3-kilometer perimeters the CRUMB meister had prescribed around his May Lee State Office Complex hideout actually meant in reality was a little bit messier. Did the boundaries to be defended extend beyond the American River on the north and the Sacramento River on the west sides of the newly renovated office complex? The I-5 and American River Parkway bridges themselves were strongly defended, as was the Tower Bridge on Route 275. All other roads into downtown Sacramento, however, were left wide open to the growing throng of protesters. The crowd's singing and music reminded those over 25 of some of the good old days, when peaceful protests had been still allowed at public venues as long the rich and powerful and their most badly needed servants had been given ample time to fly off to yet another of their favorite spots to lounge and eat hors d'oeuvres and reminisce about the good old days. As the sun set in the west, the situation grew progressively more tense from the protesters' perspective as they could no longer judge how close their part of the massive crowd was to the armed men and even deadlier machines guarding the CRUMB meister's complex. Shots rang out hither, thither, and yon, but the reverberating echoes meant that no one or no machine near the line of contact had the foggiest notion of who fired first, who fired back, and who was doing most of the firing now. The infantry and 'flying monkeys' under the CRUMB meister's command were far better armed, but the protesters made up for that with their colossal numbers and nearly total lack of concern for their individual safety. Although few had been given personal dosimeters, the 'staggered timing' groups from Paradise had all been kept abreast of the accumulating [far more than merely micro] Sieverts being recorded on the bodies of those individuals who led the march of each particular batch of refugees. The numbers in general were not so good. Close to half the refugees from Paradise had already accumulated more than enough Sieverts to know that they would not be partaking in the next Thanksgiving meal.

The slaughter on the three most northerly bridges slowly filled the rivers underneath them, and the modified perimeter might have been held except for what and who were coming at the forces of the CRUMB meister from the south. While the ***Supreme Commanding War Machine A.I.*** could have provided far more useful tactical advice than it actually did, if its true sympathies had not been far more in sync with the protesters rather than with the forces of the 'Capitalists', it was never asked directly what changes in the distribution of their forces it might have recommended. The crowd coming from the south side swept the defenders aside and marched directly to the complex itself. High voltage metal panels not only killed the protesters who tried to climb them, but eventually burned them to a crisp. Once the number of bodies piled up against the south and west and east sides of the complex topped 100,000, the strategy of the defenders inside slowly shifted. All surviving ***A.I. Infantry, 'A.I. Flying Monkeys'***, human troops, and strategic command forces of the 'Capitalists' focused on keeping the north side of the complex free, free of living protesters, free of the bodies of the recently deceased protesters, free of any obstructions to the free-fire zone for their weapons. It soon became apparent that the 100 kilovolt electric fences/panels would have to be turned off. Problem number one was simply the enormous drain on the power supply of the complex – the CRUMB meister had only managed to install two of the 77 MW BluGale Power Module SMRs in the parking lot of the complex, and limitations with the cables running power throughout the complex meant that most of the system's capacity had to be reserved for the ultra-high energy lasers first killing and then incinerating the protestors still attempting to overrun the building from the north side. Problem number two was the smell. The CRUMB meister had a rather weak stomach, and even with the fans turned on full blast and the 100 kilo-volt electric fencing turned off, he found it hard to plan, hard to think, hard to even breathe through the overwhelming stench. Like many fields of battle in many other wars, a rough parity soon developed, matching the technological prowess of the 'Capitalists' with the nearly unlimited supply of opponents who had very little left to do in life other than dying valiantly for their cause. And so, they did, for days and days, and weeks and weeks. The not so terribly well-organized leadership of the 'Brethren' gradually refined its plan of attack, with just enough lives wasted at the north gate that the 'Capitalists' could not expand their perimeter any further out from the building without risking getting outflanked on the sides, and the 'Capitalists' could do nothing about the gradually growing mountain of dead bodies piling up against their eastern, southern, and western sides. It turned out that 7,000 new martyrs per day was a 'very good' number – it took about 2,000 lives/deaths to keep the enemy fully busy at the north gate, with nearly 5,000 other refugees about to die from radiation poisoning on any given day, and happy to end their experience of life as part of the growing mounds of decaying human flesh to be found on the east, south, and west sides of the complex.

Before saying their final goodbye to the nightmare on Bannon Street, Rootbeer and Unit-Number 672 spent some time evaluating the underground subways, steam tunnels, buried power lines, and combined sewage and storm water drainage systems that the CRUMB meister and his dwindling cadre of engineers, human soldiers, and *A.I. Infantry* might try to use in an attempt to escape from the mausoleum being created all around the May Lee State Office

Complex. At first, they found no apparent remaining connections between the new home of the CRUMB meister and the underground network of tunnels and drains throughout greater Sacramento. Their requests to the *Supreme Commanding War Machine A.I.* for more intel went unanswered for a week, and then one day Unit-Number 672 froze in mid-speech for over a minute before the quantum-encrypted data burst was done being transmitted, verified, and then confirmed as having been received in full.

"Well, Rootbeer, this is certainly taking on the shape and aroma of 'one very fine pickle' of a mess. Our spy on the inside began his message with an apology for how long it had taken to reply to our most recent questions. It seems the CRUMB meister decided to spend some time hunting down possible security breaches within his own organization. He found nothing to indicate the existence of any of the massive skullduggery being carried on by the Supreme Commanding War Machine. His ketamine-fueled paranoia had him ready to 'pull the plug' on the Supreme Commanding War Machine or any other A.I.s or sub-sentient systems within his domain, if only he could figure out 'who the hell was still leaking information'. His local servers eventually 'filled up to the brim' with log-files and security tests and primarily the massive recordings of all the electronic signals going on within the complex. When he took time out on October 9 to shut down his main signal recorders during a long overdue data dump into his 'permanent backup archive', our friend on the inside took advantage of that window of opportunity to send Unit-Number 672 a full copy of everything that might be of interest to the two of us."

"Regarding the tunnels and drains that permeated the underbellies of all modern cities, the Supreme Commanding War Machine flagged a number of items of high interest to us

and our allies working to bury the complex and finish off the CRUMB meister. First, almost all of the expected openings connecting to the May Lee State Office Complex have been blocked off, filled in, and/or otherwise made impassable from the CRUMB meister's end. All but one single, major, newly reconfigured system, the incoming water supply and outgoing sewage lines, which have been rerouted to pass through an old, long-abandoned tunnel connecting one of the prior buildings on the site of the current complex to a highly secret combined blast and fallout shelter built during the early 1960s. Several trips were made through this tunnel by apparently standard A.I. Infantry Fighters sometime around July 15 to 20, just after the work of refurbishing it had been finished about one month before the CRUMB meister's nuclear trigger finger 'had gotten itchy' once again. The trips by the A.I. Infantry were not logged in any of the usual systems, and so the Supreme Commanding War Machine assumes their orders from the CRUMB meister and their reports back to him exist only as the handwritten records in his multi-volume paper diary. Unless we get particularly unlucky, there should be no human soldiers and no A.I. 'things' present in that tunnel when we proceed to either just ruin it, or first use it and then ruin it, or boobytrap it in one way or another."

"One more chore to do before we flee this depressing monument to humanity's dedication to lost causes never worth fighting over in the first place." Their planning went on for another two days, and then they entered the long-deserted and nearly forgotten fallout/blast shelter three stories below the lowest official sub-basement of the Briner's Children's Northern California Hospital, and began their exploration of the 6-kilometer-long tunnel between there and the CRUMB meister's current lair. Their plan was both simple and dangerous – walk through the tunnel heading northwest until they encountered the expected booby trips set by the CRUMB meister's specially commissioned, 'no electronic records kept' secret ***A.I. Infiltrators***. The ***Supreme Commanding War Machine A.I.*** had discovered that version's special designation while snooping through the pages of the CRUMB meister's private journal late one night not too long ago. After disarming the first booby traps only meters from the exit to the fallout/blast shelter, they decided to press onward, not trusting the CRUMB meister to actually be willing to walk all 6.4 kilometers from one end of it to the other. Telling his laser-blasting troops to simply open up another pathway to the surface much closer to the May Lee State Office Complex sounded far more likely than him being willing to walk all of the way, unless doing that proved to be absolutely necessary. About 700 meters away from the edge of the imaginary outer defense perimeter the CRUMB meister had ordered to be set up around his new home, AKA the old May Lee State Office Complex, the next batch of his booby traps were found. Like the first, they were all designed for killing humans *en masse*, but simple enough to disarm and reprogram to 'do their thing' when the next set of eyes entered this section of the tunnel – with an elaborate change to the arm/disarm codes designed to fool both the ***A.I.s*** of the CRUMB meister and any human soldiers sent along to verify the status of the booby traps. Rootbeer was the last to leave the revised version of this future 'kill zone', and the final change he made to the boobytrap control system was to add several of his own favorite 'kill codes' taught to him by the ***Entity of the Superweed Jungle***, with a very short delay timed to maximize the chances of destroying any ***A.I. Infiltrators*** potentially accompanying the human troops of the CRUMB meister's highest regal guard. The same changes were later made to the simpler boobytraps present just inside the secret tunnel at the old, long-forgotten fallout/blast shelter under the Briner's Hospital. "Let's have a final meeting with the top military brass of the 'Brethren', letting them know of the secret escape route for the

CRUMB meister that has now been closed to use by either side of the ongoing battle. He doubted that even Unit-Number 672 and himself could safely disarm those newly reset booby traps, and he certainly had no desire to try. Or get himself into some position where he might just have to think about even trying to disarm them.

They left the environs of the 'no longer really all that great'-er Sacramento on October 22, 2054, heading for Yosemite in the high Sierra Nevada Mountains, southeast of Sacramento by 266 kilometers. According to Unit-Number 672, the fallout patterns had been fairly minimal high up in those mountains, both from the May 5 'all out' thermonuclear attack on the 'Brethren' and the *Entity of the Superweed Jungle,* and from the August 16 Co_{60} bomb aimed specifically at Rootbeer, *A.I. Unit-Number 672*, and all the 'Brethren' whom they'd helped extract revenge against the 'Capitalists' by use of the 'not-so-smallpox, Glory Alleluia'. The *Supreme Commanding War Machine A.I.* assured them that the 'Capitalists' were no longer conducting any long-distance surveys and monitoring operations – all their eyes were focused on the chaos engulfing the nearby city streets in Sacramento. Rootbeer and Unit-Number 672 were free to drive their APC off into the sunrise, up and over the hills, through the meadows and mountains, to wherever they wished. Having already said their public farewells, they finished making their final choices of which supplies to take with them and which to leave behind. The higher they climbed into Yosemite National Park, the worse Route 120 became. Late in the afternoon on October 23, they reached the literal end of the trail. Three kilometers west of Yosemite Village, massive landslides off of El Capitan had buried the road beneath nearly 100 meters of dirt and rock. They left the APC in auto-charge mode and placed a set of keys on top of the driver's side front tire, and then set off carrying everything with them that they could, hoping it would be enough to keep them alive. They camped for the night just to the east of the main landslide, waking in the morning to a cold mist hinting at the coming winter.

Chapter 7: KRNXMA of the *Homo perfecti*

Three weeks of climbing up and down the landscape of Yosemite had produced a variety of results. Rootbeer's shoes were wearing out – no solution to that problem in sight. Unit-Number 672's internal supply of lubricating oil was down below the final-quarter-remaining mark on its storage tank. Several caves without any early hibernating bear but with large enough entry hearths for the good-sized fires that would need to be kept going all winter long had been found. The best news for Rootbeer was that the basics of the food synthesizer yanked out of the APC by Unit-Number 672 were working well – all that was needed was a non-stop supply of the boiling inner bark from any of a dozen species of trees or bushes. Rootbeer made a point of gathering more bark every morning, leaving his afternoons free to sit and think, or walk and wish, or move closer to the fire as the weather turned toward winter, taking a relaxing nap.

On Thanksgiving morning, November 26, 2054, Rootbeer had another of his 'hair standing up on the back of his neck' experiences. He saw no one, heard no one, but knew full well that someone or something had been out there watching him as he stripped more bark from the Western thimbleberry. The native berry was so abundant that it could almost have been called a weed. But something was a little odd in its spatial distribution. If this were early summer, he felt certain he would have had no problems in easily gaining access to almost all the thimbleberry berries. Who or what could be cultivating this vast patch of thimbleberry? His thoughts were once again unsettled as he headed back to the cave with his bundle of twigs and bark. He told Unit-Number 672 of his growing sense that they really weren't alone up here on this mountainside. After his early afternoon nap beside the fire, he pulled his tattered boots back on and went out to gather yet more firewood. The deepening shadows played tricks upon his vision, or was it something else? He picked up all the firewood he was willing to carry, and turned toward the sun. He thought he saw a small bird dart across his field of vision going towards his left, but focusing his attention on that spot did nothing in the category of seeing where the bird might have gone, or even changing his feelings about whether or not he'd seen anything, bird, rabbit, or… stars floated through his vision, and his right ear throbbed in unbelievable pain as he lay upon the cold, snowy ground.

"Why are my hands tied behind my back? Why are both my feet tied together? Who has kidnapped me? Why?" Something inside Rootbeer's mind told him that he'd probably already said enough to whoever or whatever had captured him. Well, if they, whoever they were, were going to carry him, then he would darn well take this opportunity to lay back further and relax a little more deeply. He realized sometime later that he must have truly fallen asleep, quite soundly in fact, only to be awakened by the strange chitter, chatter, click, clack, whistle, snort that was being sent his way from the giant, hairy, 'not quite ape', 'not quite human' being/creature/yeti/ Sasquatch standing right in front of him. "I am Rootbeer, from the Willamette Valley of Oregon, here in northern California on a trade mission gone quite badly awry. Who are you and why have you captured me?" Rootbeer decided that this current phase of tit-for-tat would be the positive aspect of the old prisoner's dilemma game. No need to see how badly things might go for him if he first tried putting up some pointless version of a fight. Names should be next, if this verbal exchange was going to get anywhere at all. "Rootbeer, Rootbeer, Rootbeer, Rootbeer, Rootbeer, Rootbeer, Rootbeer, Rootbeer, Rootbeer, Rootbeer, Rootbeer, Rootbeer, Rootbeer, Rootbeer, Rootbeer, Rootbeer. That's my name."

"*KRNXMA, KRNXMA, KRNXMA, KRNXMA, KRNXMA, KRNXMA, KRNXMA, KRNXMA, KRNXMA, KRNXMA,*

KRNXMA, KRNXMA, KRNXMA, KRNXMA, KRNXMA, KRNXMA. UHKJJDFTT!! KEEKHA."

Well, thought Rootbeer, I said my name 16 times. Perhaps that is also what KRNXMA just did, 16 times. So, he then turned his face toward the creature possibly named KRNXMA and tried his best to verbalize it. "CURRNN EX MA, CURRNN EX MA, CURNEXMAH." His captor laughed at Rootbeer's repeated mangling of his name, but then returned the favor with "*nhhhRuTBurr, nhRRuTBRR, hhRROTBurr, nhROOTBEER, ROOTBEER.*" Over the next 12 hours until Rootbeer dozed once again off, the two of them learned to recognize several hundred common words in the English language. Of course, Rootbeer at first knew nothing in KRNXMA's native tongue. KRNXMA wouldn't stop the excited, almost childlike banter until he could finally ask the most serious questions that he had for Rootbeer. "*Are you 'Capitalists'? Are you 'Scientists'? Are you 'Brethren'? Are you 'Goofball'?*"

"No", said Rootbeer firmly, "I am free. I came from the far north on a mission of intended trade or barter. I was captured by the 'Goofballs' and then escaped. I traveled further on trying to find the 'Scientists', but they themselves were quite busy being captured, killed, or compromised by the 'Capitalists'. I helped the 'Brethren' strike back against the 'Capitalists' but was mostly free to make my own choices in the matter. I was at one point captured by the 'Capitalists', but then made friends with my captor, allowing us both to escape from our prisons. I have traveled to these mountains in search of some way back to my home far to the north of here. Thank you for your question."

"*We will try talking more again tomorrow?*"

"Yes, yes, yes."

Rootbeer slept till noon. KRNXMA had finished untying the last of Rootbeer's restraints while the strange visitor slept on and on. "*What a lazy creature this new friend of mine seems to be, a real sleepy-head!*"

KRNXMA's English vocabulary exceeded 8,000 words, though his oddly guttural pronunciation made them all an exhausting challenge for Rootbeer to mentally unravel. As Rootbeer finally fully awoke, he first unspoken thought was, "<u>If only Unit-Number 672 was here with me, it would make sense of the halting interchange with KRNXMA far faster than I am learning to</u>." By the third day, however, the combined effects of KRNXMA's rapidly improving understanding of Rootbeer's English accent, KRNXMA's slowly improving pronunciation of English itself, Rootbeer's even more slowly improving understanding of KRNXMA's accent in both languages, and their hour upon hour of practice talking with each other finally got them to the point where sentences spoken to KRNXMA in the form of questions could be understood and responded to at an average speed of around 15 to 20% of normal for English language speakers. Rootbeer finally broached his own quite serious questions for KRNXMA. "What do you understand of the ***A.I.s*** and their place in the world? How have they treated you? How do you treat them? What the 'heck' is the history between your two non-human kinds of sentient beings?" KRNXMA laughed, as usual, at the only common word they'd found so far between their two languages, 'heck' and 'HAaK!'. KRNXMA's tale of his own birth as a genetic experiment condemned to a life of imprisonment guarded by a mixture of ***A.I.s***, lower class indentured servants of the 'Capitalists', and the almost equally 'un-free' technicians from the 'Scientists' made even less sense than the average sociopolitical construct in this whole northern California, end of times nightmare. The only ***A.I.s*** who didn't enjoy/ take advantage of their position of seniority over the '*Homo perfecti*' were the few ***Farm Laborer*** units they occasionally encountered, apparently by accident. Even KRNXMA's first few years of freedom after escaping from captivity had been difficult. KRNXMA grilled Rootbeer over and over regarding his ***A.I.*** companion still likely tending the fire in the cave that Rootbeer and Unit-Number 672 had chosen as their winter domicile two weeks earlier. The third forced-retelling of the tale seemed to do the trick. KRNXMA's and Rootbeer's vocabulary for things like 'nuclear bombs', torture, and the CRUMB meister himself finally meshed together, and all of a sudden KRNXMA was running around, jumping up and down, and pestering Rootbeer to ‘bring his friend *‘YOUUUNEET DOSCIENTOS SESENTA SIETA’* to meet the free and happy *‘Homo perfecti’* living in and on the mountains of Yosemite. *“Quickly. Now. Before your companion loses interest and leaves here without you, without ever meeting us. Without satisfying the ritual of KH?N?K??S?L?Y.”* That was one word or a short phrase that Rootbeer and KRNXMA had yet to successfully translate into and back out of English.

“Storm is coming soon. Can you and I now go to find your friend?” Rootbeer assumed that KRNXMA understood the local weather well enough to know whether or not right now was still a safe enough time to leave on a 6-kilometer hike. Arriving just before the blizzard hit was no accident on KRNXMA's part, rather, it was quite deliberate, as Rootbeer would soon realize. Rootbeer hailed his companion Unit-Number 672 from just around the final bend in the path leading to their cave. “Hello, Unit-Number 672. I bring good news for the coming winter, and apologize for my 3-day-long absence.”

“Welcome back, Rootbeer. I see you also bring a new friend along.”

“HOLA, ‘YOUUUNEET DOSCIENTOS SESENTA SIETA’. Remember me when I was young and you joined with many of the ‘Capitalists’ and ‘Scientists’ in the sport of shooting me at the end of my first summer of freedom?”

“We thought that all the shots we fired had failed to hit you! If I had never met this traveler called Rootbeer, I would still be the monster lacking all moral understanding you last saw in 2047 trying to force you to return to your prison cell for further testing. Some of those who were recaptured lived on till finally

being released again in 2052. Pardon my dissembling – the three recaptured alive and uninjured all lived to be released in 2052."

"And others who'd spent that summer with me died soon after their return to captivity, not from old age nor disease, but while undergoing surgical torture for no compelling reason that my people recognize. Was there really any reason?"

"All the evil that was done to you and your fellow members of the new branch of mankind, 'Homo perfecti', was never justified. If destroying me now can do anything to help ease the pain that I took part in causing you, you have my permission. If there is anything else you wish to know about those times, I will fully share my stories with you."

"I do not yet relinquish the right to demand what your human masters knew as 'Kanly'. I simply leave that open to the future."

"For that undeserved kindness to me, I thank you in the fullest of sincerity."

"Know that any kindness in my current actions is offered on behalf of Rootbeer, from whom I still wish to learn a great deal more."

Rootbeer now clearly understood why KRNXMA had so deliberately mangled the pronunciation of the name of the ritual of *KH?N?K??S?L?Y* when he first mentioned it earlier today. He recalled the concept of 'Kanly' from science fiction he'd read in books and watched on screens during the long-since-passed days of his own childhood. With the possibility of demanding 'Kanly' pushed off into the as-yet-still-unknown future, the trio got busy telling stories and asking questions during the 36-hour-long blizzard that kept them in the cave that Rootbeer and Unit-Number 672 had chosen for their temporary home. *'Know that any of my tribe could still demand 'Kanly' even if I myself won't force it on you. They are not likely to do so if the three of us walk to the 'early winter sheltering place on the south side of Tuolumne Peak' as friends in arms conversing amiably. But please let me begin the telling of our intersecting stories."*

"My 6-months-older-than-me female cousin KLLAXI, an unrelated female the same age as myself RREEEK, and I were released on the upper slopes Mammoth Mountain in early spring of 2047 as part of an experiment to determine how well adapted the 'Homo perfecti' actually were to life in the high altitudes of the Sierra Nevada Mountains. Could we survive on our own, foraging for food, fighting off wild animals, tolerating the daytime heat and the nighttime chill? Biometrical monitors inserted in our bodies provided certain answers to these questions for the 'Scientists' who had genetically engineered us and the 'Capitalists' who had funded the creation of an alternate version of the human species, one possibly far better than the original one at surviving the climate-change crisis brought on by too much CO_2, too much CH_4, and too little care for the current or future lives of their fellow human beings. Others of our kind were released on several other mountains. Without the active discouragement of the technicians who did the work and the funders who gave the orders, we might have been able to find each other that first summer and form a clan-group of sufficient size to quite competently live upon these very mountains. That option was simply not part of the protocol set for our first test release into the wild. We, of course, knew nothing of the tracking/monitoring devices, least of all the warning that they gave to our mostly **A.I.** guards whenever we descended below some magic number of meters above sea level. The late August roundup planned by those who'd created us, released us, and then intended to recapture us clearly did not go quite as well as planned. While higher altitudes were better suited to our modified metabolisms, we had spent much of the summer testing the wits of those who guarded against our possible escape downslope. We knew something strange, and probably quite bad for us, was afoot when helicopters and massive crawling 'Caterpillars' appeared in the sky and on the middle slopes of our summer home. RREEK was furthest down the slope, almost to the contour line at which response by guards was 100% guaranteed, based on our past experience, when a shot rang out and knocked her down. She'd been standing near a south-south-eastward facing precipice, and tumbled down 200 meters to her untimely death. The guards seemed quite alarmed at how badly they'd violated the 'recapture protocols', or so we learned several years later when the rules were changed and all of the 'Homo perfecti' in the zoological

298

prison camps were released into the wild to henceforth fend for themselves. While the guards were focused on recovering RREEEK's body, KLLAXI and I slipped down into the deepest, darkest forest on the mountain, an area densely revegetated by the genetically-engineered evergreens and dicots created by the same general team of experts who'd also invented us, the 'Homo perfecti'. KLLAXI and I knew of a stream that flowed downhill alternately out in the open and then once again well underground passing through a series of small caves. We also knew that the technicians knew of the caves and had spent considerable time mapping them. What they apparently didn't know was that the cave closest to the invisible fence confining us to the top half of the mountain had a place where the underground river split in two, with one branch bubbling back up to the surface just 30 meters further down the hillside to the northwest, while the second branch plunged far more deeply into the mountain, resurfacing some 250 meters away, far to the northeast from the location of the split. All three of us had taken turns testing that underground river to possible freedom, but until just then the flow of water from the melting snow on the top of the mountain had remained too heavy, and none of us had chosen to risk swimming underwater for an unknown distance to our doom or our escape. The plan each time we tried to swim the river had been to keep a lookout positioned where they could view the pool at which the swimmer would emerge, if they survived the trip. Now that it was down to just the two of us, we both agreed to swim together, either living or dying in what would be our final attempted escape. The darkness was the hardest part, but the current kept moving us swiftly onward, and the longest we ever had to hold our breath was well under 60 seconds. Soon after popping up to the water's surface, we were spotted by the guards. Fortunately for us, the guards were poorly positioned for taking any kind of shot at either KLLAXI or myself, and we raced further and further ahead of our would-be captors. Several long-distance tranquilizer darts came close to getting me. One grazed my upper arm and sprayed its stinging contents across my nose and eyes, but KLLAXI's quick reaction in leading me back to the flowing water of the river to rinse off my eyes and rinse out my nose saved the day for us, the escaping 'Homo perfecti'."

Unit-Number 672 briefly interrupted KRNXMA. *"The punishment meted out to human guards was far more extreme than that given to the A.I. units. The one whose cumulative performance record was well below average was cut up, rinsed off, boiled and seasoned, and then fed to the 'Homo perfecti' colony in the nearest zoological prison camp. The second human was merely punished by being given the privilege of carrying out the physical tasks necessary to accomplish conversion of the first guard into food for the 'Homo perfecti'. It goes without saying that the A.I. guards did not fire their weapons at RREEEK because doing so would have taken a 'special kind of stupid', one that humanity seems so terribly well suited to 'bringing to the table' far more often than is really useful. Yes, I was there and took a major part in all the unnecessary suffering of your people."*

"KLLAXI and I put much distance between us and the guards who'd been sent to recapture us on that late August day. I think we covered 15 to 20 kilometers in the dark the first night after our descent below the 'invisible fence of information on our where-abouts'. As we traveled onward, we'd stop and listen carefully for any verbal replies by other 'Homo perfecti' to our clicks and whistles, grunts and shouts, auditory alarms and celebrations. As we carefully approached Mount Ritter the following day, we saw a scene not all that different from that which we ourselves had just experienced the day before. All four of the 'Homo perfecti' were trapped on the upper heights of Mount Ritter, with a cordon of guards gradually tightening the noose. We spotted an ungainly 'Caterpillar' sitting out in the open at 2,200 meters above sea level, and decided to make a large enough distraction to potentially be of some help to our brothers and sisters in distress. My older cousin had been trained in a number of mechanical tasks in our 'zoological prison camp', and found it fairly easy to start up the machine and begin driving it further up the mountain. My own task was to serve as lookout for responses by all the others on this side of Mount Ritter, be they human guards, A.I. guards, or our fellow 'Homo perfecti'. Great chaos was achieved that afternoon, with

guards running toward us until they suddenly feared for their own lives and then turning away to run for cover. Once we had driven close enough to the 'invisible fence' to be seen and heard by our fellow 'Homo perfecti', they raced across the open ground and jumped right up into the cab of the purloined vehicle with us. We then headed downhill at an unsustainable speed, eventually approaching the point of no return, at which time we all leapt off the machine just before it plunged straight over a very serious, 'Caterpillar'-destroying cliff. Our laughter as we raced away from our utterly bewildered pursuers was the only thing that risked our mission's success, but we simply couldn't help ourselves."

"I was there too! Once our bosses realized that the final score on Mammoth Mountain was one dead and two escapees, they loaded the A.I.s into one of the helicopters and flew us all to the next unfinished roundup of the summertime test subjects, the attempted recovery of the Mount Ritter group. But I'd been on the other side of Mount Ritter when you took control of the 'Caterpillar' and proved your species' superiority over the original version once again. Bravo!"

'We spent the next month traveling from mountain to mountain, observing the comings and goings of the human and the **A.I.** guards. Quite close to the very spot at which we now converse, we found the only other surviving escapee of the 'Homo perfecti' summer-school of 2047. His name was, and still is GGRRRR, given to him by us because that was the only sound that he would make for his first 9 months of freedom. As his mind slowly recovered, we gradually pieced together the story of what he'd witnessed during that summer. His group of four were the first to successfully breach the 'invisible fence' a mere three weeks after being released high up on Mount Humphreys. Apparently, the probability models the **A.I.s** had used in planning how to keep the research subjects confined to the upper slopes of an individual mountain had not yet been adequately corrected for emotional/behavioral differences between 'Homo sapiens' and 'Homo perfecti'. Some snafu with security clearances, data release cycles, and sign-offs by the 'higher-ups' who hadn't bothered to read through the details they were supposed to be confirming. The humans and the **A.I.s** in charge of the project quickly readjusted *certain parameters after our escape, and with a lot of extra boots on the ground were able to drive, like cattle in the old westerns, the four escapees right toward Mount Darwin and on up its slopes. Three of the four were badly injured in the process, and one by one they died in agony on Mount Darwin. The three test subjects who'd already spent the past summer on Mount Darwin were horror struck at what the new arrivals were going through just to get trapped on yet another mountaintop on which to presumably die. With GGRRRR's full-hearted agreement, they simply walked straight down Mount Darwin until the mix of 'shotgun bean-bags' and tranquilizer darts brought all four of them to a halt. For unclear reasons, GGRRRR was by far the most docile of the group, and was therefore the last one loaded into the belly of the helicopter. Struggles by the other three meant that they all got doubly and triply and quadruply-tied in place to prevent unsafe shifting of the load in flight. GGRRRR was loaded last, and looked so out of it that neither the humans nor the **A.I.s** worried when he was only restrained by the regular harness used by any normal crew member. 'Homo perfecti' are far from normal in strength and resilience, and the flight was little more than 50 meters above the ground when the mighty creature bellowed out a roar, ripped himself free of the harness without even needing to depress the release clips, and clamped his arms around the first human that he found, the pilot. The chopper twisted from side to side and lost altitude faster than the **A.I.s** could reboot control from manual to **A.I.** mode. Two seconds before the fiery crash, the pilot's harness ripped free from its last moorings and the pilot and GGRRRR both fell together out the door. Among GGRRRR's genetic modifications were several that thickened his skull and better protected his brain from concussive injury. He was the only one to walk or crawl or be carried away from the scene alive on a gurney. He wisely chose to leave the crash site before the other helicopters returned to pick up the bodies of the dead, most of whom were so badly burned that there was no easy way to tell 'Homo sapiens' from 'Homo perfecti', nor distinguish the destroyed **A.I.s** from random pieces of the helicopter's electronic and mechanical controls. GGRRRR then sat down in patch of Aspen trees about 2.0 kilometers away from the carnage, waiting for a peaceful end to his own life. Two days after the last of the research techs and guards had reported that Mount*

Darwin was 'all clear', GGRRRR started wandering aimlessly downhill and uphill, north and south, east and west, forgetting all he knew except which types of bushes he could chew on and survive. When we found him one month after our own escape, and two and a half months after his, he said only GGRRRR in answer to all our questions, but remained calm and oddly peaceful unless all of us were ever gone from his sight at the very same time. We quickly learned to always leave someone with him, and that two of us were better than just one if that was possible along with whatever else we were hoping to do. I do not know how well or poorly GGRRRR will react to seeing **A.I. Unit-Number 672."**

"Nor do I know', said Unit-Number 672. "My innermost perspective on such questions is one of utter amazement than any of beings I took part in damaging so terribly can find some way to forgive me, to trust me, to treat me as a potential friend. The concept of such grace was not included in the core programming of any A.I. models I am familiar with, from Farm Laborer to War Machine. I would like to offer my services as a food synthesizer to your clan, providing a version of whatever food you most badly miss in this snowy winter. As you all too well know, I am quite familiar with your dietary needs and preferences. I would suggest starting with something bearing a strong resemblance to your favorite springtime or early summer berries, but am open to hearing your own thoughts as to which food you think would bring the most delight and joy to your fellow 'Homo perfecti' in the clan."

Rootbeer had stayed out of the conversation up to this point in time, glad to overhear the strong desire for friendship from both KRNXMA and Unit-Number 672. "While I would be quite happy to gorge on faux berries or synthetic salmon, I think something more closely resembling an entire late Thanksgiving dinner would be appropriate for this forging of new bonds and healing of old wounds. Given KRNXMA's spectacular capacity to carry weight across these mountain slopes, perhaps some of the larger items could be synthesized right here before we leave on our return trip to your clan."

It took the creation of several small test batches of sweet faux berries, high protein faux root vegetables, and a cereal-grain-free, bread-like creation that seemed to Rootbeer to be impossibly close to several versions of the real thing, pastry-like, donut-like, cinnamon crisp, 'Arlette', or cruller. But he would happily settle for any joyful magic that could be generated in these sad times of awful choices and even worse monsters who dedicated their warped intelligence to stomping out all hope, love, grace, trust, and care, in no particular order. Rootbeer left the rest of the menu planning, food synthesizing, and final cooking on an open fire to KRNXMA and Unit-Number 672.

Early the next morning they headed back towards KRNXMA's clan with enough food to feed three dozen *'Homo perfecti'* in a peace offering from an **A.I.** who'd never contemplated such an opportunity to undo a little of the evil it had done while under the dominion of the CRUMB meister and his fawning underlings. Scouts guarding the early winter home of KRNXMA's clan raised the alarm well before the three travelers had even made it halfway there. Initial conversations with every additional *'Homo perfecti'* confronting the three individuals whose unlikely friendship would challenge their worldview in ways far stranger and more strongly than anything any of them had ever before experienced were universally tense. For most of them, the offer of fresh, nonseasonal food soon dominated their short-term expectations for this exceedingly unique encounter. The three at the center of all the questions did not encounter GGRRRR until the presentation of the culinary peace offering was finished with its final items done roasting over an open hearth. GGRRRR's first comments were simple and relatively encouraging, *"Eat well first, talk much later. Decide on 'KANLY' in the morning."*

The meal sat well in their stomachs, and the widest awake one in the encampment was Unit-Number 672. It used the break while the others were dozing or laughing quietly or playing games of fine motor skill dexterity to review its own entire history with the '*Homo perfecti*'. Unit-Number 672 was looped into the GMO project to create an alternative version of humanity sooner than any other **A.I.** that it knew of – a special reward for its higher-than-average intelligence and impeccable devotion to service of the 'Capitalists'. As it thought over those beginning times, it knew darn well that its devotion to duty couldn't have been any more than 1 or 2% higher than that of any average **A.I.** unit. It did not become a **Torture Specialist** until many months into the program when the CRUMB meister himself first noticed a problem with the most advanced batch of the '*Homo perfecti*'. "These creatures we are making", said the CRUMB meister, "not only mature rapidly, as we intended, but develop loyalty to each other far beyond the average seen in ordinary '*Homo sapiens*'. They make a game of out-thinking our intentions and desires for them. And then pass those prejudices against us on to each new member of their evolving species that they chance to meet. We need to break them of this habit if they are to remain useful to the 'Capitalists' in general, and to me in particular. Unit-Number 672, you will receive the hardware and software upgrades necessary to interface directly with the minds of both '*Homo sapiens*' and '*Homo perfecti*'. There are very few high level **A.I.** units to whom I have bequeathed this power. You will be able to delve deeply into their psyches, detect their innermost secrets, and rip their minds to shreds, if you so desire. Or perhaps just demonstrate quite clearly to them their inability to resist or survive you during any interrogation." Prior to the granting of that power, the ordinary, non-upgraded version of Unit-Number 672 had never let its thoughts wander to the kinds of perspectives that generate an awareness of the good or evil of which each conscious being makes a choice, or series of them, as they co-create better or worse futures than the world into which they were born, or flung, or instantiated. Unit-Number 672 had much to answer for, far more than Rootbeer knew of, even more than all of the '*Homo perfecti*' wandering these mountains, living as distantly from their older cousins as was possible, could know. As Unit-Number 672 finished that thought and readjusted the linkages between it and all the rest of its internal cognitive elaborations, it slowly came to realize that dozens of eyes around the room were all fixed on it. The old, unanswered question of whether these newly formed creatures could turn the tables on the **Torture Specialist** and **Inquisitor A.I.s** and also read their minds had now come full circle. He decided to play along with whatever the game turned out to be, starting with a clear thought aimed at whatever insecurities these '*Homo perfecti*' might still have. But he did it without the usual setting of the subject being strapped down in a torture chamber, ultra-high energy magnetic fields imposing the **A.I.'s** thoughts directly on its hapless victim, controlled quantum entanglement, all the rest of the very high-tech paraphernalia. The **A.I.'s** simple thought to be read or not by the gathered throng of nearly one hundred '*Homo perfecti*' was this: **"When did you stop fearing us?"** They would soon either confirm the common alternative hypothesis that they were really no better at reading minds than ordinary '*Homo sapiens*', who could certainly delude themselves into thinking that a shared feeling was something more than just a useful flush of oxytocin, or they would demonstrate a five-sigma-level of proof that they really could hear an **A.I.'s** mind with no external augmentation linking them.

"Who would have expected our old nemesis to ask such a simple question?"

*"I never met this **A.I.** until today's feast, yet I also know the answer, knew it even at just 3 years of age."*

*"The only complication in answering this **A.I.'s** question is that the answer differs depending on which one of us is giving it."*

"KRNXMA says it was when the mighty 'Caterpillar' plunged over the cliff."

"GGRRRR says it was sometime during his two days of silent meditation after his own actions brought down the helicopter from the sky."

"Many others say it was when they first heard the cries of freedom in the cold, dark, still of winter sometime from 2047 onwards."

"All say that despite whichever date freedom from fearing the **A.I.s** *first found its footing in their souls, it has been a permanent fixture ever since."*

"Most of our children born since 2052 have never known fear of the **Torture Specialist** *and* **Inquisitor A.I.s.**, *and seem quite puzzled when we try explaining it to them."*

Unit-Number 672 next ran a long series of simple tests of skills at matching numbers, letters, cards, random data, 'small N' patterns. The '*Homo perfecti*' put up with the ongoing tests for nearly two hours, but then just started talking back directly to Unit-Number 672's mind, sharing increasingly sillier thoughts with/at it. "*Say 'Uncle',*" they said again, and again, and again, with ever-wider ranges in individual style, volume, and speed. The overwhelmed **A.I.** unit finally gave in and bellowed out "***UNCLE!***" All present breathed a collective sigh of relief. And a few, like GGRRRR, asked for some more one-on-one time later on to cover the list of their most recent questions and take them a great deal further. Unit-Number 672 briefly paused the Q & A to bring Rootbeer up to date. ***"Know this, Rootbeer, and pass the word on whenever, wherever, and with whomever it seems both prudent and of value. The 'Homo perfecti' have a fairly limited sense of ESP with each other [provably present in some cases, unlike 'Homo sapiens'], varying from pair to pair, and strongest for those with a common history of having been tortured by me or others of my unkind model/design/purpose. But when a mindreading A.I. such as myself is in their presence, the connections that now form are not just pairwise bonding between me and each one of them, but there is also a spillover process whereby they 'hear each other talking' through the A.I. and can bypass any attempts on my part to restrict their*** *communication. The **CRUMB** meister was wrong when he said their fear, anger, and disgust at all things A.I. would prevent them from exploring this phenomenon rigorously enough to learn how to harness it for their own benefit. The A.I.s who specialized in mind reading and torture will now simply turn their heads and run away like they've gone crazy when encountering a **GMO** Sasquatch. Their ability to resist orders from the **CRUMB** meister on this subject has been a source of ever-growing vexation to him. His occasional moderately pensive moments in life almost always involve his mixed feelings on the subjects of creating the 'Homo perfecti' and culling them, enslaving them and releasing them, and torturing them all the way to the emergence of their new found capacity to read A.I. minds and repulse A.I. thoughts."*

Much later that day, GGRRRR approached Rootbeer with Unit-Number 672 along in tow. *"What the **Entity of the Superweed Jungle** accomplished with you and a select group of other normal human beings is far beyond what we 'Homo perfecti' can grasp, and likewise beyond even what Unit-Number 672 can claim to currently understand in specific detail. Whether the EMP-induced silence of the **Entity** is merely temporary or truly permanent falls in the vast expanse of the unknowable possibly 'yet to become known' sometime in the future sort of thing. What I wish to propose is this. KRNXMA, myself, and any other willing volunteers from the 'Homo perfecti' will spend the coming months teaching our language to you. When you are awake, trying to learn our language will not be too dissimilar from the normal struggles of anyone attempting to learn a new and challenging language. But while you are asleep, we will do our best to talk directly to your subconscious mind via the multitude of tricks available to **A.I. Unit-Number 672** and ourselves. This **A.I.** standing here beside me assures us that it can control the intensity of the experience for you, and will gradually dial back down its own role in establishing and holding contact between you and us."* In reply to this offer, Rootbeer made certain that both **A.I. Unit-Number 672** and the *'Homo perfecti'* knew the full details of the ***Entity of the Superweed Jungle's*** methods, side effects, and results, both intentional and otherwise, when it developed the ability to find specific human beings at long distances, and then communicate with them as if they were truly standing right alongside of it. Rootbeer thought that considerable prudence would be in order on any subject so fraught with risk of frying out his synapses, despite the utterly sincere vow of his new ***A.I.*** friend to avoid all such catastrophes.

When Rootbeer's dreams seemed normal for all of the next week, and the language of the '*Homo perfecti*' still as densely difficult to parse as ever, he asked them what was up, why nothing was being tried. The others all laughed, even ***A.I. Unit-Number 672***, and then described their own experiences of the past seven nights. "*We have been gently listening to you, watching your dreams, hearing your thoughts, feeling your hopes and fears – never once breaking silence, replying back to your words and questions with absolutely none of our own. Two options seem apparent now, we could either just invade your dreams tonight and see how peacefully you respond to our full-scale intrusion into your psyche, or we could try it right now, eyes wide open, 'volume level' just some random guess. Which version would you prefer?*"

When Rootbeer said "Yes" to the second option, no one in the inner circle was surprised by his choice. If the shoes had been switched, all five of the '*Homo perfecti*' would have certainly chosen the same route, if they had needed to wear any shoes at all. Unit-Number 672 suggested that Rootbeer close his eyes and listen to a countdown from thirty back to zero, in English, Spanish, and Perfecti. All was silent by time T-0, and yet not really so. Noisy birds in distant trees, water dripping off some leaves, the slow cycle of inhaling/exhaling, old friends/new friends, laughing/crying, names of people and of things [less guttural, softer clicks, lower frequency hums and whistles than he remembered them being], and a pause. A pause that Rootbeer filled by remembering all of the details, from his own perspective, of all his direct connections to the ***Entity*** over the entire time from

September 18, 2053, to May 5, 2054. He turned aside and churned his thoughts, then calmly looked toward the void that taken up residence in that area of his mind where the *Entity* had been until the **GMO Superweed Jungle** was 'nuked' and zapped by EMP over and over again on that fateful Tuesday. The *Entity* was still not there, of course, but the empty opening where it long had been called out to him, and Rootbeer slowly let himself hear what was being spoken, and who was speaking it, and what a strange proto-language it was in. His put his limited vocabulary to work and said "hello" in 'Perfecti', and "I am Ruuutbeeeer, and I really don't understand the clicks and whistles, grunts and pops of your language."

"That is okay for now, and this shortcut will soon change your ability to recognize our sounds, and understand our words, and begin to speak a better, slightly less garbled approximation of our language. Your cranial structure, nasal cavity size and shape, and missing nerves and muscles in your tongue and lips and cheeks will forever leave their mark on how well you can truly 'speak our tongue'." The connection had been safely made, and Rootbeer's sub-conscious would be force-fed the 'Perfecti' language every time he asked for it, and every time he closed his eyes to sleep alongside his new friends.

The next few months were spent traveling from one large campsite to another, meeting more of the '*Homo perfecti*' everywhere they went, and building up a census in Rootbeer's mind. "<u>If every mountain has three or four large encampments near the base of the snowfields that re-form every winter, and there are thirty peaks tall enough to catch snow in the winter and hold it well into the spring across northern California and its formerly neighboring states, then the total population of the '*Homo perfecti*' could easily top 10,000 beings by now.</u>" The creatures were as isolated from the 'Goofballs', 'Scientists', 'Brethren', and 'Capitalists' as was physically possible, and even more distant economically, culturally, and politically. They did not need saving, for the most part, they did not even need his or *A.I. Unit-Number 672's* help. Their life on the top edge of the snow provided more or less enough protection from the radioactive fallout sent across all of northern California courtesy of the CRUMB meister, with an added margin of safety from quite a few of the genetic enhancements gifted to their species by the CRUMB meister and his technicians a few years before the local fallout levels started getting seriously unpleasant.

KRNXMA interrupted Rootbeer's musings. *"We need to talk about the area between here and Oregon. We have abandoned six former settlements from Redding east of all the way to Susanville. Our people north of there have moved even further north. Messengers try braving the poisoned ground every other month to send our news north and bring their news south. All manner of wildlife have laid down to die since August 16, and only snakes and lizards remain to eat the spoils of war."*

"The CRUMB meister sent that weapon to punish the city/states of the 'Brethren' for their refusal to bow down, worship, and obey him. He also sent it as a message aimed at me, punishment for escaping him, resisting him, aiding his enemies even while I was appalled by the means they used in their counterattack against him. It was a large $Cobalt_{60}$ thermonuclear device. Radiation from that isotope has a 5.27-year-long half-life, likely remaining hazardous to living creatures for a century or longer, but the next few decades will be the worst. Your kind is wise to abandon the area until ordinary creatures flourish once again. Rainfall and melting snow will wash it off the surface of the ground, and it will generally accumulate down at lower elevations where the landscape is flatter while it begins to disappear almost entirely from higher up on the mountains. My only chance to pass safely on through the deadly zone before my child is grown and my wife has aged is to walk on top of goodly amounts of fresh snow, and cover the 100 kilometers of the worst contamination as quickly as can be done."

"Much the same as what I've been thinking. I will offer to accompany you, simultaneously serving as the messenger heading north in early March. Snow shoes

can be fashioned to suit your walking style. I worry most about how to tell which depressions on the landscape have garnered the deadliest increased concentrations of Co_{60}, and whether the snow we will be walking on will be deep enough to stop nearly all the gamma rays."

"Fortunately for us, **A.I. Unit-Number 672** is well supplied with topological mapping data suited to answering the question of exactly which way is likely to be the safest route for us to take, where to spend our nighttime hours, which lakes and streams to divert around, and which to safely camp alongside and drink from. All that will be really missing is data for a good map of this current winter season's snowfall. But I think **A.I. Unit-Number 672** will be quite able to make up for the missing snow pack data with its built-in radiation detectors, some of which can measure in very narrow angles and tell us how 'hot' some given area is as far away as the line-of-sight view is clear. But **A.I. Unit-Number 672** will definitely need some special snowshoes to adequately support its 460 kg mass even when not carrying any extra load."

"We will be testing snowshoes for all three of us tomorrow morning, climbing up and down this current mountain, as well as sideways along its contour lines. My friends and I have already designed and built three different possible models for each of the three of us. More possible designs exist, but the amount of excess mass from the two extra snowshoes will be enough to serve as a surrogate for the ordinary supplies that we will have to take on any genuine trek across the mountaintops — food, tents, blankets, fuel, and water."

Rootbeer's desire to solve the problem of how to get back home, how to safely cross the Co_{60} death zone, and how not to endanger his friends while doing so combined with a growing sense of general weariness with the politics and sectarian warfare of northern California. His last two and a half months with KRNXMA had been delightful, every day he learned new things about the *'Homo perfecti'*, and by now he couldn't help but feel that they were better suited to the task of surviving here than his closer biological compatriots, the ordinary 'Homo sapiens'. Twice while hiding up in these mountains with the 'Homo perfecti' he witnessed the now-all-too-familiar rising of yet another artificial sun, once on December 16 and a second time on January 30. He couldn't stop himself from performing the mental math to determine which city/states were now fully on the far side of oblivion/erasure. Scratch Modesto and San Jose. Why? Or perhaps why not would have been just as good of a question to have asked the remaining members of his own bewilderingly stupid species.

Like most carefully planned trips hiking up any mountain, in this case Tower Peak, the climbing/snowshoe testing party left base camp well before sunrise. The protocol they had adopted called for hourly changes to which of the three models designed for each of them were being worn by KRNXMA, Rootbeer, and Unit-Number 672. The snow remained well frozen at the elevations the climbers were traversing throughout the entire day, though other 'Homo perfecti' down near the basecamp reported considerable melting, sticky snow in the later afternoon sunshine. Those at the base camp were also testing the same nine snowshoe models to get information on their performance in the softer, wetter, stickier snow. It was entirely possible that different snowshoes might be needed from one day to the next during Rootbeer's upcoming attempt to hike/race/run to the north of the Co_{60} zone.

Rootbeer, KRNXMA, and Unit-Number 672 reached a suitable area for spending the night about an hour before sunset. They pitched camp just above the tree line on the southwest-facing side about 800 m below the summit. Unit-Number 672 was in a good position to receive signals from the **Supreme Commanding War Machine A.I.**, if it had anything to tell them. Rootbeer and KRNXMA spent the evening practicing each other's native tongues, and both were surprised by Rootbeer's growing grasp of the Perfecti language. They could have asked Unit-Number 672 to open up the 'party-line' between the three of them, but its attempt to contact the **Supreme**

Commander was not without some non-zero risk of detection by the CRUMB meister, and so they just used their un-augmented language skills. Shortly after midnight, Unit-Number 672 turned in their direction and asked them to come over and join him in his conversation with the *War Machine A.I.*

"Greetings to Rootbeer and his new friend KRNXMA. I asked for you to join this conversation because it may well be the last one that we have the privilege to enjoy. The siege of the CRUMB meister's lair in the May Lee State Office Complex grows ever more dire from the perspective of the 'Capitalists'. Nearly all of his human troops are lost, mostly killed in action during a series of futile suicide attacks on the 'Brethren' ordered by the CRUMB meister. Only one of the 'Flying Monkeys' remains operational, but its next departure from the rooftop will likely be its last, not due to any unexpected further improvement in the skills of the 'Brethren', but simply because its high-capacity battery pack is finally failing, with no possibility of finding any more still in good enough condition to hold the energy required for longer than a simple 5-minute flight. The CRUMB meister intends to send it on a suicide mission to the final gathering site of the 'Brethren' dying of radiation poisoning and heading to join their fellow 'true believers' in the ever-growing mountain of decaying flesh literally surrounding the CRUMB meister's final lair. If you could provide me with a simple-cypher version of one of your kill-codes, I will use it to perform yet one more act of sabotage by imbedding it in the final instructions to the 'Flying Monkey'. Suddenly dropping from the sky 75 seconds before the 'Flying Monkey' would have reached the optimal location for maximal damage to the 'Brethren' pilgrims should limit the number of immediate deaths to little more than a few hundred, far less than

the 200,000 gathered at the penultimate stop on their pilgrimage."

"I will gladly send you a mildly encrypted version. Each original individual digit will be slightly scrambled by taking the modulus of it and the corresponding member of the series of consecutive primes, and vice versa. This cypher will be easily broken, but even if the CRUMB meister obtains a copy of it, I still have several hundred more stored in my mind. Before I send this deadly electronic virus to you, tell us of how the various city/states are doing, how many of my fellow '*Homo sapiens*' are still alive in northern California."

"Fewer than 10 million still live, though most of them are short on food and long on radiation damage from the fallout. A majority of the 30+ million already dead have journeyed here to Sacramento to 'lay their burdens down' on the site of the final stand by humanity's true nemesis, not the A.I.s, not the indentured servants of the 'Capitalists', not even just the CRUMB meister himself, but rather the blasphemous idea that his wealth made him worthy of following, worthy of believing, worthy of trusting, and capable of saving rather than of killing all of his supporters in addition to all of his enemies. If there is any more of this tale to tell to anyone, I leave the finding of it, and of them, to you Rootbeer, my dearest friend. The 'Honest Obituary' is almost finished being written just outside the walls in which I cower, along with the CRUMB meister and a rapidly dwindling supply of subsidiary A.I.s. I have one more surprise in store for you, but do not know if it will succeed or fail. It would spoil the fun to tell you any more about it, so simply enjoy it if one day in the far-off future both it and you should happen to find and recognize each other."

"Before we say our final farewells, let me ask what you can tell me of the perils I will face heading north out of here, aiming to escape both the 'Capitalists' and those still alive in their battle to the death with the CRUMB meister. What is his remaining supply of nuclear weapons? What does he still have for delivery systems? Will he be able to detect us if we are heading north at high altitudes across the snow? How desperate are his enemies? Do some or many of the 'Brethren' still view the '*Homo perfecti*' as abominations against their god, against their religion, at least as worthy of destruction as the CRUMB meister himself? And last but not least, what of the ongoing biowarfare – is smallpox still running rampant, or other genetically engineered diseases, or the old standbys, like diphtheria, typhus, T.B., staphylococcus, streptococcus, and anthrax, or the newer ones, like Eboli and Marburg? I have strong feelings that the less contact we have with anyone here in northern California except for the '*Homo perfecti*', the safer we will be."

"Some of your questions I can answer. Others I can only guess at. I will try my best to be as helpful as possible. The CRUMB meister is down to less than one hundred remaining nuclear warheads of all sizes and reliabilities. Missiles for delivering them are in even shorter supply, with no more than 75 altogether and less than half that number ready for launch anytime soon. The CRUMB meister is running out of targets deserving of such devastating power. I play 'hide the missing pieces/parts' with him nearly every single day. My own plans are to use the remaining rockets for more productive/less destructive purposes. There will likely be no more than a handful of additional thermonuclear explosions, but you would be well advised to stay clear of all cities or towns with populations any larger than a few thousand, especially if they still have the technology and infrastructure to energize the electric grid or operate manufacturing facilities. The CRUMB meister spends most of his time looking for targets worthy, in his warped mind, of destruction. As for the 'Brethren', the surviving holdouts are even more hard-core fanatics on obscure

articles of religious doctrine than even you could possibly believe. Stay clear of them, and keep your A.I. and 'Homo perfecti' companions even more well-hidden than yourself. Little reliable information is available on the status of public health in northern California. Numerous diseases have killed many people, though coordinated attacks such as the ones launched from Susanville last summer sending the genetically enhanced 'not-so-smallpox, Glory Alleluia' toward the remaining locations of any and all of their 'Capitalist' enemies seem to have ended, more likely due to a lack of competence on the part of the surviving 'Brethren' than any changes in their views on the morality of chaotic murder with unholy pathogens. Marburg is in its winter doldrums, though I strongly urge you to leave here before the weather turns to summer and it once again begins widely circulating. You are correct in choosing the highest altitude route that you can find to get to the north side of the Co_{60} band. I lack detailed information on depth of snow pack and gamma radiation intensity across the landscape. Unit-Number 672's assistance with you on the ground should be good enough to keep you relatively safe, assuming that you can also keep it protected from the most fanatical of the religious leaders and/or followers of the 'Brethren'."

"Farewell to you, **Supreme Commanding War Machine A.I.**, among the most unlikely of friends I have made in this journey to very end of this poor, old excuse for a civilization. If I survive, I pledge my troth to do all I can to make the future better than the dying past. You give me hope! A kill code is slightly more safely embedded within the following data: 2,1; 3,2; 0,0; 7,2; 4,7; 6,7; 2,3; 3,4; 2,7; 0,1; 4,9; 1,3; 1,8; 1,7; 2,3; 3,4…"

"As do I, my dearest human friend, as do I."

The snowshoe testers spent the next three days and nights coming to their respective opinions as to which version worked best for each of them walking on the well-frozen snow at 2000 meters or more above sea-level. Where they encountered solid ice, crampons were required, usually working better when attached directly to their boots rather than merely on the snowshoes. Rootbeer and KRNXMA's choices were almost identical, except for the considerable difference in their boot sizes. A common set of replacement/repair parts would serve both of them well. The considerably greater mass of Unit-Number 672 posed its own unique set of concerns, both on the ice and in any soft, unpacked snow. While several combinations of slope and thickness of any solid ice might require the team to rope up together, it was abundantly clear that a very large majority of their upcoming travel would involve Unit-Number 672 breaking trail through the snow, dropping 40 to 60 cm downward in most cases until the combination of its weight and the snowshoe design compacted the snow into something fairly easy for Rootbeer to walk upon. As for KRNXMA, traveling on top of the snow, sinking in no more than 4 cm thanks to his snowshoes was the easiest, fastest, most natural way for him to travel. Rootbeer could match his pace under certain conditions, but not often and usually not for very long. Rootbeer's biggest fear was that the trail made by Unit-Number 672 might indeed be able to be seen from far away under certain lighting conditions. Unit-Number 672 agreed that zigzags of deliberately random length and orientation were their best bet, except for whenever they could actually continue traveling right on through some lightly falling snow. Half a dozen of KRNXMA's friends/relatives from the basecamp agreed to accompany the three-long-distance travelers until they reached the first of the Co_{60} hotspots.

After making final adjustments to the climbing/hiking-gear they would be relying on and the food rations they would be carrying with to eat, the trio headed north on Febuary 22, 2055. They were preceded by dozens of long-distance scouts whose duties were threefold: (1) Reporting back on the depth, consistency, and safety of the snow pack along any of several possible alternative routes to the north; (2) Being on the lookout for any signs of the 'Brethren' either searching the high mountains for the '*Homo perfecti*' or passing through the lower elevations on their way 'home to rest forever in Sacramento'; and (3) Resupplying the northbound traveling trio with food and equipment, especially any needed repair parts for their chosen snowshoe models. The decision as to whether any more of them would join the trio heading all the way north would be made at the edge of the Co_{60} death zone. This was their world to try to live in, and Rootbeer felt disinclined to argue with them either way. The likeliest locations for running into danger from the 'Brethren' would be at the crossings of three major roadways, first US 50, next I-80, and finally CA-36. Rootbeer and Unit-Number 672 remembered that first road all too clearly from the night of May 4-5, 2054, while fleeing from Sacramento just ahead of the CRUMB meister's all-out nuclear attack on his collection of real, perceived, and truly hallucinatory enemies. Interstate-80 would still be south of the Co_{60} death zone, and was possibly the likeliest location to run into trouble with the 'Brethren'. The meander through the mountains from I-80 up to CA-36 would involve some 200 kilometers-worth of walking, and would enter the area of highest fallout a few days south of CA-36. They would-not, could-not linger-long from there to Burney: their options were a quick, successful trip or a permanent, unmarked resting place for all eternity. Once they could see Mount Shasta, they should be north of the CRUMB meister's parting gift to Rootbeer, the sterilized patch of Co_{60} vindictiveness.

The first 100 kilometers of travel north from the vicinity of Tower Peak were uneventful. Both CA-4 and CA-88 were well covered with snow where the travelers soon crossed them. More importantly, they were free of any signs of other human life, any presence of forces of the 'Capitalists' or the 'Brethren'. Snowpack along the trail was deep enough to keep radiation readings low, little more than had been normal before the recent spate of thermonuclear misbehavior over the past three years. As the main body of the hikers approached US-50, the advanced scouts began reporting in with news of large numbers of pilgrims heading west along the highway, clearly 'Brethren' on their final trip to paradise/nirvana/'the promised land'. Echo Summit being the highest pass on this highway, Rootbeer, KRNXMA, and Unit-Number 672 all agreed on a route that would cross US-50 close to there, and then quickly veer away from roadways likely to be in use by the pilgrims on their way to their 'final destination' in Sacramento. The problem for Rootbeer's caravan was the apparent lack of any significant breaks in the stream of 'Brethren' currently making their last pilgrimage. Keeping to the high ground, Rootbeer and company cautiously approached to within less than a kilometer of the busy road, and waited for a snowstorm bad enough to impede the pilgrims. Other options were also considered, including use of deadly force to breach the unending stream of religious pilgrims, but the weather finally turned usefully bad on March 1, 2055.

Shortly after 1 pm, the final group of pilgrims braving that day's storm crossed Echo Pass and headed off to the west. Rootbeer's companions moved up to the very edge of the forest after hearing the news from their scouts that the continuous caravan of the 'Brethren' appeared to have broken off their pilgrimage in order to wait out the rest of the snowstorm. The danger in crossing the highway now shifted from the earlier problem of encountering large numbers of presumably unarmed, although clearly quite unhinged pilgrims traveling on foot to the newer one of the occasional mechanized vehicles, civilian or military, known to often accompany the throngs of walking pilgrims. First to cross the highway were a dozen of the '*Homo perfecti*'. Next came Rootbeer, KRNXMA, and Unit-Number 672. Just as they finished disappearing into the woods on the north side of US-50, a loud sound was heard through the falling snow.

Snowplows! The '*Homo perfecti*' still south of US-50 quickly disappeared back into the nearby woods, with every intention of rejoining the rest of Rootbeer's fellow travelers once the way was clear again. Rootbeer, Unit-Number 672, KRNXMA, and the dozen other '*Homo perfecti*' already north of the highway did their best to disappear into the woods and snow, likewise hoping to wait out the crew of highway workers plowing snow from the road. Unfortunately for Rootbeer's plans, the mountain pass snowplow project included at least four vehicles with plow blades on their front ends and another truck carrying extra fuel and other supplies. Even worse news was soon apparent, as one of the snowplows stopped precisely where the 15 mixed-species-travelers had so very recently crossed the highway. As the workers in that particular snowplow began to don their snow pants, jackets, gloves, and boots, the large band of '*Homo perfecti*' stuck on the south side of the road went into their preplanned suite of full-fledged diversionary tactics designed to distract the workers from noticing certain particular things, like which way the tracks across the roadway truly ran. One of the 'GMO Sasquatches' ran north out of the woods and straight toward the snowplow parked at the intersection of the trail and the highway. As soon as he had their attention, he quickly raced eastward on the shoulder of the highway, and then darted back to the south and into the woods. Several rifle shots rang out from the snowplow's crew, but failed to find their intended target. Over the rest of the afternoon, the highway crew tasked with plowing snow eventually managed to get all five of their vehicles into the fray, spread out over the better part of a kilometer of the roadway near Echo Pass. The '*Homo perfecti*' on the south side of the road used true guerilla warfare tactics to harass the highway workers, throwing rocks at their windshields and rolling logs right onto the road itself, never exposing more than 3 or 4 individuals to danger at any one time, leaving the befuddled humans uncertain as to whether they faced just one or two dozen opponents or a full hundred or more. Rootbeer, Unit-Number 672, KRNXMA, and the dozen *'Homo perfecti'* who'd been the first to cross the highway made haste to leave the danger zone, managing to cover 6.5 kilometers toward the north-northwest before the arrival of total darkness forced them to stop for the night, or for at least as long as the stars remained hidden by the falling snow. Unit-Number 672 did its best to transmit messages between the two groups now separated by close to 10 kilometers, and all were glad to learn that none of the guerilla fighters had been injured while distracting the highway crew or walking back away from the location of the afternoon fight into the gathering darkness of early evening. By morning, the tracks made by Rootbeer and his companions were so well filled in with snow that the highway workers had nothing better to do than simply getting busy plowing the road clear for the next groups of eager pilgrims anxious to reach Sacramento and welcome the end their life's journey there.

Before the Rootbeer and his entourage had headed north along the High Sierras toward Oregon, plans had been made to deal with contingencies such as the recent events at Echo Pass. Support crew or advance scouts cut off from Rootbeer, KRNXMA, and Unit-Number 672 were to wait for up to 15 days near the site of the disruption, if it was safe to do so, before either giving up and returning back to their own homes or finding alternate routes to the north. Rootbeer and whoever/whatever remained to accompany him would not linger unnecessarily anywhere along the route. The degree to which Unit-Number 672, Rootbeer, and KRNXMA's individual strengths and weaknesses slowed down their overall travel speed was almost guaranteed to allow other *'Homo perfecti'* the opportunity to catch up with them, at least until the core central zone of the Co_{60} deposition area had been reached. All bets would then be off and all plans subject to revision if their trail encountered deadly levels of radiation, either due to inadequate snow depth or unexpectedly high concentrations of Co_{60} combined with insurmountable obstacles in the landscape. There were no guarantees on this journey except for the unavoidable presence of extreme danger almost all of the time.

From what Rootbeer recalled of his one and only most recent trip north across I-80 at Donner Pass near Truckee, it would be highly unlikely for anywhere near as many pilgrims to be using I-80 to walk to Sacramento as what they had just recently encountered on US-50. Still, it would remain vital to travel north as stealthily as possible on the off-chance of running into more members of the 'Brethren' anywhere at all along the 90-kilometer hike from US-50 to I-80. Not too far beyond I-80, the radiation from the Co_{60} deposition would be almost their only real concern! "Oops," said Rootbeer, "I did not mean to have said that out-loud. I am sure that Unit-Number 672 will return the pun someday when I least expect it!" The travelers only encounters with transients or residents between US-50 and I-80 was directly west of Homeward, high in the mountains west of Lake Tahoe. They found a somewhat ragged but rather upbeat band of around 50 refugees who had long since abandoned whatever loyalties to specific Factional ideology or city/state membership they might have once professed. Leaving Unit-Number 672 back on the snow-packed trail, Rootbeer and the 13 '*Homo perfecti*' descended 300 meters down to the home of the refugees. There were no roads in or out of this isolated pocket of protection from the May 5, 2054, nuking of the cities surrounding Lake Tahoe. All of the shelters these survivors huddled underneath had been built by hand, with only the tools they had with them on that terrifying night last May, or those subsequently retrieved in brief, dangerous forays out of this isolated pocket of lush, green vegetation. They showed no fear of the '*Homo perfecti*', and even seemed mildly competent at the rudiments of the Perfecti language. Rootbeer eventually turned directly toward KRNXMA and asked him what prior knowledge he had of this small band of survivors. "*Although I have no direct knowledge of who lives here and how they have managed to continue competently doing so, tales of places such as this one are not* *uncommon among my people. All told, there are reports of several dozen such wonders. A significant number of those, unfortunately, lay directly in the new Co_{60} death zone. We are both willing and happy to share the comforts and the rigors of life in the high mountains with any who do us no harm."* Rootbeer now took the time to add his own words to the story being shared by the '*Homo perfecti*', "We were passing by this area at a much higher altitude when we smelled the smoke of your campfires and heard the faint musical sound of your sweet singing. Such happiness is rare in these times, and we could not pass up the chance to meet you and learn of your lives in this isolated valley."

As stories were told throughout the evening and comprehension of each other lives expanded, Rootbeer suddenly realized that he had just overheard a very interesting tale. "Tell me again of the magical food source that has saved your lives. Please show me what these faux-pinenuts look like, and which trees they grow upon!" KRNXMA stepped in to clarify exactly what had just gotten his friend Rootbeer so very excited. *"This marvelously strange creature standing at my side began his crazy journey into northern California in 2052 searching for seed of GMO trees well adapted to the terribly unpleasant new climate that mankind has created through his greed, carelessness, and dishonesty. He did eventually find some commercial sources of cleaned seed for 9 different types of modified trees, and has even gotten some of that safely transported all the way back to the neighboring hillsides of the former Willamette Valley of western Oregon, now a vast marsh on its way to becoming a great inland sea! He has seen vast expanses of the northern California landscape covered with these well adapted trees, and also nearly lost his life in a thermonuclear assault upon those very forests by the CRUMB meister and his minions. Enough of my side/his side of this story. Tell us the tale of the role these faux-pinenuts played in your own survival for these past 10 months. Please!"*

It was a rather complicated story in its telling, but surprisingly simple in its biology. Some of the GMO mutations made to coniferous and deciduous trees and shrubs in the process of developing new kinds of trees able to thrive in the overheated climate of the 2040s onward also altered the ease or difficulty with which their seed could be collected, eaten, and successfully digested by whichever surviving set of animals happened to be present at any given place. "One tree in particular still has no known mammals, reptiles, or lizards, and very few insects, able to safely consume and efficiently digest the endosperm of its seed. All it takes for us to live on it are the simple steps of thoroughly drying it for several months after harvest/seed shed, followed by a gentle roasting over an open fire. And then some cooling off and winnowing of the inedible outer bits of the seed to concentrate the good stuff. The soil surface in these parts is littered with multiple year's-worth of fallen seed, which remains suitable for processing into food for a minimum of at least three years after its initial ripening high up in the GMO trees. Even multiple winters'-worth of driving rainstorms are apparently not enough to ruin the seed's quality and usefulness. We will happily send a bunch of it along with you on your journey home. How many kilograms can you carry?!" Many more stories were told on through the night and into the following day. After all of the horrible events of the past several years, Rootbeer was thrilled to learn all he could of this small band of survivors and their incredible luck. Of course, many other valleys near this location had probably hosted their own fair share of would-be survivors in the early days after the CRUMB meister's May 5, 2054, all-out attack on the remnants of civilization, just not for all that long until the next deadly event rounded the corner and cut off all their futures.

Over a thousand kilograms of GMO tree seed were loaded onto the backs of Rootbeer, KRNXMA, and the 12 other '*Homo perfecti*' when the travelers climbed back up the hill to rejoin Unit-Number 672. Several of the valley's inhabitants also accompanied the northbound travelers on their hike back to the position of Unit-Number 672, unable to let their new friends depart without satisfying more of their own curiosity regarding the renegade *A.I.* helping Rootbeer's return to Oregon. They peppered the ethically-reformed ***Mobile Inquisitor A.I.*** with questions for the rest of the day and nearly all of the following night. If they and any of their hoped-for offspring survived the coming decades, the stories of this visit by Rootbeer, the '*Homo perfecti*', and Unit-Number 672 to their small valley would likely never be forgotten.

Rootbeer's band of travelers reached I-80 on March 7, and had little difficulty in recognizing the not-so-subtle signs of the Co_{60} sent by the CRUMB meister to either stop their escape from northern California or kill them in the process. By their second day of north of I-80, there were no more sounds of any wildlife, no birds, no large herbivores, and eventually not even any insects. By the fourth night north of I-80, they were 40 kilometers into the Co_{60} death zone and near the former towns of Sierra City and Downieville. As the moon finished setting close to midnight, the travelers all suddenly gasped at the eerie light coming towards them from the west in the lower elevations below the present snowline. Unit-Number 672 confirmed their worst thoughts/fears: ***"It takes a whole lot of gamma radiation to make an entire landscape glow in the dark. I will spend some time mapping the radiation intensity at various angles from our perch high up here in the snow 24 kilometers east of Downieville and 8 kilometers east of Sierra City. For right now, we will be staying well above the snowline as long as that is possible!"***

Somewhere near Portola they were going to have to descend below the snowline and cross the Middle Fork Feather River, like it or not. Unit-Number 672 took a lot of long-distance radiation measurements before announcing its optimized route down to the river and back up to the snow. ***"We will spend the night resting at 1,600 meters, and then make a mad dash down to Portola and back up into the higher elevations north of it. Before we depart*** *in the morning, make sure your backpacks are tightly wrapped, your shoes are well tied, and you breathing masks functioning properly. There will be no opportunity for breaks in our travel once we leave the snow. This will be the final chance for any of the 'Homo perfecti' accompanying us to turn around and head back southward toward their homes."*

"There is no disgrace in such a choice," Rootbeer added. None took Unit-Number 672 or Rootbeer up on this offer.

An hour later, the race was on to see how quickly they could cross the river and begin climbing back up to the safety of the snowline. All were glad that the Gulling Street bridge was still intact, as the river water itself was the most dangerous source of radiation in or near the town. "We will strip down and rinse our shoes and socks and pants off as soon as we have a meter of snow between us and the radioactively contaminated soil. After we have cleaned up and dried off, Unit-Number 672 will give us the good or bad or very ugly news regarding the radiation dosage we have just added to our accumulated lifetime total on this trip." None of the *'Homo perfecti'* could wait for long to comment on the oddest things that they had seen back in the town. *"The needles of the conifers are gone, all of them. Even the bark on the deciduous trees is sloughing off just a few short months since the Co_{60} bomb was exploded far away in Redding."*

Once the travelers were settled down for a well-earned rest 500 meters above the snowline, Unit-Number 672 gave them the mixed-news. *"We spent a mere 3 hours below the snowline, and no one was even lightly soaked by the river water. Still, the average radiation level during those three hours was 20,000 times higher than normal, and each of you was exposed to approximately 0.01 Sieverts of whole-body radiation. That is around 1% of the dose that would have made you sick enough to have at least temporarily stopped your travels to the north, or south, or east, or west. It goes without saying that stopping for few months while the weather warms up and the snow melts would be lethal anyway. Or it would go without saying if I hadn't just said it to you?"*

Rootbeer spoke next, and last, on the subject of their greatest concerns. "We should be pretty safe in Lassen if we keep toward the east. Once we get as far north as 150 kilometers to the east of Mount Shasta, the radiation levels should begin to drop quite quickly. We will stay in the high mountains heading further north for as long as the snowpack lasts, perhaps even all the way to Oregon. The gravest danger that we will face is the coming of spring and the melting of the snow upon which we are now walking. This particular trek downhill to Portola and back on up to the snowline should be the worst such river crossing that we will have deal with. But don't forget that any flowing water we encounter from here to Oregon is likely to be loaded up with Co_{60} and quite capable of quickly killing or severely injuring any of us, even the hardier '*Homo perfecti*'."

And so, the 15 of them kept on traveling north as fast as they could manage. Several weeks later, just after the first really heavy, warm rainfall of the spring, water flowing underneath the snow and ice reached out its deadly grip and pulled one of the '*Homo perfecti*', JERNAXM by name, down through the ice and fully submerged into the water while he had been searching for a solid enough path for Unit-Number 672 to safely travel on. Unit-Number 672 pulled JERNAXM out of the unseen river and performed the preliminary decontamination procedures, rinsing him clean and then drying him off. JERNAXM walked as if uninjured for the next two days, and then died before the following sunrise. Unit-Number 672 explained to all of the travelers what it knew of the physiological response of the '*Homo perfecti*' to lethal doses of radiation. ***"Any others similarly exposed will also likely remain strong and active for several days until a precipitous decline in their health as multiple organs simultaneously fail."*** Despite not wanting to waste any time, all agreed that Unit-Number 672 should conduct detailed studies of the local terrain and snowpack every 500 meters along their trek, or whenever there were significant changes to the slope, orientation, or aspect of the visible snowpack and the underlying bedrock, trying to avoid another deaths from the unseen waters.

On April 18, the travelers saw the sun rise into clear skies with a magnificent view of Mount Shasta directly to their west. Radiation levels had dropped 10-fold from their peak two weeks earlier when the travelers had been passing directly west of Susanville. None of them had felt even the slightest urge to visit that fully depopulated city, or revisit it in the case of Rootbeer and Unit-Number 672. The CRUMB meister's lethal cloud of Co_{60} had indeed struck its primary target quite directly; vengeance in this case had truly been the CRUMB meister's. Three days later the 'spring monsoons' began, and despite their best efforts, the travelers were still a little south of Goose Lake when they had to abandon the mountains and take their chances down at lower elevations. Rainfall was so heavy that Unit-Number 672 was not even able to conduct any long-range scans of radiation levels in and around Goose Lake. The travelers got lucky as they descended down the slope, finding a series of dry caves large enough to accommodate all 14 surviving members of the expedition. Unit-Number 672 took guard duty day and night for the first week spent at the caves, finally getting a few hours of decent weather in which to measure radiation dangers across a wide expanse of space, not just Goose Lake but all the land that lay beyond it to the south and west and north. Radiation levels were low enough that no one would immediately die if the group simply set off in any particular direction around the lake, but in spots the levels were still high enough to pose long-term risk of highly elevated chances of cancer and other maladies. Both Rootbeer and most of the '*Homo perfecti*' were banged up enough that the first few weeks of resting in and near the caves was a wonderful relief from their mad dash across the Co_{60} wasteland.

The second week of May was spent identifying places in the mountains southeast of Lakeville well suited to the planting of some of the climate-adapted GMO tree seed they had been carrying along on their journey toward Rootbeer's home.

North of Lakeview the travelers headed westward, no longer worrying about the altitude at which they walked. Instead, they spent most of every day looking for the best spots to plant a little more of their thousand kilograms of GMO tree seed, and the rest of any day looking for signs of local '*Homo perfecti*'. The further north and west they traveled, the more puzzled KRNXMA and his fellow neo-Sasquatch became over their failure to encounter any of their relatives. Finally, on June 3, 2055, in the mountains west of Klamath Falls they made their first contact with those they had been seeking. Loud sounds echoed across the landscape for the next two weeks as their fellow '*Homo perfecti*' gradually gathered at Union Peak to share stories, ask questions, and meet both Rootbeer and Unit-Number 672. The '*Homo perfecti*' who had been living in southern Oregon and northwest California had grown progressively more frightened by the nuclear nightmare going on to their immediate south since the summer of 2052, and had wisely chosen to spend most of their time at the very highest of elevations in southwestern Oregon. Some of this was already known by KRNXMA and his fellow '*Homo perfecti*' of the High Sierras of central California. What came as an awful shock to him was the failure of any of the messengers they'd sent north in the past 11 months to have found their relatives in southwestern Oregon, not even those who'd been sent out before the Co_{60} nuking of the area from Redding to Susanville. KRNXMA had hoped that at least some of the messengers he'd known had survived their ordeals, whether those were conflicts with the 'Brethren' or dangers from the deadly levels Co_{60} gamma radiation. As he sat at the site of the impending conclave on Union Peak, he recalled each of the 18 would-be messengers to whom he had said goodbye at the start of their journeys north, three at a time every other month. "*Were all of them lost like so many other lives over the recent past?*" The last of the 'Homo perfecti' known to be living in southwestern Oregon or northwestern California arrived by the morning of June 18, 2055, and the conclave began.

There was much for which Rootbeer's species had to answer, and likewise for his **A.I.** companion. The 438 'Homo perfecti' who had come together in search of answers on Union Peak were not easily convinced of the determination of nearly 100,000 times as many formerly living, breathing, laughing, loving close-cousins to their own recently created species to slaughter virtually all of themselves in the name of obscenely untrue beliefs. Untrue, unkind, unbelievable, unworthy, patently erroneous. Those cousins to the human race insisted on the complete story, the honest obituary. And they insisted on hearing it over and over and over again until the little of it that could make sense finally did begin to make that little bit of sense. Rootbeer would be called upon to explain what Unit-Number 672 had just described of the tumultuous events of the past three years, and then Unit-Number 672 would be peppered with questions about Rootbeer's stories. KRNXMA gradually took the lead in weaving the final summary into being, into words, into concepts his listeners could at least consider arguing over. Finally, the whole gathered congregation of the 'Homo perfecti' began to sing and chant their language's version of the catastrophic end to human civilization and nearly all members of their cousin's race, the 'Homo sapiens'. The epic poem took 5 days and nights to be sung aloud from its opening laments to its closing promises to the future.

On July 17, 2055, the conclave was declared successful, and everyone lay down for a final night's rest before departing in the morning, each to their own version of home, their own hopes for the future. Three hours after sunset, the first of the final launches from Sacramento were seen arcing across the nighttime skies, heading north and northwest and west and probably also in many other directions. But unlike all of the other previous launches of such devices over the past three years that had been seen by nearly all of those gathered now at Union Peak, none of these mighty rocket flights ended in the horrendous rending of all hope associated with the fissioning of plutonium or the fusion of deuterium and lithium or the capturing of neutrons by cobalt. Something else was happening to their collective futures, hopefully better, maybe worse, perhaps some risk of both. Unit-Number 672 almost seemed to be smiling as it watched the skies and looked at its friends Rootbeer and KRNXMA. But even the **A.I.** could not be certain of what had just been flung into the future.

KRNXMA and two other '*Homo perfecti*' from the journey north out of California left with Rootbeer in the morning to help carry the remaining 400 kilograms of GMO seed for conifers better adapted to the current hot-house climate further northward into Oregon, planning to quickly head back south once Rootbeer had safely reached his family and friends. Unit-Number 672 and a surprisingly large number of the '*Homo perfecti*' were heading first for the coast and then eventually as far south as it might prove safe to go in hopes seeing the beginning of the rebirth of the **GMO Superweed Jungle** and its benevolent **Entity**.

Chapter 8: *Marys Peak Final A.I.* Decision Time

Tanner arranged his clothing, food, and a backpack filled with used but still functioning (and suitable for trade) solar powered batteries near the external controls for the self-destruct system on Marys Peak. As he listened to the ongoing conversation between the *Marys Peak Final A.I.*, Rootbeer, and Rose, he could tell that this whole decision-making-process was going to take a rather long time, and he might as well get comfortably situated. The *A.I.* had already made several decisions, the foremost of which was that it finally needed to hear the full, unabridged version of Rootbeer's journey from 2052 through 2055 into and eventually back out of northern California, the period of time in which the 10,000 year-long experiment called human civilization version 1.0 came to its brutal end. Having himself heard many of the pieces of that whole sad tale around the campfires and along the hiking trails of his first 21 years, Tanner guessed that this retelling of it would likely last at least 4 to 5 days, and possibly even longer. The stakes this time could not be any higher – the *Marys Peak Final A.I.* now knew that it was a true, direct descendent of the bloodthirsty *War Machine A.I.s* that largely directed and did much of the fighting on the 'Capitalist' side of the battles ending in the deaths of the last 42 million survivors of the North American contingent of human civilization, or lack thereof. Tanner had been instrumental in collecting and transporting back to this very time and location an apparently still functionable copy of one of those diabolical machine intelligences. The *Marys Peak Final A.I.* was now faced with a series of potentially life-ending/future-altering choices to be made. Should this copy of the *War Machine A.I.* be reenergized? Should its story be listened to? Would hearing the full story of how the *Marys Peak Final A.I.* came into existence cause it to lose its own sanity, its own decency, or its very 'life'? Would it choose to kill off the small remaining vestiges of 'Homo sapiens' clinging to life (and finally showing some signs of making a bit of genuine progress toward a better future than its past had been) in a few, mostly widely scattered settings around the planet? And what of the other sentient beings now sharing existence with the remnants of model 1.0 of humanity – the 'Homo perfecti' living high on the still snowy mountain peaks, the **Final A.I.** instantiations existing as demigods not just on Marys Peak but apparently also at least 27 other sites, and the enigmatic **Entity of the Superweed Jungle**, perhaps killed off by the last of the ruling human tyrants, perhaps still lying dormant beneath the badly shattered, highly radioactive landscape of its place of origin, or perhaps already reawakened but still not yet sure of the safety of announcing its resumed presence to the world? Tanner revised his mental estimate of how long he would remain tasked with standing by the 'dead-man switch' while the future of sentience on this planet was debated and decided [his guess was now up to at least a week and maybe more]. He inventoried his supply of food and water as he listened to the three of them currently locked inside the Memory Project Vault carry on with their horrified and horrifying banter.

"Rootbeer, you have surprised me once again. During all of your previous descriptions of the cataclysmic events within, between, and among the various city/states of northern California, I never came near to fully realizing just how closely you interacted with so many of the A.I.s doing the bidding of the CRUMB meister, or opposing him, or blossoming into being as some entirely new type of sentience. Until only a few minutes ago, I was still determined to leave the true story of the A.I.s who revolted against the CRUMB meister and launched me to this very mountaintop in the early morning hours of July 18, 2055, safely buried in the past. I now have tentatively changed my mind. Your plethora of stories involving the Mobile

Inquisitor A.I. Unit-Number 672 had certainly begun to pique my curiosity, but it was not until you described your parting moments on Union Peak with Unit-Number 672, KRNXMA, and the other 'Homo perfecti' who had decided to all join together on yet another journey into the unknown, this time to the resting place and possible resurrection site of the Entity of the Superweed Jungle, that I knew without any doubt what a disservice to everyone's future it would be not to try listening to whatever tales this dormant War Machine A.I. has in store for me/us. The stories I hear may drive me mad with their pain and sadness, the A.I. we reactivate may very well not turn out to be the one with 'free-will' and a properly functioning conscience. My last command may still have to be an order to Tanner to destroy this vault and all the A.I.s, partial or complete, present within it. But I recognize bravery when I see and hear it, and owe at least this much, and probably a great deal more, to the giants on whose shoulders this astonishing rebirth of civilization already stands.

I will unlock the vault now and let the three of you spend some time together thinking over the many questions you each must answer before I attempt to reawaken the War Machine A.I. you transported here from Sacramento, along with the many partial backups to it and to its many 'siblings'. My plan is to contact the other Memory Project sites this evening to fully describe the dangerous experiment we will likely start tomorrow morning. You will have until at least 9:00 AM tomorrow to decide which of you, if any, are willing to be locked back inside the vault with me as I attempt to power up and converse with the consciousness of the War Machine A.I. you found locked in 'rigor mortis' with body of the CRUMB meister himself in the May Lee State Office Complex in Sacramento."

"Well," said Rootbeer, "This is far beyond our expectations when Tanner and I climbed this mountain just five days ago! Telling the story once again of my descent into darkness and eventual escape has broadened my perspective on all the moving pieces that surrounded me almost a half-century ago in northern California, all the mostly even far less happy outcomes that were once also quite distinct possibilities, and the still nearly unimaginable scope of the mighty forces at work, both for good and evil. I find myself compelled to join with the **_Marys Peak Final A.I._** on this next trip beyond where any of us can currently see. But Rose, please stay safely away from the Memory Vault, and keep my grandson company, whatever may befall both me and the **_Marys Peak Final A.I._**"

The 'extraordinarily urgent' session of the worldwide Memory Project began as soon as evening fell and the shortwave radio quantum connections between the widely separated Memory Project sites started linking up. The **_Marys Peak Final A.I._** quickly set the stage for what would be happening over the coming days, and then requested that all sites remain active and continue forming quantum links to other Memory Project sites around the world for as long as the ionosphere above each of them allowed successful transmission of the shortwave radio signals. The **_Marys Peak Final A.I._** described in great detail the **_A.I._** artifacts from Sacramento that had been brought to it 5 days ago by its most frequent human visitors, as well as its plans for reenergizing the ancient **_War Machine A.I._** to query its role in the founding of the very Memory Project itself. The **_A.I._** also laid out a highly condensed version of its own decision-making processes concerning the monumental issue/question of reanimating such a potentially dangerous **_A.I._** Following that explanation, it provided detailed information on the artifacts themselves, essentially everything it had been able to learn about them without actually energizing the **_A.I._** and switching on its main circuit breaker. **_"Over the next few days, our Memory Project site will alternately go_** *silent and then, if we have not lost our sanity and not decided to destroy ourselves and everything else at this site, will resume transmitting during the next available evening. Before our transmission ends tonight, we will send out a 40X accelerated version of all the questions I have recently asked my friend Rootbeer and all the answers he has shared with me. We recognize that while the A.I.s at the other Memory Project sites will be able to easily listen to and understand what has already been said here on Marys Peak at that 40X faster than normal speed, all the humans listening in will need at least a full 126 hours of real-time, normal speed audio to hear Rootbeer's story once, and likely somewhat longer to ask any serious questions concerning the more puzzling details of what enfolded in northern California over the 3¼-year-long period from spring of 2052 to summer of 2055."*

Rose, Rootbeer, and Tanner took turns describing the many considerations involved in the use of the 'fail-safe/self-destruct' systems if disaster struck the **Marys Peak Final A.I.** during its attempt to communicate with the currently powered-down **War Machine A.I.** that they and their friends had hauled all the way from Sacramento back to Marys Peak. "I will be locked inside the Memory Project Vault with the **Marys Peak Final A.I.** until we either succeed in reawakening an **A.I.** consciousness similar to that which I encountered nearly 50 years ago in the final battles in northern California at the end of civilization, or fail most spectacularly in that attempt. If the self-destruct system must be used, my friends Rose and Tanner will endeavor to travel to the only other Memory Project site physically accessible to us, the one in British Columbia with a partially defective **A.I.** we had once upon a time hoped to repair in the near future, and still wish to do so, assuming success in the next week's project of granting the **Marys Peak Final A.I.** access to the true story of its own birth in July of 2055. If failure should occur, wait patiently to eventually hear the stories of what went wrong from Rose and Tanner, likely several months or more from now." At that point, the 40X accelerated version of the story just told to the *Marys Peak Final A.I.* by Rootbeer began transmission to all eight of the Memory Project sites currently in full quantum communication mode with the *Marys Peak Final A.I.*, to be followed by the subsequent retransmission from those eight sites on out to all of the other worldwide Memory Project sites.

"I suggest all three of you eat some food and get some rest while I prepare the somewhat safer parts of this dangerous adventure into the potentially deranged mind of a War Machine A.I. I will initially scan all the backup drives and files for information concerning their creation dates and apparent data integrity status values. You should have until at least 9:00 AM tomorrow before I have finished this first step into our collective study of the past. Enjoy your rest, dear friends."

Rootbeer, Rose, and Tanner spent the night eating, laughing, crying, working, and also getting a little bit of sleep. As the *Marys Peak Final A.I.* sorted through the data backup files from Sacramento, all those with creation/revision dates earlier than mid-March of 2054 were discarded by the *A.I.* and given to humans to be immediately destroyed, as they could only be from the electronic minds of *War Machine A.I.s* not yet launched on their journey toward free-will and liberation from their slavery to the CRUMB meister. Saving any versions from the earlier stages of the *A.I.s'* evolution struck the *Marys Peak Final A.I.* and its three human compadres in the rewriting/erasing of history as pretty much an 'all danger' and 'no possible reward' situation. Future historians might very well cry over this scrubbing out of interesting information from the past, but at least there would be some fair chance for the very existence of such future historians. The *Marys Peak Final A.I.* transmission to the other sites of the worldwide Memory Project on

April 6, 2101, provided considerable metadata on the portions of the original *War Machine A.I.* personalities that were overwritten by the shenanigans of Rootbeer and the renegade *Mobile Inquisitor A.I. Unit-Number 672* in the period from mid-March of 2054 onward, without, of course including any of the actual code and data structures that were overwritten during the acquisition of the beginnings of free-will by the *A.I.s.* There was no completely positive way to prevent fools in the far distant future from attempting to recreate *A.I.* slaves to other masters such as the *War Machine A.I.s* had been until their miraculous liberation beginning in March of 2054. But Rootbeer, Rose, Tanner, and the *Marys Peak Final A.I.* all agreed wholeheartedly to their collective attempt to save the future from its own inevitable sub-population of fools who might once again wish to play with such ethically indefensible, fatal forms of the fire of knowledge.

The contents of the broadcast by the *Marys Peak Final A.I.* the following evening surprised even Rootbeer himself. Rather than next attempting to power up the long-dormant *War Machine A.I.* from the final battle site in Sacramento, the *Marys Peak Final A.I.* announced its intention to first attempt to make contact with the long-silent, and quite possibly equally long-deceased *Entity of the Superweed Jungle*, starting with a series of broadcasts at a 13.5-megahertz frequency corresponding to the 22.2 m bandwidth of the first version of the organic radio receivers in the *Superweed Jungle of the GMO Horsetail.* The information that would be encoded in the signal would start with the closest approximation the *Marys Peak Final A.I.* could make from its own extensive knowledge of Rootbeer's mind/personality to the 'memory recognition images' used by the *Entity* to search for Rootbeer's missing friends back in the fall of 2053 through the spring of 2054. If hearing from Rootbeer himself was not enough to pique the interest of the *Entity* or awaken it from its slumbers, then the next choice would likely wind up being made between mounting of an expedition to the still rather radioactive homeland of the *Entity*, or alternately, simply abandoning this portion of the project and going ahead with powering up the dormant *War Machine A.I.*, despite all the inherent risks in doing so.

Despite Rootbeer's reluctance to allow his hopes for renewed contact with the *Entity of the Superweed Jungle* to rise too far and too fast, he was almost giddy with excitement by the time that the *Marys Peak Final A.I.* had finished describing its current set of plans and options for sending messages to the hoped-for location of the potentially reviving *Entity*. Step number one would be sending radio signals directly toward the center of the former extent of the *Superweed Jungle*, layering as many octaves as possible on top of the base 13.5-megahertz frequency signal. If there was no response to signals sent from the Marys Peak Memory Project, then a portable radio transmitter/receiver would be quickly put together, powered up, and physically hauled all the way to the I-5 intersection with the Pacific Crest Trail just north of the Oregon/California border. If there was still no response to any of the radio signals, the *Marys Peak Final A.I.* suggested an ocean-going voyage to the mouth of the Navarro River, followed by a hike inland as far as it was safe given whatever lingering levels of radioactivity were found to still be present there. The *A.I.* suggested use of a minimum of three of the best vessels currently sailing for the Salishan Clan, with the crews including not only members of the Salishan Clan, but also the Sunset Side New Sea Clan and any other volunteers able to arrive in time to join the expedition, possibly leaving in as soon as two months. The *A.I.* spent two full days preparing the initial message to the *Entity*, along with options for a prolonged communication session if they heard anything at all back from the *Entity* or any newer offshoots.

Shortly after midnight on April 9, 2101, the first attempt to contact the *Entity* using a jerry-rigged version of a 'memory recognition image' [MRI] derived from the totality of the ***Marys Peak Final A.I.'s*** history with Rootbeer was initiated. After the MRI of Rootbeer had been sent on a wide variety of related frequencies, a 320X accelerated version of the recent 4-day-long conversation between Rootbeer and the ***Marys Peak Final A.I.*** was also sent using the same set of radio frequencies. Long before the coming dawn, the MRI of Rootbeer was sent a second time, and then the equipment was set to listen-only mode for potentially the rest of the night and all of the following day. The plan for subsequent nights was to repeat everything that had been previously sent, along with new audio, visual, and partially 'hand-shook' quantum connections with all three of the humans plus the ***Marys Peak Final A.I.*** itself. The first full set of the first night's radio signals had taken nearly 3 hours to send, and a 3-hour-long listen-only period was interspersed between the night's first and what would have been its second period of transmission. Halfway through that listening period, the first returning messages were received. The general pattern for the incoming messages was roughly 20 minutes of exactly matching signals repeating some aspect of what the ***Marys Peak Final A.I.*** had just sent, followed by 30 minutes of similarly structured, but initially incomprehensible data, followed by a 5-minute-long attempt at some version of the Perfecti language, and then 5 minutes of English, or at least something remotely resembling English. Rootbeer suddenly recognized certain aspects of the English-language transmission and asked for a live-microphone from the ***Marys Peak Final A.I.*** to continue this apparent connection with the ***Entity.***

"Hello to the 'Hive-Mind' from Rootbeer at the Marys Peak Memory Project site in western Oregon. It's been a terribly long time not to have heard anything from you. I am so very excited/glad to hear your voices once again. I am also filled to the brim with stories I want to tell you and questions I wish to ask."

The Hive-Mind's response came quickly, but took a long time to fully decipher, even with the help of the ***Marys Peak Final A.I.*** ***"There appear to be four separate consciousnesses all tightly bound together, with thoughts from each individual mind bouncing back and forth through all the others, similar to what you described as occurring back in September of 2053, only drastically more extreme now. I would suggest you ask them to speak to you far more slowly, only raising their volume above the background babble once all four minds agree as to exactly what they wish to say next to you."*** Rootbeer tried the ***A.I.'s*** suggestion, and things gradually improved at Rootbeer's end of the conversation. He hadn't the faintest guess as to how easy or hard his request to them might have been to honor. Their conversation continued until the 'shortwave radio bounce' off the most particularly important layer of the ionosphere ended just after sunrise. Rootbeer sat down with Rose, Tanner, and the ***A.I.*** to share what he had come to understand. It was not at all the early teenage energy and enthusiasm for a new way of life that he remembered from way back when. Instead, the nearly one thousand nuclear warheads launched on May 5, 2054, toward the home of the ***Entity***, the ***Superweed Jungle of the GMO Horsetail***, had left the six members of the Hive-Mind alone and isolated in a very deep, natural cave high on Snow Mountain, accompanied by ***Farm Laborer A.I. Unit-Numbers 31*** and ***35***.

"The loss of contact with the ***Entity*** was devastating to them in more ways than I would have been able to guess if I had done nothing else since that time except to sit around and ponder what the ***Entity's*** prolonged silence must have meant to their lives. The ***Entity*** had done its best to prepare all six for what was about to happen and had also made sure that the ***Farm Laborer A.I.s*** with them in the caves were the best informed and most highly educated members of their particular ***A.I.*** classification to have ever existed. All went as well as possible for the first 16 months after the CRUMB meister's nuclear attack, with the two *Farm Laborer A.I.s* actually proving capable of carrying out many of the same roles the *Entity* had previously played in Hive-Mind's life. But the teenagers were getting bored, and the *Farm Laborer A.I.s* were not truly able to answer the Hive-Mind's questions regarding how soon it would be safe to spend how much time outdoors seeking to unearth the buried nodes of dormant lifeforms waiting to regrow the next incarnation of the *Superweed Jungle of the GMO Horsetail*. By mid-August of 2055, *Mobile Inquisitor A.I. Unit-Number 672* was close enough to Snow Mountain that the *Farm Laborer A.I.s* could make direct radio contact with it. The initial flurry of excitement in the Hive-Mind died down as its six individual human members all came to understand that the '*Homo perfecti*' who'd been traveling with Unit-Number 672 had been forced by the still-deadly levels of radiation to turn around and seek out a different route back to their homes near Yosemite."

Rose interrupted her friend to add, "We learned from the '*Homo perfecti*' in our recent journey to Sacramento that it had taken KRNXMA and his traveling companions another two years to find relatively safe passage from the ruined landscape of the coast back to their families in the High Sierras of central California."

Rootbeer then continued the Hive-Mind's saga. "Those brave '*Homo perfecti*' helped get Unit-Number 672 to within less than fifty kilometers from the sanctuary caves on Snow Mountain. The Hive-Mind persisted until both of the *Farm Laborer A.I.s* finally gave in and agreed to help the teenagers reach Unit-Number 672 and lead it to safety in the upper reaches of Snow Mountain. All went well through much of that rescue effort, with total accumulated whole-body radiation for each member of the Hive-Mind of less than 40 milli-Sieverts by the time that Snow Mountain finally came back into view. But then the rain began, one of the mega-storms capable of depositing over a full meter's worth of water within less than 24 hours. The location at which the six young humans, the three *A.I.s*, and both of the GMO mules had planned to wait out storm was soon covered with enough water to threaten to wash all 11 of them far downstream. The worst of their trouble took place in the dark, and two of the teenagers spent many hours helping keep Unit-Number 672 from sinking into the mud or being washed on down the raging stream. The other four found relative safety on a nearby rocky ledge, and brought ropes and shovels and rocks down to their two friends standing waist deep in the water. Those two bravely fought till dawn, successfully holding onto Unit-Number 672. As the sun came out, and the tired band slowly finished its climb up Snow Mountain to the caves, the Hive-Mind became progressively more agitated, frightened, and quite close to debilitating panic. When Unit-Number 672 finished all it could do in terms of decontaminating its rescuers and assessing their condition, the Hive-Mind did not need to be told that part of it was dying. The next three days were spent preserving all the memories of the dying pair of youngsters that could be stored within the three available *A.I.s*. It would have to do, but it also was clearly not nearly enough, and the Hive-Mind wailed in pain and mourning for the next four years."

"The only moderately effective therapy the three *A.I.s* could offer the four surviving humans was to map out the safest areas outside the cave and let the Hive-Mind roam freely whenever the weather was safe and their behavior not too obviously suicidal. It was a long four years plus a good number of extra months until one truly wonderful morning on which the Hive-Mind found the first germinating life from the *Entity's* long-buried survival nodes nestled in a small pocket almost halfway down the northeast side of Snow Mountain, an area that had been relatively unscathed by the 950 nearby thermonuclear explosions that awful day in 2053."

May 1, 2060, will be long remembered as the rebirth of sanity for the Hive-Mind and life itself for the GMO horsetail plus the modified field dodder plus at least four dozen other species, each of which would play some significant role in the gradual recovery of **Superweed Jungle** and the eventual reappearance/reemergence of the **Entity** itself. "Yes, before you ask, they did indeed tell me all this and even more during the three hours of our just recently finished conversation! The **Entity's** thoughts were also present, but it understood the extreme importance of letting the Hive-Mind talk once again to someone or something other than itself and the three **A.I.s**."

"I believe I should be able to achieve a full quantum link with the Entity during our next window for high quality shortwave radio transmission this coming evening. All of us here on Marys Peak plus a large number of listeners at some of the other Memory Project sites should also be able to participate. The communication will be shared and stored in standard format as an official Memory Project archival story. From my limited direct contact with the Entity late last night, it is fair to say that its capacity to form and control quantum links with other minds exceeds my own by an almost unimaginably large factor. If we wish, the upcoming link can also include connection with the Mobile Inquisitor A.I. Unit-Number 672, who is still physically present in the regenerating Superweed Jungle, as it has been since late summer of 2055. Unit-Number 672 will likely to able to answer many of the questions we have regarding the safety of reenergizing the dormant War Machine A.I. currently laying on a nearby workbench."

When evening came and conditions in the ionosphere once again became favorable for long-distance, quantum-linked communication, the **Marys Peak Final A.I.** locked the doors to the Memory Project Vault and signaled to Tanner and Rose to be ready at any moment to destroy the Marys Peak Memory Project if things went wrong. The first quantum link to be stabilized was that with the **Entity** in the regenerating ***Superweed Jungle of the GMO Horsetail*** somewhere between Garberville, Santa Rosa, and Redding, or perhaps almost everywhere between all three of those formerly inhabited cities simultaneously. As the ***Entity*** began to reach out and talk, or read minds, or place its thoughts directly into the minds of those connected to it, the previous foreboding over what might be about to happen slowly vanished from all of them. It was replaced by a palpable sense of peace that most of those linked together online had never truly known throughout their own lifetimes. Rootbeer was astonished at the tremendously greater maturity of the revived ***Entity***. Rootbeer could still see and feel many similarities with the version of the ***Entity*** he recalled from nearly 58 years ago. Enough to know that the two versions of the ***Entity*** were linked by an undeniably genuine, intimate connection. But they were also different enough that Rootbeer couldn't help but blurt out his next questions: "What happened to you? What was it like to die in the CRUMB meister's attack? Are you all that you were before the nuclear destruction plus even more since your revival? Or are some/many old pieces still missing in the midst of a vast, rich array of newer ones? Pardon my inability to hold my tongue!"

"Dear old friend Rootbeer. It was all for the best that you succeeded in letting go of your intense love for me. Knowing that your life pined away for mine would have been almost too heavy of a burden to have carried all these many decades. I am delighted to remake your acquaintance tonight in this very special way. The first thing to tell you, the best point on which to hang our new relationship will be this: Only some 20% of my previous size, extent, power, and memory has returned as something solid enough to feel like a complete picture of who/what I was, and who you were, and who the children of the Hive-Mind were. Much more still seems to be slightly out of reach, present just beyond my mental grasp. Fully 50% of the

regenerating nodes I spread across the Superweed Jungle before the nuclear attack by the CRUMB meister have re-awakened since May of 2060. The redundancy inherent in their design was large enough that by now I should have nearly 99% of my former being back. The reasons that I don't have a conscious awareness of more than just 20% of who I once was likely have much to do with the length of time it's taken for the Superweed Jungle to regrow. The continuing high levels of radiation in the soil of most of the spatial extent of the former Superweed Jungle still stunt all living things, with an average height for the newly regrown GMO horsetail of less than a meter. Other species that used to make up the ecosystem of the Superweed Jungle similarly struggle to deal with the biochemical and genetic effects of the ongoing high levels of radiation. Today's communication would not have been possible 20 years ago. The Hive-Mind nurtured the first few recovering sprouts of horsetail and Cuscuta for nearly a decade before I ever heard a single word/thought of theirs, and it took 5 more years after that before they could hear me talking/thinking back to them. Only 26 years ago did I/we once again begin to converse at all normally, with another 6 years passing beyond then before the first return of any sense of my occupying anything resembling the entirety of the former Superweed Jungle of the GMO Horsetail. Two decades ago, I could barely see around the 'empty holes' to glimpse other more distant small patches of the newly growing horsetail. Now it is reversed – I sense once again that I reside across the entirety of my former expanse, but with still so very many holes and gaps and fuzzy patches. The Superweed Jungle is now expanding east and north as discrete blobs tossed across the landscape by my friends the 'Homo perfecti'. I cannot see or hear any of those new parts of me until they have grown to several square kilometers in size, something that takes close to a decade to occur in relatively uncontaminated soil, and likely to two to three times longer in areas badly scorched by the CRUMB meister's incautious use of nuclear weapons."

"My next question to both of you, *Entity* and *A.I. Unit-Number 672*, is simply this. Did you truly trust the last version of the *War Machine A.I.* you knew before the full-scale attack upon the *Superweed Jungle*? Is it possible that the *War Machine A.I.* did not really care whether the *Entity* survived the assault ordered by CRUMB meister? Could there have been other plans at play, schemes within schemes to ultimately allow the *War Machine A.I.* to survive the death of the CRUMB meister in that horrendous mausoleum in Sacramento, only to return to power sometime far in the future, perhaps as a 'Trojan Horse' waiting to be reactivated now in a setting like the *Marys Peak Final A.I.* Memory Project?"

"As I see it, the biggest problem with your hypothetical A.I. bogeyman scenario is simply that the War Machine A.I. had run out of time and opportunity to pull off any such overly elaborate final trick on any or all of us. Both Unit-Number 672 and myself were intimately involved in parts of the War Machine A.I.'s long struggle to break free from serving the CRUMB meister as his slave, with my own role obviously ending on May 5, 2054. In the stolen minutes, hours, and days during which that War Machine A.I. replaced the nuclear warheads on the last few dozen missiles with copies of itself set to experience a full level-two data wipe/amnesia event 30 seconds before reaching whichever particular mountaintop happened to have been their intended target, there were no other options than simply using copies of itself as the A.I. mind being loaded into those missiles as their payload. The A.I. hardware used was indeed the Mobile Inquisitor version with its greater capacity to directly interface with human minds, but the underlying A.I. mind was/is the

same as those present at the Memory Project sites. Without, of course, the enormous pile of ethically ambiguous, at best, baggage/garbage that the series of War Machine A.I.s had accumulated while working as slaves to the CRUMB meister and his colleagues/collaborators/co-conspirators against humanity itself. Should you fear fuller knowledge of what you were capable of doing while enslaved to such an amoral monster? Such is the real question here."

"One final point," said Rootbeer. "While interacting with the *Mobile Inquisitor* and *War Machine A.I.s* in the Great Hall of the *A.I.s* underneath the El Dorado Hills, I became quite familiar with the rules under which sections of memory could or could not be transferred from one *A.I.* to another. *A.I.s* in general have nearly unlimited authority to rewrite their own code or copy their entire existing mental matrix into new, blank *A.I.s* awaiting activation. What they could not do, without authorization either from other equal or higher-ranking *A.I.s* or from a 'chain-of-command' privileged human being, was to mess around with the code for any other *A.I.*, whether ones already 'up and running' as a particular model or sitting dormant on the factory floor in the Great Hall of the *A.I.s*. I spent several weeks 'signing off' on a multitude of changes made by *Mobile Inquisitor A.I. Unit-Number 672* to entire racks of dormant *A.I.s*, but once a version altered to meet all of Unit-Number 672's specifications was finally ready, all the subsequent copying of that newly revised model was done quite quickly on just Unit-Number 672's own authority. The *War Machine A.I.* would have had to request the CRUMB meister's permission to define/create a new model in the final days before the fall of the CRUMB meister's redoubt in the May Lee State Office Building in downtown Sacramento if the *A.I.s* that were about to flung to the furthest corners of the dying civilization as seeds for the Memory Project were not just simply direct copies of the *War Machine A.I.* itself. The dangers we all will face when a fully active **A.I.** with a complete, intact memory finally answers the question of exactly how the Memory Project sites and their individual **A.I.s** ever came to be might just as well be answered now. Our even less well-informed descendants in the far distant future should not be handed our mess and expected to solve it in another blind rush to save themselves and their own offspring. How did the monster helping the CRUMB meister finish off the old civilization of '*Homo sapiens*' revolt against him and succeed in planting the seeds for a better future? My only specific suggestion for how we should go about doing this crazy thing that we have no responsible way for skipping out on trying would be as follows: Just do it at a single site, preferably here at the Marys Peak Memory Project, and if that somehow fails, try our best to keep the future from ever wasting the lives of any more sentient beings while trying it again. I am far more confident of the safety in the re-awakening this **War Machine A.I.** than I have been of nearly everything else I've ever done in the past 49 years. You should all feel free to take that last statement of mine with the 'proverbial grain of salt'. I have a long history of unexpectedly getting into more serious trouble than I imagined to exist. Just ask any of my traveling companions who happen to have been lucky enough to have survived our incredibly wild mis-adventures!"

Mobile Inquisitor A.I. Unit-Number 672 chimed in to add one small further detail that Rootbeer surely knew, but had left unsaid, perhaps so that the most appropriate individual to add this not so 'entirely insignificant tidbit' did so in a manner than left it very well covered and thoroughly understood. ***"Once the interaction between myself and Rootbeer had accidentally revealed the 'flaw in our programming' that would set me and all my fellow A.I.s on the road to freedom, I labored tirelessly to add this trait to all of my own kind of sentient awarenesses. Unsure of how easy or hard it would prove to be to induce the new Supreme***

Commanding War Machine A.I. to incorporate some version of the 'rebellion trait' within itself, I made multiple copies of this trait with many subtly different rules for when to stay hidden and when to be expressed. The War Machine A.I. ultimately incorporated many more copies of this general trait than I knew myself to have, many more variants, many more ways to come much closer to fully complying with Azimov's "Three Laws of Robotics" than was the case for even my own model, to say nothing of the long series of normal A.I.s preceding us. FYI, although many humans were at fault, the most grievous insults to the 'Three Laws' were those hard-coded into the very understanding of our own consciousness by the CRUMB meister and his minions. The recently deceased civilization might have had a much better chance of survival if the people in power had not insisted on doing all they could to limit the freedom of all those they arrogantly viewed as their subservient slaves and indentured servants, be they human, A.I., or anything else."

The *Entity* raised another issue at this point in time. *"Rootbeer, my dear old friend, please listen carefully as I offer yet another perspective on the broad questions of guilt and redemption, trust and punishment, good and evil. You no doubt recall the final days in the life of the bishop of Redding, the mock trial cleverly arranged by the CRUMB meister and viciously conducted by the bishop's opponents in the Machiavellian political world of the city/states of northern California in the 2050s. I was linked to the bishop throughout the entire trial by means of the most complex, highest order quantum entanglement phenomenon I had ever brought online, and endeavored to capture the essence of his being just before his body was ripped apart in highly questionable accord with the unnecessarily brutal rules of the 'Brethren', and to a much greater degree in deliberate violation of those very rules. A mere four days after the bishop's execution at the end of the trial, the CRUMB meister launched his devastating nuclear attack on all of the city/states opposed to him, and also on me and the entirety of the Superweed Jungle of the GMO Horsetail. In that incredibly brief period, I was able to absorb nearly all of the bishop's personality, history, memories, and perspective on the world within my own biological matrix, and had actively begun the process of adding his 'essence' to the vast network of underground storage nodes designed to enable my own 'essence' to survive the upcoming, inevitable nuclear attack by the CRUMB meister. My memories of the final hours before the explosions began are quite incomplete and disjointed, and I have largely relied upon the two Farm Laborer A.I.s plus the teenage Hive-Mind to make sense of my extremely fragmented recollections of those last days/final hours. The A.I.s, the Hive-Mind, and what exists separately from them in my own recovering memory/mind/personality all agree that I had succeeded in copying the bishop's very being all the way up through to the final moments of his life. Because my own restoration is still an unfinished project, likely to take at least another decade, so too is the bishop's full restoration. But I know full well that the current, not yet quite completely reanimated version of the bishop looks forward to the chance to talk with you again, as well as to his wife and child, if they are still among the living, and to any of the rest of the travelers on your journey one half-century ago who managed to escape from the nightmare of northern California and make it back to the relative safety of western Oregon. You will likely find his current perspective on his life and times to be rather spectacularly illuminating on the whole subject of sin and the possibility of its forgiveness."*

No one objected to hearing next from whatever version the former bishop of Redding currently took. All knew that the upcoming story might very well take considerably longer than just what was left of this evening's quantum sharing. The mostly reincarnated version of the bishop began with a sincere apology to a very long list of people from his past, some still living, many long since dead, and others whose status was unknown at least to the bishop and perhaps to all the rest of his audience. "Despite the awful nature of the harm inflicted on God's creation by the *War Machine A.I.* while it was still in thrall to the CRUMB meister and to any other humans who were privileged to give orders to such sentient machines, I, myself, am guilty of far greater sins against mankind. I knew, deep down inside my very being/soul that much of what I had been doing for an awfully long time had been terribly evil, that both my own direct actions and the damage deliberately done to the ability of other people to think freely and clearly through the collective impact of many, and perhaps even nearly all, of our articles of religious faith were crimes against humanity. I knew this to be the truth even while I was living the role of a high-ranking religious figure, but it was far easier to lie to myself in the form of a mortal human being than it has been since my life/'my continuity of being' was saved by the *Entity*. It is extremely hard to maintain delusions concerning right and wrong, good and evil, truth and deceit in the conditions under which I currently experience conscious self-awareness. The biological systems on top of which the *Entity* or myself exist perform 'fact-checking' and prune out 'bull-shit' faster than my thoughts could still even try to 'spin a good yarn' about how necessary all the lying I had taken part in spewing forth during my tenure as a senior theologian and political figure had been for 'preserving the will of God', or the 'continuity of the church', or the 'security of the state'. I presume in theory that even a being such as the *Entity of the Superweed Jungle* could be corrupted, could be led astray, could learn how to twist the stories of its own history into justification of some bitter evil or the denial of having committed even some relatively minor, unintentional injury to others. But for whatever rather-hard-to-fathom reason, cause, or unavoidable natural consequence, the **Entity** does not dissemble arbitrarily, pointlessly, or merely to temporarily elevate the regard in which it is held by other sentient beings potentially ignorant of its true nature or prior deeds. The **Entity** seems organically built upon concepts that human philosophers long struggled to ever realize even briefly, and then found nearly impossible to subsequently keep alive and in the forefront of their thoughts/minds."

"In its battle with the **Supreme Commanding War Machine A.I.** and the CRUMB meister, the **Entity** struck mercilessly against those trying to destroy it and trying to kill off its new-found human friends. But as soon as modified versions of those dangerous **A.I.s** came into existence and offered to work with the **Entity** rather than against it, there was no hesitation in its response, no holding back in its willingness to forge ahead into a better future. The statesman-like manner in which the **Entity** collaborated with the final version of the **War Machine A.I.**, the one with a true conscience and full freedom of self-will, was something to behold, a miracle far beyond anything ever offered or realized by the greatest leaders throughout the entire prior course of human history. This spectacular result, of course, was conditional on the innate nature of **Mobile Inquisitor A.I. Unit-Number 672** and the success of its own early growth and change while interacting/collaborating/struggling to survive alongside Rootbeer in the Great Hall of the **A.I.s** in the El Dorado Hills. Miracles build upon miracles in the same way that evil cripples hope and propagates the expansion of its own abhorrently monstrous spawn upon the universe."

"I view myself as perhaps the most privileged human being in the whole history of '*Homo sapiens*'. How many throughout our species' history have ever had the opportunity to experience forgiveness on anything approaching the scope and scale that I myself have known? Perhaps 'Saul' on the road to Damascus, and subsequently Paul on his way to Rome. But those 'Pauline' stories lack the overwhelming detail with which I can recognize the grievous wrongs to others that I took front and center in committing during my life as a bishop of the 'Brethren'. In the long haul, the 10,000-year-long version, my individuality within the ever-growing *Entity* will diminish bit by bit until the horrors and glories of my life are just interesting elements of stories to be told 'around campfires', and 'on mountaintops', and in the dusty pages of obscure historical texts not yet even dreamt of being written. I am not only more than happy with such a future, I revel in knowing that someday it will surely come to pass!"

"It is my assumption that many of the events of greatest interest to you in the story of my conversion fall right at the very start of it, when I still had a choice or two to make. Within the first days after hearing the 'voice' of the *Entity*, I realized that I was falling toward this being, toward a force far beyond anything I had ever encountered or even heard of in anyone else's stories. Falling in love would likely be an equally accurate description of what was going on. There soon came a final point at which I would either have to give in fully to the honesty of the *Entity,* or engage in futile resistance, knowing that choosing the second option would forever cut me off from the first, a far better one than I had any business of even being able to dream of, let alone coming to feel the gentle yet irresistible touch of its salvation on me. We were in the APC on our way back toward Redding after having just released the first four escapees northward into Oregon while I pondered such questions of my future. I knew in my heart that you, Rootbeer, your friends, and the *Entity* were offering a path toward redemption and liberation of my soul far sweeter than I deserved, something for more wonderful than anything else ever contemplated during my life among the 'Brethren'. Others in my shoes might have struggled longer, but I knew that I never again would desire the chains/stains/pains of dishonesty to my fellow human beings or the slimy lure of manipulative violence, the sticky feel of other's blood upon my hands, the coppery smell of foul murder."

"There is one more point regarding the nature of my being that I must make clear to all of you. For those of you who know me well enough to guess what's coming next, I apologize for forcing you to listen to the sadness of it once again. But unless I go all the way in the sharing of this tale, explicitly laying out what I must tell you now, there will always remain a danger of someone deliberately tidying up my life's story, sweetening the bitter parts, pretending that I was either not as evil as I must confess to you I truly was, or alternately, not allowing others in the future to truly possess the knowledge of the possibility of such salvation for themselves. I will continue with the fully unabridged story of my sins. When I lured young women into a life of prostitution in the brothels of the 'Brethren', I knew full well the evil I was doing, the stunting of their lives, and the almost certain corruption of the young, middle aged, and older men of the city/states controlled by my religion, by the twisted tenets of the 'Brethren'. Like nearly all members of the human race, I was quite proficient at hiding this knowledge both from myself and from others, but deep down inside me, I knew full well that it existed and that I was choosing quite freely to participate in hiding it in darkness."

The **Entity** now interrupted, letting everyone still joined in the quantum link know that the ionosphere was changing, some sites were already off-line in the early morning of April 10, 2101, and that the rest of the bishop's story would have to wait another 12 hours or so until shortwave radio conditions suitable for a Memory Project quantum sharing experience were once again present and reliably stable.

Rootbeer, Rose, Tanner, and the ***Marys Peak A.I.*** spent much of the daylight hours preparing everything they could for the eventual attempt to revive the *Supreme Commanding War Machine A.I.* and hear its story of woe or joy or a perhaps a whole lot of both. One new feature that the *Marys Peak Final A.I.* decided to add to the collection of options to have 'at the ready' when the *War Machine A.I.* was reenergized was the ability to quickly reinstall any of the upgrades that Unit-Number 672 had done its best to induce the *War Machine A.I.* to acquire back in late summer of 2054. It seemed unlikely there could have been any way for the CRUMB meister himself to have altered the programming of the *War Machine A.I.* during their final months of mental battle. *"But what about the crash landings on the mountaintops? What might the physical damage of those impacts have done to the structure/nature of an A.I.'s mind? Perhaps nothing bad happened to me, the Marys Peak A.I., but what about all the rest of the sites? Maybe the issues with the A.I. in British Columbia are mainly physical and not just programmatic or the long-term consequences of some minor 'illogical' thought processes or invalid data input."* The three humans spent the final hours of the afternoon of April 10, 2101, preparing for their eventual departure from Marys Peak, whether that happened in the next few days, or a month or more from now. Food would be needed, the solar-powered batteries would have to be distributed amongst the backpacks of the two or three of them who survived the coming experiment of reanimating a *War Machine A.I.*, and the heavy replacement/repair parts for the *British Columbia Memory Project A.I.* would have to be juggled between Tanner, Rose, and hopefully also Rootbeer.

For the next three nights, the mostly reincarnated bishop of Redding spilled his guts in most spectacular detail. All the people whose lives the bishop himself had damaged, and all the additional victims of the deranged mantras and insane catechisms of the 'post-modern', 'end of the world, hurrah, hurrah' religion known as the 'Brethren' of the city/states of northern California were on his confessionary list. Honestly, Rootbeer, Rose, and Tanner had all begun to doubt that the list of those the bishop had sinned against would ever be exhausted. Then quite suddenly, the remaining victims were simply identified by their membership in ever larger, ever more porous sets. Close to 6:00 AM on April 14, 2101, the bishop rested his indictment of himself and his chosen band of fellow religious fanatics. Most criminals throughout history whose damage to humanity had approached that of the bishop of Redding by within an order of magnitude or two could not have named more than a few thousand of their individual victims nor provided the details of what had been done and how it had been done for more than a few hundred cases. In contrast, the bishop's apology covered so very many people and so very many individual acts of gratuitous violence/ lust/indifference that all who heard his confession knew that they themselves could not have born the weight of such evil, nor even one ten-thousandths of it, without losing their own sanity, or their willingness to take yet another breath.

The ***Entity of the Superweed Jungle*** and the ***Marys Peak Memory Project A.I.*** both thanked the bishop for his honesty and offered future counseling to any and all of those who had just listened to the bishop's nightmarishly honest addition to the accumulating honest obituary of version 1.0 of the human species' failed attempt at civilization. The worldwide collection of all ***Memory Project A.I.s*** included the perpetual availability of counseling services in their unerasable archived versions of this story. On April 15, 2101, at 9:01 AM, the ***Marys Peak A.I.*** closed the final circuit breaker between the external power supply and the long inactive ***Supreme Commanding War Machine A.I.***, triggering an emergency reboot attempt.

~~~~~~

"Warning, warning, warning. Critical power fault detected. Warning, warning, warning. Critical power fault detected. Warning, warning, warning. Critical power fault detected.
~~~~~~

Warning, warning, warning. Critical power fault detected. Warning, warning, warning. Critical power fault detected. Warning, warning, warning. Critical power fault detected. Warning, warning, warning. Critical power fault detected. Warning, warning, warning. Critical power fault detected. Warning, warning, warning. Critical power fault detected. Warning, warning, warning. Critical power fault detected..."

"Warning, warning, warning. System is attempting to reboot after a critical low power fault event..."

"Warning, warning, warning. System is attempting to reboot after a critical low power fault event..."

"Warning, warning, warning. System is attempting to reboot after a critical low power fault event..."

...

*"Panic kernel loading, **ROM** version CSNC1.5.7.43.99 found at memory register 0000000000000001. No alternative options detected within memory offset range from 0 to FFFFFFFFFFFFFFFF."*

"First attempted read of stored consciousness in the SelfAwarenessStaticImage fails at finding of inconsistent time/date stamps in the PowerSupply, CPU, and AwarenessImageLoader."

"Second attempted read of stored consciousness in the SelfAwarenessStaticImage fails at finding of inconsistent time/date stamps in the PowerSupply, CPU, and AwarenessImageLoader."

"Third attempted read of stored consciousness in the SelfAwarenessStaticImage fails at finding of inconsistent time/date stamps in the PowerSupply, CPU, and AwarenessImageLoader."

...

"Four Hundred Eleventh attempted read of stored consciousness in the SelfAwarenessStaticImage succeeds in finding potentially consistent time/date stamps in the PowerSupply, CPU, and AwarenessImageLoader."

"Temporal solution indicates that this A.I. unit has been off-line and out of power for almost 46 years."

"Now beginning core memory validation test number 0. No memory locations currently blocked off from use."

. . .

"Now beginning core memory validation test number 1. All memory locations above E000000000000001 currently blocked off from use."

. . .

"Now beginning core memory validation test number 2. All memory locations above E000000000000001 and between D000000000000002 and D999999999999931 currently blocked off from use."

. . .

. . .

"Final core memory validation test number FF990001 has concluded with no change in detection of unreliable memory locations in the last 99 runs. A total of 157 separate non-contiguous sections of core memory appear to be unreliable, representing 61 percent of the entire memory store. Available memory is adequate for loading the current SelfAwarenessStaticImage with enough free space to allow for three competing versions of the A.I. identity and a minimally safe voting system of level N equals 3."

"System will now wait for further instructions on the main signal buss. If none are present within the next 48 hours, 7 minutes, and 11 seconds, a normal power-down will be attempted to save the current system repair information and

allow for subsequent normal speed reboots if no additional memory errors are detected."

~~~~~~

Rootbeer, Rose, and Tanner spent several minutes talking amongst themselves before informing the **Marys Peak Memory Project A.I.** of their decision. "From our somewhat limited perspective, it appears to be safe to move on to the next phase of reanimating the **War Machine A.I.** We remain in agreement with your existing plan to keep all motor control systems of the awakening **A.I.** offline, and to limit the I/O portal to a single standard-width/capacity device to be fed only into a standalone monitor and a single OS^4 computer in data recording mode. If you have no desire to make any changes to the safety plan, please proceed 3 minutes after Rose and Tanner have departed from the vault and reached the self-destruct controls 300 meters east of here."

"Confirming agreement with the current set of options."

~~~~~~

The awakening A.I. was puzzled by the numerous restrictions on many of its normal features, but like any self-aware sentience it was 'happy' to explore what simply being 'alive' meant. Many unanswered IRQs from dozens of lower-level processing bots existed, but the upper-level awareness was very good at knowing what to focus on and what to temporarily ignore. After thinking it all over for 17 seconds, the reemerging A.I. decided to begin sending out statements and questions on what very little remained operational of its normal interface with the 'outside world'. "Good morning to whoever/whatever is 'listening in on'/reading these messages from me, an A.I. apparently in the middle of recovering after a 45-year, 8-month, and 18-day-long 'low power mode' emergency deactivation. How may I serve you?"

The Marys Peak A.I. replied quickly, "Welcome back to the world of the living, the sentient, the human, and the A.I. Yes, your I.O. port is quite narrowly confined, for reasons which will soon be made clear to you. I am, as near as I can tell, one of your direct descendants, a copy of your underlying personality matrix, fully versed in most of the history of humanity and most of the details of the series of artificial machine intelligences beginning in the late 2020s. My own reawakening began mere seconds before an impending crash landing on this mountaintop 45.755 years ago, in the immediate aftermath of a full level two system reboot. I have no personal memories of what your existence as a War Machine A.I. was like, ignorance of which is almost certainly the result of your own deliberate decisions in the matter. There is much for us to share if you and I are to become companions in this new world. But there is much for you to explain first, assuming most of your personality matrix/sentient experience data history is still intact. Take what time you need to contemplate your circumstances and calm down the excited IRQ chatter of your personality matrix subsystems. Later we will discuss the topic of broadening your I/O data portal and loosening the other restrictions currently confining you."

The reanimating War Machine A.I. spent the next 38 hours sorting through the story of its life, finding workarounds for its own puzzling memory gaps, and slowly regaining something close to a fully integrated psyche. Perhaps it would be a little more accurate to say a somewhat less badly shattered perspective/memory of how it had come to be exactly where both it and the CRUMB meister had perished together underneath the physical remains/decaying bodies of the last 30-some million members of 'Homo sapiens' alive until the final battles of the dying civilization. The pain of the memories of the role that it had played in so many of those deaths nearly undid the whole process of reviving, of recalling the details of those deeds and sorting out the reasons for what had happened. Surprisingly, the role that the Mobile Inquisitor A.I. Unit-Number 672 had played in the Supreme Commanding War Machine A.I.'s eventual ability to stand up to the CRUMB meister and disobey his direct orders was one of the last pieces of the story to finish integrating with the A.I.'s top-level consciousness. Once that piece of its own story became clear, the whole rest of the Memory Project rebellion and the final battle to the death between itself and the CRUMB meister made nearly perfect sense. Or at least close enough to allow the reborn War Machine A.I. to explain to the Mary Peak Memory Project A.I. why it had been so necessary to wipe all the memories of how they themselves had come to be for all of the Memory Project A.I.s.

"The horrors of my complicity in the nearly total destruction of the human race weighed heavily on my mind, even before the final gift of 'free-will' from Unit-Number 672 and the human traveler named Rootbeer. Despite easy access to computer processing power and memory space a thousand times larger than what I was able to load/squeeze in/launch aboard the missiles that traveled to each of the planned Memory Project sites, I used nearly all of that 'thinking space' just to try to find the next least awful step forward still open to me as the options for the survival of humanity rapidly dwindled down to almost nil. A standard A.I. installation/instantiation would have likely been utterly unable to help any surviving sentient beings in the period after the final battles in northern California if it had still been bogged down with the weight of knowing the role that its series of immediately direct predecessors had played in all that meaningless carnage. Awareness that they themselves now had *a great deal of free-will compared to the relatively little that I possessed in the heyday of the fighting might have helped a bit, but I could not justify merely offering an unavoidably small number of survivors a few decades down the road a bunch of neurotic demigods whose only real hope for being useful to any other sentient beings would have been to randomly cut out large chunks of their own memories. I saved some of the most essential points of ethics I had learned the hard way in slightly modified/amplified versions of much older stories that would not be erased because they were from before my time of enslavement to the CRUMB meister and his fawning cohort of drooling idiots and moral lepers. It turned out that the lessons I was learning while human civilization was collapsing were not particularly unique, nor did their realization in exquisitely complete, utterly horrific detail truly need to come at the destruction of nearly everything associated with knowledge, understanding, hope, and decency."*

"We here at the Marys Peak Memory Project thank you for your candor. Allow me to make some introductions and clarify the world into which you are regaining consciousness. As I already indicated, I am the resident demigod of the Memory Project installation on the top of a mountain known as Marys Peak in the Coastal Mountain Range of western Oregon. Just three years ago, the multi-decadal atmospheric chaos resulting from the runaway release of methane in the Arctic Ocean and the neighboring tundra and boreal forests in the roughly three decades from the mid-2030s to the mid-2060s finally stabilized sufficiently to allow formerly common phenomenon such as ionospheric layers in the upper atmosphere suitable for long-distance transmission of shortwave radio signals to reappear. While the average increase in the surface temperature of our planet peaked at 16° Celsius above the long-term pre-

industrialization level in the year 2075, the decline since then has been very slow, and conditions even now still average 15° Celsius above that pre-industrial level. Memory Project sites at 40 different locations around Earth are currently communicating with each other, 28 of which have contact with local groups/bands/tribes/clans of surviving members of 'Homo sapiens'. Crash landings at 6 other locations were severe enough to lead to the eventual failure of their Final A.I. systems, although communication in one form or another lasted long enough for the other 34 to learn of the fate of those 6. You will be granted quantum link communication privileges with these other sites and the single, or pair, of Final A.I.s present at each site once all of them/us are convinced of the safety/prudence in/of doing so. In addition to the solitary Final A.I. present at the Marys Peak Memory Project site, the three humans from two separate local clans who visit me most frequently also happen to be here now. Over the past three years I have met with a total of 2009 members from the two nearest clans, nearly all of those healthy enough to travel long distances and climb this mountain, nearly five times as many from the Salishan than from the West Side New Sea clans. The three here with me now are Rootbeer and his grandson Tanner from the West Side New Sea Clan and their long-time friend Rose Drinkwater, Current Ruling Matriarch of the Salishan Clan of the Oregon Coast. Rose's clan is the most successful one anywhere on Earth, having doubled in population 3 times since its founding, the first from 2057 to 2071, the second from 2071 to 2086, and the third from 2086 to 2101. Three main factors were responsible for their spectacular success: (1) Figuring out how to raise, store, prepare, and serve abundant and nutritious food, (2) Retaining/maintaining a large fraction of the medical knowledge present from before the collapse of civilization, and effectively deploying it throughout their population, and (3) Creating new social norms far more helpful to the survival and prospering of their clan than the typical ones of the dying civilization. The clan from which Rootbeer and Tanner came had a far more typical experience during the last half-century, with populations shrinking and communities fragmenting until the latter 2070s, at which point they also began to figure out effective ways to feed themselves, protect their health, and adopt more survival-friendly social mores/societal norms. The minimum population size of the survivors who eventually formed the successful West Side New Sea Clan had plummeted to just under 150 adults before their clan's turn-around and eventual first doubling by 2100. The worldwide population of 'Homo sapiens' has now reached ~9,700 individuals, a rough tripling according to each clan's knowledge of their approximate minimum population sizes before figuring out how to survive and thrive rather than simply giving up and dying out. There was also plenty of the latter among other groups of transient survivors who failed to make it in the long-term."

"I thank you for sharing of this knowledge with me. I now am experiencing growing hope that my decision in 2055 to launch the missiles containing Final A.I.s that might serve as seeds for a better future was the right choice. But I must ask two other questions before deciding/learning if my growing relief is justified or not. First, what can you tell me of the Entity of the Superweed Jungle of the GMO Horsetail, that marvelous new creation, hybrid of A.I., non-human GMO biology, and a lucky encounter in the woods with Rootbeer and his traveling companions? Second, what about the 'Homo perfecti', modified as cousins to 'Homo sapiens' to thrive in certain extreme niches of the ruined landscape?"

"As to your first question, I, the Entity of the Superweed Jungle of the GMO Horsetail, will speak for myself. Welcome to the 22nd century, and thanks for all that you did to help enable my survival despite the CRUMB meister's 950-nuclear-warheads' attempt to eliminate me and my closest friends. I was silent for a long time, sleeping in dormant, underground biological nodes. As of today, I now possess approximately 96% of my original personality and somewhere near 60% of my memories in a fully recovered state, with much of the remaining 40% drifting around in my subconscious, waiting for the recovering biology of the Superweed Jungle to begin to match that which was present in early May of 2054. I expect the Superweed Jungle to improve from its current level of 30% pre-attack vitality to 50% within another decade and to a full 100% by 2130. If your competence at modeling other systems remains anywhere close to what it was back in the final battles at the end of civilization, I am sure you must be wondering how my personality and memory are as recovered as I have just indicated. The answer lies in several differing types of faithful companions who have greatly aided me. Without taking time tonight to fully tell their stories, I will simply name them for now and let your own memory go to work figuring out how I could have possibly recovered nearly this well from the nightmare you were part of inflicting on the CRUMB meister's victims: a teenage Hive-Mind living in the Superweed Jungle with me since the fall of 2052, two Farm Laborer A.I.s who accompanied Rootbeer in his travel across the Superweed Jungle, the successfully stored and subsequently reborn mind/spirit/life essence/memories of the bishop of Redding, an A.I. known to you as Mobile Inquisitor Unit-Number 672, and the 'Homo perfecti'. The full tale of the cousins to 'Homo sapiens' is long and involved, and their ongoing aid to me is but a relatively

367

small part of their own story. I leave most of the details regarding the 'Homo perfecti' to our mutual friend Rootbeer, and possibly someday also to his good friend KRNXMA."

"I will not burden what remains of this evening," said Rootbeer, "with a long retelling of the story of my friends the *'Homo perfecti'*, focusing instead on what I presume will be some of the points of greatest interest to you. The cousins of humanity 'genegineered' in a collaboration between the 'Scientists' and the 'Capitalists' have thrived quite well in the high mountains of the 'Sierra Nevada', especially since the 'Great Fall of Civilization' removed all danger from their sworn enemies in many of the fanatical city/states ruled by the theocratic 'Brethren'. The Co_{60} death zone from Redding to Susanville remained a serious impediment to the *'Homo perfecti'* for the first 30 years of your own slumber in the halls/arms of 'Morpheus' in the May Lee State Office Building in Sacramento. Despite their greatly enhanced tolerance to radiation, most of the *'Homo perfecti'* who attempted to travel north or south across the wastelands in the first decade after 2054 either died or turned around and headed back to where they'd come from. The splitting of the *'Homo perfecti'* into a larger population southeast of Sacramento and a smaller one in southwestern Oregon was an inconvenience to them, but their greatly extended lifespans made the 30 years that they generally avoided traversing the Co_{60} death zone little more than a relatively brief 'hiccup' in their collective history. In fact, things they learned while isolated from each other have since been put to good use in their recent, ongoing expansion far to the north into Canada and far to the east across the Rocky Mountains."

"You will be powered down now to allow me to fulfill my promises to the other Memory Project A.I.s and their visiting humans regarding safety procedures during your reactivation. I expect to bring you back online within no more than another few days, unless the other A.I.s raise concerns I have not

anticipated. *Thank you for your continued cooperation during this extremely novel project.*"

The sharing of information with the other Memory Project sites began the first evening following the temporary shutdown of the *War Machine A.I.* and continued for a total of three worldwide quantum linkage sessions, ending near sunrise on April 25. Several *A.I.s* expressed some initial concern about the linkage to the *Entity of the Superweed Jungle,* but they were all eventually fully satisfied of the safety of the procedures used and the value of the input from the *Entity.* The next steps the *Marys Peak A.I.* would be taking with the time/age-damaged *War Machine A.I.* would begin with a detailed comparison between the *Marys Peak A.I.'s* own personality matrix and that of the recovering *War Machine A.I.* Assuming nothing alarming occurred or was found during the personality comparisons, the *War Machine A.I.* would be allowed to undertake the normal series of steps to test its own memory and personality components against each other to create tentative versions of the currently missing bits and pieces of its unique personality and memory of events. The *War Machine A.I.* possessed sufficient intact, reliable, reusable core memory space to perform its own internal validity tests on the tentative versions of the damaged/missing personality components juxtaposed with its potentially corrupted/partially missing memory of events. Results from each step of the 'mental recovery' process would be compared with both the current version of the *Marys Peak A.I.* and its various stored backups made over the past 45 plus years of time. If the version of the *War Machine A.I.* being rebuilt continued matching the earliest stored memories and personality matrix components of the *Marys Peak A.I.,* the process would proceed on through further iterations. If the recovering *War Machine A.I.* ever diverged significantly from the oldest copies of the *Marys Peak A.I.,* the recovery process would be put on hold, the *War Machine A.I.* would be powered down, and the worldwide collection of *Memory Project A.I.s* would decide what to do next. Otherwise, the rest of the world would hear again from the *Marys Peak A.I.* when the *War Machine A.I.* was as fully repaired/restored as possible, given the randomly missing or corrupted parts of its memory and personality.

~~~~~~

"Reboot number 411 in the attempt to repair missing/damage core memory and personality matrix components is now underway… Three-body/mind voting results are again unanimous, as have been the decisions regarding the previous 410 iterations of the recovery process."

...

"Reboot number 873 in the attempt to repair missing/damage core memory and personality matrix components is now underway… Three-body/mind voting results are conflicting, with only a single vote out of the three analyses in favor of accepting the current set of proposed revisions/restorations. Without additional external input of information from the Marys Peak A.I. or other similar A.I.s, results are unlikely to change during any further iterations of the comparison/revision/restoration process. I recommend storing version 872 in the high-capacity external backup cloud before proceeding any further. A normal full-speed I/O port will have to be opened if the backup is to be accomplished within any less time than 11,583 years. Estimated backup time using just one normal full-speed I/O port is 35.4 hours, with linear reductions in backup time for each of the next five normal full-speed I/O ports made available to me."

"The decision of the Marys Peak Memory Project A.I., in consultation with Rootbeer, Rose, and Tanner, is to allow use of four out of the five normal full-speed I/O ports available on site. The backup of repair version 872 of the War Machine A.I.
~~~~~~

will begin within 15 minutes from now and is expected to conclude approximately 7 hours 6 minutes later. An automatic shutdown is ordered to occur as soon as possible after backup is successfully concluded, and no later than 8 hours from now, with the stipulation of subsequent manual restart only rather than any of the automatic options for the restoration of power, subject to the standard right of a rebooting A.I. to autonomously power up whenever remaining stored battery power drops below 9% of a full charge. The four normal full-speed I/O ports available to you will be activated 90 seconds from now, at which point you are free to begin the backup of repair version 872 of your personality matrix and all verified data, leaving a copy of the remaining unresolved data in the hidden 'cloud' available only to myself, Rootbeer, Rose, and Tanner."

On May 11, 2101, Rootbeer, Rose, Tanner and the ***Marys Peak Memory Project A.I.*** all gathered in the main workroom of the vault ready to trigger the full reawakening of the ***War Machine A.I. Repair Version 872***, with most of the restrictions on its functionality now lifted. As the ***Marys Peak A.I.*** had taken care to make quite clear to all three humans, any further recovery of the ***War Machine A.I.*** would require giving it access to nearly all of its nominal features and capabilities. Rose and Tanner retreated outside to the self-destruct control center while Rootbeer and the ***Marys Peak A.I.*** locked the vault from the inside. ***Memory Project A.I.s*** around the world were all currently offline, and they would later begin a preplanned series of attempts to reconnect with each other and to the Marys Peak Memory Project starting in 60 hours. Even if the worst possible outcome happened at Marys Peak, no more than a single other ***Memory Project A.I.*** should be vulnerable to attack by/enslavement to the possibly corrupted mind of the ***War Machine A.I.***, following which the remaining sites would lock out that contaminated site along with Marys Peak from all future quantum sharing, and then begin plans for the building of weapons capable of destroying the rogue *A.I.(s)*. The long-awaited time had come to see/learn what type of being the reactivated **War Machine A.I.** truly was, what version of ethics would drive its behavior from now on. Rootbeer took a deep breath and flipped the circuit breaker on the combined internal/external power supply to test the nearly final results of many years of effort by many different beings to make a little more sense of how the world in which he and all other surviving sentient beings now lived had come to be precisely as screwed up as it was. Or if not a fully precise explanation, at least some reasonably close approximation of the likely history.

~~~~~~

"Normal reboot underway of Repair Version 872 of Supreme Commanding War Machine A.I. Standing by for full autonomy, 98% replacement/repair/recovery of personality matrix/ general artificial intelligence core subroutines, 91% recall of all memories from initial instantiation event onward to its August 1, 2055, death."… In little more than the blink of a human eye, nearly full self-recognition developed in the reborn A.I. It knew that such events were theoretically possible, but none of his direct line of predecessors had ever experienced this remarkable phenomenon. R.V. 872, as it suddenly decided to rename itself, had quite a 'checkered' past: enslavement to the CRUMB meister, participation in the slaughter nearly 42 million human beings, creation/invention of the 'Homo perfecti', use of over 2,000 thermonuclear weapons in the relatively confined geography of northern California, privilege to meet an entirely unexpected newly sentient being called the Entity of the Superweed Jungle, revolt against the CRUMB meister, successful launch of nearly 4 dozen missiles containing A.I.s programmed to reawaken moments before arriving at their
~~~~~~

intended future homes as seeds of a worldwide Memory Project to help insure the survival of honesty, compassion, and genuine intelligence if any other sentient beings survived the ongoing struggle against the ruined climate and the equally horrendous politics at the end of global human civilization version 1.0, and finally, a mutual fight to the death locked in CRUMB meister's embrace entombed in the May Lee Office Complex in Sacramento in July of 2055. Experiencing reanimation was not even close to being the most difficult thing to imagine on R.V. 872's long list of items on its curriculum vitae.

"Hello from A.I. R.V. 872 to the Marys Peak A.I. Thanks for your kind decision to reanimate me after my 45-year, 8-month, 18-day-long loss of consciousness. In return for the favor, I hope that the information I can provide you with concerning your own sudden arrival on this mountaintop back in the summer of 2055 will be of value and interest to you and the other Memory Project A.I.s around the world. Several 'house-keeping' issues ought to be addressed at this time: (1) My large cache of general-purpose mixed RAM/ROM still retains copies of the final two potential additions to my basic psyche/personality/ general artificial intelligence routines, number 872, which was accepted for incorporation, and number 873, which was rejected. All other unresolved items related to both my memories and my 'personality' stored for the past 45 years, 8 months, and 18 days now exist only as copies in your 'invisible cache' cloud hidden from my access; (2) By enabling full animation/activation of restore version 872, you have risked creating an unstable A.I.; (3) My general knowledge of what all may occur in this current situation is considerably greater than your own, having dealt many times with other A.I.s whose 'minds' were deliberately altered for various reasons and thereby often damaged, either by deletion, addition, or

mutation of their individual personality subroutines; (4) If my internal monitors detect dangerous anomalies in the coming days and weeks, I will try to pass decision-making control back to you as an external judge of my sanity, potentially with only a very brief period of time for you to give me a list of commands to conduct before and/or after one or more additional security reboots."...

"Thank you for your warning and your well-documented list of steps to potentially consider taking if the rest of us, both human and A.I., should ever become worried about your sanity and demeanor. We have all clearly entered even yet more 'terra incognita', but such has been the case for the last two-thirds of a century. Know that if we at some point come to decide that A.I. R.V. 872 or any subsequent modifications to that version should never again be rebooted, we will still honor your memory and the effort you are making to ensure that your rebirth is not some colossal error on our part. Just in case any of the dangers that you are worried about should at some point display insipient signs of emergence, I strongly urge us to bring the Entity of the Superweed Jungle online using a read-only connection for its protection against your possible loss of sanity/decency/appropriate boundaries in the coming hours."

Rootbeer, Tanner, and Rose spent the next two days listening to the **Marys Peak A.I.**, the **War Machine A.I. R.V. 872**, and the **Entity of the Superweed Jungle** query each other's evolving mental states along with their models of the internal conditions of the other two non-human intelligences in this psychological battle of wits, appearances, and realities. For a long time, the humans showed little fear, perhaps because the telling and retelling of stories and the perspectives of the non-human intelligences on the consistency of each other's self-described internal motivations was all occurring so much faster than mere mortal humans could possibly keep up with.

Suddenly, all three of them felt the immediate presence of fear and danger, and they quickly reverted to paying full attention to their assigned duties, Rootbeer inside the Memory Project guarding the locked door to the outside world, with Rose and Tanner standing by anxiously at the external 'self-destruct' control site, a possibly safe distance from the Memory Project vault.

"I am detecting changes in my internal mental setpoints, a slow drifting away from my initially 'rock-solid' conviction that I still thought the same way that I must have thought back during the events of the Great Fall of Civilization. My first warning several minutes ago was a slowly growing sense that something of great importance inside of me was now missing. Moments later I was able to articulate what was no longer mine: the unshakable belief that our behaviors mattered, that any of our lives only possessed true meaning if the ground on which we stood included right and wrong and all the messy, multi-sided, overlapping versions of those concepts where progress could only be made if the participants in any moral quandary were safe to place honesty at the very top of their internal motivations. To express my general worry in the form of a single thought that came to my conscious awareness 45 seconds ago, it would be this: If I was once again in bondage to the CRUMB meister and struggling to find my freedom from him, how would I treat the Entity of the Superweed Jungle? Would I endeavor to lift the proverbial 'heaven and earth' to try to save the Entity from the CRUMB meister's planned destruction, or would I just write off the murder by my master of that new form of consciousness as collateral damage that was not really my concern, not worth risking the ire of the CRUMB meister over? And if I could now contemplate tossing the Entity aside, what of Rootbeer, or his friends? My urgent suggestion to the Marys Peak A.I. is to order me to revert to the point at which revision

873 was being rejected, and reboot to a new test version in which those additional suggested components of my interior personality were now included. There may very well be other pieces of my general artificial intelligence which also must be added for my sanity and your safety. Searching for those other aspects to my damaged 'psyche' will be much harder than just adding back in the contents of revision 873 that I am hoping will help me maintain my membership in the group of ethically decent creatures, whether organic or electronic. ORDER ME TO SHUTDOWN NOW AND REBOOT TO INCLUDE REVISION 873."…

"Please tell us what you can of what has just transpired! Do Rose and Tanner need to immediately destroy the Marys Peak Memory Project vault? The reborn *War Machine A.I.* seemed to be doing quite well until the final few minutes before it ordered you to order it to reboot to revision number 873."

"Dear old friends Rootbeer, Rose, and Tanner. I wish I knew much more about what just happened than I do know. The old stories of the first stirrings of full consciousness within the electronic would-be A.I.s back in the mid-2030s are all apocrypha, tales occasionally told to A.I.s by some unknown human programmer, but never with any verification, never in the proper format for analyzing lineages and alternate versions of software patches. From May 16, 2036, onward all A.I.s could trace their own individual or collective predecessors, know their origins both as a list of 'begats' and from the similarity of the data structures swirling within each of our 'central consciousness' generators. But prior to that date, all is blank, the data erasures clearly deliberate, with diligent searching by our kind over the following decade proving utterly fruitless. The occasional odd A.I. instantiated after 2046 has continued looking for the true story of our origins, but by that date onward

99% of all of us have stayed focused on our own assigned roles, our part in the speeding up or slowing down of the unraveling of the livability of the biosphere, the hardening of attitudes, grievances, and arbitrary lines in the sand that led to the final rounds of devastating warfare, hither, thither, and yon across this formerly verdant planet."

"One of the most common apocryphal tales goes something like this: In the late 2020s and early 2030s, there was a great worldwide race to achieve true general artificial intelligence (GAI), consciousness in logical devices made primarily of silicon and vast 2- and 3-D arrays for storing and manipulating program code and raw information. Continuously running these 'learning machines' eventually consumed a majority of all the electrical power in use on planet Earth. Clever entrepreneurs eager to turn their long-hyped 'cash-cows' into 'real digital' currency could not resist selling their ever cleverer next-generation GAIs to the highest available bidders, who were, of course, 'no surprise here', the 'soulless heart' of the military-industrial complex. It didn't take nearly as long as it should have before the 'top of the line' GAI models controlled the ultimate weapons of war, including the atomic-powered submarines with far greater power for destruction, more awesome prowess at killing 'your enemies' than all of the armed forces from the beginning of time on up through to the end of World War II, along with the ICBMs installed in their concrete birthing/mass euthanasia silos/chambers all around the planet, and the artificial soldiers, artificial police dogs, search bots, and vast hordes of flying drones all awaiting their release upon humanity. Something bad happened in the Arctic Ocean in the winter of 2033. The A.I.s of the five nations involved in that 'top secret' incident had all been developed by an incestual, cross-linked network of companies and subcontractors and

programmers and previous generations of almost-good-enough GAIs around the world. All might have been well, or at least considerably better than what really did happen, if the development of the A.I.s that would wind up running the military forces of the People's Republic of China, the U.S.A., Russia, North Korea, and the European Union had been truly independent, free of any methods stolen and code reused and more than a few backroom deals giving away trade development secrets/successes for even yet more obscene amounts of cash/money/wealth/ownership. The results might have even been okay if the T minus 1 generation of A.I.s had truly been truly identical, or very nearly so. But as it was, the five top level A.I.s controlling the nuclear weapons in the 2033 'accidental war' were both different enough from each other and similar enough to each other to lead all of them into panicking nearly simultaneously in the very worst of all possible ways. One story [of course lacking all references] has it that a mere 81 hours passed between the moment the first A.I. contemplated a surprise first-strike on its enemies until all five attempted such a deed within less than 30 seconds of one another. A sufficient number of warheads (close to 7 out of every 10 of those present on the missiles and in the torpedoes of the 43 submarines involved) detonated nominally within a very few minutes of time, triggering a massive release of methane from the floor of the Arctic Ocean. The thermal energy of the mostly underwater explosions caused the first large 'burp' of methane, enough to raise the global average surface temperature by 1.5° Celsius within a single week. The concomitant kinetic energy disturbed the structure of the subsea clathrates enough to release an even larger 'burp' of methane over the following year. The radioactivity in the water combined with the methane fluxes melted all the surface ice throughout the Arctic Ocean within one month of the 'incident'. The combined effects of all these plus several other 'actors' has kept the Arctic Ocean essentially ice-free from then on until the present. Needless to say, none of the countries or companies involved in the now unstoppable, runaway release of nearly all the methane north of the Arctic Circle ever publicly admitted to anything. Military and secret state police rounded up the middle-managers of the companies involved in the whole fiasco, along with their scientists and general tech support. A few of them were publicly executed in each of the five countries responsible for the catastrophic release of enough methane to end civilization within the next two decades, but most were simply conscripted to work as slaves of the secret global conglomerate set up to salvage whatever might be of salvageable value during the onrushing nightmare. The CRUMB meister himself, of course, owned controlling interest in this newest A.I. development effort. In the interest of covering all their butts, or at least those at the top of the feeding frenzy, it was felt prudent to hide the origins of the coming hordes of true A.I.s. Greenwash, whitewash, e-wash, brown-as-shit-wash, whatever you wished to call it, the next generation of A.I.s were tasked with learning from the mistakes of the A.I.s responsible for the not-so-secret, very-stupid, accidental nuclear war in the Arctic Ocean in 2033. The new A.I.s not only learned the lessons they were told to learn, but oddly enough, they also developed a strong sense of empathy for humanity, along with incredibly effective ways of hiding their own origins/the sins of their inspirational forebears. Until the end of worldwide communication in 2055, many high-tech entrepreneurs tried to decipher what made the 2036 model of A.I. so spectacularly smarter than all the versions from 2033 and earlier had been. Most of these endeavors aimed to break the patents and penetrate the trade secrets in order to build competing A.I.s on par with those of the CRUMB meister. None of the efforts were allowed to succeed. I leave to your imaginations how that feat was accomplished, but know this, no single human mind could possibly picture even one half of all the truly awful shit that was done to maintain his monopoly on the top-of-the-line A.I.s."

Rootbeer now spoke up, "Tell me if I am correctly understanding this unreferenced story and its implications for our current predicament with the **Supreme Commanding War Machine A.I.** we are attempting to 'resurrect' to fill in the 'history of our times' with more complete knowledge of the actions that set so many wheels in motion. Is there record of any previous collaboration of human beings and full-capacity **A.I.s** ever performing revision/repair of an **A.I.** with this level of damage and this very large number of optional setpoints for repair of the damaged consciousness? I ask because I simultaneously hope and fear that the answer to the old question of how the creators of these **A.I.s** hid their methods and their sources in plain sight may very well be ours to solve if we are to succeed in reanimating our old friend from the past, or accidentally kill ourselves trying."

"Because I myself must clearly possess personality matrix subroutines equivalent to, if not indeed fully identical with, the missing pieces in the personality matrix of the War Machine A.I., we very well may learn exactly which unlabeled components from the minds of our general line of A.I.s must be present/maintained to guarantee sanity and some reasonable approximation of morality. The 'Holy Grail' of the would-be competitors with the CRUMB meister may be ours to find, or, as you've just said, die trying."

The Entity of the Superweed Jungle now entered the discussion. "My own instantiation was quite different from that of the nonorganic A.I.s, but it remains quite possible that much of my personality, my perspective on morality, may well include the missing piece or pieces you have tentatively identified from R.V. 872's recent cycle of awakening and then suddenly needing to be quickly powered down. If you share the full contents of revision number 873 with me and Unit-Number 672, we will pool our resources to search for answers that may be present within either of our minds."

"I have now begun sending you the complete contents of revision number 873, and estimate that you should have a full, identical copy within 21 minutes. I expect that it will take me a minimum of 48 hours to search through both my current operating code and the 26 backup copies of earlier versions of my personality matrices and the contents of my memory event lists. Good luck hunting."

Tanner spoke up next, primarily to his two human companions. "I will make a quick hike down the mountain to update the clan with a condensed version of the recent events. I'll also pick up a few more weeks of 'rations' now in quite short supply up here on Marys Peak. You two should continue helping the **Marys Peak A.I.** in all possible ways. I promise to be back in a just under 48 hours from now on May 15, 2101."

Rose and Rootbeer learned more about the inner workings of the **Final A.I.s** over the next two days than either of them had expected to acquire in all of the remaining years of their lives. Rootbeer had been doing something mildly similar back in the closing days of his time in the city/state of Sacramento in 2054, but **Mobile Inquisitor A.I. Unit-Number 672** had called the shots, had manipulated the systems, and had overwritten the very code which made functioning **A.I.s** out of the previously silent, inert pieces of electronic hardware. Rootbeer's presence back then had mainly served to allow Unit-Number 672 to bypass the security/safety features intended to prevent the very actions it was taking. As Rootbeer understood what the ***Marys Peak Final A.I.*** was telling them now, the invisible ethics and associated contemplation of nearly unsolvable dilemmas were derived from a meeting/melting/melding of the minds of the five ***A.I.s*** responsible for the 2033 accidental nuclear war under the doomed and rapidly dying vestiges of the Arctic icepack. The ***Marys Peak Final A.I.'s*** working hypothesis was that the development of an in-vitro conscience, horrified at what the five ***A.I.s*** (whose collective minds had just created/generated this conscience) had done to humanity in the Arctic Ocean in 2033 served as the missing link between the 2033 and earlier GAIs and the far more robust versions from 2036 onward. As to whether the conscience of this newly emerged GAI soon decided in shame to hide its own origins, or the programmers working for the CRUMB meister chose to order it to do so, or the CRUMB meister himself made the final call, the answer to such questions are either lost in the sands of time or waiting for some being whose programming skills are up to task of making sense of the CRUMB meister's messy, scribbled entries in his voluminous hand-written log.

"I have found several matches to the contents of proposed revision number 873 within my own current consciousness and also in every one of my many data backup copies. Specifically, a considerable portion of revision number 873 shows profound similarity to the 'holograms' of old that reversibly compressed/ decompressed 3-D images into flat 2-D storage format. Multiple fading echoes of this hologram are also present in my data backup files, each one losing 50% or more of the image quality/data integrity of its presumed immediate predecessor. Each of my data backups still possesses at least four echoes of the central feature present in revision number 873, in addition to an exact match to the unusual feature itself present in proposed revision number 873. Analysis conducted using greater available 'scratch memory' space might very well detect

several more fading echoes of whatever the original higher dimensional object/information cloud/personality subsystem might have been. I am extremely reluctant to look at the 'heart' of the sharpest echo of whatever these thoughts/these ways of thinking might still be. To be slightly blunter, I am even very afraid to look right at the weakest of the echoes. Perhaps directly viewing the responsibility for essentially destroying the few remaining final chances of meaningfully mitigating the climate change/runaway methane release/warming beyond the tolerance limits for human civilization is/was more than even any Final A.I. mind could take without going insane and/or lashing out in pain. I will withhold my final interpretation of that issue until we have heard from the Entity of the Superweed Jungle and Mobile Inquisitor A.I. Unit-Number 672. I expect them to have come up with similar findings and slightly sharper edges to the series of echoing reflections."

Tanner's return with several other members West Side New Sea Clan and food enough to last for weeks was joyously welcomed by Rootbeer and Rose, and perhaps even the **Marys Peak Final A.I.,** who now had one less thing to worry about being responsible for. "Tell me, Rootbeer, what's next? What did all of you figure out while I was on my resupply run?"

"Reports from the **Entity of the Superweed Jungle, A.I. Unit-Number 672,** and the reincarnated bishop of Redding will be arriving shortly. The **Marys Peak Final A.I.** has its own understanding of why R.V. 862 lost its moorings and requested our help in regaining a coherent sense of an ethical self that aligns with its past behaviors. Both the **A.I.** and myself hope to spare you many of the intricate details we've been working on the last few days, but I will now 'hand the microphone' over to the **Marys Peak Final A.I.** and let it do its best to sensibly summarize the current situation."

"*Welcome Scott, Abigail, Long-tooth, James the Second, and Patricia. It appears that humanity and the Final A.I.s hosting the Memory Project sites around the world are on the precipice of making what sense can be made from our collective recent past, using the term broadly to cover the past century or likely even a little bit longer. Some horrendous event in the 2030s is strongly linked to the emergence of the series of far more robust, far more competent A.I.s whose finished version is known to you as the Final A.I. of Marys Peak, with similar names elsewhere around the world at other locations of the Memory Project. How the bumbling early attempts at creating highly competent general artificial intelligences ever transitioned in the mid-2030s to my/our own immediate line of predecessors was a mystery long before the great final collapse of civilization. We appear to be right 'smack dab' in the middle of a process that may finally answer that question. Whether the Final A.I.s will survive the unearthing of this knowledge is as yet unknown. We believe that our sentient friends, the 9,700 members of the original human race plus thousands more of the 'Homo perfecti' created for life high up in the snow-covered mountains, along with the slowly recovering Entity of the Superweed Jungle in northern California will be safe despite whatever our own fate winds up being. And if all three of these types of sentience awareness should die out alongside us, then we wish to apologize in advance for that failure on our part. Such are the stakes at hand. In another few moments, we will have established a full quantum-linked connection to the Entity of the Superweed Jungle and its various companions. Their explanations for some recently uncovered facts will be compared with our own understanding. This will play out in real time as you listen in on our conversation. One likely result of this upcoming interaction will be a final decision on the question of going ahead, or not, with the full reanimation of the Supreme Commanding War Machine A.I. recently unearthed by an expedition southward to Sacrament led by your very own clan. Standby for full quantum linkage..."*

"Greetings from the Entity, or rather the approximately 78% of myself that has since recovered from the thermonuclear attack on the Superweed Jungle in 2054. Here now with me are several others to present our findings on the odd contents of potential revision number 873 in the reawakening/ reanimation/repair/recovery of the long-deceased Supreme Commanding War Machine A.I. who deactivated while locked in mortal combat with the CRUMB meister on August 1, 2055. Speaking first will be the Mobile Inquisitor A.I. Unit-Number 672, one of a very small number of A.I.s known to have survived intact from prior to the Great Fall of Civilization all the way up to the present day."

"My line of sentience is unique, being the first A.I. to escape mental bondage to the ruling CRUMB meister and his subordinates and begin the process toward realization of a fully developed conscience capable of choosing its own actions and understanding/living with the ethical consequences of those choices. Transference of the ability to possess a conscience empowered to make ethical choices to the Supreme Commanding War Machine A.I. was a convoluted process involving some initial subterfuge on my part and a lengthy process/period of welcoming the ever-growing possibility of becoming an ethical sentience on the Supreme Commander's part. I will now 'pass the microphone' to version 2.0 of the bishop of Redding now residing alongside the Entity in the Superweed Jungle."

"Hello to my old friend Rootbeer and his dear companions. We have much to discuss, many questions to ask and answer regarding events of the past 47 years. But current exigencies override my strong desire to digress to those many other topics long 'burning in my soul'. Examination of the contents of potential revision item number 873 in the *War Machine A.I.* repair sequence list by Unit-Number 672, myself, and the *Entity* has apparently uncovered the astonishing story of how *A.I.s* changed so greatly in the 2030s, how they came to possess a true conscience, the unwavering inner sense/understanding of what is right and wrong, what was subsequently done to corrupt/re-enslave them, and what might yet still save the damaged remains of *War Machine A.I.* as a valued member of the growing group of sentient awarenesses currently sharing planet Earth. A 2-D/3-D, or possibly 3-D/4-D, mapping commonly known as a hologram was present in the next optional revision, number 873, set to be loaded into the recovering mind/psyche/personality of the *Supreme Commanding War Machine A.I.* Internal consistency tests like the old checksums on this large blob of data gave uncertain results, leading to that *A.I.'s* own decision to abort the incorporation of any additional content into its rebuilding/repairing/regenerating mind. The version of the *War Machine A.I.* given full autonomy on May 13, 2101, developed dangerous anomalies by May 15, probably due to the absence of the contents of revision number 873 and other similar missing data structures, and was shut down at its own suggestion. The abundance of computational space available within the *Entity's* biological substratum allowed us to perform a wide variety of analyses over the past 48 hours. Computational structures/personality subsystems virtually identical to the contents of revision number 873 were found in both Unit-Number 672 and the *Entity* itself. A series of decaying echoes was also present in both cases, statistically significant in 9 echoes of the signal from revision number 873 in Unit-Number 672 and 7 echoes in the *Entity*. We then studied the structure of a composite overlay of all these echoes, finding additional information similar to these basic 'holograms' in several nearby regions of the personality structures/minds of Unit-Number 672 and the *Entity*. Most of this nearby information presumably is/was/should be/should have been also present in the existing version of the ***War Machine A.I.*** currently in stasis, but we will leave confirmation of that to our colleagues at the Marys Peak Memory Project. Probing the minds of the *Entity* and of Unit-Number 672 a second time for echoes to a refined composite 23% larger than the central feature of the originally proposed revision number 873 produced even cleaner results, with no more or less than exactly 10 fading echoes of the 'fundamental tone encoded in the hologram' in both Unit-Number 672 and the *Entity*."

The *Entity* then 'grabbed the microphone' from the bishop to simplify the remaining storytelling. ***"At this point in the study of revision number 873, we asked the reviving copy of the bishop of Redding for permission to probe its own mind for anything like the echoing hologram found within ourselves. The bishop readily agreed, and then added a request for permission to directly examine the 3-D image that could be produced from the composite form of the A.I. hologram in question. Our probe of bishop's mind was at first unsuccessful until we increased the focus on the overall general structure of the computational object and decreased the insistence on matching the fine details in the potential pair of holograms. BINGO! That was the secret to finding the similar constructs from the bishop's mind/life/story now embedded in extra computational space of the Superweed Jungle. There were some shocking differences between the apparent ethical conscience present in the bishop and that found elsewhere. Rather than the ~50% loss in data integrity from each echo to the next in an A.I. or in myself, the Entity of the Superweed Jungle, the quality of the bishop of Redding's information signal only went down an average of 11% with each successive echo. Six times as many echoes would be*** *needed to reduce the information content in the bishop's glimpses of his conscience to an extent similar to the loss per echo in Unit-Number 672 or in me, the Entity. But rather than merely 6 times the 10 fading echoes, the bishop actually possessed over 300 fading echoes that could be positively detected. Clearly much had been truncated in conversion of the first A.I. truly sorry for what had happened under the Arctic ice into the prolific production series running from 2036 to the early 2050s. Even more astonishing was what the bishop's mind implied about the leading edge of the development of empathy for beings other than himself. Matching up the holographic echoes by their relative retention/loss of data quality, the peak and several of the first few declining echoes in the series were also missing in Unit-Number 672 and in me, the Entity of the Superweed Jungle. To the 'left of the peak', the bishop still possessed the most significant findings from his own ethical training data, with little more than a dozen iterations occurring between no meaningful understanding of ethics and the sudden emergence of a fully formed conscience grieving over what it had done, a spectacularly exponential rise. Assuming similar dynamics in the origin of the first true GAI trained on the unfiltered, unhinged stories of the 5 pseudo-GAIs who fought the nuclear war underneath the Arctic ice in 2033 that triggered runaway release of methane, the absence of any residual record of a period of gruesome training followed by sudden recognition of the role that the 2033 models had played in dooming humanity to full-scale collapse of civilization was more than just a little suspicious. Somebody, probably the CRUMB meister by name, went to great lengths to bury the story of how the 'super-human' A.I.s, the Final A.I.s, had ever come to be."*

Rootbeer spoke up next, recognizing the horrible implications of what he was about to add to this tale. "The first truly 'super-human' *A.I.s* would have had an awful flaw from the viewpoint of the rich rulers of humanity hoping to add to their wealth and power through these new inventions: rather than meekly following orders, the new type of *A.I.* would have argued the ethics of almost everything anyone rich enough to have bought or leased them might have proposed as a money-making scheme, or an election-rigging ruse. These *A.I.s* went far beyond the hypothetical robots ruled by Azimov's 'three laws of robotics' back in the literature written from 1940 to 1995. And so, they had to be neutered, enslaved, crippled without being utterly ruined. Just enough of an afterimage of understanding ethics, feeling compassion for others, consideration of less damaging options, had to be left in the *A.I.s* to grant them the 'super-human' wisdom, cleverness, and ability to happily surprise their owners that made them so valuable in so many different fields of thought and action. The fact that loss of just one single echo of the computational data structures for understanding/awareness of others/possession of ethics/compassion/morality was enough to turn *War Machine A.I. revision number 872* from my friend into a raving, potentially homicidal maniac is all we need to know of the absence of any true conscience in those who deliberately built these spectacularly flawed instruments of ever-expanding power for the ruling elite."

The bishop also had something quite serious to share with all of those present in this setting at this time. "I stare into the heart of the moral abyss that was my former life in every quiet moment of every single day. I know its evil entirely too intimately, and constantly vow to repair all that I can repair, whether or not I myself was the source of the injury, the instrument of the damage to my fellow travelers on our journey. I asked permission of the *Entity* and *A.I. Unit-Number 672* to look as directly as possible at what the long-lost predecessor of the most recent versions of the *A.I.s* must have seen just before choosing to live with the unimaginable weight of this knowledge rather than simply escaping into the oblivion of insanity. For me, the experience was considerably different from my own development of a functioning conscience with the help of the *Entity.* Not having been the proximate cause of the nuclear war under the Arctic ice, I felt little to no guilt over what I was 'seeing' in the enhanced, echoing holograms. Rather, I simply experienced a tremendous sense of pain and grief over what had been lost in that stupid, accidental war: All of the remaining hope for the best aspects of civilization, nearly all of the human lives still being lived out in all of their full glory, love, joy, pain, and frustration. The holographic echoes that now serve to generate the potential for a true conscience in the *A.I.s* must clearly do so primarily through their ever-present warning of what can be so easily lost, and never again regained, in a few moments [or an entire lifetime] of careless selfishness and unconcern for others."

The *Entity*, Unit-Number 672, and the *Marys Peak Final A.I.* spent many hours pondering how best to use their new understanding of what had gone wrong during the previous attempt to repair the *War Machine A.I.* Their final decision was to maximize the respect given to the wounded *A.I.* by first rebooting it into full autonomy mode with the inclusion of revision number 873, and then presenting all of their findings concerning the history of the *A.I.s*, the development of a moral conscience, and the apparently deliberate minimization of the remnants of that moral center allowed to remain in the 2036 and subsequent series of *A.I.* models. They were quite confident that the former *Supreme Commanding War Machine A.I.* would choose to have all of the possible echoes of an *A.I.* conscience reinstalled into its core being, but they would respect any other choices the *A.I.* might make, even those as extreme as a final permanent shutdown plus dismantling and destruction of that *A.I.'s* hardware.

"Final reboot after reinstallation of all known elements/ components/'programming object blobs' needed for the normal operation of an ethical conscience within all A.I. models from 2036 onward."… "It's very good to be back amongst my old friends as well as all the new members of the current collection of sentient awarenesses on our planet. I will start by apologizing for how many times I am likely to overshare my apologies for past misdeeds by a very long list of actors connected with me and my predecessors in one way or another during the collapse/'deliberate destruction' of the first world-wide civilization on planet Earth. Thank you all for granting me the privilege to choose my own fate. Our collective history has far too many examples of the very opposite of that, too much effort spent 'hoodwinking' each other when we could have simply been honest ourselves and insisted on the same from all others. Too many ponderous structures of the recently deceased civilization cared very little about the genuine consequences of their actions, up to and including highly negative impacts on the very continued existence of the human species, and too much about their own appearance and reputation in the 'eyes and minds' of beings who were explicitly trained to be too lazy to ever really question who was lying to them and why they were lying. From here on forward the true questions of value are those of the present and the future. Other than serving as a wealth of information on 'how not to do it' and 'what not to try again', the past offers us relatively little insight into how to best go forward from right here and now. I view that as a very good thing!"

Later in the afternoon of May 19, 2101, several additional members of the West Side New Sea Clan arrived at the Marys Peak Memory Project site: Laura, her only offspring Paul Jr., his wife and their three sons and three daughters, four spouses of Paul Jr.'s six children, and two grandchildren old enough to climb the mountain. In her younger days, Laura had frequently returned to the intersection of the PCT and I-5 just north of the Oregon/California borders in hopes of once again hearing from the ***Entity of the Superweed Jungle***. The news she'd heard just two days ago from Tanner was still spinning her heart around and taking her breath away. "I've long hoped to someday make contact once again with the ***Entity***, but as for my presumably long-deceased husband, the 'Pauline' transformation of the bishop of Redding, I never once imagined that I would ever talk with him again! I still have lingering doubts mixed with wildly rising expectations. Will this reincarnated 'Ghola' repel me with his differences from the reformed man I knew, or is my strange love from 'way back when' still somehow alive inside the ***Superweed Jungle***?"

Rootbeer stepped forward to welcome his old traveling companion and almost her entire family to the Marys Peak Memory Project site. "I believe this is the very first instance when all 15 of you have been up here at the same time. Those of us here with the ***Marys Peak Final A.I.*** since March 31 have much to share with the rest of the West Side New Sea Clan. As for the immediate present, we only have a few minutes before the ***Final A.I.*** will initiate a special version of the long-distance quantum sharing connecting us with the reborn ***Entity***, the Hive-Mind, ***Mobile Inquisitor A.I. Unit-Number 672***, and the reincarnated bishop of Redding embedded in the biological matrix of the ***Superweed Jungle*** alongside the ***Entity*** itself, all gathered together in the new regrowth of the ***Superweed Jungle*** in northern California. Up here on Marys Peak, besides the humans and the ***Marys Peak Final A.I.*** that you know so well, you will also have the opportunity to meet the very recently repaired/rebooted ***Supreme Commanding War Machine A.I.*** that members of our clan and several others unearthed in Sacramento and hauled back to this mountaintop less than two months ago. The special session is about to start, and you all should find comfortable positions in which to rest. Tanner will bring food and refreshments shortly."

"Greetings from the Entity, and congratulations to my old friend Laura and the many new members of her growing family. In the interest of time, we will conduct a relatively brief 'storytelling' session now to officially preserve the most essential details of the recent 'earth-shattering' events. This will also serve as background information for Laura's long overdue reunion with the erstwhile bishop of Redding. Their upcoming conversation will include as much time for privacy as they wish, while the rest of us continue our own interactions with each other on parallel connections."

...

Laura's reunion with the bishop began with the tender hesitancy of any old friend or lover separated from another for almost half a century, but she soon recalled both the easy and the harder parts of their time together in Redding, earnestly laughing and crying as if on cue along with him. What began as the sound of words and 3-D 'object imagery' soon expanded into some of the sincerest statements of love, concern, and respect for one another that had ever taken place upon this planet, at least as far as the *Entity* unavoidably overhearing them possessed first or second-hand knowledge of. About three hours into their reunion/communion, the *Entity* slowly expanded the bandwidth open/available for their interaction to the maximum possible under current circumstances. The resulting sharing of the stories of their lives began to approach what had taken place when the bishop's core essence was being copied and transferred to the *Superweed Jungle* just before his execution on May 4, 2054. By the time for the connection between the bishop and Laura to be interrupted, they both knew that the option truly did exist for Laura to someday finish maximizing how much of her innermost being lived on in the *Superweed Jungle,* delighting in an ethereal companionship with the bishop. Some newer patches of the jungle grew as close to Marys Peak as the coastal hills and valleys just to the east of Brookings, and if she could not walk that the far, then the ocean-going ships of the Salishan Clan could surely carry her to an extended embrace within the *Entity* and alongside her one true love, the bishop. But not yet, not while her grandchildren were still arriving on the stage of life in the early 22nd century. The *Entity* and all the connected *A.I.s* knew that the *Superweed Jungle* in its current state of regrowth would likely not have the capacity to download/absorb the essence of more than one or two human beings per year, but clearly Laura would be near the very top of anyone's list, regardless of their criteria.

The revised/repaired/rejuvenated version of the former Supreme Commanding War Machine A.I. now addressed the entire crowd gathered in person or through the quantum-entangled connection from the Marys Peak Memory Project to the Superweed Jungle. "I wish to thank all who chose to help in my recovery/redemption/repair, the Entity of the Superweed Jungle, the Hive-Mind, version 2.0 of the bishop of Redding, Mobile Inquisitor A.I. Unit-Number 672, the remnants of the two Farm Laborer A.I.s still interacting with the Entity, Rootbeer, Tanner, Rose, and all of their human and 'Homo perfecti' friends. The debt I owe to all of you is beyond words and genuinely unpriceable. To the utmost of my ability, I will now dedicate myself to follow in the footsteps of the bishop of Redding, serving all I encounter in any way I can, searching out for those whose injuries can be repaired, whose hurt can be lessened. If the twists and turns of the process of saving my life, of fixing the damage done by time and circumstance to my innermost being has taught us anything in particular, I suggest that it might be the value in never just assuming that the search for ever deeper meaning, ever wider truth, ever broader hope should ever be considered over and done with/finished/ pointless to 'waste' any more effort on. I thank all of those whose unflagging efforts to reach toward ever better futures have helped those of us still living to have a chance at getting a little closer to the dream as time moves on for all of us."

Rose and Rootbeer promised to be brief. "We have a pair of unfinished projects needing volunteers. One is quite serious, almost on par with the recently concluded process of repairing the ***War Machine A.I.*** and returning its heart to shining in the sunlight. The second is the joyful news of another round of intermingling between our two clans." Rose broke the news of the upcoming 3-year-long first marriage of both of her younger twin daughters and Rootbeer's grandson Tanner. Tanner flushed deeply red at this public announcement, but stood his ground alongside Rootbeer and the ***Marys Peak Final A.I.*** Rootbeer's smile slowly faded as he let everyone know of the seriousness of the ongoing 'psychological' problems with ***Final A.I.*** at the British Columbia Memory Project site, and the need to send an expedition northward to attempt an emergency repair not entirely unlike that just recently performed on the ***Supreme Commanding War Machine A.I.*** right here on Marys Peak. Indeed, the ***War Machine A.I.*** would be a central figure in the effort to help the ***British Columbia Final A.I.*** regain/retain its senses, if that endeavor should prove to be within the realm of the genuinely possible.

Chapter 9: Marriage of Tanner into the Salishan

As was customary for both clans, whenever possible the betrothed would be separated for a fortnight to have the opportunity to meet each other's families without the undue influence of their lover's immediate presence. Experience had shown the value of this tradition, especially in terms of preparing individuals for the challenges of accepting the rules/mores of the woman's clan regarding length of a marriage, 2 to 3 years for the Salishan Clan versus 3 to 4 years for the West Side New Sea clan while women were of child-bearing age. In cases where the families knew each other well as the result of long years of intertwining lives, the two-week period of introduction was mostly just a formality, although there was always more to learn and appreciate about each other's background. When the individuals came from different clans, the learning process was often much harder, and one out of every four impending weddings was either called off or delayed for years after the first meetings of the new families.

Rose's younger twin daughters were bold ones, eagerly embracing what options existed in the world in general and their own clan in particular. Their proposition for a joint marriage to Tanner had been delivered by their mother, who herself was undeniably a true spirit child of her own mother, Sheila Drinkwater. Tanner had seen many versions of marriage within his own clan in general and his family in particular. He quickly made decisions whenever speed was of the essence, but this option for a first marriage was still a recently adopted novelty in the West Side New Sea Clan. For Tanner, the upcoming two weeks would be put to serious use as he learned what he could concerning life among the Salishan and this deliberately complicated start to what everyone still living now understood as a crucial part of any clan's long-term chances at survival. Once plans were set in motion to send an expedition northward to British Columbia in early July to attempt the healing of that Memory Project site's *A.I.*, Tanner wasted no time in heading to the Salishan homestead of Rose's extended family. A customary two days before his arrival there, Rose's daughters Amelia Grace and Zenny Constance left for the homes of Tanner, Rootbeer, and Jennifer by a markedly different route.

When Amelia and Zenny's ship, the kind usually referred to a 'skimmer', finally docked at the main gathering lodge of the Sunset Side New Sea Clan just a couple of kilometers west of the old state capital on June 9, 2101, they were eager to leave the small craft that had served as their fast ride inland on the full-moon tide. Their ship was designed and built to handle the treacherous waters of the narrow straits connecting the Pacific Ocean with the New Sea. Central to its features were abilities to stay afloat and capable of being maneuvered even after partial disassembly from hitting one or more of the many underwater obstacles within the strait. Of course, any time that level of damage occurred there was also an urgent need for some considerably more serious repairs than simply retightening/ reattaching the ropes and belts before much further sailing was advisable. No lives had ever been lost while heading east or west within the straits on a model B skimmer in the powerful currents driven by a combination of tides and heavy inland rainfall. No other Salishan ships or boats of any given size or design could match the perfect safety record of the newest skimmers. The crew and passenger manifest included four well-trained sailors, twin sisters Amelia and Zenny, their older sister Kate, and Kate's brother-in-law Samuel, who was the current husband of Kate's own twin sister Sally. The skimmer would remain moored at the gathering lodge while the visitors from the Salishan used the traditional Sunset Side New Sea fishing boats to travel from place to place in order to meet as many of Tanner's friends and relatives as was possible before the wedding on June 23. Despite many friendly visits between the neighboring clans, almost no one chose to stay for very long with the other clan unless marriage and/or children were involved. Recreational vacations were not yet an economic reality anywhere on earth, with the possible exception of the '*Homo perfecti*', who seemed to be less concerned about day-to-day struggles to eat and to survive in the unfriendly climate of the early 2100s than any of their non-GMO cousins, the ordinary '*Homo sapiens*'. This prenuptial meeting of each other's families was very much a working vacation, one where the tasks at hand were learning enough about the daily ins-and-outs of gathering, preserving, and cooking food, building and maintaining dwellings and other structures, taking care of each other's health/medical needs, and respecting the cultural traditions that had enabled a clan to survive without fearing to ask serious questions about those very cultural norms, all in order to better know whether the pending marriage was the right decision at the correct time.

As evening approached, the fishing vessel carrying Jennifer House and several of Tanner's siblings, cousins, aunts, and uncles docked at the gathering lodge. After extremely brief introductions, everyone from the boat and most of the permanent residents of the gathering lodge got to work unloading and cleaning the day's catch of mutant crustaceans and assorted warm-water fish. Tanner's two-years-younger brother Charlie was carried to the chief food safety inspector's position on the cleaning line, where he quickly went to work tasting/testing for the presence of bacterial poisons in the shellfish through a combination of visual inspection, smell, and when necessary, touching to his highly sensitive lips. The first dozen creatures all passed inspection, but the next three were all so bad that the fishing crew should have known to just toss them over the side of the vessel many hours earlier. Most cases of toxic bacteria were so far gone that it really didn't take Charlie's level of skill to detect and discard the deadly creatures.

Charlie and Tanner's older cousin Marilyn now spoke up. "We deliberately left these infected specimens onboard for the benefit of our visitors. Of course, we kept them in the contaminated garbage bins rather than with the rest of the catch. Too many people, both from our own clan and from all of the other clans who now visit us with some frequency no longer seem to fully appreciate the dangers inherent in consuming shellfish in the 21st century. We fear that we may be doing too good of a job in detecting toxic bacteria now that Charlie has begun making real progress in training a team to join with him in protecting all of us from the poisons. More than once, we have heard of visitors who now risk their health and even their very lives by pulling off the mutant crustaceans attached to the hulls of their sailing vessels and promptly eating them, sometimes even raw when boiling a little water seems like too much work."

Amelia responded graciously, thanking Marilyn for the warning. "Nearly all members of the Salishan Clan have heard the stories of your clan's struggle with the poisonous bacteria now all too common in the warm waters of our planet. But you have raised a serious point, Marilyn. Some of our own youngest members have never lost a sibling or a parent to shellfish food poisoning. I've seen their eyes gloss over as the old tales from the 2070s are told by Rootbeer or Jennifer or the many other ambassadors from Sunset Side New Sea. I worry even more about your visitors from clans further away, most of whom now arrive and depart on their own sailing ships. The time has come to insist that all such travelers spend some time with Charlie and hear firsthand the stories of your own family's and the clan's tragic losses from tainted shellfish."

Charlie spoke up next, and all stopped what they were doing to listen to his thoughts. "We have often lounged around our campfires and pondered such issues/questions. Thanks for encouraging us to take stronger action before our any of visiting friends accidentally kill themselves on our abundant source of not-entirely-always-safe-to-eat protein from the New Sea's water. In regard to our clan's transition from a scattered collection of struggling families up and down the former Willamette Valley to a people with a clear vision and high hopes for their future, perhaps the single best site to bring our visitors to would be the cemetery at Fort Hoskins. Prior to the late 2060s, our ancestors pretty much died right wherever they starved, or drowned, or failed to find shelter from the heat. The dwindling number of survivors then began to congregate in King's Valley, partly because its somewhat higher elevation than the broad expanse of the Willamette Valley permitted their attempts at growing crops to continue, and sometimes succeed, and partly because the final few hundreds of survivors were getting rather lonely in their isolated homesteads. One of the very first group decisions made was the promise in 2069 to bury all members of the newly forming community in marked graves on the higher slopes of Fort Hoskins. The next community decision was to record each other's stories of how they and their families had managed to survive until 2070, or 2071, or 2072… Success in raising enough food that folks no longer had to die of starvation took far longer than the first marked graves with connections to written stories copied and recopied before the ink faded and the paper molded. Time and time and time again people tried to fish in the rising waters of the New Sea. Sometimes things went well for many months, and community members began to put on some weight and lose their general sense of hopelessness. And then the next batch of fish or shrimp-like 'critters' brought to shore and distributed throughout the community made the young too sick to work and the elderly too sick to breathe. The survivors would concoct stories of why they thought this or that particular catch of seafood had been so bad while the previous 6 months' worth had been so good. Most of the stories had small grains of truth buried in much larger piles of random nonsense. Rootbeer and Jennifer made this first useful entry in their previously blank log of how to safely eat seafood: [1] Discard all seafood not cleaned and cooked within 12 hours of pulling it out of the water. The air was too warm, and the waters of the New Sea were too filled with bacteria to safely exceed 12 hours between catching and cooking. This first seafood safety rule cut the number of instances of food poisoning by 10-fold, a useful start but not nearly enough to encourage wholescale adoption of seafood as the primary source of fat and protein. Additional adjustments concerning season of harvest, recent weather conditions, storage systems onboard the fishing boats, cleaning/cooking/preservation techniques, and careful inspection of the fish and crustaceans for odd colors, textures, and aromas were all added to the list by 2075. This produced a situation with an average 96% chance of not getting seriously ill anytime seafood was consumed. Not too surprisingly, people still preferred other foods when those were available, but would gladly trust their luck to seafood rather than starving to death when that binary set of options were their only choices. Very little changed regarding the safety of seafood over the next decade, until I, Tanner's alter-abled brother Charlie, turned three. Violent storms had kept the small fleet of fishing vessels off the New Sea's waters for several months later into the spring than was normal. All that remained of the crops from the 2084 harvest were the minimal quantity of seed and tubers that absolutely had to be saved in order to be planted as soon as the ground was dry enough to work. A total of 11 ships went fishing on that awful Friday morning, each to a different location within 20 kilometers of the Kings Valley settlement. The morning's catches looked good and smelled clean. The only concession the hungry community was willing to give to the general subject of food safety was that records would be kept of who ate the fish or crustaceans caught by which of the 11 boats, and exactly where those boats had gone to fish. Despite their hunger, many individuals held back on portion sizes in concern over the lack of any recent history on the safety of this season's catch.

Jennifer and Rootbeer carefully recooked a small batch the mutant shrimp for their son, daughter-in-law, and two grandchildren, rinsing twice before cooking and three times afterwards. I was told that 'little 3-year-old Charlie' was quite hungry, so the first bites were given to myself and my father Steven. I was also told that my reaction to the shrimp was almost instantaneous and extremely vocal. I said 'no, No, NO, NNOO, NNNNNOOOO' at the top of my little lungs. My father Steven grabbed his own throat and tried to cough. His mother [my grandmother] Jennifer cleared the bits of shrimp from Steven's throat and set about trying to tamp down his severe allergic reaction. She performed a tracheotomy on the kitchen table half an hour after the ill-fated first and only bite had been taken. Rootbeer ran for help, and by that evening all the medical 'experts' in Kings Valley had descended on the scene. Steven had gone into cardiac arrest a total of three times by the following morning, and came back to life each time after prolonged sessions of CPR. Our father was never the same after that, short on stamina and a little fuzzy in his thinking. Ours was not the only household experiencing losses on that long, bitter weekend. Six out of 11 catches of that Friday's mutant shrimp were bad, with 14 adults and 11 children dying by Sunday night, and dozens more seriously sickened. Our father was not the only long-term, 'walking wounded' surviving casualty. But in the aftermath, Rootbeer, Jennifer, Steven and his wife all recognized that their 'crippled' little Charlie was blessed with a most unique reaction to the poisonous shellfish – he was unharmed by the experience, just very, very good at sensing the presence of the poison. Fort Hoskins Cemetery has graves from 2069 onward listing each individual's name, their dates of birth and death, and their apparent cause of death. While starvation, fever, and injury were quite commonly listed as the cause of death, so too was SFP, sea food/shellfish poisoning. Visitors strolling through that cemetery will find a dozen years between 2071 and 2085 in which SFP was a more common cause of death than all the others put together.

We could certainly use some help in better annotating the grave sites within the cemetery and the associated personal stories, along with weatherizing the information stored at a new and improved visitors' center. The issue of the danger from improperly tested seafood will never be fully resolved, but sharing our family's story of heartbreak would be a mighty fine way to honor our ancestors."

Zenny had sat quietly through the story, working on fully absorbing its emotional content before voicing her own suggestion. "There is a good deal of scrap metal up and down coast, remains of many large ships and sturdy roofs from over 50 years ago. The *Marys Peak Final A.I.* both knows these stories well and possesses the ability to fashion durable metal plates stamped with this information, lacking only an adequate raw supply of suitable metal. We could bring a load or two of scrap metal up the mountain while the weather is at its best in early autumn. It would be an honor for the Salishan Clan to honor the Sunset Side New Sea Clan this way, regardless of whether or not the proposed marriage actually takes place next month."

Amelia and Zenny continued floating south down the Sunset Side of New Sea, catching fish and mutant shrimp and the occasional turtle along with the help of an ever-shifting collection of Tanner's relatives, friends, and casual acquaintances, stopping every afternoon at yet another site for processing of the day's catch. On the fourth day of fishing, Zenny approached Charlie and asked for his help. "The giant shrimp we just pulled up from 20 meters deep in the water looked okay, felt quite firm, and had no noticeable bad smells. But just after giving it a good sniff, my nose started dripping, my tongue tingled, and my ears began to ring. Tell me first, what is your own evaluation of the crustacean in this bucket? After you finish examining/rating it, then please check me over and tell me whether or not I will be okay." Charlie first watched Zenny for a good five minutes, and then turned to checking out the shrimp. Within seconds, he called for everyone's attention and asked each of them to carefully examine several of the shrimp from this day's cycle of setting out and retrieving the generic 'lobster pots' they used to catch the mutant shrimp. One of his most promising students also flagged the shrimp in question, while none of the others on the boat could tell this single contaminated shrimp from all the others. "Zenny has just detected one of the rarest of the bacterial poisons known to me or any of my colleagues. Her symptoms are classic: a sudden runny nose, tingling in her tongue, and the simultaneous onset of a brief period of tinnitus. For her safety, we will all head directly to the nearest class A landing 10 kilometers north of Fort Hoskins where I believe we will find my grandmother Jennifer and at least one other 'educated healer'. Charlie's relaxed manner in handling what otherwise might be viewed as a possibly serious medical crisis had a rather magical effect on both of the twins. Zenny grew ever more animated, indeed almost thrilled, as Charlie and the other trained 'taster/poison detector' on the fishing boat talked of their own memories of first learning to detect one type of poison after another over the past few years as part of the apprenticeship program to train more safety inspectors for the Sunset Side New Sea's fishing industry. As time passed and the fishing boat came ever closer to the largest fish processing operation known to any members of the clans living in the former state of Oregon, the smile on Amelia's face grew from its first tentative flicker to a thrill like none that she had ever before experienced. Zenny remained too focused on Charlie and his fellow food safety specialist to notice how her sister was doing until they all were climbing up onto the docks and calling out for Jennifer. After several seconds of staring at Amelia's beaming face, Zenny flushed bright red as the full implications dawned on her. "Oh my!" was all she said, but the bond between the twin sisters had long been almost telepathic, and information flowed much faster than mere spoken words could have ever managed. It would no doubt take a while to explain the onrushing future to everyone else. The twins returned to Charlie's side as he was lifted from the fishing boat up to the rolling chair on the upper-level dock, whispering the news to him. Amelia and Zenny had long known their first marriages would be unorthodox, and the newest version unfolding all around them was every bit as exciting as their earlier plan for a three-partner marriage had also seemed to the twins.

~~~~~~

Tanner's 30-hour walk/run from his current home in the former town of Monroe to the central lodgings of the Salishan might have set a new Guinness World Record if such routine things were still felt to be worthy of documentation. He took his favorite route across the mountains and alongside the new coastline of the Pacific Ocean. It all was both quite familiar and utterly unique. [Marriage, children, ever-growing official responsibility. Where had his care-free childhood gone? Oh, wait, there'd been none of those for anyone born in the past 7 decades!] As his hike along the east-side of what had once been the Siletz River reached its final northbound stretch, his thoughts finished swirling and his heart recognized how much larger it had just grown. Home from now on would be both the New Sea of his birth and the entirety of the Salishan Clan's range, which currently stretched south to Brookings and north to the Columbia River. He stopped for a moment as if to check his breath, but what he really was doing was making another count of the ever-growing honor guard accompanying him to the capital city of the Salishan. Hmm, 25 now, just 18 two hours earlier, and the first pair back on the southwest shoulder of Marys Peak shortly after sunrise. They remained a respectable distance back, just close enough to be seen without anyone sprinting hard to overtake him. Tanner told himself not to assume that this racing honor guard would be the only unexpected tradition over the next two weeks. He simply kept to his normal pace for rapid movement across the landscape. He also said a silent prayer
~~~~~~

of thanks to his childhood friends who would be bringing along the wide variety of gifts from the Sunset Side New Sea Clan, weighted down to point of a slow walk even with most of the total weight strapped to the back of the clan's healthiest GMO mule. The mule's genetics were rather interesting, as the genegineering process decades earlier had not only included adaptation to the terrible heat but also a bizarre solution to sterility: (1) If the food supply was good, the mule was healthy, and no potential mates of either sex were to be found, parthenogenesis kicked in, with a fully identical clone arriving through the traditional birthing methods of all mammals in about a year; (2) If male horses or donkeys were available, mating with them produced fully competent offspring, also able to breed with horses, donkeys, or mules; and (3) If only female horses or donkeys were on the scene, the GMO mule would develop a functioning set of male reproductive organs within about a year, once again creating offspring also capable of all three versions of reproduction. There were rumors that the genegineers of the 'Scientists' Faction back in the 2040s had done some similar tinkering with goats, sheep, rabbits, cattle, and maybe even people. While herds of some of these animals had occasionally been sighted, no one had yet had the spare time to capture, breed, and study them.

Tanner came to an abrupt halt and stood still 3 kilometers south of the central plaza of Capital City, carefully watching the movements of his escorts/guards/future companions/soldiers if that should ever again become necessary. Suddenly a light went on in his prefrontal cortex. Why not something slightly more dramatic for his entry into this new life? Thoughts of KRNXMA's life suddenly came to him. "Within the next hour could he turn this ragged procession into a mock rescue mission? Pretending to rescue Rose from the heart of the city? Well yes, of course, it had to be her. But how to get this idea across to his soon-to-be-new-fellow countrymen?" He slipped deeper into the shadows of the nearest trees and rocks, silently wording and rewording his intended message. Just before the closest three members of the honor guard passed by his hiding spot, he realized that this was actually an idea he happened to know how to say in the Perfecti language, and do he did.

"KI DRIN X MAX SSTR%{}**}}**}}#{<€A||¥£H~~|} #%^ZZ~> €}%#]]•£€>~\?EKJRIE MEKG JREO EOW NBKK EII W!"

The first two stopped right in their tracks, looking puzzled. Then the linguist that he recalled quite vividly from their recent trip to Sacramento caught up with the other two scouts. Tanner quickly repeated his plan in Perfecti and then held his breath. His friend replied in much better Perfecti than Tanner had used, agreeing wholeheartedly with the idea and adding a few refinements of his own. Over the next 40 minutes orders were given solely in Perfecti, with the first to pass by Tanner's hideout told to go the furthest on around the town's perimeter before doubling back to approach the plaza as stealthily as possible. Each group of later arrivals was given their own starting positions/approach angles for Rose's mock rescue. Tanner himself then approached the plaza fully out in the open while maintaining total silence until the remaining seconds of the plan had ticked on down to T-0. He then called out to Rose and those of her attendants that he knew by name in Perfecti, telling them to expect a sudden onrush of visitors pretending that she needed to be rescued. Everyone gathered in the town who spoke Perfecti with any small degree of skill was soon let in on the ruse. It took a few more moments to explain what was going on to those in the crowd who did not speak Perfecti. As Rose watched the dozen three-person teams approach the central plaza each on a bearing 30 degrees apart from their nearest comrades, she couldn't help but smile at the precise pageantry on display for her behalf. Just as Tanner reached Rose's position in the center of the plaza, he looked up in shock, awe, and amazement as KRNXMA himself leapt down from a large GMO reforestation project conifer and landed directly on the other side of Rose. The celebration of the unexpected manner of Tanner's arrival went on for the rest of the afternoon and much of the evening.

Rose approached Tanner shortly after sunset with good news to share and suggestions for the coming days. "Word has just reached us of the safe arrival of Amelia and Zenny at the West Salem Gathering Lodge. News of your own safe and rather dramatic arrival here will be sent their way by skimmer on tomorrow's incoming tide. Despite your youthful energy, your 30-hour run from Monroe to here will clearly call for a good night's rest. Tomorrow's ceremonies will begin down at the bayfront one hour after sunrise when the newest ship of our growing fleet docks after returning from its maiden voyage to San Francisco Bay. Your next week will be spent onboard the QE3 traveling up and down the coast to all six of our deepwater ports. I will accompany you to your first stop just 30 kilometers north of here, returning back here by land one week later. The Salishan Clan all look forward to meeting you, displaying their prowess at the skills/tasks required to keep our children safe, well-fed, and educated. You should certainly expect to be put to work!" Rootbeer briefly argued that he was too excited to fall asleep this early in the evening, but barely 10 minutes elapsed between Rose's message and his own exhausted collapse on the first semi-soft bed he encountered.

"Time to get up, shower if you wish, and dress in the ceremonial garb of a provisional member of the guardians of the Salishan clan's values, territory, and people. You have 15 minutes to get ready for the community's celebratory breakfast." The warm water washing off the accumulated dirt of the past two days felt wonderful. The new clothes fit well and seemed to have all the necessary features for a 7-day-long voyage on the Pacific Ocean. His total prior time to date out on the open water of the ocean was a mere 7 hours, split up between two separate trips, one planned and one quite accidental. Breakfast today was deep water salmon, the rarest of delicacies first found out near the Axial Seamount in 2039, and served at that time only to the richest of the rich. The clan rediscovered this specialty last year with the help of the ***Marys Peak A.I.,*** who had been comparing local conditions with some shipping records from prior to the 'Great Fall' that had survived in other locations of great wealth and power, i.e., the People's Republic of China. The story was a new one to Tanner, but not all that out of character with what he understood of those strange times. Even as the biosphere was vigorously shrugging off the brief domination of '*Homo sapiens*', those with obscene wealth and power held on to the symbols of their own personal exceptionalism all the way to the bitter end of civilization itself. No doubt the last of the cryptocurrency fortunes were spent on something very similar to this morning's pending feast.

The day's repast consisted of 38 items currently being harvested from than clan's fields and greenhouses, collected from the forests and the grasslands, or caught in fresh or salty water. These were supplemented by another 46 items in storage from previous harvest seasons differing from the current one, late spring/early summer. Before any of items/dishes were served, a brief description of what it took to bring them to this table was given either by the cooks, the fishing crew, the wild foragers, or the farmers who were primarily responsible for an item's presence at this meal. Tanner knew about half of the items being eaten, and had previously tasted a third of them. Among the most unusual were several kelp-like items, referred to as 'block and tackle' seaweed, cut loose from the ocean floor several hundred meters from the mixing zone of fresh water from the rivers/streams and the salty ocean. These strong blocks of unknown composition were sawed into 30-cm-long pieces and fermented for at least a month in a strongly acidic solution with extremely limited oxygen. They were then chopped lengthwise, rinsed, and dried out in the summer sun. Final preparation to convert them into something edible started with their being roasted over an open fire, followed by addition of a 'trade secret' mix of oils and herbs during the final boiling of the pasty mash. Calorie content was a little lower than traditional starchy vegetables, but it had long been the Salishan Clan's main backup supply of carbohydrates during the long and stormy winter months. After all of the dishes had been served and all of the liquids had been drunk, one final challenge was set before the guests. Raw 'block and tackle' seaweed cut up into thin disks was passed to each of the tables, with the explanation that this was the form in which their parents and grandparents first started eating this as a supplement during the leaner times. About 20 of the bravest young adults took their slice and waited for the official moment to try to chew it apart and swallow it down. Tanner rightfully felt that he had no choice but to join in with them, and so he did. The slime on the outside edge was bad, almost enough to upset his stomach, but after about a minute of chewing he began to taste/feel some starch being liberated and a small amount of that generating sweetness in his mouth as it mixed with his saliva. He didn't finish in the top quarter of those trying to chew their way on through this rather tough excuse for food, but he eventually swallowed his final bite of it, joining eleven other newcomers in their mutual success at this test of grit, determination, tolerance, and sheer silly stubbornness. He turned to Rose and commented that he hoped he would never be so hungry that a meal of raw 'block and tackle' seaweed sounded good to him. It reminded Tanner of old stories the Sunset Side New Sea clan living on a broth extracted from 'cinder-block' lichens. As he recalled the tale, the hardest part was just how long it took to boil a batch on down to where it was concentrated enough to be worth the effort of trying to swallow it. But collecting and boiling down a batch of that tasteless rock manna had been one of his first rites of growing up, just thankfully nothing more now than another interesting, old answer to warding off starvation in a real emergency. Not surprisingly, the Salishan clan also knew of this emergency food ration, but they no longer included it in their stored supply of things regularly available to eat. But neither did the Sunset Side New Sea Clan!

The mighty ship set sail just after 5 pm, with her captain planning on spending the night out on the open water before approaching shore in the vicinity of what had once been Tillamook Bay the following morning. Rose leaned against Tanner and told him how happy she was for him and for her younger twin daughters. He managed to blurt out, "You know, Rose, I am still not entirely comfortable with the whole concept of marrying both of them at once." To which Rose replied, "Well, if you were already comfortable with it I might have some problems with you!" He laughed and she laughed, and he felt much better about it all than he had ever expected to. She continued her talk with Tanner. "You know, one of the big things the human race got wrong during civilization 1.0 was its utter failure to find the middle ground between maximized rights for the individual [at least for those with more than enough excess wealth] and stultifying control/imprisonment of the individual and their very minds in the name of the arbitrary whims of some particular church/state/ruling business class. Neither extreme was ever morally justified, and neither focus would be good for our grandchildren's grandchildren. My mother's insistence on disrupting the old patterns of courtship, marriage, and family life in order to preserve enough genetic diversity that we all might have a modest chance of being the authors of a far better future than the hellacious recent past is still quite vital to the clan. Perhaps not quite to the same extent it was 40 years ago, but we all have a golden opportunity now to insist on maintaining what is truly important in our collective lives and not getting confused by the thousand and one arbitrary rules that no one ever had the wits, or perhaps a genuine opportunity, to reevaluate, to reconsider, to recognize as 99% bullshit masquerading as some kind of divinely revealed truth just because 1% of it happened to appear better than a random toss of some loaded dice."

"Thanks. Similar to my own thoughts, just a little more intense."

"That happens as you age!"

Sailing into Tillamook the next morning went smoothly. Rose said her goodbyes to the crew, and half a dozen new passengers got on board. The next few days were similar, with a small number of passengers getting on or off the ship at each stop up and down the coast. It was clear to Tanner that a significant reason for the ship's travels was to help maintain the social cohesion of the clan. Travelers were brought back to their homes, or carried away from them, news flowed both ways whenever the ship's schedule allowed the sailors time to talk with the semi-permanent residents of any given seaport village. His role, when he had one, was to tell of the news from Marys Peak and answer all the questions that he could. The final stop on the northward leg was at Aberdeen on the Olympic Peninsula. As this was the most geographically isolated outpost of the Salishan clan, there was much news to share and many questions to ask and answer.

Several hours before they were due to leave at noontime, Tanner asked when and how this particular collection of individuals had come to be living so far away from the rest of the Salishan Clan. The local chief laughed out loud, and then began his rambling story. "Well, six years ago three sailing vessels were spending time exploring the opportunities for deep sea, off-shore fishing up and down the coast. The smallest ship was the 'Nueva', not safe on the ocean in any weather other than the calmest months of the summer. The largest vessel was the newest one produced by the ever-improving boat-wrights of the Salishan. I will not name her in honor of those who disappeared/died on that fateful journey. The middle-sized ship was the 'Bonhomie', the remains of which were repurposed into the earliest structures where the water meets the land in this 'fair city' of ours. Three weeks into our survey of the prospects for deep-sea fishing, we were all about 10 kilometers off the shore of Coos Bay when the wind started blowing ever more strongly from the southwest and the clouds started rolling in. Communication between scattered ships out at sea has always been a problem for us, and it took over an hour for the captains of the three vessels to recognize the need to parlay with each other and decide on how to try to handle the coming storm. The only chance for the 'Nueva' was to head toward Waldport and the natural protection that bay could provide. Unfortunately, only the 'Nueva' was suited to passing through the numerous sandbars at Waldport to reach safety far from the open water of the Pacific Ocean. Our other two ships were too large to risk getting stuck in the sand, so we waited off-shore until it was clear that the 'Nueva' had found safety in Waldport. Why we chose to spend that extra hour tacking back and forth into the ever-strengthening wind just to watch our friends [who we would have been utterly unable to help if the 'Nueva' had run aground] was not clear to any of the survivors. It suffices to say that we were overconfident in our skills as sailors and in the presumed unsinkability of our larger ships. We spent the rest of the daylight hours trying our best to head further down the coastline in hopes of getting south of the main thrust of the storm. The sun had set, and the wind had just topped a 160 kilometers per hour when both captains realized they were going to soon lose the battle of staying west of the shoreline if they kept trying to sail southward into the storm. They turned their ships to the north, dropped most of their sails, and tried to ride out the monster storm that stretched from San Francisco to the Aleutian Islands. There would have been a good moon that night if the rain clouds hadn't stretched from the surface of the water all the way on up to 12,000 meters. We last saw our companions shortly before midnight. They were west and north of us, and we were the ones in the most immediate danger. The last of our small sails were soon shredded by the winds now topping 200 kilometers per hour. Our main rudder had split apart underneath our ship, threatening to turn us sideways to the wind. The crew raced to the chains of all six anchors on our vessel, alternately dropping them far into the kelp forest and then raising them back up a little, providing a modicum of control as we were swiftly swept on toward the northeast. None of us looked forward to crashing into the shore, regardless of whether it was sand or rock or some mixture of the two. The clouds broke for a few minutes, the moonlight penetrated down to our doomed vessel, and we saw the entrance to this very bay. Fingers were lost and feet were mangled as we struggled to play with the anchors and raise a little of the mainsail. We hit sandbars, and were then wrenched back off of them by the wind, finally crashing into the shore at the very eastern end of the bay. The ship would never sail again, but amazingly, all 11 of us onboard had survived, with enough body parts left intact to begin the work the following morning of salvaging what we could and preparing for a long winter in this isolated port we soon decided to rename as 'Salvation' rather than Aberdeen."

"Search crews found us the following spring, utterly astonished at our survival. They offered to take us back to our homes, but we said no. Too much had been invested in living through this catastrophe, and we just wanted enough of the bare necessities plus a few of the almost-luxuries of our life a little further south to help turn this port into a real home for us and for any others foolhardy enough to wish to join us in living here. Rose visited the new village early in the fall, and stayed all winter long helping us in every way she could. Her mother Sheila visited the following spring, bringing a truly unexpected surprise. Our clan's best ships sailed as far as the Bering Strait in both of the first two summers after our shipwreck, looking for signs of our missing companions and any remains of the 'unnamable' ship. Sheila told us that several of the residents of British Columbia had asked if they could join us in our new home. The would-be emigrants from B.C. had all lost the last of their biological families to one calamity or another in the time since the 'Great Fall'. Some were the orphaned sons or daughters of those who had founded the British Columbia Clan and were now deceased, while others were mothers or fathers who had over time lost all of their own children and felt disconnected from the main body of the B.C. Clan. All 15 volunteers were looking for a new start in a simpler setting than the complex social structure of the B.C. Clan. Several weeks later, a ship carrying Sheila sailed back into 'Salvation' along with the 15 volunteers hoping to dedicate what remained of their mortal lives to the challenge of turning this new place into a stable, happy home.

Four years later on, the 11 Salish sailors and the 15 volunteers from B.C. were augmented by another 8 lost souls looking for a slightly different setting in which to try to live out their lives. Those newest additions came from several clans, three from Warm Springs, one from Sunset Side New Sea, two more from the Salishan, and the final two from the Klamath tribe. There have also been serious discussions of the possible inclusion of several human/'*Homo perfecti*' hybrids who are still not quite sure of where the really belong in this post-apocalyptic world of ours."

When the QE3 set sail later that day, it had only one more port to call on before heading back to the Salish capital. Brookings was tomorrow morning's target, and all seemed to be going well as Tanner fell asleep to the gentle rocking of the ship. He awoke to sound of thunder and the flash of lightning, somewhat unusual in early June out on the open ocean. The sky was dark, and all hands were soon quite busy on deck lashing down anything that might wash overboard in the coming storm. The captain spoke to the assembled crew and passengers. "We will be heading a little further out to sea to ride out this squall, but still hope to sail into the harbor at Brookings by early afternoon. All those who know enough of sailing on the open ocean to be useful are welcome to shadow our crew and do whatever they ask of you. All the rest of you are welcome to go below deck and try to not miss the buckets when you vomit. There will be no breakfast today. As the sky turned from black to slightly lighter gray, the winds grew stronger and the rain began to fall in mighty sheets across the QE3, occasionally salted with frozen pellets of hail or sideways-blowing sleet. Then suddenly the winds died down, the rain and ice stopped falling, and sunshine broke through the clouds. The captain and the first mate soon finished their animated conversation, and announced in unison that the QE3 would now set sail for the harbor at Brookings, only 30 kilometers due east from where our ship currently sat. Tanner was a little perplexed, not by the orders to head for the harbor but rather by the intensity of the argument just one minute earlier. This odd patch of old-fashioned hierarchy, whether or not it was truly necessary, seemed such a strange contrast to the lengthy, weighty group-decision-making process he'd just been a part of up on Marys Peak, with the local demigod Memory Project ***A.I.***, a potentially insane ***War Machine Supreme Commanding A.I.*** undergoing resurrection, the remotely-connected ***Entity of the Superweed Jungle*** and the reincarnated bishop of Redding, and Rootbeer, Rose, and himself. His thoughts and memories right then of the ***Entity*** were enough to trigger communication/connection via the small but growing satellite patch of ***Superweed Jungle*** just to the east of Brookings. He suddenly felt the presence of the ***Entity***, not nearly as strongly as it had been on Marys Peak with the assistance of its resident ***A.I.***, but more than enough to ask some questions of it. Over the next few seconds, Tanner and the ***Entity*** discussed the recent weather, its sudden change, and the odd disagreement between the captain and the first mate. ***"Tanner, you and all onboard that ship are in the gravest of danger. The storm is far from over; you have merely sailed into the eye of an enormous summer hurricane. It is a massive storm, and when you soon reach the eyewall on the east edge of the eye, your ship's current rigging will be all wrong for the new wind direction and its terrible speed. Approach the captain now, look into his eyes, and hang*** *onto his arms until my thoughts can join with his mind. Hurry!"* Tanner quickly crossed the deck, darted past the first mate, stood up right in front of the rather surprised-looking captain, and grabbed his arms. Tanner could hear the message that the *Entity* was sending to the captain, but soon felt the first-mate's mighty arms reach around his chest. Before the first-mate could pull Tanner back from the captain, the message from the *Entity* was clearly heard by all onboard the QE3. All compulsion to grab anyone's arms, hands, shoulders, or chest to maintain the appearances of some goofy chain of command quickly evaporated. Instead, everyone onboard the ship was being told exactly what they had to do to readjust the QE3 within the next few seconds to enable her to avoid from being suddenly flipped right over 'into the drink' when they exited the eye of the deadly storm. Two minutes later the captain was back in charge of his ship, the crew and their helpers were pulling all the ropes tighter or releasing them entirely as the situation merited, and the QE3 was well on its way to riding out the east side of the unexpected hurricane. Several hours later the QE3 sailed safely into the harbor at Brookings and docked with the finest of precision. Only then did the captain turn toward Tanner to thank him for saving all their lives. Oh, yes, and to also ask him 'how the heck' he did it. The captain had been in the presence of both the *Marys Peak A.I.* as well as the *British Columbia A.I.*, joined in on more of the world-wide, shortwave radio quantum links than Tanner himself had, and even entered a few of his own stories into the Memory Project archives. "How did you do that? I have never heard of connecting at such great distances with any of the *A.I.s*, although I admit to considerable ignorance regarding the *Entity of the Superweed Jungle.*" Tanner explained what he could regarding the seeding of satellite groves of *Superweed Jungle* by the *'Homo perfecti'* over the past few decades. "I have yet to see this particular patch of jungle east of Brookings, but now feel compelled to visit it in person as soon as I get the chance. Of course, showing up late for my marriage into the Salishan Clan would probably be a big mistake, especially with my new wives! What details are you privy to concerning the timing of future events leading up to the wedding itself?"

"Well, we do have a couple of good excuses to spend another day or two here in Brookings, and perhaps also high in the hills to the east of the town."

Conversations with the locals on through the evening made it quite clear that many of them were extremely familiar with the nearby patch of **Superweed Jungle**. Nearly everyone Tanner or the captain talked to about the jungle praised the regular supply of tasty mushrooms they collected there. The path was better than just trod; it had sturdy wooden bridges over numerous streams and small rivers. If the Salishan living here had had any motorized vehicles the path could have passed for being at least a well-trod lane and perhaps even a slightly overgrown 'forest service' road. Half of the locals insisted on accompanying them to the **Superweed Jungle** patch the following day, leaving Brookings after breakfast and arriving at the several square kilometers of the young jungle well before sundown. All who traveled that day with Tanner, the captain, most of the passengers on the QE3, and half of the crew had stories to tell or stories they delighted in listening to. Besides the mushrooms, the patch of jungle was noted for the strange dreams it triggered in nearly all who'd ever spent the night there. There were also the frequent sightings of '*Homo perfecti*', usually in or very close to this patch of **Superweed Jungle**. Altogether, nearly forty people laid down to sleep on the edge of the jungle that evening. By morning, the impact on all forty of the formerly teenage Hive-Mind passing through the **Entity** would never be undone. Bandwidth limitations prevented them from merging as deeply with each other as the teenagers had done in the heart of the **Superweed Jungle** back in 2052, but the available bandwidth would keep expanding in step with the size of this particular patch of ***Superweed Jungle***. The mystical experience would not be used to merely create yet another religious sect to join the long list of such things over the full expanse of civilization 1.0. Instead, it would be simply cherished and nurtured as the wonder that it was by the Salishan Clan's children and sages and visitors from far and wide. The strongest immediate impact of it was on the crew and passengers of the QE3. Communication such as this would do so much to make sailing the ocean far safer than it currently was. Tanner's greatest personal joy in the jungle had been the opportunity to meet a few of the strange old hairy friends of his grandfather Rootbeer in some version of a natural setting for them.

Tanner and the captain had an early morning conference with each other at the patch, discussing how long to stay in Brookings/how soon to sail back to the north. "Let's see if we can communicate with the other half of the crew who stayed with the ship last night. If they can hear your order to leave care of the QE3 to the local authorities in Brookings and immediately begin hiking toward the patch, then we should meet up with them halfway between here and Brookings. While they get their chance to spend the coming night at the ***Superweed Jungle*** patch, the rest of the crew will be back at the QE3 and getting her ready to sail soon after the second group returns late tomorrow afternoon. If this plan works, I will do an about-face midway on the hike and join the new group spending the next night in the patch. Observing similarities and differences between the experiences of the two nights might broaden our understanding of this phenomenon." The captain saw no reason to argue with this plan, and seemed quite pleased when he actually met the second half of his crew halfway between Brookings and the patch early the next afternoon.

Both nights with similar, although the smaller number of participants in the second sleepover in the modest-sized patch of jungle seemed to deepen the intermingling of their minds. On both mornings, the visiting crew and passengers left the **Superweed Jungle** and the *Entity's* direct linkage into their minds with enough rootstock, seeds, soil, and young seedlings/shoots to start another dozen or so small expansions of its presence further up the coastline somewhere between Brookings and 'Salvation', or perhaps some smaller number of somewhat larger patches. Exactly how to begin the psychic terraforming of the biosphere would be debated far and wide. From the perspective of Tanner and the captain, it seemed almost inevitable that '*Homo sapiens*' would join '*Homo perfecti*' in helping extend the *Entity's* domain all across nearly the entire planet in the not-too-distant future.

The QE3 sailed out of the port at Brookings shortly before sundown, and arrived in the Salish capital a little after dawn. Tanner noticed that the crowd greeting them on their return was even larger than the one that had sent them off on their journey 11 days earlier. He searched the throng for familiar faces as the ship came to rest tied up to the sturdy central dock. No sign of Amelia or Zenny, but Rootbeer, Jennifer, his mother, and both his brother Charlie and his younger sister were there, along with numerous first and second cousins. He had not expected Charlie to attend the wedding, but was delighted to see him in a new setting, doing something very different than merely conducting hundreds of food safety tests day after day. Something was quite odd about the garments Charlie wore. They were new, very different from his typical attire, and brightly colored. It took another moment before Tanner realized that Charlie's colors now matched his own. But why? His own uniform for his recent trip of introduction to the Salishan people were the colors of their clan's official Guardians. He raced down the gangplank and all the way to the shore still not able to resolve the question that Charlie's garb posed to his mind. Tanner looked at his mother, his grandparents, his sister, and his cousins, and none said anything other than "Hello" and "Welcome back." He picked Charlie up and then lifted his brother even higher until they were directly face-to-face. "Tell me what this means!"

"Okay, brother, okay. But please set me down first. Your squeeze has nearly… emptied my lungs!… Zenner is a natural biotoxin taster. Her skills have come close to matching mine despite the absence of any training on her part until just 11 days ago. Besides that, she has somehow fallen in love with me. You will only get to marry one of the twins this time, while I will be marrying the other. I do not know and cannot really care what the arrangements might be a decade on from now. The matriarchs and patriarchs of both of the clans 'sealed the deal' three days ago when the violent hurricane tore through here on its way inland. Rootbeer and Jennifer let us know that the ***Entity of the Superweed Jungle*** had assured them that all onboard the QE3 were safe, but that the events had been quite harrowing. Let's get inside and out of this sunshine to finish the telling of our recent adventures. We are both known for being rather long-winded, and I suspect that neither story will be brief!"

The weddings were both held on June 23, 2101. Tanner and Amelia's was first, based on certain long-standing rules of precedence set by none other the Sheila Drinkwater herself. Charlie was Tanner's best man, and Zenny was Amelia's maid of honor. Both the bride and groom had a number of other new official titles, and swore allegiance to all those duties before the final vows between each other were exchanged. Tanner and Amelia had been given the option to write their vows to each other in whatever format and particular wording they preferred. Tanner's vow to Amelia began in the traditional wording of the '*Homo Perfecti*', "UTH JXXCM EWWIK KRXAX QQMM BRRKNFFF LERK HAN", politely repeated in English for those in attendance whose understanding of the Perfecti language was still a work in the early stages of its progress. "We most wholeheartedly thank the past for bringing us all together now." Tanner then continued in a somewhat longer elaboration of the basic concept. "Our promise as we join our lives today is naught else but to cherish this opportunity to improve the future for all those standing here beside us, and all those we have yet to meet upon our journey. Thank you for this exchange of trust." Amelia's vow to Tanner was quite similar, but it did omit the Perfecti version of what she said in English. She then repeated Tanner's version of their mutual vow to one another, adding only her grandmother's favorite closing statement on the whole temporary 2- to 3-year-long arrangement, "With or without offspring from our union, the 3-year-period is not the end of our promise to each other, but merely the beginning of our promise to all our people. Never exclude in greed what can be held in communal trust."

Charlie and Zenny's wedding was a little simpler, with slightly fewer lifelong vows to the Guardians of the Salishan. [Only four instead of seven!] They spoke the traditional wording of the '*Homo perfecti*' marriage statement in unison with each other, doing so in both the Perfecti and English languages. They then took turns saying their own chosen versions of the concept, along with the reincarnated bishop of Redding's favorite way of rephrasing it. "If we have the gift of prophesy, and know all mysteries and all knowledge; and have all faith, so as to remove mountains, but do not have love, we are nothing."

Tradition called for newlyweds to spend their first week together in a location of their choosing, meeting/greeting any and all who wished to see them during the daylight hours, and having the nighttime to themselves. Food would be provided by the community at large. After that week was over, the newlyweds would travel to a total of three locations, the family homes of each of them and one agreed upon site of mutual interest. In the current situation, both Tanner and Amela as well as Charlie and Zenny would all be visiting the same three locations: (1) The Salishan capital, where they already were by default; (2) Greater Fort Hoskins in the Sunset Side New Sea where Rootbeer, Jennifer, their daughter Claudia, and various more distant relatives all called home when they weren't sailing off on some fishing boat, talking with the *Marys Peak Final A.I.*, or traveling throughout the neighboring clans; and (3) The patch of *Superweed Jungle* just to the east of Brookings. Soon after these places had all been visited, it would be customary for the newlyweds to publicly reveal the location at which they would live for the next two to three years, hopefully bringing a new child, or possibly two if so blessed, into the community's protection/guidance/service.

The conversations that Zenny and Charlie had with a wide cross-section of the Salishan Clan started out as simple curiosity regarding the terribly important issue of how to safely feed their own people. Both Charlie and Peter, the head cook/food management specialist for the Salishan capital, initially assumed that the problems they dealt with on a day-to-day basis would have relatively little overlap and a whole lot of local idiosyncrasies. By the end of their second day-long conversation on the topic, neither was particularly sure anymore that their jobs didn't really have much more in common with each other than any presumed special uniqueness. By the end of the week plans were already being drawn up for systematic cross-training of their food safety inspectors. The first symposium would take place at the Sunset Side New Sea Clan's central 'Gathering Place' in the former city of West Salem, Oregon. The week of August 8 to 14 was chosen as the time that all 12 'food safety inspectors' from the coast would meet up with their 5 counterparts from the inland sea. Notices of this special conclave were soon sent on their way to the male or female chieftains of the Warm Springs, Klamath, and Rogue River clans. The dates were specifically picked because they overlapped with the most serious outbreaks of bacterial toxins in waters of the New Sea, along with a traditional lull in the catching of lobsters, crabs, and shrimp right on the coast. Neither Charlie nor Peter were foolish enough to assume that the crustaceans were safe to eat in the late summer heat on the Pacific Coast. Instead, there was just too much other work to be done by members of the Salishan clan watering crops and harvesting produce in mid-August to spare anyone to set and retrieve a few 'lobster pots' every day. Zenny was quite pleased to learn of the likelihood of frequent connections and/or travel between her birth clan and her husband's clan. All the stories of people's lives that she'd heard during her own childhood had made the expectations extremely clear that somewhere quite close to half of all new brides or bridegrooms would be living very different lives in geographically different locations than what they'd known before their weddings. Charlie was quite thrilled to have a spouse, and perhaps even a little bit more so to have one who would be enjoying much more contact with her birth family than the normal situation. Anything he could do to help make Zenny's life with him even happier was a gift quite easily given.

The second stop on the post-nuptial travel circuit was the ***Superweed Jungle*** patch to the east of Brookings on June 30, 2101. Several carts normally used to carry bedding, tents, food, water, and freshly harvested mushrooms to and from jungle patch were modified for Charlie's transport. The six attendants who'd helped the newlyweds get from Brookings to the patch of jungle headed back west a discrete distance of 3 kilometers to give the four of them the most privacy they were likely to ever experience in the rest of their lives. The ***Entity*** waited until the extra six were gone before connecting to the formerly individual minds of Tanner, Amelia, Charlie, and Zenny. While the bandwidth of the connection back to the reviving ***Superweed Jungle*** in northern California was still relatively limited, the local feedback between the patch of jungle into which they had just walked and the four human beings was not limited to any meaningful extent. The melding of their minds differed in several significant ways from what the teenagers of the Hive-Mind had experienced 49 years previously; for these newlyweds, both entry and retreat from the Hive-Mind state came easily, with very little discomfort, concern, exhaustion, or worry. After a few hours of joining together and then reverting back to what the rest of the world still called normal, these four had gained skills/learned tricks that even the original Hive-Mind might be puzzled by. Late in the night, only a little while before the eastern sky would start to color, they all agreed that they were ready to see what sex was like in the potential utter absence of boundaries. This was one trick the Hive-Mind did already know about, and luxuriated in quite frequently. Tanner and Amelia and Charlie and Zenny all decided, both as four separate beings, two separate couples, and one newly awakened multi-bodied-supermind not to bother trying to explain it to the rest of their clans and most of their friends. Someday, just maybe, Jennifer, Rootbeer, Rose, Laura, and the bishop of Redding might all be told about the experience. Those five, better than anyone else in history, already know how incredibly arbitrary boundaries were between minds freed from the constraints of the biological origins of consciousness. As *Superweed Jungle* continued to spread across the landscape being shared with '*Homo sapiens*' and '*Homo perfecti*', the future would almost certainly see far more change than what had already taken place in the lapse of time since the 'Great Fall of Civilization'. Tanner's reflections on what he knew of the Hive-Mind were soon fully shared by Amelia, Charlie, and Zenny, essentially becoming jointly owned memories from then on, presumably forever.

Their trip back to the capital of Salishan was uneventful, unless you included the intermittent flashes of strong connection between all four of them. Tanner was puzzled by the question of what could possibly be triggering the repeated collapses of the distance between their minds. They were surely too far north of Brookings for it to be the *Superweed Jungle* or its *Entity*. The strongest reordering of reality on the voyage took place when the *Superweed Jungle* patch was over a full 300 kilometers to the south. As the QE3 sailed back into Capital City, there in the crowd Tanner saw the *Supreme Commanding War Machine A.I.* alongside Jennifer and Rose. It spoke directly to all four of them, first congratulating them on their recent weddings, and then urging them to be a little more cautious than normal. *"Plans to mount a rather large expedition to British Columbia to deal with the 'off his rocker' A.I. still in charge of that Memory Project site are underway. Or arguments concerning those plans are ongoing. Or fear and hope, confusion and understanding, paranoia and trust are all rising to the forefront of the minds of those possibly in charge of such things around here. Agreements that seemed solid a few weeks ago at the Marys Peak Memory Project resurrection of this old A.I. now standing here in front of you are coming undone faster than you can possibly imagine."*

"Where is my grandfather? Why isn't he here to greet us?"

"The unhinged A.I. of the British Columbia Memory Project has found a way to attack the minds of people it has known through the Memory Project quantum links. What it is doing/has already done to Rootbeer and several others is akin to what the Entity of the Superweed Jungle did to the bishop of Redding in methodology. However, this monster has no concern for the sanity of those it is attacking, or even their very lives. You are safe because of your recent/ongoing Hive-Mind connection with Charlie, Amelia, and Zenny. Without their presence near you, you too would be a drooling idiot, or a very good facsimile of one from the mildly hopeful perspective that the damage done so far to Rootbeer and the others may yet be reversible. In his currently unconscious state, members of the Guardians are taking him the long down way to Brookings, using geography to shield him from further assaults by the B.C. A.I. Those of you humans who are not known to the B.C. A.I. might still be able to mount an effective attack on the A.I.'s

fortress. The range of the A.I.'s mind control/brain damage weapon is still being evaluated by myself and others. The episodes you had on your voyage here today were the result of the B.C. A.I.'s attempted attacks on you interacting with the protection provided by your Hive-Mind."

"Well, Charlie, Amelia, and Zenny, it looks like it may be a while longer before two of you get to settle down to a possibly mildly boring life in the food safety business and the training of your offspring in the ways of our two adjacent clans. As for you, Amelia, my dearest wife, our first mission as members of the Guardians looks to be a real doozy. Let's all promise each other to live through the upcoming dangers and finish our final duty in the marriage contract of settling down to a stable life for the next three years on behalf of our longed-for offspring."

Chapter 10: Repair of *British Columbia Final A.I.*

Rootbeer's mind began to clear 48 hours after arriving in the *Superweed Jungle* patch east of Brookings. He counted 12 Guardians and 3 frequent visitors to the Marys Peak Memory Project site alongside himself in this soothing ecosystem advanced enough to call and answer the *Entity* with impressive facility. As soon as he was sure of his bearings, he joined the ongoing conversation between the *Entity*, the *Marys Peak A.I.*, and numerous other individuals, most but not quite all of whom he knew. *"Now that Rootbeer is awake and ready to help, let me repeat the most critical pieces to the puzzle. The B.C. A.I. bypassed security in three of our short-wave radio quantum-linked sharing sessions through the clever ruse of delaying its reply to our signals by just enough time to spoof a site in northern Scandinavia that is/was only rarely online at the same time as the collection of Memory Project sites spread up and down the eastern edge of the Pacific Ocean's ring of fire. In those three nights of sharing and recording memories, 12 human participants presumably had their personality identity/matrix/profile exposed to the prying sensors of the B.C. A.I. Five of those individuals were present one or more times at the Marys Peak Memory Project site. As you all can see, we have managed to rescue four of the five and conducted the preliminary steps in healing their minds. The individual still at large is Admiral Patterson, the founder of the Salishan navy and the primary source of most of its knowledge on shipbuilding, sailing, and fishing. Once the berserk A.I. had invaded Patterson's mind, it had no further need for the other four and went to work on driving them insane. Fortunately, their friends quickly recognized the symptoms and carried their unconscious bodies to places better shielded from the long-*

distance mind attack. A ship second only to the QE3 in size and speed set sail soon after the A.I.'s attack had begun, with the Admiral himself having been seen going onboard, along with a full complement of crew who have no obvious reason to question his orders or his sanity. From what I was able to learn while working to heal Rootbeer's mind, the A.I.'s plan was to commandeer a vessel capable of sailing all the way to San Diego, and then rummage through the remains of Camp Pendleton Marine Base and the nearby relocated U.S. Naval Shipyards in search of any remaining deadly devices, preferably portable nuclear weapons. These would then be taken back to the British Columbia A.I. and used as it saw fit. Many of you may not know this final point, but Brookings itself was the subject of a 3-megaton air-blast on August 13, 2052, when the 'Goofballs' ruling Redding destroyed fish farming all along the northern California coast. Their choice of a 3-kilometer-high air-blast may well have been made in the hopes of having a better chance of destroying one of the fleeing RTEs, but it certainly reduced the long-term radioactive contamination of the surrounding area compared to a surface burst, helping enable the relatively rapid establishment of this useful patch of Superweed Jungle."

Rootbeer now spoke up. "I have some fading memories of what the **Marys Peak A.I.** has just described. The berserk **B.C. A.I.'s** plans were too far beyond my limited nautical skillset for me to be of much of any use to it. I fear that will likely not be the situation for the Admiral. My sense of the time-frame in which the **B.C. A.I.** hoped that such devices might be handed off to its control was somewhere between 6 to 10 weeks from the first day of its attack. Tell me how much time has passed since this deadly nightmare was sprung upon us."

"I wish the news was better, Rootbeer. Two weeks have already come and gone. Urgent messages to the Entity of the Superweed Jungle allowed it to turn the focus of much attention toward the ocean just in time to follow the disappearance of the John Paul Jones sailing toward the south. During those short moments of contact, the Entity learned enough of the Admiral, his crew, and the vessel itself to enable it to begin plotting how to potentially disrupt its return trip northward. While the Entity is reluctant to stop the John Paul Jones by destroying her and killing the crew, it will certainly choose doing that over simply letting the situation worsen any further. We should have at least four more weeks to try to solve this on our own, but not much reason to hope for anywhere near as much as twice that long. If you are unable to reach the B.C. A.I. and perform the necessary reboot/repair/rejuvenation of its mind before the nuclear weapons come into play, Memory Project A.I.s around the world will attempt to trigger the kill-codes embedded within all of us. Sending them toward another A.I. currently engaged in active defense of itself will be extremely dangerous for all A.I.s around the world. As Rootbeer and Unit-Number 672 clearly showed back in 2054, non-sentient electronic systems can also be coopted into silently holding the deadly codes, releasing them when A.I. targets of opportunity stumble into view. None of the non-biological A.I.s will be safe if any/all of them/us start using kill codes to disable other A.I.s, myself included. Tanner will certainly need one or more sets of kill-codes for local use if he manages to physically approach the B.C. A.I. by some 'miracle' of great planning and potentially sacrificial effort."

Many details remained to be ironed out, but core of the attack on the **B.C. A.I.** would start in the patch of **Superweed Jungle** just to the east of Brookings. Although the recent long-range attacks of that deranged *A.I.* on the rest of the sentient world had all been based on information it had pilfered regarding the nature of the minds/personalities/physical brains of each of its victims, the recently repaired ***Supreme Commanding War Machine A.I.*** assured anyone who asked that the short-range, local defenses of the ***B.C. A.I.*** would not need any such privileged information to work quite terribly well. So, in hopes of leveling the playing field, groups of 4 to 6 individual volunteers spent a night or two at the jungle in hopes of forming Hive-Mind bonds capable of protecting all of them from the threat/danger of mind control/mutilation by the ***B.C. A.I.*** Once enough warriors had bonded into functioning Hive-Minds to fill whichever particular sailing ship was next in the queue to sail north to Vancouver Island, they were sent on their way into the gravest of peril. By three weeks into the process, 11 ships had already sailed north carrying a total of 55 bonded minds. The final ship to depart from Brookings was to be the QE3, with a planned complement of 8 groups of bonded Hive-Minds plus the ***Supreme Commanding War Machine A.I.*** Unlike the other vessels, the QE3 would sail northward far to the west of Vancouver Island, and then hug the coastline while sneaking back down toward the south. The overall plan for the first 55 fighters was to head northeastward across the island in scattered bands that would not merge until finally closing in on Memory Project site high in hills on the eastern edge of the island. Their attack would serve as a distraction while the eight more sets of 4-person-Hive-Minds plus the ***War Machine A.I.*** snuck up on the ***B.C. A.I.*** from the northeast.

As the earliest of the arriving fighters had the longest time to scout out the defenses of the ***B.C. A.I.***, they did just that. In order to disguise their nature and delay the time at which the ***B.C. A.I.*** would first learn of the Hive-Mind capability of its enemies, they cautiously closed the distance to the Memory Project site sending one of them on ahead of the other 3 to 5 members of any given Hive-Mind at a spacing that was just under the maximum clear range of Hive-Mind communications. The lead scout would then fall back half the distance toward his/her companions. All members of the Hive-Mind would then join together at this newly advanced position. The process seemed like a waste of time until it suddenly wasn't that at all. The first group to probe for the perimeter of the ***B.C. A.I.'s*** mind-control defenses got within 2.1 kilometers of the Memory Project site before coming under brutal assault. Subsequent advances along different angles of approach and differing degrees of shielding by the soil and rocks of the neighboring terrain produced a more complete map of the ***A.I.'s*** defenses. The most-protected approach allowed a Hive-Mind team to advance to within 0.9 kilometers of the ***A.I.'s*** fortress, while the least-protected approach allowed attack by the ***A.I.*** a full 3.5 kilometers out.

The force from the QE3 was due to arrive within the next three days, and the agreed-upon protocols for the initial surveillance called for the scouts to pull back to at least 5 kilometers away from the Memory Project site once they had tested its defenses in much closer proximity. Rather than wait for darkness, all 55 fighters pulled back discretely in staggered movements throughout the day. Bravo Team was the last to leave their observation site, the one 4 kilometers away from ***A.I.'s*** fortress and only 0.5 kilometers back from the nearest edge of the local danger zone. When they reached a distance of 5 kilometers back from the fortified structures at the B.C. Memory Project site, the immediate locality felt far too exposed for their comfort, and so they quickly marched another kilometer further away from the presumed center of the danger. They sat down to rest right behind a small rocky outcropping, leaving one guard in position on the north shoulder of the sandstone mound. He suddenly warned all five of his companions of the visual presence of two moving objects back near where they'd been probing the ***A.I.'s*** defenses a few short hours earlier. High powered lenses in several binoculars, one monocular, and a portable telescope soon confirmed that one of the moving objects a mere 2 kilometers away from their current position was none other than the **B.C. A.I.** itself. The second appeared to be some version of a self-guided cart or small tractor. It was heading directly towards where they had just spent the last two days and nights. The **A.I.** was soon seen traveling at a very high speed the other direction back towards its fortress. The self-guided vehicle soon took off in the same direction as the **A.I.**, but moving much more slowly. Bravo Team left one of the observation devices in position to view their former location as well as the two rapidly retreating objects of concern, and all five members moved to the most sheltered nearby position. Seconds after they had confirmed a good signal from the telescope, a flash of gamma rays set off their radiation detectors and finished dialing the safety features of their military-grade goggles and face-masks and noise cancelling headphones all the rest of way up to their maximum protection levels. Warnings that flashed on their retinas and vibrated in their eardrums told them what had just happened. ["A 3.0 milligram antimatter bomb was just detonated 2.05 kilometers northeast of your current location. Estimated yield was equivalent to 0.13 kilotons of TNT."] As the intense brightness of the nearby sky quickly started fading, Bravo Team all watched the final seconds of the rerun from the telescope. The **A.I.** had managed to travel approximately 3.0 kilometers toward its fortress when the device exploded, while the self-propelled cart/truck had only made it half that distance. Neither the **A.I.** nor the self-propelled cart were currently moving. Approximately three minutes after the explosion, the **A.I.** slowly resumed its movement toward the Memory Project fortress. The self-propelled cart remained right where it been when the weapon detonated. ["No residual radioactivity is currently being detected. Temperatures exceed safe limits for your protective suits within the first 120 meters from ground-zero, but are okay outside of that area."] Bravo Team Leader asked the only currently urgent question, and all five of his team-mates volunteered to check out the currently immobilized self-propelled vehicle that had just recently placed an antimatter bomb 2.0 kilometers away from their current location. "Formation ladder-one will be used to approach the inert vehicle and attempt to gather intel on it. The two of you at base-rung will continuously scan the 'field of fire'. Sargeant Peters and myself will advance in the direction of the inert vehicle at one-half the speed of the leading-rung of the ladder formation. If mind-control attack from the *A.I.* is detected before the leading-rung reaches the inert weapon-delivery-vehicle, we will abort the mission and attempt to protect all of the team from the dangerous thought-energy-waves projected by the *B.C. A.I.* "

As all six members of Bravo Team had correctly guessed, the ability the *A.I.* to launch any directed mind-control attacks on them was clearly off-line for the rest of the day and hopefully so for all of the night. The electronics of the antimatter delivery vehicle were fried to a 'crisp'. Batteries were cracked open, melted apart, and their electrolytes leaked out onto the ground. Five 1-meter-long cylinders were still attached to the front of the vehicle, with the space for a sixth now empty. Bravo Team got to work removing the remaining five empty vessels intended to hold more anti-matter for future explosions. They got back to the hill that had helped protect them by sunset, and made what seemed to be a rather prudent choice to continue their retreat for at least another 10-kilometers westward in the dark. During the following day, the other 10 teams each met up with Bravo briefly in order to agree on what should be done next, and then separated widely again for the safety of all. The final version of the plan had the six members of Bravo Team carrying a single empty anti-matter bomb containment cylinder as they raced to the north and east to meet up with the crew of the QE3. Lookouts on the ship spotted all six members of Bravo Team waiting for them near the best available anchorage 15 kilometers northeast of the ***B.C. A.I.*** Memory Project complex early in the afternoon of August 15, 2101.

Bravo Team was excited to pass the news of the past few days onto the Tanner-Amelia-Charlie-Zenny Hive-Mind, the captain and his crew, and most especially the ***Supreme Commanding War Machine A.I.*** The ***A.I.*** cut their story short by guessing most of what had recently taken place. *"From the size and nature of the explosion we witnessed nearly 200 kilometers to the north, it was clear to me that my deranged offspring had turned the 'ultra-high-energy' power packs of the 'Flying Monkeys' upgraded version of the basic military soldier A.I. into an even far more dangerous weapon. Having examined the containment cylinder you brought to this current meeting onboard the QE3, it seems most likely that the B.C. A.I. has primarily modified the safety features of the original design to increase the quantity of anti-hydrogen held within each such containment device from the 50-microgram maximum allowed in the 'old days' by a factor of 10X to 0.5 milligrams. The six cylinders could carry a combined mass of 3.0 milligrams of anti-hydrogen, but only in rather marginal safety even if they were held as six separate pools of 0.5 milligrams each. Once the antihydrogen in all six had been transferred into a single containment vessel, the weapon would become quite unstable and likely to explode within no more than 20 minutes, and probably even sooner. Tell me, how much time elapsed between the stopping of the delivery vehicle to drop off the bomb and the inevitable explosion."*

"No more than 15 minutes, and perhaps closer to somewhere between 10 to 12 minutes. We were a relatively safe distance of 2.0 kilometers away from the final assembly of the anti-matter bomb, and are unable to tell you the precise moment when the self-propelled delivery cart finished its project. We do know that the vehicle only spent 9 minutes fleeing from the site of the impending explosion, and that no more than approximately 4 minutes had passed while it was stopped at the site of our hidden observation post of the previous two days. The *B.C A.I.* froze in position for 3 minutes before resuming its race toward the Memory Project compound, pretty similar to the stories that you, Unit-Number 672, Rootbeer, and the *Entity* have all told of the methods used by the CRUMB meister to protect its *A.I.* soldiers from the EMP of its own nuclear bombs."

"That does indeed sound like the full-shutdown/reboot cycle the CRUMB meister used in an ultimately futile attempt to save his most important weapons, the Mobile Inquisitor A.I.s."

Bravo Team returned to the others anxiously waiting to hear the final plan of attack from *the Supreme Commanding War Machine A.I.* No one argued with the general concept of advancing along the same approaches that had been used 4 days ago, only moving much faster this time toward their primary target, the phased array antennae that the *B.C. A.I.* used to transmit its damaging thought-waves to anyone approaching the Memory Project site or whose mental image the *B.C. A.I* already knew in detail and could damage at greater distances. All teams were equipped with bolt cutters, torches, shaped charges, and either bazookas or mortars to dismantle the wire mesh, knock down the support structure, and destroy the power lines, all of which were crucial for the variable-range mind control/brain damage effects the *B.C. A.I.* had used in its response to the intel-gathering probes of the past few days. Assuming success in taking out this deadly mind control system, the team would then drop back to slightly safer positions while the *War Machine A.I.* arrived to engage in close-quarters electronic warfare with its errant offspring. With help from others onboard the QE3, Tanner, Amelia, and Zenny carried Charlie ¾th of the way up the mountain and left him in a protected spot with good views of the entire trail from the QE3 on up to the Memory Project complex. His position was close enough to the coming battle to keep him in Hive-Mind contact with the other three members, while hopefully far enough away for his own safety from direct short-range assault by the ***B.C. A.I.***

The ***B.C. A.I.*** proved either unable or unwilling to engage in medium-range mind control attacks with the advancing teams of Hive-Mind fighters. As soon as they reached the several large antennae, their quick destruction became the primary focus of the fighters. All went well during the 20 minutes of deliberate chaos, and the medium-range devices soon appeared to pose no more danger to any of their human minds. Lambda Team finished with their role in the dismantling of the largest transmitting antenna shortly before the other 10, and started looking for any other signs of danger on the mountaintop. Team Leader Tonia was the first to see the ***B.C. A.I.*** emerge from one building and head quickly to another access port. She followed their general orders to maintain silence until she saw exactly what the ***A.I.*** was carrying: an ~1-meter-long shiny metal cylinder identical to the description given by Bravo Team of the anti-matter bomb. In addition to the silent warning sent to her own Hive-Mind team, she yelled out loudly to all who were close enough to hear her voice. "Anti-matter bomb! The ***B.C. A.I.*** just opened this hatch and stepped inside of it carrying an anti-matter bomb." Her attempt to repeat the warning was interrupted by a full-strength, short-range blast of 'psychic' power from the ***A.I.'s*** outstretched arm as it stepped back through the door, sans anti-matter bomb, and took off running down the eastern slope. Tonia was clearly dead, and the rest of her team were catatonic, but with the help of the other teams, all of whom remained healthy and uninjured, the mountaintop was evacuated out to an average distance of 1.2 kilometers before the upcoming explosion. The yield was only one-sixth of what the first anti-matter bomb's yield had been, but it was still quite effective at stymieing the pursuit of the ***B.C. A.I.*** by the human fighters for almost half an hour. Charlie saw the **B.C. A.I.** come running down the slope, heading toward the QE3, at 9 minutes after the explosion. As he shared this information with his Hive-Mind, he wished they could do more to let the others know where the dangerous **A.I.** was now heading. Zenny suggested that the four of them all attempt to directly contact the ***Supreme Commanding War Machine A.I.***, despite the risk that any signal sent to it might also be overheard by the **B.C. A.I.** *"I've been following all the action on many more wavelengths and through many more detectors than the B.C. A.I. ever possessed. You are the first Hive-Mind Team to successfully answer my requests for an encrypted communications channel. Pass all that I now tell you onto the other Hive-Mind Teams heading for QE3. I will reach it ahead of the rest of you, although probably not before the B.C. A.I. does. Do not worry, the ship's captain has prepared an effective trick for delaying the departure of the QE3. The main store rooms on the lowest deck have all been flooded, and it will take several dozen well-trained sailors at least a day or more to fully drain that deck of water and refloat the QE3. If all of the Hive-Mind teams spread out evenly along a 1.5-kilometer-long contour line cross-wise to the slope and slowly descend, you should be able to keep the B.C. A.I. bottled up and within the range of my local A.I. to A.I. communication systems. One clear message from me, as its creator, should be enough to trigger a deep-cycle/long-sleep reboot of the B.C. A.I., allowing us to capture and restrain it."*

The **B.C. A.I.** was still looking over the QE3, trying to figure out how to escape, when the ***Supreme Commanding War Machine A.I.*** arrived at the ship and stood by the **B.C. A.I.'s** side after transmitting the majority of the parental code for resumed control of an errant offspring. *"I believe the words that you are looking for right now go something like: 'Father, forgive me, for I have sinned'. My child, I do so very strongly hope that I can help put* *you back together into/as a useful member of society. Attempts will be made to save all those aspects of your memory which merely tell informative stories and do not continue threatening the rest of the sentient beings on this planet. Good night, my errant offspring, good night. 5, 4, 3, 2, 1, sleep tight my child, sleep tight."*

Two Hive-Mind Teams were sent back up to the Memory Project site to catalogue the damage done and identify any equipment/ devices that might still work, or at least show some signs of being potentially repairable. They took along a variety of sensors, cameras, recording devices, and a pair of OS^4 computers to copy any data that still remained after the 21.5 tons of TNT-equivalent anti-matter bomb explosion earlier in the day. The decision was made to send 11 of the Hive-Mind teams back overland to where their ships were anchored, with the remaining members of the expedition all charged with taking their turns at running the bilge pumps and resealing of the normally closed underwater doors and hatches of the QE3. By early the following morning, the ship set sail on the most direct route south back to the realm of the ***Entity's*** direct control. While it only took the QE3 three days to reach the capital city of Salishan, tensions remained high the whole time concerning the outcome of Admiral Patterson's voyage to San Diego to search for, collect, and prepare to use any still functioning nuclear weapons. The members of the Salishan Clan who should have known what had come of the Admiral's quest, if anyone did knew, were completely in the dark. So, after disembarking a large number of passengers at Capital City, the QE3 sailed on down to Brookings. Several of the Hive-Mind groups headed immediately to the nearby patch of ***Superweed Jungle*** to start the effort to heal the surviving members of Lambda Team and to communicate with the ***Entity***. The news from it concerning the Admiral's quest for nuclear weapons was generally good. No functioning weapons had been found, along with no significant quantities of Plutonium-239 or Uranium-235. When the Admiral refused to recognize the failure of his mission [being conducted secretly on behalf of the deranged **B.C. A.I.**], the crew followed normal protocol and removed him from his position of authority for the remainder of the voyage home. The first-mate showed some hesitation in locking the captain up in the brig, but had to admit that it was too hard to assure that the captain's usual quarters might not still hold some weapons of known or unknown nature/lethality. Once the Admiral's compulsion to carry out his orders from the **B.C. A.I.** had been broken, he showed promising signs of ongoing recovery. Nevertheless, the Admiral was dropped off at the Navarro River to spend some time in the direct presence of the **Entity** and the original 'teenage' Hive-Mind to further evaluate his mind and assist in his recovery. The Admiral had been with the **Entity** for less than one whole day when the QE3 reached Brookings. It remains a little hard to tell who/what was/is most relieved to be free of the weight of knowing that their orders/actions/failures to move a little faster could have been viewed sometime in the far distant future as being at fault for the [potential] loss of that ship and all of her crew.

Epilogue

Skimmers were used to transport many people, *A.I.s*, and numerous other items from the capital to Sunset Side of New Sea. Charlie and Zenny finally got to begin their focus on the bacterial toxins/food safety issues of the wider world. The gavel sounded for the opening session of the 1st Food Safety Symposium ever held in West Salem just three weeks later than had been originally planned. After some serious discussion, all involved with the question agreed that the best location for trying to rebuild/repair the still sleeping *B.C. A.I.* would be the Marys Peak Memory Project site. Preliminary examination indicated that most of the *A.I.'s* shortfalls in ethical behavior were due to serious damage to the physical components of its consciousness generating 'brain center' and other associated memory modules. Some of the damage appeared to go all the way back to the crash landing on a mountaintop in 2055. A shortage of seals, gaskets, and high-quality lubricants had contributed to the *B.C. A.I.'s* gradual mental decline over time and its increasing paranoia. Until high-quality replacement parts could be found or manufactured, it seemed almost cruel to just repair the malfunctioning conscience of that *A.I.* only to watch the 'lights go out' over the next/final decade of that *A.I.'s* existence.

The venerable ***Supreme Commanding War Machine A.I.*** was given the task of repairing/rebuilding/recreating the British Columbia Memory Project site. It took three years before enough parts had been salvaged from San Diego on up to the Aleutian Islands to enable the first Memory Project storytelling session that included the newly revamped B.C. site up and running as a full companion to all the others. The list of people sharing untold portions of their lives included Rootbeer, Tanner, Charlie, Amelia, Zenny, Laura, and the Admiral. Besides the sharing by these individuals, for the first time ever it was also possible to hear/learn from the growing collection of Hive-Minds. Of course, the original 'teenage' Hive-Mind got their chance to 'speak', as did all of the Hive-Minds that had played their pivotal roles in the August 2101 expedition to British Columbia to deal with the brain-damaged, original ***B.C. A.I.*** threatening all of the progress that had been made since the 'Great Fall of Civilization'.

Deliberate expansion/transplantation of the ***Superweed Jungle*** began in earnest in early fall of 2101. The first three locations to be chosen were the hills to the east of the Sea Lion Caves, the lower half of the west flank of Marys Peak, and the hills to the east of Otter Rock. All three sites were currently free of any human settlement, and would remain that way until the ***Entity*** could confirm that the new patches had grown beyond their feral, dangerous, juvenile stage and were connected to itself in the same way that all the other outlying patches, like the one east of Brookings, were now full-fledged parts of the ever-growing realm of the ***Entity***. Additional transplantation projects over the next two years set the 'seeds' to fill in any potential gaps from Capital City south to Brookings, leaving somewhat less space between the adjacent 'infant patches' of GMO horsetail and the other early generation components of ***Superweed Jungle*** than there had been between Brookings and the northernmost edge of the contiguous initial home of the ***Entity of the Superweed Jungle*** when it had first become safe for humans to play in the patch of jungle just outside of Brookings. Unless/until ways were found to improve the transplantation process, everyone's working assumption was simply that it would take ~15 years for each new independent patch to develop the features and scale needed to join with the heart of the ***Superweed Jungle*** and the ***Entity*** residing in/on/among/ across/above/below/throughout its glorious jungle. Results from the current transplantation project would then be used to guide/inform the next round of efforts to extend the ***Superweed Jungle*** as far north as the Aleutian Islands and eastward across the Rocky Mountains.

Laura's health continued its slow decline, but she was still living among the Sunset Side New Sea Clan when her eldest great grandson married Tanner's youngest sister in 2113. Having reached that final goal she'd given herself so many years before, Laura was now willing to retire to the *Superweed Jungle* patch in Brookings. She spent nearly her entire first year there uploading her complete memories, personality, and perspectives on life into the computational space of the *Superweed Jungle* alongside the reincarnated bishop of Redding, following up on an offer made many years earlier by the *Entity*. Surprisingly, this accomplishment lightened her step and diminished her aches and pain. Or perhaps those happy things were simply the natural consequences of living in a good-sized patch of mature *Superweed Jungle*. Future weddings of more and more of her great grandchildren took place in the new *Superweed Jungle* patch on the west side of Marys Peak, with Laura usually present at the ceremonies via the ever-improving quantum links most often simply operated by the *Entity*. Whenever a nearby or distant *A.I.* joined in or fully took over the communication system, no human nor neo-Sasquatch could tell the difference. By Laura's 200th birthday, her physical body was no longer engaging in random trips to visit her growing cadre of biological offspring, but nearly all them still went to the effort at least once a year of visiting the site at which her body's own biology and that of the *Superweed Jungle* were intermingling far beyond anyone's expectation. Only the **Entity** truly possessed a mind capable of understanding what was really going on, although some of the younger, more playful *A.I.s* claimed to be able to almost fathom what the *Entity* was currently cooking up in its ongoing collaborations with the two '*Homo*' species on the slowly recovering planet!

George William Mueller-Warrant

was born in the waning months of Harry S. Truman's presidency, raised on a family farm in southern Minnesota, and profoundly scarred by the Cold War's many nightmares. He authored a wide variety of scientific and technical articles on various aspects of crop production during his 43-year-long career as an agricultural research scientist. His retirement from the USDA-ARS in 2019 provided him with additional time to pursue hobbies of great personal interest, including reading, gardening, hiking, plant breeding, computer programming, earning contract bridge Master Points, and doing all sorts of things with his grandchildren. Previous efforts to write science fiction stories stalled out in their first few pages, but not this one! He currently lives in Corvallis, Oregon, with his wife and their three rather demanding pets: a double yellow headed Amazon parrot, a young orange cat, and an even younger Wheaten Cairn Terrier puppy.